A Love of My Own

Also by E. Lynn Harris

INVISIBLE LIFE

JUST AS I AM

AND THIS TOO SHALL PASS

IF THIS WORLD WERE MINE

ABIDE WITH ME

NOT A DAY GOES BY

ANY WAY THE WIND BLOWS

A Love of My Own

a novel by
E. LYNN HARRIS

DOUBLEDAY

NEW YORK   LONDON   TORONTO

SYDNEY   AUCKLAND

PUBLISHED BY DOUBLEDAY
a division of Random House, Inc.
1540 Broadway, New York, New York 10036

DOUBLEDAY and the portrayal of an anchor with a dolphin are trademarks of
Doubleday, a division of Random House, Inc.

ISBN 0-385-49270-7

PRINTED IN THE UNITED STATES OF AMERICA

In celebration of this being my eighth novel,
this book is dedicated to eight amazing women
whose love and friendship I treasure.

Charlotte "Cindy" Barnes

Regina Brown Daniels

Garbo Watson Hearne

Yolanda Starks

Robin Walters

Sybil Wilkes

Dyanna Williams

Brenda Braxton Van Putten

❀ ❀ ❀

In Memory
Victims of 9/11

Gerald Douglas

Calvin Gooding

Aaliyah Haughton

Orville Henry

Jon Richardson

Arletha Stapleton

Lorraine Haynes Wilson

Acknowledgments

My, how time flies when you're having fun. It has been ten years since I entered the world of writing, and I'm just as grateful today as I was when I was selling copies of *Invisible Life* out of the back of my rented car.

I'm grateful to God for allowing me to enjoy a successful career with the support of my family and friends. I have mentioned a lot of these people before in past acknowledgments, but I must mention them again because I realize now more than ever that nothing can be taken for granted. Faith, family and friends are so important to me.

So here goes. My mother, Etta W. Harris, and my aunt, Jessie L. Phillips, for always supporting and loving me unconditionally all my life. I'm thankful to Rodrick L. Smith for his love and support for creating a place I can call home. Thanks also to Rodrick and Stephanie for sharing your daughter, Desiree, with me. I must thank all of my family: my sisters, nieces, nephews, cousins and my new godson, Sean Harrison Gilmore.

I have the best friends in the world. People I've known for twenty-plus years and have loved me before I became "E. Lynn, the author." These friends understand when I can't come out and play and are always sending encouraging words of support and prayer. They include the amazing eight ladies mentioned in the dedication and Vanessa Gilmore (known from now on not as Judge Gilmore, but Sean's mom), Lencola Sullivan, Troy Donato, Sean James, Blanche Richardson, Carlton Brown, Rose Crater Hamilton, David and Tracey Huntley, Debra Martin Chase, Lloyd Boston, Derrick Thompson, Brian Chandler, Keith Boykin, Anderson Phillips, Reggie Van Lee, Ken Hatten, Brent Zachery, Tavis Smiley, Steve Barnes and Hugh Watson.

I've made some new friends lately—some of whom had a big part in helping with this novel. Thanks to Chris Bequette, Derrick Gragg and Sanya Whittaker Gragg, who make me proud to be a fan and graduate of the University of Arkansas-Fayetteville.

The year 2002 also marks my ten-year anniversary with my publisher, Doubleday/Anchor. This is something I'm most proud of. I look forward to spending my entire career with the best in the business. I realize how lucky I am to be published by a company who treated me from the beginning like I was a best-selling author. I extend my heartfelt thanks to: Stephen (the great) Rubin, Michael Palgon, Bill Thomas, Jackie Everly, Linda Steinman, Suzanne Herz, Jenny Frost, Pauline James, Laura Wilson, Ari Jones, Emma Bolton, John Fontana, Ann Messitte, Luann Walther, Jen Marshall, Meredith McGinnis, Carol Lazare, Judy Jacoby, Gerry Triano, Dorothy Boyajy and Rebecca "Still the Magician" Holland.

As always, I offer special thanks to my publicist extraordinaire, Alison Rich, a wonderful woman I'm proud to also call my friend. Thanks for all your hard work and always going the extra mile for me.

Although not a part of Doubleday, I give special thanks to Chris Fortunato and his staff.

They say good friends don't make for a great staff. For me nothing could be further from the truth. I am grateful to the following people for being special friends and helping me hold my life together: my assistants, Anthony Bell and Laura Gilmore; my agents, John Hawkins, Moses Cardona and Irv Schwartz; my attorney and friend, Amy Goldson as well as my Atlanta attorney Joe Beck and accountant Bob Braunschweig. Special thanks and much love and respect to Tony Hillery of TZR. I must also thank Shannon Jones, Janis Murray, Taurus Sorrells, Matthew Jordan Smith, Patrik Henry Bass, Smith & Polk Public Relations, Bobby Daye, Roy Johnson, and Amy DuBois Barnett of *Honey* magazine for schooling me in the magazine industry.

Thanks to the entire staff at my home away from home, the Trump International Hotel and Tower, with special thanks to Elizabeth, Rose Marie, Carlos, Dennis and Suzy. Thanks to Dr. Ian Smith for the medical information.

There are also several people and organizations that have supported me with each and every book. I realize they don't have to, and I'm extremely grateful. My thanks to Stanley Bennett Clay, David Star, and *Essence, Ebony* and *Savoy* magazines. Black Radio has been a big boost to my career. I wouldn't be here without *The Tom Joyner Morning Show, Doug Banks and DeDe McGuire, The Steve Harvey Show*, Frank Ski, Ryan Cameron, Donnie Simpson, Wendy Williams, Skip Murphy and his wonderful, crazy team, and Cliff and Jeanine on the West Coast. Special thanks to the CBS *Early Show* for giving me national exposure.

There are also several organizations that support me with a great deal of love: booksellers (a special shout-out to the black booksellers, since it all started with you), librarians, and book clubs the world over; Carol Mackey and the Black Expressions Book Club; Sigma Gamma Rho, Alpha Kappa Alpha, Zeta Phi Beta, Delta Sigma Theta, Kappa Alpha Psi, Alpha Phi Alpha, NAACP and the Links. Thank you all very much.

I have two wonderful outside editors whose friendships and talents I treasure. Charles Flowers and Chandra Taylor made writing this book fun, and I couldn't have done it without them. I will miss our Saturday get-togethers.

Thanks to all my writer friends, published and unpublished, for your friendship and support. I'm so proud to be a part of this community.

I must also thank the cast of *Dreamgirls; The 20th Anniversary Benefit* and The Actors' Fund of America for my Broadway debut. You were all so warm and loving and made the dreams of a little boy from Little Rock, Arkansas, come true. Special thanks to the directors, Brenda Braxton and Danny Herman, and the musical director, Seth Rudetsky.

I've saved the best for last. I have the best editor in the world, who happens to be a wonderful woman and great friend to all fortunate enough to know her. Janet Hill takes my words and stories and molds them into best-sellers. She is the one person I depend on for making my career so special. I couldn't do it without her. I wish all my writer friends have the same experience. Thanks, Janet.

In closing, I want to thank the fans who have supported me with each and every novel. I don't take you for granted. We've been through a challenging year as a country and as human beings living in a world that's constantly changing. Still, just the thought of all you marvelous fans makes me deliriously happy to turn on my computer every day and ponder, "What can I write today?" Thank you for that pleasure and privilege. I wish you all love, all the time.

e. lynn harris
New York City
June 2002

Prologue

That's the Way Love Goes

JANET JACKSON

Sometimes the beginning of a story starts at the end.

It was December 2001, a few days before Christmas.

Mr. and Mrs. Raymond Tyler Sr. had just come from the mall loaded down with presents and decorations. This was going to be the first Christmas they would share with their adult sons, Raymond Jr. and Kirby, in their new home in Naples, Florida, which they had built to enjoy their retirement.

It would be different from the cold-weather holidays they'd spent in Birmingham, Alabama. In Florida, Christmas Day wouldn't be spent in front of a roaring fireplace but maybe on the beach where they could watch the sun descend slowly in spectacular shades of orange and pink. Christmas would end with a twilight swim under the stars.

While Marlee was placing gifts under the tree, Raymond Sr. was at the bar preparing cocktails. Once he finished mixing the drinks, Raymond placed a drink on a sterling-silver tray for his wife of forty-plus years as the phone rang.

"You want me to get that, baby?" he asked.

Marlee loved that her husband still called her baby and smiled and said, "Sure, Papa."

She opened a box of Christmas cards and gazed lovingly at her husband as he answered the phone.

"Yes, this is Raymond Tyler. Slow down. I can't understand a word you're saying."

Marlee took a pen and started to write special messages to her sons when she heard the tone of her husband's voice change.

"You said your name is Zola. Oh God, no! What hospital?" Raymond Sr. asked. His wife looked at him and noticed that the pleasant expression on his face had changed; a mask of joy had been replaced with one of horror. Marlee dropped the cards and pen to the floor and rushed to her husband's side.

"Raymond, honey, what's the matter?"

He removed the phone from his ear and placed it against his heart and cried, "Baby, our son Raymond's in ICU, we've got to get on a plane right away."

What had happened to Raymond Jr.?

Zola Denise Norwood

I finally discovered the formula for having love in my life. I call it the power of three. Let me explain: find three different men and together you'll have the perfect man.

Every year I would review the list of things I found important in a man. I wanted someone who would be my best male friend and even appreciate my hobbies like playing classical music on the piano, watching my favorite television shows, going for drinks and having tea. I wanted a man who was comfortable in his own skin, and making a difference in the world. A powerful man. And I wanted someone who'd make my toes curl every time he touched me. A man who knew how to make love to a woman's body completely.

But after being a part of the dating scene for more than three years in New York, I realized my perfect man was going to be hard to find. Besides, love had already tricked me—and once is always enough.

I know love is like the lottery; you take a chance and at most there are only a few winners. I don't like to gamble, especially with my heart. I'm like Janet Jackson; I've got to have "control."

I love men, but they wear me out with all their confusing issues. One day they say they love you and the next they see someone with a bigger ass, bigger breasts and a prettier face and suddenly they forget about love—or at least loving you. I've had enough, and I'm not having that kind of madness in my life anymore. I got places to go and things to do without love keeping me down like a set of weights. Finding real love was more difficult than catching stars.

When I meet a man who has a powerful and dazzling bank account, he is usually boring and consumed with obtaining more power, which means he doesn't have a lot of time for me or my needs. On those occasions when I find a guy who makes my body rock, he usually has the ambition of a determined picnic ant—he is interested in one thing only, in getting into *my* goody basket.

When I meet a guy who listens to me and I trust as a friend, he usually turns out to be gay or bi-curious at the very least.

So I've finally accepted the power of three, and let me tell you, Zola Denise Norwood is one happy lady. Most times.

First, I have Hayden (no last name, like Cher and Madonna). He's an unemployed Broadway dancer and just one of the best friends I've ever had. We met in a yoga class when I first got to New York and we've been close friends ever since. He's cool for when I want to go dancing, see a play, or go to an independent movie that I can't convince my girlfriends to watch. Hayden is a handsome escort when I have events and I don't want to go alone. He's a Gemini and he can be very masculine one moment and soft and caring the next. He's also very funny, and a sense of humor is important. I can also trust Hayden with my secrets, something, I hate to admit, I can't always count on with my good, good girlfriends. It's my belief that if your girlfriends promise you they won't tell anybody, they usually mean that they won't tell anybody after the first three people they've blabbed to.

As my number-two man, I have Davis Vincent McClinton. He is not only the man who made my dream of heading a major magazine come true, he's also an invaluable source of information. You see, Davis owns the largest African American media company in the world and he's always passing on useful tidbits about investments and generously provides leads on inside stories of what's happening with the black elite, not only in New York but in the entire world, be it South Africa or Paris. He's smart and well respected and powerful with a big "P." He's only five eight in his Gucci loafers, but Davis McClinton commands attention everywhere he goes, whether he's in the boardroom or the barber shop. He uses his money and influence to help people of color—not just if you have a dream, but if you have a viable business plan as well.

A lot of women would think Davis is the perfect catch for a husband, and I'm sure his wife, Veronica, would agree every time she lays her American Express black credit card down on the counter and says, "Charge it." Now, even though I wasn't raised to date married men, it doesn't bother me a bit that Davis is married. Besides, he really doesn't seem that sexual to me. On those nights when he can escape from home, he likes spending time in bed with me, but he also spends a great deal of time reading *The Wall Street Journal* and business magazines.

I've gotten use to the lack of quality time I spend with Davis, just like I've gotten used to his generous nature. I've received so many exquisite gifts that I could loan out more jewelry than Harry Winston on Oscar night.

Last, but certainly not least—what does Vanessa say in her song? "Save the best for last?"—there's guy number three, Jabar Taylor, my one-man wrecking crew who has a body God created just to cause havoc here on earth. I met Jabar at a gym I go to every once in a while. When he would walk onto the floor, the room would get as silent as a library during finals. Women would start sweating, and not because of the workouts. Jabar's a beautiful milky brown, with short hair that looks like peach fuzz on his perfectly round head. He's tall and muscular and is so popular as a personal trainer that it's a year's wait before he considers taking on a new client. But with Davis's help, he made sure I was moved to the top of the list. What's that saying? *Money talks and bullshit walks.* But a girl's got to keep a secret or two for herself, so I didn't think Davis needed to know that Jabar provided training in other areas as well. The boy is both blessed and gifted, with body but not brains. Aside from being a trainer, Jabar doesn't have much ambition. Once when I asked him about his dream job, I was hoping he would at least say he wanted to be a policeman or something. He quickly replied, "To be Jennifer Lopez's personal trainer and valet." I didn't have the heart to tell him women didn't employ valets. But who am I to take away someone's dreams? I just wish Jabar knew the difference between dreams and fantasy.

Now, I know a lot of my sisters may not agree with my methods. Some might even go so far as to call me a user and even a slut. I don't care what you think or what you call me, just as long as you call me happy!!

❖   ❖   ❖

I have the dream job of dream jobs. I'm editor in chief of a new urban culture magazine called *Bling Bling* and Davis made it all possible. I met Davis on an American Airlines flight from Chicago to New York when I was on my way to interview for an associate editor position at *Vanity Fair.* I knew who he was because he's always in the media. Open any *Fortune, Wall Street Journal* or *Forbes* and there he is. He's rich, powerful, and somewhat handsome in a nerdy kind of way. I was working as an associate editor to my mentor Linda Johnson Rice, the publisher of *Ebony,* and I figured maybe an article on how Davis had built his empire and a photo spread on some of his homes would be a great story, even though Linda said Davis McClinton didn't do black press.

As I was boarding the plane, I looked down and I stared at Davis while he was reading a newspaper, his glasses resting on the edge of his nose, and asked him how he was doing. Davis removed his glasses and looked at me from the tip of my leather boots up almost every inch of my five-eight, one-hundred-twenty-eight-pound body, lingering at my honey-brown eyes, and in a very deep and cultured voice asked, "And you are?"

"Zola Norwood, with *Ebony* magazine, soon to be publisher and editor in chief of my own magazine. I just wanted to say I think what you're doing is great. Keep it up," I said.

I moved toward the back of the plane and my coach seat. I didn't have anything against coach, but since I flew on American Airlines so often, they should have upgraded me no matter how much I had paid for my ticket. When I saw important people like Davis sitting in first class, I wished I could afford first class all the time.

I put my laptop and garment bag in the overhead and took my seat in Row 27. Just as I was getting settled, the flight attendant approached me and said in a firm voice, "May I see your boarding pass?"

"What?" I asked.

"I need to see your boarding pass. I think you're in the wrong seat."

"Please tell me you're kidding."

"Miss Norwood, your boarding pass, please."

I reached into my bag and of course I found everything but my boarding pass. I wanted to tell Miss Flight Lady to just throw me off the plane, when she looked at me and said, "Please get your luggage and come with me."

I was getting ready to throw a black-girl hissy fit complete with hands on hips and head rotation, when it hit me that a lot of other important people besides Davis McClinton flew the Chicago-to-New York route regularly, and perhaps this wasn't the best moment to show out, so I decided to revert to my Miss Porter's correspondence course behavior and act like a lady.

I followed the flight attendant down the aisle, smiling like I hadn't done anything wrong. Once we were a few feet from the cockpit door, the attendant turned to me, smiled and said, "This looks like your seat."

"What?" I asked as I looked at the third row and the very sexy smile of Davis McClinton.

"You heard the lady," Davis said as he patted the large leather seat.

As I was lifting my luggage into the overhead, Davis barked, "Thomas, get the young lady's bag." A tall, lean white man swooped up from the seat in front of me and placed my luggage in the overhead. I suddenly realized I was sitting next to the opportunity of a lifetime.

By the time the plane arrived in New York, I knew I was right. During the two-hour flight, I told Davis about my big plans for starting my own magazine. I wanted to do something like *Vanity Fair* and *Ebony* combined. I even had a name for my magazine, *U.S.*, short for *urban soul*.

When I was a girl around thirteen, I spent my allowance not on music like most of my friends but on magazines. By the time I graduated from high school, my room had become a fire hazard from all the magazines I just couldn't part with. I would read copies of *Jet* and *Right On!* at least three times before protecting them with plastic covers I made from freezer bags. I would write "Property of Zola" in Magic Marker and the name of the store where I purchased the magazine.

I told Davis the mini-version of my life story and he listened intently and would ask questions when I would take a breath and sip some white wine.

"So you grew up in Nashville? Nice city," Davis said.

"Yeah, it was a great place to grow up. I went to Tennessee State University and majored in journalism. I worked for a few years for *Memphis* magazine as a fashion editor and then I went to graduate school at Northwestern. After that I worked as an intern at *Ebony* and was later promoted to associate editor," I said.

"Did you work for Linda Johnson Rice?"

"Oh, she is my shero, and I've learned a lot from Linda. Sort of like a law school grad working for a Supreme Court justice," I said.

"Then why do you want to leave?"

"Because I'm smart enough to know that I'll never be editor of *Ebony*, and it's time to move on," I said.

"Sounds like a good reason," Davis said.

When we arrived in New York, Davis had his driver take us to my hotel. I invited Davis to the bar for a drink, and to my great surprise he accepted. Five hours and two very expensive bottles of wine later, Davis had convinced me to skip my interview and start a magazine for him.

I thought this was the birthday for Urban Soul but Davis said that was a nice title but he already had a title, *Bling Bling*. It didn't knock me off my feet, but Davis explained that we should do something hip and on the cutting edge. He said young people bought magazines these days and were the first generation of African Americans who expected to do well and have nice things. Davis also pointed out how young white teens were fascinated with Hip Hop and African American culture.

I agreed, and the next afternoon Davis had me sitting in a conference room with a group of business planners, interior decorators, and employment counselors. Two months later I was having my first staff meeting. A week later I signed an employment contract, a high six-figure salary with perks, the most important being the chance to buy the magazine from Davis after five years. That night, to celebrate, I showed Davis how thankful I was, and he was very impressed with my talents.

Now, don't think for one minute I used my body to get my job. I am very attracted to Davis, although I have to admit it might be the power thang. Besides, I got skills.

I was raised in a solid middle-class family. Both my parents were educators. My daddy, Edward Norwood, was dean of students at Fisk University, and my mother, Virginia, was the first black female to receive a doctorate degree in education from Vanderbilt University and taught there.

I studied piano and ballet and was president of Jack and Jill. I won several piano competitions and won the only pageant I ever entered, Little Miss Black Nashville.

My parents always told my sister, Pamela, and me that we could do anything we dreamed and encouraged us to dream big. I listened. My sister, Pamela, didn't because she was too busy whoring around and doing drugs.

Bling Bling is going into its third year of publication with a circulation of more than 250,000 a month, and despite the competition has been growing at a rate of over 20 percent a year.

I just love my job! I get to go to movie premieres, fabulous parties, and meet interesting characters almost every day. So what if some of them are ill-informed rappers, BPWTTR (Black People Who Think They're Rich) and DWDs (divas with drama)?

Raymond Winston Tyler Jr.

Children should be the only ones allowed to believe in dreams with happy endings. It sure would save a lot of grown-ups so many sleepless nights.

I don't remember when I gave up on happy endings and can't really explain the sadness I felt for months when life dealt me my latest disappointment.

Just when I was thinking my love life was going to end up in the happily ever after way I'd dreamed it would, I was once again reminded how cruel life and love can be. If I'd just hung up the phone a moment earlier, maybe my life and my love for my partner, Trent could have gone on the way it had for more than seven years. If only I hadn't had a craving for a pepperoni pizza.

I was in the family room, looking over some contracts I was reviewing on a freelance basis for a firm in Seattle. I don't think Trent realized I was home. Why else would he risk having a phone conversation that would cause our relationship to end?

When I picked up the phone to satisfy my pizza jones, I heard a female voice screaming, "When are you going to tell him? I can't and won't wait forever." She was shouting so loud that they didn't notice I'd picked up the phone. I started to hang up but thought they would hear the click, so I just held the phone close to my ear. I then heard Trent say "Okay, baby. Okay. I'll tell him." I knew I shouldn't be listening, but I was intrigued . . . Tell who what?

"Well, if you don't tell Raymond, then I will, 'cause I am not doing this alone," the female voice said. Well, now I knew who "him" was. But I couldn't help wondering what she wouldn't do "alone."

"Michelle, you can't do that! I told you I would tell him. Give me a couple of days. I've got to go," Trent said.

"You've got twenty-four hours. If you don't tell him by then . . . I'll file my paternity suit," Michelle said.

"I told you, don't worry! I'll take care of it," Trent said before he hung up the phone.

For a few moments I just held the phone close to my chest, hoping I was in a crazy dream. Had I heard what I thought I heard? I just hung up the phone and stood silently, deciding what I should do next.

I could hear Trent moving around in our bedroom and thought maybe I should march upstairs and demand to know what was going on though a part of me didn't want to know.

But when I heard Trent coming down to the family room I decided I needed an explanation. Immediately.

Trent bounced into the room with his usual wide grin. There was nothing unusual about that. Trent was one of those people who always seemed to have a smile on his face and made anyone who saw him wonder what he was so happy about. It was one of the things I loved about him, even though right now I hated to admit it. But when he came toward me with his lips puckered, I felt a sharp pain, like someone was driving a dagger through my heart, and then jiggling it around for good measure. I pushed him back and said, "Trent, we need to talk."

"Don't I get a kiss?" he asked playfully.

"Trent, who is Michelle?"

"Michelle? Are you talking about Michelle Adams?"

"I don't know her last name. Who is Michelle Adams?"

"She works with me. Remember? We worked together on the new ballpark. She joined the firm about two years ago. She's from Miami," Trent said with a puzzled look.

"Was that who you were just talking to on the phone?"

For a few long sounds Trent didn't respond. When he finally spoke, his voice was accusatory. "So, you're listening to my phone calls?"

I started to defend myself, but instead I screamed, "Why is she talking about a paternity suit?"

"Michelle is pregnant," Trent said calmly.

"Yes, and what would that have to do with you?"

"I'm the father."

"What?"

"Michelle and I are going to have a baby," Trent said as he glanced around the room to avoid looking at me.

I was telling myself not to give him drama, to remain calm even though I felt my life disintegrating before my eyes. I remained silent, but my eyes looked at Trent and said, "Mutherfucker, you have *got* to be kidding me."

"Raymond, talk to me. Let's talk about this," Trent pleaded. I still didn't say anything, and Trent got nervous and started talking so fast he erupted like a geyser letting loose for the first time in years.

"You know this is just as much your fault as it is mine. If you'd been here at home with me instead of running back and forth to Alabama and San Diego, this wouldn't have happened. I needed somebody. I didn't want to hurt you, but I was lonely. Michelle and I didn't plan to have a child."

While he was talking I was thinking about returning to my undergrad alma mater, the University of Alabama, to teach at the law school for a semester. Was this the same man who told me what an honor it was for me to be asked to return and teach there and that I'd be a powerful role model for minority students? Was this the same man who told me I should get on a plane to go and comfort my baby brother while his marriage was crumbling?

I suddenly felt like Trent was sucking all the air out of the room and that if I stayed there listening to him, he was going to suck the life out of me, too.

I walked toward the stairs, and suddenly Trent grabbed me and shouted, "You've got to listen to me. Let me explain. This doesn't have to end our relationship!"

I could no longer remain silent. As I pulled away I said, "Trent, what relationship?"

I walked slowly up the stairs, praying he wouldn't come after me, but hoping somewhere in my heart he would.

He didn't.

❖   ❖   ❖

I spent the night in a hotel, where I had cold pizza and warm beer. I couldn't sleep, so I watched a lot of Nick at Nite and ESPN. I started to call Trent several times to ask him to explain himself. How could he have done that to me? To us? Infidelity is infidelity, so at first I didn't focus on the fact that he'd been unfaithful with a woman, but I now wondered if his infidelity had included men as well.

I wanted to call my baby brother, Kirby, and tell him what had happened, but he was still nursing his wounds from his own divorce. I thought of calling my mother, who I knew would make me feel better, but she would tell my father and he would tell her, and maybe me, "I told you so." Calling my best friend, Jared, was an option, but I knew after he'd let me have my say, he'd start talking about the kids and how wonderful married life is, and I would be cursing the day I accepted the fact that I was gay, that I would never really experience the joy I heard in Jared's voice when he talked about Nicole and the kids. Besides, they were in the throes of moving from New York to Atlanta.

Maybe Trent believed he could risk taking a chance since he knew about my "three strikes you're out" theory when it came to relationships. As far as I knew, he only had one strike against him. Several years ago his transgression with an undercover cop had cost me a chance to be on the federal bench. But now, it was time for me to move on and not risk being shocked by what strike three could be.

A few days later Trent and I finally got together. I was still angry, but I had invested too much in the relationship to at least leave with Trent as a friend, and he'd been a great friend for as long as I'd known him when we were fraternity brothers at Bama.

We didn't talk a lot about what had happened as we sat around the round glass table where we often shared dinner. He kept telling me how sorry he was. Since I'd been away so much, Trent had started to feel sorry for himself and used the rationale that he didn't want to be with another man, because he didn't want to jeopardize our relationship. He didn't think that being with a woman would harm the relationship, especially if I never found out. The baby had been a huge surprise to both him and Michelle. When I quizzed him about safe sex, he said the condom broke.

"So what are you going do?" I asked.

"I want to work this out with you because I still love you," he said.

"What about Michelle?"

"Michelle said she loves me and wants to marry me."

"What are you going to do?" I repeated.

"I want to do what's right," Trent said, looking away.

"So you want to take a wrong and make it right. Sounds like there is no place for me in that solution."

When Trent remained silent and didn't reassure me there was room for me in his *situation*, I knew my so-called good thing had come to an end.

We decided to put the house on the market, and agreed to let some time pass before we resumed our friendship. When he asked me if I was going to stay in Seattle, I really didn't know the answer. Seattle held so many memories for me. Trent and I had moved there because we thought it was such a beautiful city. It was. Still, I knew that every restaurant, shopping mall or gym would remind me of Trent. Seattle meant Raymond and Trent, and since we were no longer a couple, I thought I should move on.

❖   ❖   ❖

A week later Trent moved out. I don't know where. I assume with Michelle. I contacted a headhunter, Heather Sparks, whom I had met while teaching law school at the University of Washington. When Heather asked me what city I wanted to live in, I told her anywhere but Seattle. I was thinking about San Diego and even Los Angeles. Anywhere but here.

A couple of days later Heather called me and said, "I think I have a wonderful opportunity for you."

"I'm listening."

"Have you ever heard of a magazine called *Bling Bling*?"

I thought for a moment and said, "I don't think so."

"Have you heard of a man named Davis McClinton?"

"Sure everyone has heard of him," I said. "We studied him in business school."

"Well, he owns a publication called *Bling Bling*. It's a hot, up-and-coming Hip Hop magazine. He also owns more than one hundred radio stations across the country and a couple of television stations in South Africa. A real media mogul," Heather said.

"I think he's one of the richest men in the country," I said.

"And he's African American," Heather added.

"No, stop!" I said, kidding Heather. I remembered how proud I was when we studied Davis McClinton when I attended the University of

Washington executive MBA program. I was the only African American male in the class and I loved hearing how Davis had bought several radio stations on the brink of bankruptcy and turned them into huge moneymakers. He took his company public and made millions. Later, in a shrewd move, Davis McClinton purchased the stock and turned it back into a private company, bigger and more powerful than before. I thought it would be great even if I got the chance only to meet Davis McClinton. Now, the prospect of working with him was just as exciting.

"So, what's the job?" I asked.

"CEO of the publishing arm of his business. I've already talked with the search firm in New York, and they love your background. They were really impressed that you had both a law degree and a MBA," Heather said.

"What's the next step?"

"I thought this would be perfect for you, so I've already set up the initial interview."

"Where is the job?" Since Davis McClinton owned a media company, I assumed it would be based in either New York or L.A. I was hoping for the Big Apple.

"New York," Heather said.

"New York," I repeated. When the words came out of my mouth I felt like somebody had told me I had a chance to go to heaven. I felt a sense of relief. I knew there was only one place I wanted to be: New York City. I needed the city with the big arms and heart. I hoped it needed me.

Welcome to *Bling Bling** Confidential . . . the private website with observations and information on characters in *A Love of My Own* too busy causing havoc to speak for themselves.

To Unsubscribe, follow the instructions at the end of the novel. Otherwise, enjoy and remember *Bling Bling* for those who want everything!

*bling bling: jewelry; material show off; the glitter of diamonds.

(From *The Hip Hoptionary*, by Alonzo Westbrook)

From *Bling Bling* Confidential

They were beginning to wonder out loud, at the architectural firm where Trent Walters worked. How could this attractive man who was in his late thirties, with the body of a college football player be single?

Sure he had a teenage son from a college relationship. But this black man was making six figures and he needed a wife and kids. You know it just didn't look right. Michelle was more than willing to help a brother out.

BOOK ONE

I Wish I Didn't Miss You

ANGIE STONE

1

"Cyndi, let's go over the articles I need to assign," I said. I was in my office with my executive assistant, Cyndi Jones. I met her when I gave a speech at the Howard University School of Communications, and I hired her immediately after she graduated because she was ambitious and aggressive. It seemed like every other week I was getting an update on articles Cyndi had written for the Howard University newspaper. She's been with me for more than three years now.

"The Halle Berry and Yancey B. stories have been given to Kirsten Dawson. I'll make sure we have the signed contracts. The only one that hasn't been assigned is 'Divas return to the Great White Way,'" Cyndi said.

"Refresh my memory. Who are we featuring?"

"Vanessa L. Williams and Sheryl Lee Ralph," Cyndi said.

"Are they in the same show?"

"No. Sheryl is in a new musical, *Millie sumthin'*, and Vanessa is in a revival of the musical *Into the Woods*."

"Now, Cyndi, I know the show isn't called *Millie sumthin'*—make sure you have the correct title before we talk to writers about a story," I said. "You know I hate stuff like that."

"I'm sorry. I'll be sure to do that. Do you have any writers in mind?"

"Maybe we should go with a guy. See who's available. By the way, how are things coming with the Sexiest Brothaman Alive contest?"

"The contest is coming along great. We've gotten some fantastic submissions. I'll investigate and get back with you. Don't forget your breakfast meeting in the morning," Cyndi said as she stood up. She was wearing a black semitransparent silk blouse that truly wasn't appropriate for the office. I started to say something, but the last time I spoke to Cyndi about her wardrobe she got a little sensitive. I realized she was young and she didn't know quite how to dress in a corporate environment. I had even taken her on a couple shopping trips, but she always seemed to be drawn to the tight and the transparent. Every Wednesday, Cyndi would use her lunch break to go to Century 21 and somehow always managed to find the tacky items left from the previous week. I was just praying that Davis didn't come down to the office today, because he wouldn't be able to bite his tongue. He'd tell me to send Cyndi home to change posthaste.

"Cyndi, who am I eating with tomorrow morning?"

"Eunice, the ad manager, and the guy who handles all the national advertising for Wal-Mart," Cyndi said.

"Oh yes. Eunice has been trying to land that account for months. I need to make a mental note to wear my red power suit," I said.

"You look fierce in that suit," Cyndi said as she walked out.

❖   ❖   ❖

I was looking over the agenda for the weekly staff meeting when Cyndi walked back into the office carrying a vase of white orchids and said my mother was on the phone.

"Thanks, Cyndi," I said as I picked up. I smiled to myself, thinking that after three years Davis still remembered to send me a token of his affection once a week. I loved flowers almost as much as the aqua-colored boxes from Tiffany's.

"Zola, did I catch you at a bad time?"

"No, Mother. You know I always make time for you. What's going on?"

"I hate to bother you, but I just didn't know who to call," Mother said.

I knew from the sound of her voice that she was calling with bad news and had a feeling that it involved my older and troubled sister, Pamela. Everybody in my family always said Pamela had a few drama problems. I called her what she was, an emotional vampire sucking the life out of everyone she came in contact with. She caused chaos whenever she pleased.

"What did she do now?" I asked.

"Pamela has been missing for about a week. Nobody's seen her, and I went over to her apartment and there was an eviction notice on her door," Mother said.

"I'm sure she'll turn up soon, Mother. Don't worry about it," I said as I looked out the huge picture windows of my office and observed wisps of high clouds against a May blue sky.

"Zola, I'm just wondering if I should file a missing persons report with the police."

"I don't think so. She's probably met some new junkie and will show up any minute and act like nothing has happened," I said.

While my mother talked about all the bad things that could have happened to Pamela, I was having swirling recollections of some of my sister's previous antics, like being arrested at one of Mother's Links meetings for writing hot checks. To make matters worse, she had a vial of cocaine in her purse when she was searched at the police station.

The last time I was home—to attend the funeral of my Aunt Sophie Lou—Pamela showed up at the funeral sloppy drunk, threw herself into the casket, and started screaming and crying like a madwoman. The sad thing was that Pamela was not crying because Aunt Sophie Lou died, she was crying because the well had run dry: She could always count on Aunt Sophie for money for her bad habits. I remember pulling Pamela out of the coffin and taking her into one of the back rooms of the church and telling her, "When this is over I'm going to kick your ass for embarrassing the family once again, and I want you to take it like a man."

When my mother had finally finished listing the places where Pamela might be, I asked her what Daddy thought she should do.

"I didn't want to bother him. You know he's worked so hard all his life and I just want him to enjoy his retirement," Mother said.

"Mother, that's what I think you should do too. Enjoy your retirement. You've raised us and you did a great job with me. Pamela is a grown woman and she's responsible for her own actions," I said.

"I've got to do something. She's my daughter," Mother said. Her voice sounded flat and lifeless and not like the Nashville educator and socialite many of her friends thought she was.

"Mother, I'm trying to understand how you feel. But I am not a mother. I'm a sister who has been wronged by Pamela time and time again, just like everyone else in this family. I don't mean to sound cold, but we can't live her life for her," I said.

"Zola, I love you, baby, but I just wish you could be more forgiving."

"I am," I said quickly.

"Then please forgive Pamela. She never means any harm."

"Mother, let's face it. Pamela wakes up every morning thinking about what kind of mayhem she can create."

"I just hope nothing bad's happened."

"If it had, you would have heard something by now. Why don't you plan a trip up here to New York? It'll take your mind off things. We could go see some shows, do some shopping, and there are lots of new restaurants that the owners are dying to have me visit. If I keep taking Hayden when I go out to eat, he's going to be so fat, he won't be able to get a job," I said, laughing.

"Visiting you would be fun. But I need to find out what's happened to Pamela first."

"Just let me know when you want to come, Mother. I'd love to see you."

"Well, I'm always here in Nashville, and I know your daddy and I would love to see you too," Mother said.

"Let's both think about what will be best as long as it involves me getting a hug soon from the woman I love the most," I said as I walked back to my desk and sat down.

"I love you, Zola," Mother said.

"I love you, too, Mother. Promise me you're going to stop worrying."

"I'll try."

"Promise."

"I promise," Mother said, and we both hung up the phone, drained by an ungrateful Pamela.

❖　　❖　　❖

Later that evening, around seven-thirty, I was reviewing the details of a cover-shoot schedule for pop star Yancey B., who was making her movie debut and getting ready to release her second CD. Yancey B. was at the top of her game, but I was beginning to wish I'd selected someone else for the December cover. A couple of designers had mentioned that they would love seeing Yancey B. wearing their clothes, so I acquiesced.

Yancey B. and her manager were carrying on like she was a diva with a capital D. They had a list of requirements two pages long. I wanted to assign the story to Veronica Chambers, one of the best writers in the country, but I knew she'd never agree to Yancey B.'s demands. We had to use the photographer of her choice as well as her stylist and her hair-and-makeup guy. But it didn't stop there. The list of food we were required to have on the set included caviar, green seedless grapes, Fiji bottled water, Grich Hills Chardonnay, DeLoach Merlot, and Sunkist orange soda in addition to cold shrimp, which each needed to measure at least two inches.

Normally I would have told Yancey B. and her people where to go, but they had chosen *Bling Bling* to do an exclusive promotion with our readers that involved screening her new movie at Yancey B.'s South

Beach penthouse. We had beat out several of our competitors, including *Sister 2 Sister, Essence, Honey,* and *O* and we'd never been in a position to compete with them before. I saw this as a tremendously positive sign that we were a few issues away from increasing circulation.

Just as I was making sure I had my two-way pager in my bag, Cyndi came in with a look on her face I didn't like.

"There's a phone call for you," she said dryly. I knew this wasn't a good sign, because she usually just buzzed me. When she came into the office, I always knew something was wrong.

"Who is it?"

"You're not going to like this."

"Cyndi, tell me who it is."

"It's Lena Ford, Yancey B.'s publicist. When I asked if I could help, thinking it had something to do with the shoot, she said she had to speak to you. I told her I was handling all of the arrangements, including that tacky white limo they requested. She said she needed to speak to you no matter where you were." Lena Ford was a powerhouse publicist who was known in the industry as being more difficult than many of her high-profile clients.

"Thanks, Cyndi. You're right, this doesn't sound good," I said, and picked up the phone. Cyndi gave me a sour look as she left the office.

"Hi, Lena," I said cheerfully.

"Zola, I've got some bad news," she said quickly.

"What?" I asked as I sank to my seat.

"There's a problem with the shoot."

"What problem? Is something wrong with Yancey B.?"

"No, we'll be there bright and early," Lena said.

"Then everything's fine. What's the problem?"

"Is there any way we can delay the cover?"

"What do you mean?"

"We can still do the shoot tomorrow, but I was wondering if we could move the publication back a couple of months."

"A couple of months?" I asked, raising my voice.

"Yeah, just a couple of months. Since magazines are always on the stands a month early, it shouldn't matter anyway. Some scheduling issues have come up."

"Has the movie been moved back?" I asked.

"No," Lena said quickly.

"Then what's the problem?"

"I wish I could talk to you in person, but here goes: Yancey B. just got a wonderful opportunity," Lena said.

"A wonderful opportunity? What are you talking about?"

"*Vanity Fair* wants to put her on the cover. She'd be the first African American woman to grace the cover solo. Also, Donatella Versace is designing several gowns just for Yancey B. Isn't that just fab?"

"What does that have to do with our shoot?"

"They want to do it for September and to have an exclusive for thirty days after the issue hits the stand."

"An exclusive?" I said, laughing in my best diva voice. "We already have an exclusive, remember?"

"Yeah, but I was hoping you'd reconsider and let us move forward with *Vanity Fair*," Lena said.

I started to feel warm as I looked around my office for something to focus on. I had to get myself together quickly before I lost my temper. I knew this woman wasn't calling me at the last minute to tell me she'd already secured another deal for her client.

"Lena, why would I want to move my cover back? It doesn't make sense. I thought you turned those other magazines down before you chose *Bling*. We have a deal," I said.

"I know, Zola, but this is big and I have to look out for what's best for my client, and being on the cover of *Vanity Fair* is something Yancey B. has dreamed of all her life. I'm sorry, Zola. We can still do the shoot, but publication will have to wait until at least thirty days after the *Vanity Fair* cover is off the stands."

"Woman, have you lost your mind? Do you know how much work we've put in to pull off this shoot? How dare you call me at this late date and ask me to do this. The answer is no. Hell no. We will move ahead according to plan," I said firmly. I was willing to bet that Lena wasn't telling the entire story. I was certain there were a few little trinkets lined up for both Yancey B. *and* Lena. Probably a few Donatella Versace originals, and other perks, had made them change their minds about doing the *Bling* shoot.

"So you're going to play hardball, Zola?"

"Call it what you want, but I'll see you in the morning."

"I don't think you should expect us."

"What?!"

"If you don't agree to my terms, Yancey won't be there. You'll have to find someone else for your cover," she said.

"I tell you what . . . don't show up. I'm sure we can find a nice stock photo of your client. I bet there are lots of not-so-flattering pictures out there of her, and I'll run one on the cover. So, Lena, don't play with me. I'm the wrong one," I said.

"You wouldn't do that."

"Wouldn't I? Try me. Matter of fact, rather than the glowing story we were going to run, I'm going to take another angle."

"Another angle?"

"Oh, yeah. I know a little more than you think about your client. We've done our homework, and there's lots of interesting information floating around about Yancey B. Maybe I'll have LaVonya the gossip columnist write the story instead of Kirsten Dawson. You can't stop us from running the cover, nor do you have a say on what writer we assign if you break the original agreement."

"Can't we work something out?"

"We've already worked something out. Deal with it," I said, and slammed down the phone.

2

On a lovely June morning, I stepped into a dream office on the forty-sixth floor of a Times Square high-rise, and it belonged to me. The office building housed several record companies and a large publishing company. Davis leased two floors for the staff of *Bling Bling* and maintained corporate offices on the top three floors of the building.

I got off the elevator and was greeted by a large, fragrant floral arrangement and my new assistant, Bristol Barnes, who once was the executive assistant to Davis's executive assistant. Bristol was a tall, lanky white man with sandy-blond hair and a sparse goatee.

"Welcome to *Bling Bling*, Mr. Tyler. I'm Bristol," he said.

"Nice meeting you, Bristol. Davis, I mean Mr. McClinton, told me all about you. Impressive résumé," I said. I wanted to ask Bristol, with his credentials, why he wasn't looking for a management position, but I knew a lot of graduates took lower-paying jobs to gain entry into corporations that didn't always post job opportunities, choosing to hire from within the organization.

"Thank you, sir," Bristol said. Bristol's résumé had been in a package I'd opened upon my arrival in New York. I'd learned that he was from Houston, had graduated from Rice University with a degree in English and had gotten an MFA from New York University.

"So, is this my office?" I asked as I looked over Bristol's shoulder and saw a large office through the glass in front of his work space.

"Yes, sir, it is," Bristol said as he opened the door and waited for me to walk in.

The office was large; I would guess maybe more than 950 square feet, the size of an apartment. It had blond parquet floors that were polished to perfection and an Oriental rug strategically placed under the desk. There were built-in bookshelves on each side of a closed cabinet, which looked to be an entertainment center. I opened the door and out popped a thirty-six-inch flat-screen television. I also found a six-disc CD player, a video recorder, and a DVD player. Through a huge window I took in the view of Times Square, which included several large bill-boards advertising everything from current Broadway shows to cologne and underwear. I paused for a moment and thought about calling Trent and telling him about this office, but wondered if he would appreciate my success. I wondered if he'd ever been proud of me.

My new desk was large with oval leather in the center and wood surrounding it. My chair was blue leather and steel. I looked around the office and saw a comfortable navy blue leather sofa with two matching chairs and a glass-and-steel coffee table covered with issues of *Bling Bling* and several other magazines. I couldn't believe my eyes when I noticed a black-and-steel wet bar in another corner.

"Is everything okay?" Bristol asked as he walked into the office.

"Everything looks fine," I said as I looked at not one but two computer screens on my desk. I guess I really had made it big.

"Did you see the spectacular view?"

"How could I not see it," I said, laughing.

"I'll give you a chance to get comfortable, but if you need anything, just push this button," Bristol said as he pointed toward a phone that had more buttons than I'd ever seen.

"Thanks, Bristol. Give me a little time to get used to everything," I said.

"Sure. Do you have a Palm, Mr. Tyler?"

"I sure do."

"Why don't you let me have it so I can transfer your old data to the new one I purchased for you. It's updated with all the most recent entertainment and service information for New York City," Bristol said.

"Sure," I said as I reached into my briefcase, pulled out my Palm, and handed it to him.

"Thank you, sir. Oh, and I took the liberty of picking out some CDs for you to start off your office collection. If you'd like some other selections, please let me know. There's a record store in the building, and I'd be more than happy to run downstairs and pick up whatever you like."

"Great, Bristol. I'm sure your selections will be just fine," I said.

When Bristol left my office I walked back over to the window to watch the throng of people moving through the streets below and tried to muster the sense of triumph I thought I'd feel when I dreamed of reaching this type of success, but the only thing I felt was an overwhelming sadness inside. I never thought being so successful would feel so lonely.

Standing there, looking down at Times Square, I realized that everything in my world had changed. My life was like a puzzle in a box, and I had to figure out a way to put the pieces together. Again.

From *Bling Bling* Confidential

Davis McClinton didn't like all the press African Americans like Richard Parsons, Sylvia Rhone, Kenneth Chenault and Stan O'Neal were receiving by heading Fortune 500 companies and spent a great deal of time thinking about how he could return to the front pages and covers of some of the top business magazines. He'd spent a great deal of time in the late nineties competing with Earl Graves, Cathy Hughes, and Robert L. Johnson. There had to be an area of business where once again he could reign supreme.

3

I could tell I'd already missed the first round of drinks when I entered the dimly lit restaurant, Rosita's, and heard Justine laughing. I spotted her and Kai and another woman I didn't know munching chips and salsa and sipping from half-filled margarita glasses.

"Hey, ladies. What'd I miss?" I asked as I took the empty seat at the corner table illuminated by the plum-red glow of a covered candle.

"Bitch, where have you been? I told you six-thirty," Justine said.

"I have a magazine to run," I said as I turned to the stranger and extended my hand and said, "Hello, I'm Zola Norwood."

"Hi, Zola. I'm Roberta Garrison Elmore, president of the Greater New York Panhellenic Council."

"Nice meeting you," I said. "And how are you, Kai?"

"Honey, I am doing just fine. What's going on at *Bling Bling*?"

"Same ole same ole. The second week of September is Fashion Week, and my assistant spent most of the day begging a bunch of white designers assistants for tickets and decent seats to their shows. I guess they think my readers don't buy designer clothes," I said as I looked around one of my favorite Mexican restaurants for our regular waiter, Hector. I loved the atmosphere but didn't like eating a meal there unless I was depressed or had lost a few pounds. Mexican food was just too fattening.

Justine Rice was my best friend from way back. We'd grown up in Nashville and attended school together from fourth grade until we parted ways after high school. Justine attended Memphis University because she got a full scholarship and after graduation moved to New York. She was a professional events planner and moonlighted at one of the posh hotels, catering to the needs of their special clients.

Justine was a heavyset beauty with a strong sexual presence and confidence when it came to men. She had wonderful deep-set brown eyes and a soft round face. One moment she could be as calm as a Sunday-school teacher, but after a few drinks her personality and voice would suddenly change, and she would become more sure of herself and sound like an emcee at a raunchy strip show. The girl could cuss like a comedian.

Justine and I met Kai Davidson at one of the events Justine had planned. Recently divorced from her doctor husband, Kai was the only child of an upstate New York federal judge and a clinical social worker. Kai graduated from Sarah Lawrence with a degree in Art History but hadn't worked a day in her life, unless you counted all the volunteer work she did. She was now living off a hefty divorce settlement and occasionally took classes in interior design. Her ex, whom we called "the good doctor," was more than happy to part with some of his money when Kai discovered he had gotten not one but two nurses pregnant within months of each other. Kai was so hurt that since her divorce she had sworn off men and sex and now called herself a second-chance virgin. She was as tall and slender as a fashion model, which both Justine and I couldn't understand because Kai ate nonstop like she smoked blunts all day and had perpetual munchie mania.

Kai had helped me navigate the New York social scene and had been invaluable in helping me decorate my renovated Harlem brownstone, including a music room which held my treasured baby grand piano.

Hector brought more chips and salsa to the table and a glass of white wine for me. We clinked our glasses in unison and took a sip of our drinks. Roberta looked at her watch, took another sip and said, "Been nice meeting you guys. I've got to run. Have to catch the next train to Mount Vernon."

"What, no car and driver, hon?" Justine said, laughing.

"I wish," Roberta said as she pulled out two twenty-dollar bills and laid them on the table. She looked at Justine and said, "I'll look over your proposal and get back to you in a few days."

"Do you have a card? I'd like to send you a copy of my magazine."

"Sure, that'd be nice. Maybe it'll earn me some points with my teenage stepdaughter from hell." Roberta laughed as she pulled her card from her wallet and passed it to me.

"Smooches to you, Roberta. I hope I'm invited to your big shindig," Kai said.

"Your invitation will be in the mail. See you ladies later," Roberta said as she walked out.

When Justine was certain Roberta was out of the restaurant, she took another sip of her drink and said, "The shit I have to go through to make a dollar."

"What are you talking about? She seemed perfectly nice," I said.

"She's a snobby bitch from a middle-class ghetto trying to make a dollar out of fifteen cents. That type of woman just drives me crazy. If I don't get this event, I'm going up to Mount Vernon to kick her ass like she stole my paycheck," Justine said.

"Right . . . right. I got your back, girl. Just let me know so I can get my Vaseline. Can't risk getting this face damaged," Kai said, laughing as she pulled a pack of cigarettes from her purse and glanced around to see if anyone was looking. "Do you mind if I smoke?"

"Yes, I mind," Justine said.

"I thought you stopped smoking?" I said.

"I did."

"So?"

"I started back," she snapped.

"Well, you know you can't smoke in here," Justine said. "I don't know why your crazy ass is trippin'."

"I'll take care of the tip and Hector will let me do whatever I want," Kai said.

"So I guess it doesn't matter what we think, or if we get cancer from your secondhand smoke," I said.

"If you get cancer, I'll get you gift certificates for free visits with my ex," Kai said, laughing.

"That shit ain't funny," Justine said.

"So what's wrong with Roberta?" I asked.

"You know the type—she thinks because she's got a little clout she can make a sister jump through hoops and then turn around and give the business to some dizzy white girl," Justine said as she broke a tortilla chip in half and dipped it in salsa.

"Sisters got to jump through hoops every day for everybody," I said. I was thinking about all the calls I had made, the crying and pleading I had to do to get my entertainment editor into premieres, not to mention sleeping with Davis to make sure he kept pumping money into *Bling*.

"Do you ever wonder what you'll be wearing when you're lying in a casket, getting ready to be put into the ground for eternity?" Kai asked.

Justine and I looked at each other and rolled our eyes. It was one of the things Kai did that drove us crazy. We could be having a completely normal sister-girl conversation and Kai would look away and release these stupid-ass questions about life. Sick questions. After about six months of actually trying to answer some of the questions, Justine and I figured that if we didn't respond, Kai would return to earth and stop acting so wacky.

A moment of silence followed, and sure enough Kai came back around. "So what are we doing for dinner before I stuff myself with these chips?"

"I feel like some jerk chicken," I said.

"That sounds good to me," Kai said.

"Then let's finish our drinks and get to stepping toward Island Spice," Justine said.

From *Bling Bling* Confidential

Davis greets his tea-colored reflection with a smile each day after finishing his shave. He's not happy because of his wealth and power but because every day he wakes up he moves farther from his past.

4

On my fifth day in New York I had a long lunch with my new boss, Davis McClinton, at Le Bernardin, on West Fifty-first between Sixth and Seventh avenues, one of the city's toniest restaurants.

The maître d' had a strong French accent and greeted us with a warm smile. He clasped Davis's hands and said, "Monsieur McClinton, so great to see you again. I have your regular table ready for you. How's business?"

"*Très bien, Henri,*" Davis said. "*Et la famille, comment ça va?*"

I followed Davis and Henri and noticed several of the lunchtime patrons staring at us. They probably recognized Davis's face from the covers of both *Fortune* and *Forbes* magazines. Finally black men were beginning to be recognized for their business smarts instead of for playing sports, or being in entertainment or being associated with crime.

We reached our table and Henri pulled out the leather chairs for Davis and me and said, "I'll send Tucker right over."

"Thank you," Davis said as he removed his glasses and put them in a snakeskin case. The waiter came over and warmly greeted Davis with a smile and an amber-colored drink resting over several ice cubes. He looked at me and asked, "And what can I get for you, sir?"

"Just some iced tea," I said.

Davis looked at me with a frown and teased, "Are you trying to impress the boss? Order a drink."

I didn't know if I should follow his instructions, but I remained firm and said, "No, iced tea will be fine. I want to get some work done this afternoon." When Davis nodded, I was happy to see that he wasn't one of those egomaniacs who thought things should be his way or no way.

"Are you glad to be back in New York, Raymond?"

"Yeah, I am," I said.

"New York, the most exciting city in the world. I wouldn't live any-place else, even though I have homes in Paris, The Hamptons, Tel-luride and Miami. But if I'm away from the city for more than a month, I start to get a little crazy," Davis said.

"Yeah, I must say I've missed the city a lot," I said as I looked out on the busy sidewalk.

"So tell me about yourself. I mean, the stuff I don't already know," Davis said.

"Like what?"

"Your family?"

"You know I'm from Birmingham, Alabama. I have a younger brother who plays for the San Diego Chargers. My parents are retired and live in Naples, Florida. My father was a civil rights attorney and my mother was a teacher. They're both retired and enjoying life. What about you? I mean besides the stuff you read in magazines?" I asked, try-ing to turn the tables on Davis.

"My family is from New York," Davis said.

"Harlem?" I suggested. There was very little personal information about Davis in the case study.

"Fuck no," Davis snapped. "I grew up on the Upper East Side."

I started to apologize, but Davis didn't give me the opportunity as he began to speak proudly of parents who were second-generation millionaires. He told me they had made their money selling insurance and burial polices to African American families all across the country, but mainly in the South. Davis told me he attended prep school in Boston, then went to Harvard undergrad and Harvard Business School. He created his first business while he was a student at Harvard, a messenger service for students in the Boston area. He described it as a ground FedEx for students at Harvard, Radcliffe, Boston University, and Tufts. After graduation Davis sold the business and bought his first radio station, a country-western station in Huntsville, Alabama, and turned it into one of the top R&B stations in the South. When he talked, he glowed with boundless pride. I wondered how Davis had gone from insurance to media.

"Who did you hire as messengers?" I asked.

"Some black kids from Roxbury. At least it kept them from begging on the streets in Cambridge," Davis said as he shook his head in a mixture of frustration and disappointment. Then he added, "Our people. Can't do with them. Can't do without them. This is a great country. I just wish more of our people realized that."

I didn't have a proper response for Davis's statement, so again my eyes roamed the spacious restaurant. I was relieved when the waiter returned with my drink and the menus. Davis didn't look at the menu, he just instructed the waiter to bring him the usual. I knew that didn't leave me much time to decide, so I just asked for grilled salmon and a vegetable.

"Would you like a salad, sir?" the waiter asked. Before I could answer, Davis told him to bring me a green salad.

"So, you're married?" I asked.

"Yep, been married more than fifteen years. Some good and some bad. I have two perfect children, Morgan and Logan," Davis said proudly.

"How old are they?"

"Logan is thirteen and he's away at prep school in Connecticut, and Morgan is eight going on twenty-eight and she attends the Chapin School here in the city. Do you plan to have kids? Even though you're gay? Not that it's a deterrent, especially in a city like New York," Davis said calmly.

I raised my eyebrow in surprise, even though I figured it would come up sooner or later. My sexuality had become public several years before, when I was nominated for a federal judgeship.

"I didn't realize I'd put that on my résumé," I joked.

"Raymond, now, you don't think I'd hire someone for such an impor- tant position and not know as much as the best investigators in the world can find out. Besides, I have no problem with it. I think it's best to tell the truth about yourself so no one could ever blackmail you," Davis said.

"Was my being gay something you thought about when you offered me the job?" I asked.

Davis responded quickly, "Hell, yeah. You're a double minority, black and gay. I get a lot of points for that when I go after government contracts. Now, if I can just find me a handicapped black lesbian, I will have hit the jackpot," Davis said, laughing. I was shocked by Davis's insensitive remark and suddenly I felt as if I were being entertained by the devil himself, but instead of challenging him, I decided to change the subject.

"Tell me about Zola Norwood, your editor in chief," I said.

"Smart girl, Zola. I think she's doing a good job, but she's made the mistake most women do, she thinks her pussy can take her places in the world of high-powered people, and it's good pussy, so it can, but only so far. She'll learn," Davis said, leaning over the table, whispering as though he wanted to make sure Henri or the other waiters or patrons heard the sudden change in his language from business-speak to straight from the 'hood.

"So your relationship isn't strictly business?" I asked.

"She's one of my women," Davis said. "But someone like me got a lot of bitches who think they can serve me up some good pussy and get over because I got both wealth and power. Women love that shit. Even though they think they're the only one, they don't know I have more than one box of diamond studs in my safety-deposit box. My assistant makes sure everyone gets fresh flowers every week, especially my wife."

I didn't know what to say next, so I changed the subject again.

"So what sports do you enjoy besides golf?" I asked.

"I like sailing and riding horses. I just bought a new mare. She's a beauty," Davis said.

"I'm anxious to improve my tennis and golf games, but it doesn't look like I'm going to have a lot of time, between getting adjusted to the new job and the temporary living situation."

"You don't like the corporate apartment? I can get a designer to come and redo it to your taste," Davis said.

"Oh no, it's great. But I know I can't stay there forever."

"Stay as long as you like. It's a write-off, but when you're ready to find your own place, let me know. I have a great real estate guy," Davis said.

"Thanks," I said, knowing full well I couldn't afford anyplace Davis's real estate agent might show me, even on a good day.

The waiter served the meal, which ranked as one of the best I'd had in a long time, not counting my mother's fried chicken. Our lunch was interrupted several times by Davis's two-way pager and his cell phone. Once, during the meal when both were in play, the waiter brought a phone over and said he had an urgent call for Davis.

Davis took the phone and after a "Yes. Sure. I can make it happen," he asked, "How much do they want for it?"

Then Davis hung up the phone and said, "I need to get back to the office. If you want dessert, you can stay, and don't worry about the bill. I have an account here, so everything's taken care of."

"No, I'm fine. I'll just head back with you if it's okay," I said.

"Sure. My driver's out front."

We walked out of the restaurant and were greeted by two young lanky black guys with their pants hanging off their butts, holding boxes of candy.

"Excuse me, sir. Would you like to help support our youth basketball team by buying a box of candy? We're trying to buy new uniforms."

As I stuck my hand in my pocket to see if I had any singles, I was disappointed when I heard Davis's response.

"What are you kids doing out here harassing this restaurant's clientele? Where are your parents?" he demanded.

"What?" one of the kids asked. He looked like he was ready to challenge Davis to a duel.

"Don't question me. Why don't your parents pay for your uniforms?"

"Dawg, you gon' let him talk to you like that? Who dat short niggah think he is?" the other one asked, laughing.

"Davis, is that your driver over there," I asked, trying to intervene.

Davis made eye contact with a middle-aged white man dressed in a black suit and black hat and said, "These little project people better be glad I've got business to handle, or else I would show them. Raymond, do you want to ride back with me?"

"Uh, I think I'll just walk back," I said. I didn't know what had made me angrier, Davis's behavior or the young boys' foul language and disrespect. Still, I couldn't resist giving each boy a ten-dollar bill after Davis's limo had pulled off.

5

I walked into the bar, greeted by the chalky glare of fluorescent lights and a warm smile from a man who I knew would never disappoint me: Hayden.

"Hey, Miss Zola. What are you drinking today?" Hayden asked as he took a swig from a green beer bottle.

"The usual," I said.

"Bartender, a white wine for the beautiful sistah in green," Hayden yelled as I scooted into a booth near the bar. I leaned over the table, gave Hayden a kiss on the cheek and said, "Good seeing you, baby boy."

"You, too. You smell good. What are you wearing?" Hayden asked.

"After eight hours? I guess it would be funk mixed with a little Angel," I said.

"Oh, I love that scent. You know they make that for men, too," Hayden said.

"I know. Which one do you wear, the funk or the Angel?" I teased.

"It's too early in the evening to come for me. My reading skills are sharp since I've had only one beer," Hayden said, laughing.

Thursdays were reserved for my best male friend. Right after I leave the office, Hayden and I would usually meet at our favorite hangout, Joe's Pub, in the village on Lafayette and Astor Place. We'll have a couple of drinks, then head uptown to my place or over to Brooklyn, where Hayden lives. We watch *Survivor* and *Will & Grace*. Most times we fall asleep and wake up in the middle of night and talk about life and the perfect relationships neither one of us have but secretly dream of.

Joe's Pub was a cute little spot that featured live entertainment of up-and-coming R&B groups and poetry slams. It was also a place where both Hayden and I felt special because of the attention we received from the male patrons.

Hayden was from Pittsburgh and had moved to New York to perform with the Dance Theatre of Harlem and was later a principal dancer for a new group called Evidence. He had injured his knee and was now concentrating on acting and Broadway. He was tall, almost 6'5" with a well-proportioned dancer's body and sculpted biceps. He had an angular face with unusual gold-flecked dark brown eyes.

"So what did you do today?" I asked as the bartender brought over a glass of white wine for me and another beer for Hayden.

"Nothing special. Went to the gym after all the gym bunnies left. Dropped my pictures off at a couple of casting agents and then I did a little broke shopping, looking in the windows, since I don't have any money to buy anything," Hayden said.

"Anything look promising?"

"Are you kidding? Child, if I don't get a callback for *The Lion King*, then I can forget about Broadway," Hayden said.

"Didn't you say something about auditioning for *Oklahoma!*?"

"Yep, but it didn't go that well. I must admit that ole Hayden can't high kick like he used to. I'm getting old."

"Please, you're not even thirty," I said.

"For a dancer I might as well be fifty. Besides, I don't care what the doctor said about making me as good as new, I still feel a little pain after I've danced for more than thirty minutes. That won't cut it on the Great White Way."

"But you're not going to give up, are you?" I asked as I squeezed Hayden's hand.

"Naw, I'm not going to do that, but you might have to fire that assistant of yours and let me come work for you," Hayden said, smiling.

"But you can't even type," I said.

"Yeah, but I'd look good trying," he said, laughing.

"You got enough money?"

"I'm okay. I'll let you know before I head to the soup kitchen."

"So how's your love life?"

"You mean my lust life?"

"Whatever."

"I've hit a dry spell. I was hoping there would be more prospects in here than this," Hayden said as he surveyed the room with one scope. His eyes suddenly lit up when a handsome, brown-suited UPS man walked into the bar, carrying a box.

"Hayden, don't embarrass me," I warned. Hayden approached *any man* in whom he took an interest. It didn't matter if the man was gay, bi, or straight. In fact, Hayden preferred men who were somewhat confused, and I had been captivated by his stories of seducing so-called straight men. When I protested, telling him if he had them they couldn't be straight, he would tell me what he told them: As long as they messed around with only him, then they kept their straight status.

Hayden didn't have time for romance with gay men because he said they brought him too much drama and heartache. I knew his current dating strategy was just a phase he was going through and that one day he'd give true love a chance. I was also a little concerned that he had such an easy time meeting and having sex with men who were either married or living with a woman. I was comforted by Hayden's promise that he wouldn't let me date any man who swung both ways, and whenever I had a concern I made sure Hayden met the guy before I became intimate. I remember how mad Hayden was when I introduced him to Jabar and Hayden had to admit that he didn't stand a ghost of a chance to get him to cross over, even for just one night.

"So how is my man?" Hayden asked.

"Who?"

"Zola, don't be coy with me. You know who I'm talking about."

"Jabar?"

"Yes."

"You know I don't see him but once a week. Twice if he's lucky." I smiled.

"Stop frontin'. If you get that dick twice a week, then we both know who the lucky one is," Hayden said.

"As Jabar would say, 'That's what's up,'" I said, laughing.

"Tell me about it. What time is it?" Hayden asked as he looked around the bar for a clock.

I checked my cell phone and realized that it was almost seven-thirty. I gulped down my wine, dropped my phone in my bag, and told Hayden to drink up, that it was time for us to dash.

From *Bling Bling* Confidential

When Davis met Veronica Meadors during orientation at Harvard, it was love at first sight for him. For Veronica, the leggy beauty from Philadelphia it was love at fifth sight—once she learned from his close friend Seth, that Davis came from old money. She was even more interested when she discovered that both of Davis's parents were deceased and there were no siblings to share his inheritance, which he would receive once he turned twenty-five. Since Veronica had her own trust fund, she decided she could wait.

6

It was a humid Tuesday evening in early July, and I jumped from the taxi to the street and then through a gold and glass door. A nervous anticipation bounced in my stomach as I rode up the elevator with an attendant to Davis's Fifth Avenue apartment. I wondered if I'd be dressed appropriately since I'd only changed my shirt and tie and had kept on the suit I'd worn to the office that day.

Davis's wife, Veronica, had insisted on giving a small dinner party for me to welcome me to New York City. I was hoping that Davis had told her I was gay so I wouldn't have to spend the evening entertaining some beautiful woman she had invited just for me.

When I reached the penthouse I took a deep breath and rang the doorbell. Seconds later, an older white man in a tux opened the beveled-glass door and greeted me with a very stately, "Welcome to the McClinton residence. And you would be?" as he looked me over from head to toe as if he were measuring me for a better suit.

"I'm Raymond Tyler."

"Yes sir, you're the evening's guest of honor. Please follow me, Mr. Tyler," he said as he turned to lead me down a long hallway covered by a colorful Persian rug. I could hear the buzz of conversation and laughter coming from the end of the hall.

I was led into a large mahogany-paneled room with three chandeliers that looked like dripping diamonds. It was the size of a small ballroom, grand and gilded, with built-in bookshelves and gold-trimmed books. A shiny baby grand piano occupied a space next to a life-size marble statue. When I walked into the room, Davis saw me and signaled for me to join him. He was holding a monogrammed brandy snifter with an amber-colored liquid and smoking a cigar. He was also dressed in an elegant navy blue tux with a white shirt sans tie. As I moved toward him, I suddenly wished I had at least changed suits. I felt like the Eddie Murphy character in the movie *Trading Places*.

"Raymond, over here. I have someone I want you to meet."

"Davis, how are you doing? This apartment is amazing," I said as I looked around the spacious room with its high ceiling. It was so large that calling Davis's place an apartment didn't sound appropriate.

"I don't think you'd call this an apartment," a large lady said as she chuckled with the musical laughter of a bubbly socialite. I guess she was a mind reader.

"It does have more than twenty-five rooms," Davis said as he smiled at me and the lady.

"I'm Danielle DuBois," the woman said as she extended her plump hand, flaunting a large diamond on her ring finger.

"Nice meeting you, Miss DuBois," I said as I took her hand and shook it gently.

"The DuBois of Philadelphia and Newport," she added. I didn't know what she meant by that exactly, but I just nodded and smiled like I knew.

"What are you drinking, Raymond?" Davis asked.

"White wine," I said.

"Tell me you're kidding? I've got some fifty-year-old scotch that you must try," Davis said.

"Maybe later. Just some wine right now," I repeated.

"What about some champagne? I know my butler keeps the Cristal chilled," Davis enticed.

Since it seemed like getting a glass of wine was going to require an act of Congress, I quickly agreed. Davis disappeared, and I started to walk slowly around the room, admiring the books and artwork. I glanced out a large window, which looked out onto a busy Fifth Avenue, when I heard a female voice say, "You must be Raymond."

I turned around quickly. I was facing a tall, beautiful lady with an egg-shaped face and long auburn hair. She was wearing an elegant egg-yolk-colored evening gown and an emerald necklace surrounded with diamonds the size of Spanish peanuts.

"I'm Veronica Meadors McClinton," she said as she gave me a quick peck on my cheek and handed me a drink. "My husband asked me to give this to you."

"Thanks," I said, accepting the glass. "Nice to meet you."

"Come, let me show you around. I also want to introduce you to our daughter and some of our guests. I invited only eight people, and I just hope none of the gossip columnists find out about this little dinner. I'll have hell to pay if some of my *B-List* friends find out I had a dinner party and didn't invite them. I find it best to ask people to only one or two events a year or else they get a little too comfortable," Veronica said as she offered me the soft hint of a smile. There was an impatient edge to her voice, but I could tell she was trying hard to be nice.

I followed Veronica back down the long hallway as she pointed out different rooms, including a music room and a twenty-five-seat screening room. Veronica led me to what seemed like another part of the house, where she gently opened the door. I could see that it was a child's room, and I noticed a white lady wearing a modest uniform, with a book, sitting on the edge of the full-size canopy bed.

"Is she sleeping?" Veronica asked, and the lady nodded. Veronica then turned to me and put her slim finger to her lips and whispered, "Maybe you can meet her next time."

"I'll look forward to it," I said as I noticed the face of a young girl with small hands covering her nose.

I toured Veronica and Davis's apartment in awe. The master suite was larger than my temporary residence and included a thousand-square-foot closet with floor-to-ceiling drawers and a special chilled area for furs and cashmere sweaters. I discovered that he had a staff of six that lived in the residence—a nanny, a chef, and two maids, one for the day and one for the evening, as well as a butler and Davis's personal valet who was on twenty-four-hour call.

"So, where did you go to school?" Veronica asked.

"The University of Alabama and then Columbia Law," I said proudly. "I also have an MBA from the University of Washington."

"What about prep school?" Veronica asked.

"I attended public school."

"Oh, you poor thing, but you're from the South, right?"

"Yep, a proud son of the new South," I said.

I could tell Veronica was not impressed with my education or Southern upbringing, and I suddenly felt like I should repeat my Ivy League law education but decided against it. I was sure Veronica was trying to make me feel ashamed of my public school background, so I raised my eyebrow to let her know she had said something insulting, but I wasn't about to go off on the boss's wife in her own house.

Just as it seemed Veronica was getting ready to ask something else about my background, another white lady with a plump, pleasant face approached us and said, "Madame McClinton, dinner is served."

"Thank you, Marion," Veronica said as she looped her arm through mine and led me to the dining area. It looked like something out of a British murder mystery, with a long table covered with a white linen tablecloth and adorned with blue Wedgwood china and crystal goblets.

I listened intently to the guests' conversation, which mostly included yachts, summer homes, and parties, losing money on technology stocks, and how hard it was to find good personal assistants. When I didn't join in, there was a friendly silence interspersed with more comments about wealth and the silliest of people, especially black people who actually thought earning a million dollars might make one a millionaire. I suddenly missed Trent and recalled how we would enjoy talking about different guests at events like this, even though I couldn't ever remember a dinner party like this in Seattle.

After courses of soup, salad, and tuna tartare, one of the guests complimented Veronica on the food. She took a sip from her wineglass and said, "Thank you, darling. I slaved over a hot checkbook all day." Most of the guests laughed, and I gazed into my empty soup dish, wishing I hadn't emptied it so fast.

Based on the gentleman sitting next to me during dinner, I figured Davis had told Veronica I was gay. He was a tall, brown-skinned man with thick eyebrows that looked like they had been painted on. He told me his name was Mathis, and when I asked if he had a last name, he laughed and said, "I used to before my parents disowned me. It's a very interesting story and I would love to tell you sometime."

I smiled back like I might be interested, and he whispered, "My place, of course. If I can decide which one."

"Must be nice." I smiled.

"Where do you summer?" Mathis asked.

"Excuse me?"

"I mean, do you have a place in the Hamptons or the Vineyard?"

"No, I just moved back east," I said.

"Then I'll have to invite you to one of my soirees this summer at Fire Island," Mathis said.

"I see you two are getting along wonderfully," Veronica said. She had left the head of the table and looked pleased with herself and the party as she circled her guests like a socialized vulture.

"Oh, Veronica, darling, you didn't tell me that Mr. Tyler was so handsome," Mathis said.

I looked away in embarrassment while Veronica said, "Who knew."

Then Mathis and Veronica both laughed and touched hands. The laugh sounded fake. Who was I kidding, it was fake.

I turned to my left and was looking in the face of Danielle and decided to engage in a little small talk.

"So, are you from New York, Ms. DuBois?" I asked.

"Darling, please call me Danielle. I used to live in New York, and I still have a place here, but my husband and I live in Paris."

"So, what brings you to New York?"

"The evening, of course. Veronica and I go way back, and when she calls and tells me she needs me, well, I just call my pilot and head across the waters," she said, laughing.

"So, you just came for the evening?"

"Yes. I might do a little shopping in the morning and then head back to the most fabulous city in the world."

I smiled politely and finished the rest of the excellent piece of beef the chef had prepared.

After dinner Davis and Veronica led us into the music room, where they had a frail man with glasses playing the piano and a lady in a red velvet dress playing the violin. The music was beautiful, but I was ready to go back to my apartment.

I was hoping the servants would move faster with the coffee and after-dinner drinks, but they didn't seem in a hurry. All the men were smoking cigars and one of the ladies was smoking and coughing at the same time. I was getting ready to bolt, when a tall, well-built white man walked over to me, extended his large hand and said, "I was sitting at the end of the table, I wanted to introduce myself before I left. I'm Chris Thomas."

"Thanks, Chris. How are you doing?"

"Davis has been bragging about how he had convinced this hotshot lawyer from the Northwest to come and oversee some of his interests," Chris said, smiling. He looked like a corn-fed football player and had a handsome face, curly brown hair and sparkling hazel eyes.

"So, that's what he's been saying. What do you do, Chris?" I asked. I suddenly wished I hadn't, because it seemed like the question I had been asked more than my name by the other guests. I assumed Veronica hadn't bothered with providing her other guests with my bio.

"Oh, I'm a lawyer."

"What kind of law do you practice?"

"Very little these days. I'm a partner in Cook, Johnson, and Kahill. We specialize in employment discrimination cases. Have you heard of us?"

I vaguely remembered a large firm from when I had practiced in New York in the early nineties, so I said yes. Chris and I continued our conversation, and one of my impressions had been correct. Chris, who was from Lincoln, Nebraska, had played football at Harvard and later for the Chicago Bears. I told him about Kirby, and he recognized his name. When I asked how he knew Davis, he told me they had met at Harvard. He also said that his wife, who was unable to attend dinner this evening, was one of Veronica's best friends.

I found out Chris and his wife, Debi, had created a foundation for AIDS prevention that serviced minority neighborhoods. When I told him about More Than Friends, the foundation I had set up in memory of my best friend, Kyle Benton, Chris suggested I send him some information on it. Chris also told me that his wife was a doctor doing AIDS research and felt like they were coming awfully close to a vaccine.

When I told him about Kyle and our wonderful friendship and eventual loss, Chris pressed his large hand on my shoulder in a very comforting gesture. It was as if he understood that I missed my friend still after all these years. "Time doesn't always cure everything," Chris said.

I wondered why Chris and his wife were so interested in AIDS, but I decided to save my questions for our next meeting, since Chris insisted that I have dinner with him and his wife very soon. There was something warm and humble about Chris. I found myself drawn to him and agreed immediately to meet for dinner. I thought it was interesting that the only person I enjoyed conversing with was the lone white guest.

When Mathis cornered me as I was getting ready to leave, I was thankful I had given my last business card to Chris.

From *Bling Bling* Confidential

Davis didn't have any African Americans as members of his household staff or as executive assistants. He was concerned that the lines between professional and personal were so easily blurred when it came to his own people. Besides, he knew if they saw how he and his family lived it would breed jealousy and contempt.

7

"Zola, I'm sorry I'm running a little late," Kirsten Dawson said as she sat down at a corner table at Judson Grill in midtown.

"That's all right. I know you're busy. Thanks for agreeing to have lunch," I said as I took the last sip of my club soda. Kirsten was a tall and lean brown-skinned sister with beautiful locks down her back. She was wearing a thin peacock-blue sweater that was filled to capacity and a shapeless black skirt. She had earrings in both her ears and her nose and wore very little makeup. She had a delicately pretty face, but I wondered why it had never occurred to her to pluck her eyebrows.

I had arranged the lunch with Kirsten, who was one of the city's top freelance celebrity writers, to convince her to do a rewrite of a cover story on Halle Berry that we had pushed back several months. Her name alone on the cover of a magazine could mean at least an additional twenty thousand in sales. Still, she had the reputation of being notoriously late with stories, was resistant to being edited, and always required final approval on her stories. Perfect for Yancey B., I thought.

You had to handle Kirsten with kid gloves like she was more important than the talent. Cross Kirsten, and she and her agent might disappear for months, holding the story hostage.

"Yes, I am. I just left a meeting with *Vibe*, and when I leave here, I'm headed for *In Style*. Bringing in the benjamins," Kirsten said as she grabbed one of the menus standing on the table.

"What's good here?" I asked.

"Everything. I love the shrimp and avocado salad. Delicious, and the onion rings are the bomb," Kirsten said.

The waiter came over and asked Kirsten what she wanted to drink, and she ordered a martini. I never understood professional people who could cocktail during lunch and then expect to be productive in the afternoon. It was an off-the-record policy at *Bling Bling* that staff members didn't drink during lunch. I knew I couldn't expect the same from freelancers, even though I was paying the bill.

"So, how much time do we have?" I asked.

"I've got a couple of hours. What do we need to talk about? I know you loved the story," Kirsten said confidently.

"Yeah," I said softly. How was I going to tell her the feature needed some major work? This was one of the reasons I didn't really like hiring the heavy hitters, but they could get to the major celebrities that neither I nor any of my staff writers could snag for a one-on-one interview. The best some of my staff writers could get was a phone interview. Kirsten was the type of writer who was regularly invited to the sets of movies and into the homes of stars. Her access really allowed the readers to feel like they were there at the interview.

"When will the article run?" Kirsten asked as she removed the martini olives and laid them on her bread plate. She finished the drink with two long gulps while waiting for me to answer.

"Well, we're still waiting for some pictures. Do you think there's any way we could get some pictures of Halle and Eric's wedding? No photos have run yet, so it would be major a coup for *Bling*," I said.

"I don't think we can get any photos," Kirsten said. I guess she had forgotten how she boasted about being so tight with Halle's publicist that she could get anything out of them she wanted.

"Do you think we can talk to Eric's daughter about what a great mother Halle is?"

Kirsten rolled her eyes and looked at me like I had called her a bad name and said, "I don't talk to children."

"What about some of the people Halle went to high school with? I mean, if we could talk to the girl she had to share the title of prom queen with, well, that would be just priceless," I said.

"How am I going to do that?" Kirsten asked as she motioned for the waiter. Before I answered, the waiter came over and Kirsten ordered another drink, but this time she requested a double.

I wanted to tell her it was called reporting, but all I could think about was the beautiful and talented Halle Berry gracing my cover with Kirsten's name running across some amazing outfit Halle would wear for the photo shoot.

"What about some of her ex-boyfriends?" I suggested.

"Why?"

"I just think the story needs some more quotes. A little more depth," I said cautiously.

"More depth? I thought you said you liked the story," she said, her voice edged with surprise.

"Oh, I do. I just think it could be stronger."

"I don't know about that. Besides, my schedule is tight. I don't know when I can get around to it," Kirsten said. I could tell she wasn't exactly feeling good about me right about now.

"What if I got someone from my staff to help out?"

"I don't work well with other people. That's why I freelance."

"Oh, I understand, but I was just thinking of maybe getting a researcher who could find some of the people I think would make the story stronger and then have you do the interview," I said.

"I hope you don't expect me to be going to Cleveland or some-place like that. I really don't like traveling to small towns. Let's order."

"Okay," I said, hoping maybe a meal might soak up some of the vodka Kirsten had gulped down and suddenly make her more reason-able. I didn't really know what the next step should be. I was already paying her four dollars a word, which was going to really put a dent in my budget for future projects. I justified paying her the large amount of money because of the additional revenue the issue would bring in. I decided that I should maybe change the subject from Halle and the rewrite and talk about something a little more pleasant.

"Did you get the invitation to the dinner party for some of our adver-tisers and top writers?"

"Oh, yeah. I'm really looking forward to it. I've got my dress nar-rowed down to three," Kirsten said.

"I know you'll look beautiful," I said.

"Well, you know I won't come in there half stepping. You never know when Mr. Right Now might show up," Kirsten said, laughing.

The waiter placed our entrées down, and I was relieved I no longer had to make small talk. A dull silence covered our corner of the large dining room, broken when Kirsten ordered a glass of Merlot. I figured I would just rewrite the story my damn self.

8

I had been in New York over a month before I made the phone call I knew I would eventually make, dialing the digits of John Basil Henderson. He was a man I had a love/I-think-you're-out-of-your-mind relationship with. Basil was a super-sexy gray-eyed ex-professional football player I'd had flings with at different times in my life. I called him a friend, although we rarely saw eye to eye on anything. Still, there was something about the sexy Mr. Henderson that maintained my curiosity, and I knew the feelings were mutual. He's so cocksure, and he routinely turns the heads of both men and women.

The moment I'd gotten to the city I had thought about calling Basil, but I decided I should get my bearings in my new position before I brought any John Basil Henderson confusion into my life. Besides, I figured there was nothing like a good-looking man to make me forget about my troubles. The last time I had seen or spoken to Basil, he'd been in a great deal of trouble, but I suspected he had somehow made it through since I hadn't heard from him in a while.

I grabbed my PalmPilot and located Basil's numbers, but I didn't know if I should call his office or apartment. I really just wanted to leave a message and let him contact me.

Basil answered after two rings.

"What's going on?" I asked.

"Raymond Tyler, what are you doing in New York? Looking for me?" Basil asked.

"How did you know I was in New York?" I asked.

"Now, you know a brotha like me gonna have caller ID. It's good hearing your voice," Basil said.

"So that's why you call me all the time?" I joked.

"I've been meaning to call you," Basil said.

"Sure, sure. I bet you tell that to all the boys and girls," I said. Basil was terribly confused when it came to his sexuality, or maybe he was truly bisexual.

"So we got a lot to catch up on. A lot has changed since we last spoke. How long are you here for?"

"A while. I've taken a job here," I said.

"What? Man, that's great. When's your boy getting here?"

"I'm not certain," I said quickly. "What's going on with you?"

"I'm in love again, and this time it's the real thing. I can't wait for you to meet her," Basil said. There was an excitement in his voice I had never heard, so I was thinking that maybe he had finally met the woman who could tame his wild ways.

"That's great. What happened to Rosa? More important, whatever happened with that Yancey lady?"

"I don't know if I should tell you this over the phone or in person," Basil said.

"You must have big news if you don't want to talk about it over the phone. What's going on with the firm?" The last time I had spoken with Basil, he was trying to decide whether he was going to leave the sports management company he co-owned.

"It's big, and things couldn't be better at the firm. We've signed some of the top talent coming out this year and we got rid of that asshole Nico," Basil said.

"Nico. I think I remember you talking about him. Was he one of the partners?"

"Yeah, that's the niggah who thought he was going to get me to leave the firm. I did some checking on his dealings with some of our clients' finances and, well, let's just say it was either leave the firm or spend some time in jail," Basil said.

"Dude, what's going on with your brother's agent? The guy in Florida is getting ready to go on trial. I guess I won't be so judgmental the next time I see some black athlete signed with a white agent."

"I hear you. But I don't want to talk about that mofo. I can't wait for you to meet Talley Henderson," Basil said.

I was wondering if I had heard Basil correctly. Did he say the new lady in his life shared his last name? Was Basil married?

"Talley Henderson," I said nervously. I didn't know why it even mattered who his new lady was. I always assumed Basil would end up with some beautiful lady and keep an equally good-looking man on the side.

"Yes, Talley, and she is beautiful," Basil boasted.

"I can't wait to meet her," I said weakly.

"What are you doing this evening?"

"I've got to meet with my new boss. You might know him, or maybe you've heard of him. Davis McClinton."

"Who hasn't heard of him? I mean, that brotha is the big dog. I heard he might be the first black billionaire. Is that true?"

"Possibly," I said, feeling very small that I had lied about my plans to Basil. I just didn't want to spend the evening watching him fawn over some beautiful playmate of a woman.

"Maybe we can get together for breakfast or lunch. It might be hard for you to meet Talley because she'll be in nursery school," Basil said.

"Is she a teacher?"

"A teacher?" Basil asked with a deep laugh.

"Did I say something funny?" I asked.

"Who do you think Talley is?"

"Your new lady," I said.

"True, but it's not what you think," Basil said.

"Who is she?"

There was a brief pause and then Basil said proudly, "Talley is my daughter. Ray, I'm a daddy."

"What? When did this happen? The last time I spoke with you, the biggest thing in your life was telling your father the truth about you. Now you're a father? I can't believe this," I said.

"It's a long story, but I can't tell you how happy I am, Ray. Talley is just beautiful. She's changed my life."

"Sounds like it. Who's the mother?" I asked. I hadn't read anything in the entertainment magazine about Basil's ex, Yancey, having a baby. Besides, she knew the real deal about Basil, and I didn't know a lot of women who would knowingly take a chance with a man who slept with both sexes, unless you were Michelle Adams, Trent's baby's mama.

"Rosa. Remember the flight attendant I used to hang with? It's a long story, and I can't wait to sit down and tell you."

"Are you still hanging with her?"

"No, not like that, but we're cool. Trying our best to be great parents to our daughter," Basil said. I couldn't believe how mature and serious he sounded. Maybe this parenting thing was more powerful than I could have ever imagined.

"Let me give you my number. I've got to run, but I can't wait to meet your little girl," I said.

"Do that," Basil said.

I gave Basil my office numbers and suggested that we get together soon. I didn't know if I was looking forward to seeing him, but I knew it was something I had to do.

9

I tapped gently on Raymond's office door and I heard a voice say, "Come in."

When I walked into his office, I smelled the strong scent of food, like somebody had been slaving over an oven or grill.

"Zola, glad you could make it. I hope you like ribs," Raymond said.

"I do," I said as I looked to my left and noticed a table with a red and white tablecloth covered with a wooden picnic basket. There was a bottle of red wine standing beside the basket with two wine glasses. I hoped my new boss wasn't trying to get me drunk in the middle of the day and try and have his way with me. I would hate to have to sue him for sexual harassment during his first month.

"Great. I thought instead of going to a noisy restaurant we could have lunch here in my office. I want us to have a chance to get to know one another," Raymond said as he pulled out a chair. Hmmm, I thought to myself, I like this. Raymond was a gentleman, unlike that fool Seth

Matthews, who held the position of CEO before he went wacko and was quickly escorted out of the building.

"Thank you." I smiled as I took my seat. "Whatever's in that basket smells good," I said.

"I hope so. I ordered ribs from a place around the corner called Virgil's. Bristol said they have great food, although I'm sure their ribs aren't as good as the ones we cook down in Alabama," Raymond said.

"So, you're a Southern boy. I should have known," I said, wondering if Raymond would be insulted by my referring to him as a boy.

"True and true," Raymond said.

I breathed a sigh of relief that I hadn't offended my new boss. "I'm from Nashville," I said.

"I know. Davis gave me a copy of your bio," Raymond said.

"Why am I not surprised," I said.

"Zola, I don't really want to talk a lot of business over our little picnic. The two of us are going to be working pretty closely together, and I want to get to know the real Zola. Not the magazine editor or the person in the bio," Raymond said as he took a seat and opened the basket and the scent of the meat became stronger. It reminded me of my parents' kitchen when they had just brought meat from the grill on holidays or summer evenings when Daddy had a taste for beef.

"Sounds good, although I'll tell you, I've never had a picnic before like this in my career," I said.

"What was your relationship with the guy who had my job before me?" Raymond asked as he pulled a plastic container from the basket that looked like it held coleslaw.

"Seth and I really didn't have a relationship. He was Davis's right-hand man, but he was too weak and let Davis literally drive him crazy. Maybe it wasn't Davis but his wife and girlfriend," I said, laughing. I didn't know why, but I felt totally comfortable talking with Raymond. I looked over at him and scrutinized his face. His smooth skin glowed like a warm stick of butter, and his eyes were a startling shade of grass green.

"You're kidding, right?"

"About Seth?"

"Yes."

"I wish I was. Everybody in the office knew he had a mistress, and sometimes she would come up to the office when he thought everyone was gone. He let this job and Davis get to him. Mr. McClinton's shadow can be cold and overpowering. There are some stories I could tell you, but I'll wait until I get to know you better," I said.

"Would you like both baked beans and coleslaw?" Raymond asked.

"Sure. It looks good. Did black folks make this?" I asked.

"I'm not sure. I took a peek at the ribs and they looked like they'd pass the Slap-Yo-Mama's test," Raymond said, smiling. He was wearing a starched white shirt with a rose-red tie with a thin strip of royal blue. I noticed a navy blue pinstriped suit coat on a hanger over the door that led to the private bathroom and shower, which I had actually used when the office had been empty while Davis found a replacement for Seth.

"What kind of wine is this," I said as I picked up the bottle and read something in French. I thought about Davis and how pompous he sounded when he ordered in French.

"A very nice French Merlot. Can I pour you a glass?" Raymond asked.

"Sure, but just a little corner. I got a lot of work waiting on my desk," I said.

Raymond walked over to the bar area and picked up a corkscrew and then went back over to the table, where he opened the wine. He smelled the cork and then poured a little taste in my glass like we were at an expensive restaurant.

I took a sip and enjoyed the dry fruity taste.

"How is it?"

"Wonderful," I said.

"I'm glad the lady approves," Raymond said as he poured me half a glass and about the same into his and sat down and gave me a polite smile. I guess the no cocktail rule was made to be broken.

"So what do you want to know about me?"

"Who came up with the name *Bling Bling*?"

"I tell you, it wasn't me. Davis came up with it. I hate the name, but Davis thought that young kids spend more money on music and the products we advertise in the magazine. I guess I've gotten used to it. What do you think of it?"

"It's different," Raymond answered quickly.

"So is that the only business question? Nothing about future issues, advertising revenues, or personnel issues?"

"That's it. Now it's Raymond and Zola."

"So I'll ask again. What do you want to know about me? My family? My friends? What I do for fun or have I been involved in covert activities?" I teased.

"Tell me what you want me to know. Did you pledge while you were in college?" Raymond asked.

"No, I didn't." A surprised look crossed Raymond's face. "I just knew you were greek," Raymond said.

"I started to, but I couldn't decide. At first I wanted to pledge Delta, but their lines were always so long. I didn't want to be a small fish in a big sea. Then I was stuck on pledging AKA and really liked the girls on the yard, but they were a large group as well. The fish theory again. I had this professor who I just loved and she was a Zeta, and I decided that's what I wanted to be. Just when I thought I had made up my mind, I became really close with a Sigma, Lorraine, who was majoring in journalism. That sista was bad. She was one of the smartest girls at Tennessee State and could dress her butt off. In the fall, girls couldn't wait to see what Lorraine was wearing the first few weeks of school," I said. I couldn't believe I was sitting there, chatting easily with Raymond, but there was a warm quality about him that made me feel comfortable and safe. Nothing like being around Davis. With him I always felt I had to think about everything I said before it left my mouth.

"I guess I can understand your not being able to make a choice. They're all great organizations. I also know a lot of it depends on what school or part of the country you're in," Raymond said.

I took a bite of the rib, which was so good that the meat was falling off the bones. I poured a little of the barbecue sauce and dipped the meat in it like I was eating chicken wings. Raymond was using the black and gold china with the official McClinton Enterprises crest that Veronica, the wife, had insisted that Davis purchase for the few formal dinners we held at the office.

"Did you pledge?" I asked Raymond after I had finished one rib and dipped my hands into the box for another one.

"I'm a member of KAQ," Raymond said calmly.

"Why am I not surprised?"

"Why do you ask that?" Raymond asked.

"Two words. Pretty boy," I said. I noticed Raymond blushing and thought maybe I had crossed the line, but I still thought it was wonderful to know my new boss was bashful and seemingly not conceited.

"That's not true," Raymond protested.

"Raymond, this is one thing you need to know about me. I am brutally honest. I call them as I see them. I'm sure your wife or girlfriend would agree with me."

"I'm not married and I don't have a girlfriend," Raymond said matter-of-factly. I stopped eating my food and gazed at him for a moment.

"Zola, is there something you want to ask me?"

"Is there something you want to tell me?"

"I just broke up with my partner of several years," Raymond said.

I was thinking he didn't have to hit me over the head with a rib bone. My new boss was gay, which certainly didn't bother me. Still, I didn't think I should tell him I knew just yet in case Raymond wasn't comfortable talking about his sexuality. If he was, then it would be quite refreshing if he was open and honest and not trying to trick a sister by living his life on the d.l., which I called the d.l.d.—dirty low down.

I wondered for a moment if Raymond would be somebody Hayden might be interested in but quickly remembered my friend was interested only in the low down.

"I'm sorry to hear that. Are you okay?"

"I'm a big boy. I'll be fine," Raymond said.

"Breakups can be a bitch," I said.

"Yeah, they can," Raymond said as he stood and walked over to his desk and picked up a photo. He came back and sat down and asked me to look at the picture. It was a sepia-toned picture of two African American boys and two girls on the back of a truck. It looked like a photo taken in the fifties or early sixties.

"Who is this?" I asked as I studied the photograph closely.

"I don't know. I thought you might know. I found it in my desk, mixed in with some letterheads," Raymond said.

"Did you ask Bristol?" I noticed the names Norman and Scooter printed in a child's handwriting.

"No, these people look black," Raymond said.

I looked at the picture again and said, "Yeah, they're light but not white. Even though sometimes I think Bristol might be an undercover brotha. You know, passing," I said, laughing.

"You're crazy. But Bristol does have a sense of what's right about our culture. He picked up all these great CDs for me. Maxwell, Joe, Angie Stone. I guess he reads your magazine." Raymond laughed.

"Yeah, Bristol is cool people. I talk to him every now and then. Did he tell you he used to work at *Vibe* and *Vanity Fair*?"

"Yes."

"I'm pretty sure Davis stole him from over there by offering him a lot of money and making a lot of promises," I said.

"Do you think it belongs to Seth?"

"What?"

"The photograph," Raymond said.

"I doubt it. Seth was very dark, blue-black," I said. "I personally love every shade we come in. From light-bright to blue-black."

"I hear you. Are you sure it's not a family photo that belonged to Seth?"

"Besides, he was an only child like Davis. The two of them started off really tight. I think they went to college together. You should have seen the two of them together when they had a couple of drinks. Styling and profiling, smoking big cigars, talking about the good old days at prep school and Harvard," I said.

"What happened to them?"

"Just between you and me, I think Seth resented Davis's success. I think he wanted to be just like him, but Seth wasn't as confident or aggressive as Davis and gradually got annoyed by that. He knew Davis was looking to replace him because people in their social circles were talking about it. His job was so important to him he couldn't take the pressure. I guess that's why old Seth lost it. I wasn't here when it happened, but office lore has it that when Seth cleaned out his office he did it in a yellowed T-shirt stained with coffee, a tie around his neck, and plaid boxer shorts," I said.

"That's sad," Raymond said.

"Yes, sad would be the word. Just make sure you don't leave here that way," I said.

"Thanks for the warning," Raymond said.

"Thanks for the ribs," I said as I got up to go back to my office.

From *Bling Bling* Confidential

People often spent so much time looking at how beautiful Raymond's green eyes were that they never noticed they were stained with loneliness.

10

I located the gothic brownstone on Eighty-eighth Street between Columbus and Amsterdam avenues. I pulled a yellow piece of paper from my suit jacket pocket and looked at the number 105 and then the number on the building. I walked up slowly, like I was getting ready to enter a haunted house, took a deep breath, and rang the bell.

After a couple of weeks of restless nights, I decided I should get some help before I quietly had a nervous breakdown. At first I thought I was having trouble sleeping because I missed having Trent's warm body next to mine, but I realized I had some anger brewing inside. Many of those nights it took everything I had not to pick up the phone and call Trent and yell at him about what he'd done to our relationship, what he'd done to me.

A few moments passed and I rang the bell again. This time I heard a buzzing sound, and I pushed the door open and found myself in a cluttered foyer with several newspapers lying on the floor and a coatrack that held several jackets and a couple of nondescript umbrellas. I saw three doors and a set of buzzers with last names on two of them. Dr. Carolyn Few was on the bottom. I pressed the button and heard another buzzing sound and the release of several locks. A few moments later, a medium-size white lady with a pale complexion and long, stringy black hair opened the door. She was wearing a pale green top with a matching skirt.

"Are you Raymond Tyler?" she asked.

"Yes."

"I'm Dr. Few. Come on in. You're a little early, but my appointment before you canceled, so we're fine," she said.

I looked at my watch and realized that it was ten minutes before six. I'd left my office early to make sure I was on time after Dr. Few told me she didn't take kindly to latecomers. I had found her through a referral service on the Internet, and she had been the fifth doctor I'd called. The first four weren't taking new clients, and I felt I really needed to talk to someone quickly, and didn't have the luxury of finding an African American doctor.

I followed Dr. Few into her office, which looked more like the living room or work space of an artist. There were several paintings on easels, a comfortable-looking melon-colored sofa with pastel pillows, and a rocking chair in which Dr. Few promptly seated herself.

"Have a seat," Dr. Few said.

"Thank you," I said as I sat down and crossed my legs and laid my hands across my lap, but I didn't feel quite comfortable.

"Since this is your first visit, I need to go over some housekeeping details. I charge a hundred and fifty dollars an hour. I expect to be paid at the end of each fifty-minute session. I accept insurance, but that's only after you have been a patient for three months. I have a forty-eight-hour cancellation policy, and if you don't show up or call, then you will be billed. Leaving a message on my answering machine is okay, but I would prefer to speak with you when you need to cancel. Do you have any questions for me?" Dr. Few asked.

"No."

Dr. Few picked up a yellow legal pad and pen from a cloth covered ottoman next to her chair and asked, "Have you been in therapy before?"

"Yes."

"How long ago?"

"Oh, about eight years ago," I said.

"Do you mind sharing the circumstances?" she asked.

"It was after the death of my best friend," I said.

"Did you take any medication?"

"Briefly. The doctor gave me something to help me sleep."

"Are you on any medication now?"

"No."

"Do you drink?"

"Socially, maybe a couple of glasses of wine to relax," I said.

"So tell me why you felt the need to resume therapy," Dr. Few said.

"I've been having trouble sleeping, and my stomach always seems full with nervous energy when my day ends at the office," I said.

"What do you do?"

"I'm a CEO of a magazine."

"And you moved from where?"

"Seattle."

"For your job?"

"Sorta," I mumbled.

"What does 'sorta' mean?"

"I sought out the job."

"You didn't like Seattle? I hear it's a beautiful city," Dr. Few said. I didn't remember my last doctor offering editorial comments. But this was New York, where everybody had an opinion.

"I love Seattle. I didn't like the situation I was in," I said calmly.

"Why don't you tell me about it?"

I spent the next ten minutes telling Dr. Few about my relationship with Trent. I also told her how I'd found out about his affair, his pending fatherhood, and how basically he had made the decision to end the relationship.

"How did that make you feel?" she asked when I had finished speaking.

"Like shit," I said.

"Are you still in love with him?"

Was I still in love with Trent? The question startled me, because I wasn't expecting it and didn't really have a yes-or-no answer. I thought about Dr. Few's question for a few minutes and then I said, "I guess you've heard this before, but here goes: I still love Trent, but I don't think I'm in love with him anymore."

"Are you angry with him?"

"Yes," I said quickly.

"Have you told him?"

"No."

"Why not?"

"I didn't think it was important. I thought it was best to move on."

"Do you have any problems with your sexuality?"

"No."

"That's good," Dr. Few said. I guess she was thinking that would save us some time, but I thought there were some things she needed to know about my self-acceptance.

"I dated women for most of my young-adult life. When I was a senior in college, I realized that I was attracted to men when this football player seduced me. For several years I hated being attracted to men and continued to date women. When I fell in love with Trent, all the feelings of shame seemed to go away," I said.

"Was it a good relationship?"

"It was a great relationship ninety percent of the time," I said. "We both had very demanding careers. Besides practicing law, I was also teaching and working on my MBA. Trent's job required him to travel, and mine did also for extended periods. But we always talked with each other, trying very hard to keep the lines of communication open," I said.

"Are your parents still living, and do you have any siblings?" Dr. Few asked. This question also caught me off guard, because I tried not to think about a time when my parents might not be alive.

"Both of my parents are alive and I have a younger brother."

"Do they know you're gay?"

I started to tell Dr. Few I didn't necessarily like the word *gay*, but then she would want an explanation of why and that would take up too much time.

"Yes, they know and they're very supportive."

"What did they say about the breakup?"

"I haven't told them yet."

"Why?"

"I don't want to burden them," I said softly.

"If they're supportive, then why would it be, as you say, a burden?"

"I don't know."

"Have you told your brother?"

"No."

"Why?"

"Same reason."

"Is that really the reason?" Dr. Few asked.

I didn't answer. I just glanced around the room, focusing on her bookshelf, looking for books I might recognize, and then back at her. I wondered if she could help me deal with my feelings without involving my family. I wanted to prove that I could handle this on my own. Dr. Few didn't repeat her question, but after some time had passed she looked at her watch and said the four words all therapists must love: "Your time is up."

From *Bling Bling* Confidential

Davis loves women for the same reasons a lot of men do. They make him feel strong and powerful. His wife, Veronica, is the love of his life, but he finds her life as a black socialite boring. So there's Zola, who he enjoys because of her looks and the fact that if he or any man raised a hand to her, Zola would cut it off. There was also Annabelle Boyd, a white socialite friend of Veronica's who Davis enjoys because she totally believes the myths about black men, you know the one about size. He is amused by LaKecia because she's straight-up ghetto, thinks five hundred dollars is a lot of money, talks shit, doesn't like to cuddle and gives the best head in town.

11

I was running about ten minutes behind, and Davis didn't like my being late. He didn't understand that sometimes it was just as hard for a sister to get a cab as it was for a brother. Besides, he usually sent a car for me, but had paged me about an hour before I left the office and suggested I get a cab because his driver had to take his wife and daughter to dinner. I started to say "You're rich and you know the rules. Get another driver to cart your wife and kid around."

I raced through the lobby of the Four Seasons hotel and went to the front desk and told the clerk there should be a key waiting for me under the name Mrs. McClinton.

A few minutes later she came back with a smirk and said, "Oh, yes. Your husband is waiting for you in the Presidential Suite. I'm sure you know where the elevator is."

"Thank you," I said as I snatched the card key and raised my eyebrow and gave her my best *don't-try-me* look.

Moments later, I was in the marble foyer of one of the best suites in town. Davis and I had stayed there once before. He'd bragged how he'd once forced Michael Jackson to cut his stay short or move to a smaller suite. Another time he said Michael Jordan and his family were in the suite when he wanted it, but he decided to take something smaller since Michael Jordan was one of the few men he had respect for as an athlete and businessman. I told him Michael Jackson wasn't a slouch in the business department either, since he'd bought the Beatles' music catalogue.

I heard soft music playing, and as I entered the master bedroom I saw Davis sitting on the bed in a cobalt-blue robe with his computer on his lap. There was a Palm, two cell phones, and several files on the side of the bed where I would eventually end up laying my head. Davis wasn't handsome, but he wasn't unattractive either. His body was firm and well proportioned with powerful shoulders and a nice chest. Davis wore his hair short and he didn't have any hair on his face, which was the color of a toasted bagel.

"Sorry I'm late," I said as I leaned over and kissed Davis on the cheek.

"No problem. I just kept myself busy by making a few more million," Davis said.

"How was your day?" I asked as I took off my jacket and heels.

"Now, Zola, you can make better small talk than that. You sound like a suburban housewife who just came in from cheating on her husband," Davis said.

"Cool. You're going to make love to me tonight the way I like it, big daddy?" I asked.

"Now you sound like some ghetto whore," Davis said.

I didn't answer. I just stared at him for moment. I don't know why I let him bother me at times. He could be such a split personality. Sometimes he would talk to me like the lover he thought he was, and there were times when he sounded and acted like a judgmental father.

"Would you like something to drink? I had room service bring up a couple of bottles of Cristal," Davis said.

"A little later. Is that what you're drinking tonight?"

"I'm sipping hundred-year-old cognac my valet found for me on the Internet."

"I guess that sounds good," I said. Davis looked at me firmly. I became uncomfortable under his stare, and soon I stood and turned and faced the huge picture windows and unzipped my skirt from the back. I loved the view from this room. I recalled the first time I had met Davis here and how we watched the sun drop down slowly and beautifully and the dusty yellow light cover the city.

That night was one of the times when Davis seemed interested in my life. He'd asked about my parents even though I had told him more than once what they did for a living. He seemed to understand why I didn't hold my sister in high regard.

Once he asked me if I was saving any money and I proudly told him how much I had in my checking and savings accounts. Davis told me I should take the money out of my accounts and invest it. I told him I had some money in mutual funds, but Davis suggested I live a little and play the market. "Invest your money in companies who make products or provide services you can't live without. Stick by them until you notice the products are slipping or receive negative publicity." I loved the fact Davis had an ego and brain that matched.

"Are you going to shower and start my show soon?" Davis asked, interrupting my thoughts.

"I'm on my way," I said.

"Take your time," Davis said. "We've got all night."

"Oh, Veronica's out of town?"

"I have all night," Davis repeated.

I walked into the bathroom, which was as big as my bedroom. There were three marble vanities, two tubs, and a shower for two. The room was mirrored, and there was a closet lined with maple and teakwood. I noticed three sets of panties and bras all lined up side by side.

On each visit, Davis would have someone purchase expensive silk or satin lingerie for me. Most times there would be three sets and he would have me model each one before picking the one he wanted me to wear to bed. I didn't mind his little crazy fantasy because I got to take all the items home and wear them for Jabar, and they were always beautiful things that I would never buy for myself. I wondered if this was the type of clothing Davis's wife wore to bed every night.

I didn't know a lot about Davis's wife, Veronica, or their marriage. I had heard she was a snob who could go ghetto if needed. She was cute, but you could tell she'd had some work done. Her face looked like she was always excited or surprised, and her breasts were a little too perky for a mother of two.

I had met her on only a couple of occasions, once when Davis gave a big party at Cipriani to celebrate the first year for *Bling Bling*, and again at the Black Charities annual black-tie event, which was one of the major social events of the year. Davis had given me a pair of tickets at the last minute, so I didn't have time to search for the proper outfit. I had worn a little tomato-red dress with spaghetti straps. I thought I looked good and so did Hayden, my date. I went into the bedroom to touch up my makeup, and as luck would have it, I ended up putting on fresh lipstick next to Veronica.

Veronica smiled at me and acted like she didn't remember my name. I could tell she had a personality similar to her husband's when she went from business polite to bitchy black girl in a matter of minutes. I told her how much I loved her dress and she turned toward me and thanked me and said my dress was cute and then asked if I had made it myself. If I hadn't been worried about causing a scene and making the gossip columns, Veronica would still be in that bathroom, picking up her face.

I took off my clothes and started the shower and walked over to feel tonight's selections. There was a white set the color of wedding-dress satin, a pair of soft pear-green panties and a bra with embroidered pearls and fringe, and a bright yellow set. I knew deep down that Davis was really a black-and-white kind of guy, so I decided to wear the white ones last.

I was feeling a little tired and thought a warm shower might put me to sleep, so I turned the water to the lowest level of cold. I stepped into the shower and felt it drowning me like cold ocean waves. When I got out of the shower trembling like a fragile leaf after a rainstorm, I realized I had left the address of my breakfast meeting on my desk. I knew Cyndi, my assistant, was working late, so I picked up the phone to call her and ask her to send the address to my pager. I heard Davis's voice on the phone, and he didn't sound happy.

"What do you mean, they won't cash the checks? Why did you wait so long to tell me?"

"Mr. McClinton, I . . ." a male voice said.

"Damn. Figure out a way to make sure they take the money. Make sure they don't know where it's coming from. Do you understand?"

Who was Davis paying off or buying, I wondered as I hung up the phone, hoping Davis didn't hear me pick it up.

I put on the pear-green panties and bra and walked down the long hallway and back into the bedroom. Davis's eyes traveled up and down my body with the speed of a subway train. He was still on the phone, but he put his hand over the receiver and said, "Those are okay. Put on the ones you know I like and I'll meet you in the library."

I smiled and walked back to the bathroom so that I could change for the second act.

From *Bling Bling* Confidential

Some days, Davis will leave his office and have his driver take him to visit his fourteen-year-old son, Logan, at his Connecticut boarding school. Davis makes sure his visits are unannounced, because he wants to make sure Logan is following not only the school's strict rules but the ones Davis and Veronica have set up as well.

Davis won't accept second best for, or from his son. Logan is expected to maintain a grade point average that will rank him among the top five in his class. Logan can't participate in common sports like football or basketball but is only allowed to master elite sports such as tennis, lacrosse, swimming and golf.

Logan is only allowed to listen to classical music. Davis instituted this rule when an eleven-year-old Logan told his father he wanted to be a rapper. Davis Vincent McClinton was not going to let that happen.

On the way back to New York he instructs his driver to take him through some of New York's underprivileged neighborhoods in Brooklyn, the Bronx and Yonkers. Davis locates a playground or basketball court and passes out hundred-dollar bills to kids curious enough to inspect the black man riding in the immaculate black Mercedes sedan.

12

"So why don't you and me kick it on a regular basis?" Basil asked. He had stopped by my apartment on his way to pick up Talley.

"What are you talking 'bout, niggah? You don't want a relationship with a man," I said as I playfully punched his rock-solid left biceps.

"I'm not talking about no relationship. I mean you and I have always been tight and I think we could roll pretty good on the down low, but the only relationship I want is the one I have with Talley."

"I feel you. But I'm still trying to figure out what I'm going to do next. Getting hooked up with you in a DL relationship is the last thing I need. Let's just keep it like we got now. Friends. Real good friends," I said.

"You sound like a—"

"Hold up. Don't use the word *bitch*. I told you about that shit," I said. I still didn't understand why when men wanted to get their way or show power they resorted to calling somebody a bitch or a faggot.

"I hear you. I sometimes forget some hardhead might be using that word to describe my little girl one day," Basil said. "Some habits are hard to break."

"And you're not going to like it either."

"Damn straight. So you think you gonna get back with ole boy?"

"Trent?"

"Yeah."

"Why is it so hard for you to say his name?"

"Say his name? I can say his name. Trent. Trent. The mofo don't mean shit to me," Basil said, sounding a little bit defensive. I always smiled to myself when he acted jealous.

"Cool. So you can say his name. I don't know if we'll get back together. I really don't spend a lot of time thinking about it. I mean, he got his hands full," I said.

"I still can't believe ole boy . . . I mean Trent . . . came out of the box like that on you, Mr. Raymond Winston Tyler, who's also preaching about telling the bitches and letting them decide if they want to spend some time with a dude. That's bullshit, 'cause once they get a taste of the jimmie, it don't mean shit. I could tell them I was from outer space and it wouldn't matter," Basil said.

"Trent broke the commitment we had to be in a monogamous relationship. That's the problem."

"Did you know he was still interested in females?"

"I never thought about it. He said he was in love with me," I said.

"How did she look?"

"Why does that matter?"

"Was she beautiful?"

"I don't know."

"Do you ever think about hittin' it with females? I know you used to be a first-team ladies' man," Basil said, laughing.

"Basil, let's talk about something else. Isn't it time for you to go pick up Talley?" I asked, wondering why I let myself get into conversations with him about my personal life, or, at this point, the lack thereof.

Basil looked at his watch, gave me a sexy smile, and said, "Yeah, it's getting close to that time. But we gonna talk about this some mo'."

"I don't know why you're so interested in my relationship with Trent."

"I'm not. I just want to know why you won't hit it with me," Basil said.

"You need to be honest with yourself, Basil, before you try to get in a relationship with anybody, and that includes the mother of your child," I said.

"Rosa ain't even trying to hear that shit."

"You should tell her before somebody else does," I suggested.

"If I told her, would you think about hittin' it with me?"

"I don't know, but I don't have to worry about that because you ain't going to ever tell her," I said with a cocky smile.

"I might surprise you one day," Basil said as he got up from the sofa and headed toward the door.

"That would shock me," I said.

"Later," Basil said as he opened the door and gave me a wink that registered with a certain part of my body.

13

I was at home in my den, looking over the competition. I was sipping tea and reading copies of *Teen People, Entertainment Weekly, Sister 2 Sister* and *Honey*, when the phone rang. I looked at the caller ID and saw Justine's number.

"Hello," I said.

"Zola Denise Norwood, what am I going to do with you?" Justine asked.

"What are you talking about, sweetheart?"

"You got me sitting here on my bed in tears, bitch," Justine said.

"Why?"

"I just got your gift and read the note," Justine said.

"Isn't that a great book?" I asked. I had sent copies of *Sisterfriend,* a picture book with stories that I had first seen in the book editor's office at *Bling.* I picked it up and became captivated with the pictures and stories of African American women talking about their friendships and love. I had picked up two copies and sent notes to Justine and Kai, telling them both how much their love, support, and friendship meant to me.

"I can't put it down. Thanks for always thinking about me," Justine said.

"Thanks for always being there for me. How was your day?"

"It was long. It just ended. I had to do several proposals for some big-money events coming up and had a four-hour shift at the hotel with those crazy motherfuckers," Justine said.

"It was long for me too. But I'm going to take a warm bath and get up and play the game again tomorrow," I said.

"Well, at least it's Friday. Did Kai say something to you about dinner?"

"I know there's a message on my machine from her about a surprise."

"Then maybe I'll see you tomorrow."

"Most definitely."

"You sleep well. I love you, Zola," Justine said with such tenderness in her voice, and I felt a wave of sisterly love. I was grateful for the day so many years before when I had invited Justine to sit and eat with me the first day of school at the University School on the campus at Vanderbilt. It was not only the beginning of the school year but a lifelong friendship.

"I love you too, Justine," I said. "Good night."

❖   ❖   ❖

Friday evening, Kai pulled off another one of her surprises that I am certain took her weeks to plan. The three of us had met at Lola's, a restaurant in lower Manhattan, for drinks. As soon as Justine and I walked into the bar area, Kai whisked us off into a waiting limo. We headed to Kai's apartment on the Upper East Side.

When we arrived, Hayden had on a pastel-blue robe, drink in hand and greeted us by saying, "You bitches holding up progress."

Kai had arranged a pamper party. She had hired a masseuse, manicurist, an aesthetician and a handsome Brazilian waiter to cater to our every need. Each of us received massages, facials, manicures and pedicures while drinking cosmopolitans and listening to Diana Krall.

The tuxedo-clad waiter served caviar-covered deviled eggs, crab cakes, and shrimp wrapped in bacon and flirted with the four of us.

"Does he have his papers?" Hayden asked. "'Cause I think I want to marry him if only to see if there's any bite in that bulge in his pants."

"Leave the hired help alone," Kai said.

"Bitch, you sure do know how to spend money, and I'm not hatin', especially tonight," Justine said.

"Right, right," Kai said.

Deliciously exhausted, we retired to Kai's terrace with champagne replacing the cosmopolitans. I was enjoying the soft summer night air on my skin and I gazed at the streetlights, brighter than the tiny stars in the sky. I was thinking how lucky I was to have such great friends who shared not only material gifts but who offered me a love I could depend on.

I was getting ready to voice my appreciation when Hayden said, "I sure wish my daddy could see me now, laid up and made up with you three beautiful grown-ass hoes."

"Why is that, Hayden?" Justine asked.

"So I could show him the difference between love and lust, cause I sure do love y'all."

"I don't know if that's a compliment, Hayden, since you're a full-fledged homosexual," Kai said.

"Baby, we're just like Visa, we're everywhere you want to be," Hayden said, laughing.

"Tell her, baby," I said.

"Hayden, how can I be a ho if I'm not having sexual relations?" Kai asked.

"Being a ho ain't about getting dick on a regular basis. It's an attitude. I've been a ho for as long as I've been Hayden."

"Sweetheart, I appreciate all the effort you've gone to. But just think, if you did this for a man. You'd have dick lined up in your lobby," Justine said.

"I don't know if I agree with that. Men don't know how to appreciate being pampered."

"That's where you're wrong, girl. I can't tell you how many men I've gotten giving facials and braiding hair," Hayden said.

"Do you think they'll ever invent a robot that can give you an orgasm?" Kai asked.

I should have ignored Kai's question, but I couldn't resist and said, "They have, sweetheart. It's called a vibrator."

Hayden and Justine were laughing so hard, they both ended up spitting out their champagne.

After we had regained our composure, I asked each of my friends to share a moment from the previous week that they would always remember.

Hayden asked, "Does it have to be something serious?"

"It can be whatever you like," I said.

"Then that's easy," he said. "I kicked out this fine man I've been dating for about two weeks, perpetrating like he was all man, construction-worker type, when lo and behold, he started kissing me all over my body, and girls, I do mean all over. It was nice when it was my neck and chest, but when he got down around my navel, I pulled his head up and said, papi, ain't no poo-nanny down there. I told him he had to put on those dungarees and get out. I'm strictly dickly."

"I did something really bad this week," Kai said.

"What did the princess of the East Side do?" Justine said.

"I was having lunch at Le Cirque the other day, and this white man kept staring at me. At first I didn't know if it was one of those what-is-this-black-bitch-doing-up-in-here-alone stares, but when he smiled at me, I knew he was trying to make a move. A few minutes later the waiter brought over a bottle of Veuve Clicquot with a business card. He was a CEO of some company."

"Did he come over to your table?" Hayden asked.

"No, I don't think he was quite happy with me."

"Why?" I asked.

"Because I sent the bottle back and had the waiter bring out a bottle of Cristal instead. Did he think because I was black I was going to go for the cheapest bottle of champagne on the list?"

"Girl, that's not what he was saying. He just probably thought you were a cheap ho. It didn't matter if you were black or white," Justine said.

Then Hayden turned to Justine and said, "What happened in your little life?"

"I bought my mom a linen suit from Saks Fifth Avenue."

"What was the occasion? Was it her birthday?" Kai asked.

"There was no occasion," Justine said.

I looked at Justine and smiled, and she smiled back. I wanted her to tell Kai and Hayden that her mother had never had a suit from a store like Saks.

Hayden playfully hit Justine and said, "You trying to make us look bad, aren't you. Come on, Miss Zola. Don't you go Goody Two-Shoes on us."

"My most pleasant memory of the week won't be over until we kiss each other good-night and I'm back at home, turning the key to my door."

Justine and Kai affectionately touched my shoulder while Hayden smiled at me and mumbled, "Bitch."

14

Bristol walked into my office with a file and said, "Davis wants to talk to you about this."

"What?" I asked as I looked into a file with the name Sasha Cartwright printed on the folder. Sasha was one of my former students from the University of Washington Law School whom I wanted to hire for the legal staff. She was one of my favorite students. Sasha was one of those friendly white Southern girls who never met a stranger she didn't like talking to. When I first met her I could tell she was from the South because of her thick accent. When I asked her how she landed at the University of Washington, Sasha told me her education had carried her to several parts of the country. She'd spent her first two years at Valdosta State in Valdosta, Georgia, and then a year at the University of Wisconsin, a summer at Harvard, and finally graduated from UCLA. Sasha told me she knew there was a big world waiting after she discovered New York City when her high school band had been selected one year to participate in the Macy's Thanksgiving Day parade. Sasha boasted about how the Bainbridge Marching Bearcats band had beat out several other large high school bands in the state for the honor.

When my new position at *Bling* was announced in the *Law Journal*, Sasha had called to congratulate me and then asked if I had any openings because she was finally ready to work in the city that had opened her eyes to what the world offered.

"Has the offer package been sent out?" I asked Bristol.

"No. I was getting ready to do it, but I got word from Davis's office that he needed to talk to you before he could sign off," Bristol said.

"Then get Davis on the line," I said.

A few minutes later, Bristol buzzed me and told me Davis was on line one.

"Good morning, Davis. How are you doing?" I asked.

"I'm doing just great," Davis said.

"Bristol said you have some questions about Sasha Cartwright," I said.

"Sasha?"

"Yes, we sent her information up to your office. I really want to get an offer to her before somebody else snaps her up," I said.

"Where did she go to law school?" Davis asked.

"The University of Washington. She was one of my students, a really sharp young lady," I said, wondering if Davis had even looked at her résumé.

"Is she the one from Georgia?"

"Yes, from a small town named Bainbridge. A great little Southern girl, but I promise you she'll fit right in," I said.

"I don't think it's a good plan," Davis said.

"Why not?"

Davis paused for a moment and said, "I don't think we should hire your former students. Besides, I think we need to be looking at Ivy League grads with some big-firm experience," Davis said.

"I agree we should go for the top candidates, Davis, and I feel Sasha fits in that category. I still need to hire a few more lawyers, and I will definitely look at candidates with an Ivy League background," I said.

"Then that's what you should do. I know I told you that hiring your staff would be up to you, but something about this girl doesn't feel right. I reserve the right to use my veto power, and I'm going to use it here," Davis said.

"I don't understand. Will you at least sit down and meet with Sasha? I think she'll change your mind," I said.

"Raymond, we're wasting time here. I've made my decision. Have the headhunter send you more candidates. I'm sure you'll find some soon. I've got to run," Davis said, and then he hung up.

I was pissed and didn't know what I should do. I had given Sasha my word, and now it looked like I had to call her with bad news after I had told her to expect the offer package before noon.

Bristol stuck his head in the door and said there was a woman on the phone who didn't want to give her name and that he was taking some files to the corporate conference room. He wanted to know if I wanted to get someone to cover the phones.

"How long will you be gone?"

"Five minutes at most," Bristol said.

"No, I'll be fine," I said as I picked up the phone. I was hoping it wasn't Sasha.

"Raymond Tyler speaking," I said.

"Good morning," a cheery female voice said.

"Good morning. With whom am I speaking?" I asked.

"You don't know me, but I just wanted to call and congratulate you," she said.

"Congratulate me on what?"

"I read in *The Wall Street Journal* and *Adweek* that you've taken the job as CEO at *Bling Bling*. I just love seeing good looking brothers working it out and heading companies," she said.

"That's very nice of you. You say I don't know you, but you just wanted to call and congratulate me?" I asked.

"Yes, that's right."

"Who are you?"

"Let's just say I'm the fairy godmother to the talent tenth. You know the press would have us think today that we don't even have a tenth of our people who know how to do anything but act a fool on television or play sports," she said.

"Do you have a name?" I asked, wondering why I didn't just hang up the phone.

"Yes, sir, I do, but that's not important."

"Why not?"

"Don't worry, I'm not some kind of crazy stalker who is going to be calling or following you around. I have a life. Although from that picture of you, I bet a lot of women will be on your heels. But they don't know what I know," she said, laughing.

"What's that?"

"That you don't really feel us that way, but you might want to rethink your position."

"Who is this?" I demanded. This call suddenly wasn't encouraging or funny.

"Now, baby, I told you. You sound like you're getting a little hot under the collar, but before you hang up on me, please, for your own good, listen to this little bit of advice. Don't be foolish enough to hook up with Basil Henderson again between the sheets. If you do, wear double rubbers or you'll be receiving a call from the health department with the message 'welcome to the world of HIV,'" she said in a voice that sounded unstoppable. Then she hung up before I could.

From *Bling Bling* Confidential

Although Zola met Jabar at the gym, she still hides her jewelry, credit cards and cash in a safe in her closet when Jabar visits. It's one thing for a man to try and steal her heart, but material possessions are entirely different.

Zola had another rule about the men she dated. Never date a man who didn't know every inch of the female body was a treasure that always needed polishing or any man who would be intimidated by her collection of vibrators.

15

Mondays are usually boring, but now I live for them because they mean Jabar and the sheets. He is always on time. Eight o'clock straight up. I had left the office a little early and come home to take a leisurely bath in warm, scented water. Afterward, I put on some light makeup and pulled my hair up and back. I was wearing a pale sandy-pink panties and bra set that Davis had bought me from La Perla. Davis liked seeing me in the set; Jabar loved taking them off slowly with his teeth and large hands.

I lit the candles in my bedroom and brought a silver tray with fresh orange juice for Jabar and a glass of Chardonnay for me. I didn't know why, but I was feeling a little wicked that evening. I'm not into whips and chains, but I wouldn't mind a little tap on the ass, a little controlled forcefulness by Jabar. I'd tease him, resist him at the right moment, and refuse to give him what he wanted. That, I hoped, would be his cue to take charge. While Jabar was no rocket scientist, he usually picked up on my clues as to how I'd like the evening to go. When I wanted him gentle and tender, I invited him into the bath with me. Jabar knows how to lather a sista up and down and then pat me dry gently, taking his time at just the right spots.

In many ways Jabar is like Play-Doh to me. I can mold him any way I want to fit my desires for the evening. With Jabar there are no pretenses, no token declarations of love, and very little romance. That's why I have to be totally in charge of foreplay. Once I jokingly ragged him about his youthful "slam-bam" technique of lovemaking. I told him I wished he'd engage in a little more foreplay before the straight-up in and out. Maybe, I suggested, he could treat me like one of his workouts: a little stretching, some warm-up exercises before, and then on to the heavy stuff. He looked at me like I'd just asked him to recite the Declaration of Independence. So I showed him what I wanted. Great thing Jabar was good at following demonstrations.

The doorbell rang and I could feel my body getting warm with excitement. I sprayed a little fragrance between the twins for good measure and walked slowly to the door. I was ready for my slumber party for two.

I opened the door and I felt blinded by Jabar's dazzling white teeth when he smiled upon seeing me. He had on a tight-fitting white T-shirt and a warm-up suit that wasn't black but the darkest possible navy blue, with "Phat Farm" in crimson. I looked him up and down and I was a happy girl. I couldn't wait for Jabar to be naked and magnificent in my bedroom. I'd spent the last couple of weeks mulling over photos for *Bling Bling*'s Sexiest Brothaman Alive contest, but I knew I had him right here in my home. If I were the sole judge, the search would be over.

"'Sup, Z. You ready for a brotha?" Jabar asked as he walked past me without a kiss, carrying a black leather gym bag.

"Jabar, how are you?"

"I'm fine, boo. What up?" Jabar asked without looking in my direction. He unzipped his bag and started rummaging through it. A few moments later he pulled out his portable CD player.

"Jabar!" I shouted. He turned around quickly.

"What up, Z?"

"Come here," I said.

Jabar dropped the CD player back into the bag and walked toward me with a quizzical look on his face, and when he was standing a few inches from me, he asked, "What I do?"

"Baby, let's start over," I said as I took his hand and moved him toward the door.

"Hey, Z, you not fixing to put a brotha out. What's up with that?"

"No, I'm not putting you out. We're just starting over."

"Starting what over?"

"Repeat after me. Damn Zola, you look fly or hot; use whatever word your boys are using. Tell me how my panties and bra make you feel," I said.

Jabar looked at me and licked his full lips and gently took my hand and kissed it.

"Damn, yo, them panties makes me want to do some things. Yo, that's what's up. How you feel 'bout that, boo?"

"Now kiss me," I said.

"Where?"

"Anywhere you want," I said.

Jabar kissed my forehead, then my cheeks, neck, and lips as he squeezed my nipples gently. I felt like my legs were going to give out on me.

"How does that feel?"

"Wonderful," I moaned.

"Thought so," Jabar said.

"Follow me," I said as I grabbed Jabar's hand and headed toward the bedroom. I was literally pulling him like he was a toy with wheels. Once I reached the bedroom, I turned back the bedspread, hit the CD player button, and took a sip of my wine. When I turned around, Jabar was naked, and not only could I smell his excitement, I could see it.

"Yo, sweetness. 'Sup?" Jabar's voice had almost a childish triumph, like it was the first time he realized how large his manhood could grow.

"Jabar! You look great. I've been waiting and thinking about you all day."

"Waiting?" he says, a little startled. "Am I late?"

"My body says yes but the clock says you're right on time—as usual. I was just anxious to see you, feel you."

"Yo, Z, you know I ain't even trying to be late, not to see you." He came close to me and placed his hands on my behind, pulling me close to him. I smelled citrus and masculinity, a potent aphrodisiac. He leaned down and kissed me lightly, barely brushing my mouth. He pulled me firmly, gently, to his chest and massaged my lower back. I could feel his erection against my abs. He slid one hand between us, under my bra, and fondled my breasts. His hands were huge, like the size of a clothes iron. I felt like I was on fire. I had never known a man whose mere presence made me feel like I could make love 24/7.

I placed my hands on his heavily muscled shoulders. Jabar's body is layered with muscles like hot butterscotch on French vanilla ice cream. Pure perfection, I thought. I looked at him with a half-smile playing on my lips.

"Z, what?"

Jabar didn't get it yet. He pulled me back to him. "Yo, boo," he said, "let me taste you and give you what you want." He put both hands on my breasts, kissing one nipple and then the other.

I pushed him away again. I took both his hands and put them at his sides. When Jabar reached for me again, I put his hands firmly back at his sides and held them there. This time, he left them there and smiled, his beautiful bald head cocked to one side, one brow lifted in question.

I touched his hairless hard chest and erect nipples. He turned his head as I walked behind him and rubbed his shoulders. I loved being naked with him. Jabar turned around with a raging erection. He doesn't feel like Play-Doh, but like granite. I decide to stop the game short and let Jabar take over, but not just yet.

"Z . . . damn yo. This is torture. What do you want me to do?"

"Just stand there," I commanded. I circled him, running my hand across his erection, across this taut, round butt and back around, and said, "Do what any *real* man would do with all this." I bent over and stepped out of my panties.

I saw the light come on in his deceptively sleepy amber-brown eyes. He grasped my wrists and pulled me within an inch of his handsome face. He stared deep into my eyes, then suddenly pressed his mouth hard onto mine, nipping my lower lip before pushing his tongue between my lips. He slapped me on the behind and then scooped me up into his arms like I weighed less than a feather. I could hear Usher begging for love on the CD player, and I laughed to myself thinking Usher and Jabar were probably the same age. Jabar dropped me on my king-size bed. I leaned back on my elbows, knees up and apart with a devilish grin.

"Stay there!" he said, and he went to the door of the bedroom to retrieve his warm-up suit. I was looking up at the ceiling, ready to feel him inside me for the rest of the evening.

Jabar sat on his side of the bed, picked up the orange juice and drained the glass in one long, slow drink. He stood and began to dress, putting on his warm-up pants, his socks.

"Jabar!"

He looked down at me on the bed. "Beg me to stay, yo," Jabar said, slipping his T-shirt over his shoulder. He looked serious.

Was he playing with me? Zola does not beg. Would he really walk out on me? Who's the Play-Doh now?

"Jabar, come to bed, baby," I said, as I tried to beg and seduce him simultaneously. "I'm sorry."

Jabar moved closer to the bed, pulling off his warm-ups. I noticed his erection was still around in the flickering light from the candles, which threw his shadow across the bed and over my body.

"Will you be good?"

"I will be very good," I said as I gently touched my nipples.

"Yo, you got to stop so much playing, Z. You know, I been thinking 'bout this all day," Jabar said as he placed his face at my center, kissing me until I felt as wet as a gushing spring.

"Don't you want to come in from the cold?" I whispered as I stroked his erection.

"Yo, Z . . . in a minute. Don't this feel good?"

"It feels amazing," I moaned.

"That's what's up," Jabar mumbled.

Moments later he entered me. I felt like he was using my body like he was seeking refuge in some secret space that only I possess. I felt like I was going to explode as I enjoyed the sound of Usher's sensual voice and the rhythm of Jabar's heavy breathing. They both sounded like I felt: magical and magnificent.

16

"Have you been sleeping, Raymond?" Dr. Few asked just as I was getting comfortable on her sofa.

"Somewhat," I said.

"What does that mean?"

"I stay at the office pretty late. I come home and watch a little television, or it watches me, eat dinner, and maybe have a couple of glasses of wine, and I'm in bed by ten. The problem is I wake up around three-thirty, wide awake. I go to sleep again around maybe six. I know it's six because I have the television on TV Land and *Mannix* comes on at that time. I guess I fall asleep and I wake up again when the alarm goes off around seven-thirty," I said.

"Do you want me to prescribe something to help you sleep?"

"I don't know. I don't think I'm ready to do the drug thing," I said.

"What do you think about when you wake up?"

I thought about her question for a few moments and then I began talking. "I think about the fact I can't believe I'm living in New York

City, working for one of the most powerful men in the world. A black man whom I can't figure out if I like or not. I respect Davis, but something isn't right. I don't know what it is. I think about Trent, our relationship, and what went wrong. I wonder if I'm ever gonna really have true love in my life. A love I can depend on. I know I'll have people who will say that they love me. Might even love me for that moment in time. I want an everlasting, unconditional love, someone who's gonna love me forever like my parents and my brother. And then there are moments when I think I don't want anything to do with love. I just want to go and date, have fun without feelings or emotions attached. Like a male version of *Sex in the City*. Damn, what am I talking about? Men have always lived their love life like that," I said as I paused and took a swig of the bottled water I was holding near the not-so-lean part of my stomach.

"So you're saying there isn't much difference between heterosexual men and homosexual men?" Dr. Few asked.

"Not really. We're both accidents waiting to happen," I said causally.

"What do you mean by accidents?"

"The opportunity to fuck up. Mistakes," I said.

"Have you ever made mistakes in your journey toward manhood?"

Damn, that's a deep question, I thought. Should I come clean? Yeah, I was paying Dr. Few to tell the truth and not worry about judgment.

"Yeah, I have."

"Are there any mistakes that stick out in your mind?"

I thought for a few seconds and said yeah.

"Would you like to talk about it?"

"I've made a lot of bad decisions in my love life. Done a lot of dumb things in the name of lust. I remember one time I was in Florida and I don't really recall if I was there on vacation or for business. Anyway, I was staying at a motel, which means I was most likely spending my own money. It was some kind of motel with the two double beds, cheap furniture, and the television standing on the low end of the dresser drawers. Small rectangular soap that didn't have any kind of fragrance to it or much lather for that matter. I digress. I woke up one morning with nothing but my underwear on and I get out of bed and walk over to the curtains to see if it's going to be a sunny day or a rainy day; you know, with Florida you can never tell. I think I was yawning and had my hand in my drawers rubbing on my sex like I'm digging for gold, and I suddenly notice this man getting in his car. He stops and he's just staring at me. It was early morning, which means I probably had a hard-on. I don't like the way he's looking at me, so I push back the curtains. I must have been heading for the shower or to the bathroom, when I suddenly hear a knock at the door. Still in my underwear, I walked to the door and opened it and there's the man from the car standing at my door. He has on a skinny tie with a short-sleeve shirt. I don't know why I remember that, but he looked like a geek," I said. I took another swig of my water and wondered if I should continue.

"What did he want?"

"He just looks down at my crotch and says, 'Can I suck your dick?'"

"What did you say?"

"I just laughed and said, 'Not now, come back in an hour,' and then I shut the door," I said.

Dr. Few gazed intently at me for a few moments and then asked, "Did he come back?"

"Yeah, in almost an hour on the dot. I let him suck my dick, got off, and asked him to leave," I said.

"How did you feel?"

How did I know that question was coming?

"I was young, so I didn't feel guilt. That was a time in my life when I thought about sex a lot and it was nothing for me to have sex three or four times a day. It didn't matter if I was alone," I said as a grin came across my face.

"What are you thinking about?" Dr. Few asked.

"Looking back, life was so simple then. I thought it was tough, but I didn't have a clue," I said.

"How so?"

"I was so busy trying to live up to the expectations of my parents, peers and the world. I made life harder than it needed to be."

"Do you think you're doing that now?"

"I'm trying my damnedest not to. That's why I'm here," I said. I noticed Dr. Few look at her watch, and so I lifted my body and prepared to leave.

17

A ringing phone woke me from a deep sleep. I rubbed my eyes and looked at my caller ID and saw Justine's number. I fumbled to pick up my cordless phone.

"Hello," I said in a voice still filled with sleep.

"Zola? Have you heard?"

"Have I heard what?" I asked as I sat up in my bed.

"Girl, Aaliyah is dead," Justine said. "Can you believe that shit?"

"Aaliyah who?"

"Aaliyah the singer. Didn't you have her on the cover once? Remember, you told me how pissed off you were that she was so sweet, beautiful and nice."

"Justine, don't believe everything you hear. There are rumors all the time about famous people being dead. Remember the Luther Vandross death lies," I said.

"If you don't believe me, then you need to turn on your television, because all the major networks are running the story. If it's a joke, then it's a sick motherfucking one," Justine said.

I grabbed my remote control and clicked on the television, which was already on CNBC. There on the television was a photograph of Aaliyah and then a shot of plane wreckage.

"Justine, let me call you back," I said as I turned up the volume on the television. I sat with my back against my pillows in a stunned silence as I learned of Aaliyah's demise on a small plane in the Bahamas.

My thoughts went back to a few months before, when I sat in the suite at the Ritz-Carlton hotel in Washington, D.C., and interviewed Aaliyah. I went in expecting another over-hyped diva. I left wishing I had a little sister with the inner peace and beauty of Aaliyah. I recalled her quiet confidence as she talked about her dreams to be a multitalented performer. She had plans to not only make hit albums but to do movies and Broadway as well. When I left my interview, I was convinced that nothing could get in the way of Aaliyah achieving all her dreams.

I hopped out of bed and got down on my knees and prayed for Aaliyah's safe passage to the next life.

Then I jumped into the shower, put on some jeans and an oversize shirt, and grabbed my bag. I had to get to my office fast.

❖   ❖   ❖

Two days after Aaliyah died, I experienced one of the longest days of my life. It was Tuesday, and one of those heavy summer days when the sun looked as though it had found a permanent spot in a blue blue sky. I still couldn't believe someone so beautiful, kind and talented was no longer with us.

My staff and I spent most of Sunday and all of Monday trying to pull together a tribute issue for the young singer. This meant a new cover and moving some stories to the December issue. Miraculously, we pulled it off and put the issue to bed. Now came the fun part, informing our cover girl Yancey B. that we had to change plans. I was hoping she and her publicist would understand, but if the photo shoot was any indication, I knew the phone call wasn't going to be easy. But it had to be made.

I located Lena's phone number in my Palm and quickly dialed the number.

"Lena Ford Agency," a cheery female voice said.

"Is she in?"

"Who may I say is calling?"

"Zola Norwood of *Bling Bling*," I said.

"Hold on. I'll see if she's available."

A few moments later I heard Lena's voice. "Zola. How you doing, girl?"

"Fine, considering everything that's happened," I said softly.

"What happened?" Lena asked.

For a moment I wondered what rock Lena had been hiding under. The story of Aaliyah's plane crash had been on all the news programs and on the front page of several New York newspapers.

"Didn't you hear about Aaliyah?" I asked.

"Oh, that. Yeah, that was real sad," Lena said causally. "Did you like the pictures of Yancey B.?"

"They're beautiful," I said, slightly annoyed that all this lady could think about was her client.

"I told you Anthony was just fabulous. I know you're happy we insisted on using him instead of whoever you were planning to use. When is the issue hitting the stands?"

"That's why I'm calling. We had to make a change," I said calmly.

"What kind of change?" Lena asked. I could hear impatience in her voice.

"Well, I—I hate to tell you," I said. It was as though the words were jammed in my throat.

"You hate to tell me what?" Lena demanded.

There was an uncomfortable silence. I grabbed a bottle of water that was sitting on the edge of my desk, took a long swallow, and then said, "We're putting Aaliyah on the cover."

"What?"

"We're going to have to move the Yancey B. cover story back a month. We've decided to do an Aaliyah tribute issue," I said.

"Tell me you're joking," Lena demanded.

"No, I'm sorry. We'll put Yancey B. on the next cover," I said.

"You need to stop trippin'! Yancey B. is going to be on the cover of the December issue. Need I remind you that we gave up a chance to be on *Vanity Fair* to do the cover of your little magazine? I bet they aren't going to do some morbid tribute issue. So whatever plans you've made, change them. Dead singers don't need publicity," Lena said coldly.

My body began to feel warm, and I was thankful that I was in my office and not with Lena face-to-face, because I would have slapped her silly. I couldn't believe how cruel she was.

"Lena, I understand why you're angry, but my decision is final. I suggest you call Yancey B. and tell her that she will be on the cover in December," I said.

"I'm not telling her shit. If she isn't on the cover as planned, then she won't ever be on the cover of your magazine."

"Suit yourself. But I can put her on the cover whenever I please. Have a nice evening," I said. As I was preparing to hang up the phone, Lena started screaming and swearing.

"Bitch, don't hang up on me. Change that cover! We spent all day doing that shoot. Do you know how valuable Yancey B.'s time is? You can't do this. I'll ruin you *and* your magazine."

This woman had cracked my last good nerve. I had had enough! "Lena, you need to check yourself. At least you and Yancey B. are alive. She'll have plenty of cover stories in the future, including *Bling Bling*. You need to look in the mirror and check yourself," I said, and slammed down the phone. I was surprised by the tears flowing down my face.

18

I was getting ready to go and pick up a pizza before calling it a day, when my phone rang. I looked at the caller ID and saw the 858 area code and figured it was Kirby.

"What's up, li'l bro?" I asked as I laid my keys down on the kitchen counter just in case I was getting ready to settle in to one of those long conversations about life.

"What's poppin', playa? How's the new job?"

"I'm getting into the groove of being in the world of publishing," I said. "How are you doing?"

"Everything is cool. We lost again this week, but I guess you saw that. I've been talking to my coach about getting me involved in more plays. The head coach thinks since he got a first-rounder in the backfield he needs to get their money's worth, but they're paying a brotha like me a bunch of benjamins too. I want to feel like I'm earning my keep," Kirby said.

"I hear you. I've got to get me one of those DirecTV packages so I can see your games. They don't ever play them here in New York 'cause you guys start so late," I said.

"I know. Pops was saying the same thing, but he went out and got one of those satellite dishes because he didn't want to miss nothing. He's come to three games already, and Mama told him if he was going to get on a plane every week to come out here then she was going to start looking for a home out here," Kirby said.

"How would you feel about that?" I asked, laughing.

"I don't have to worry about that. Mama isn't moving again," Kirby said.

"I know that's right," I said.

"Besides, she would be treating me like a baby."

"You're always going to be her baby. She worries about you just like me. Which, by the way, are you sure everything is all right?"

"Yeah . . . yeah. I'm fine. Dating a different honey every other night. Not about to leave my heart with anyone just yet. I called because one of my buddies is coming your way, and I wanted you to meet him and see if you can help him out," Kirby said.

"What's up?"

"His name is Sebastian Lewis. Cool dude, played backup to me during the exhibition season and he crashed with me during training camp. Dude busted his knee, so his season is over and most likely his career. He's dating this honey from Jersey, so he's going to shack up with her for a minute until he gets on his feet," Kirby said.

"What does he want to do?" I asked.

"Sebastian is going to do the trainer thing, and he's interested in becoming an agent. I thought you might hook him up with your dawg Basil to see if he can help out. You know, just look out for him, make sure he keeps his head on straight and doesn't get in trouble in the big city."

"Where's he from?"

"Pensacola, Florida. Seb played ball at Florida State and he was giving your li'l bro a run for the starting position until his knee problems cropped up. He's got his degree in business and was really interested in meeting you when I told him you were working for that McClinton dude," Kirby said.

"Hey, what do you know—a football player with a college degree? Sounds like somebody I need to meet," I said, joking.

"Don't come down so hard. Man, now I realize how lucky I was that Pops stayed on my ass about hitting the books. If I hadn't graduated like I promised, I would have to hear about that shit every day of my life," Kirby said, laughing.

"Yeah, from both Pops and me," I said.

"So can I give him your digits?"

"Yeah. Give him my office number and the one here at the crib. I'll take him to dinner and introduce him to Basil. Who knows, Basil's firm might be looking for some young blood," I said.

"Thanks, bro. I appreciate that and you. Sebastian is becoming like a little brother to me, like family, so I was hoping you'd look out for him."

"Like he's family. When's he coming East?" I asked.

"I think in a couple of days, but I'll holla back when I get the exact day," Kirby said.

"That's cool."

"Ray, can you believe the sad news about Aaliyah? Man, you don't ever know from one minute to the next what the universe has in store for you," Kirby said.

"Man, that was really sad. I remember playing that Isley Brothers remake she did, "For the Love of You." That song was tight," I said.

"That song was the bomb. My big brother is more in the know than I figured," Kirby said.

"Dude, good music is just good music. It has no age limit," I said.

"I hear ya. Let me get off this phone. I love ya and miss ya," Kirby said.

"I love you too, Kirby. I hope you make it to the East Coast real soon."

"Me too. Holla!"

❖   ❖   ❖

I was running about fifteen minutes late for my meeting with Kirby's friend Sebastian Lewis. He'd called me the night before and we'd agreed to meet at B. Smith's restaurant in the theater district. I'd made the mistake of going to the old location on Eighth at West Forty-seventh and had to call my assistant to get the correct address, almost two blocks away on West Forty-sixth.

I walked into the spacious restaurant that had the feel of an upscale art gallery. I rushed past the hostess and headed toward the bar, where I saw a handsome peanut-butter-brown man standing at the bar alone with an apple-red sweater and some nice-fitting straight-leg jeans. Sebastian had told me he would be wearing a red sweater.

"Sebastian?"

"Raymond," he said.

"Yes, I'm Raymond. Nice meeting you," I said as I extended my hand to shake his. I was startled when Sebastian reached for me and pulled me close to his broad chest in a brotha-man hug complete with the two pats with closed fists on my back. Once he released me, I moved back a few inches and smiled weakly.

"What're you drinking?" I asked.

"Just a brew," Sebastian said.

"Do you want to get something to eat?" I asked.

"I had something to eat before I came into the city," Sebastian said.

"Where're you staying?"

"Over in East Orange with my girl, but that won't be for long," Sebastian said. "I want to find me a small place in the city, but I got to make sure I get a gig before I start spending my money," Sebastian continued with a slight smile. He had near-perfect teeth and a diamond stud in his left ear. His was wearing his hair in cornrows, but the lines between each braid looked like a perfectly manicured lawn, not scraggly like I had seen on some brothers wearing the seventies hairstyle that was making a comeback with the younger crowd.

"Kirby told me you were thinking about being a trainer," I said.

"Yeah, but I got to get certified and find a good gym," Sebastian said as he looked at a beautiful Latina woman who had walked into the restaurant and captured the attention of a couple of other male patrons. I let Sebastian finish checking her out, and when he looked back in my direction, I said, "How much are you going to charge?"

"For what?"

"Training."

"I don't know. This ain't Pensacola, where folks used to bitch and moan over twenty-five dollars an hour," Sebastian said.

"I think you can get a little more up here," I said as I turned toward the mirrored bar to get the attention of the bartender.

"Man, I hope so. Kirby tells me you work for Davis McClinton," Sebastian said.

"Yeah, I do."

"What's he like?" Sebastian asked.

"Hold on a second," I said. The bartender came over and I ordered a glass of Merlot and then continued. "Working for Davis has been a new experience, and most days I like working for one of the world's most powerful black men," I said. The waiter placed my glass of wine on top of a white linen napkin and then went over to the cash register.

"Does he need a trainer?"

"Who, Davis? I'm sure he's probably got about three or four working for him already," I said.

"So he got it like that, huh?"

"Davis is a true example of living large. Why are you so interested in Davis?" I asked. Sebastian slightly shook his head and rolled his large brown eyes and said, "I just read an article about him in *Black Enterprise* and wondered if rich and famous black folks were different from the rest of us," Sebastian said.

"Would you like to meet him?" I asked.

"I don't think Davis McClinton wants to meet me," Sebastian said as he took a long swig of his beer.

"Kirby mentioned that you might be interested in becoming an agent. Is that true?"

"True dat. He told me you're tight with Basil Henderson, who actually tried to get me to sign when I left Florida State," Sebastian said.

"So you've met him?"

"Yeah. He was a cool brother. I almost signed with him."

"Why didn't you?" I asked.

"You know that mentality we youngbloods sometimes have. I thought the white boys could get me a better deal. You know there ain't any black men in management positions in the NFL signing checks, but I must say I was impressed with Basil Henderson. He tried to sell me on how important it was to get with somebody who was interested in making sure I was taken care of once my playing days were over. I had no clue I'd get to spend only a couple of seasons in the league," Sebastian said.

"So what round did San Diego draft you?"

"They didn't. I was drafted by Dallas in the second round and then traded to San Diego after the first season. I was like cool, because Troy Aikman wasn't slinging the ball like he used to and the Cowboys were stocked with wide receivers, so I figured I'd have a better chance with the Chargers."

"So what do you need me to do?"

"Whatever. I mean, you could introduce me to some of your peeps like Basil, and if you hear of any cheap apartments, that would be cool," Sebastian said. He lifted an empty beer bottle in the air toward the bartender.

"What about your lady friend?"

"Dude, I'm cutting her loose as soon as I get on my feet. It's not like she's somebody I'm going to marry. We dated for a little while when I was in school, broke up, then I moved to Dallas and we just reconnected lately. It's just a little something to do while I need a place to lay my head," Sebastian said.

"How are you going to advertise your training services?"

"I need to get some pictures taken. You know, let the people see what I got. Nobody wants a trainer who can't keep his own shit together," Sebastian said.

"I feel you," I said, thinking how old I was when I tried to use the catchphrases of the youngbloods.

"Do you know any photographers?"

"Not personally, but I'm sure the editor of *Bling* can recommend someone," I said as I took a sip of my wine.

"*Bling Bling* has some nice-looking honeys in there, especially their swimsuit issue. I look through it to see what the hardheads are wearing and what the honeys aren't," Sebastian said, laughing. "It doesn't matter that I can't afford half that shit."

"Who's your favorite designer?" I asked. I could tell from Sebastian's well-groomed appearance that clothes were important to him and most likely one of the reasons he and my clothes-crazy little brother had hit it off.

"I like me some Sean John, FUBU, and Phat Farm. Yeah, that's what's up," Sebastian said.

"You know, I've been thinking about hiring a trainer. Maybe we should give it a shot and see how it works out," I said.

"You look like you're holding your shit tight for an older dude, but I could put some more muscle on you," Sebastian said as he reached over and squeezed the top of my arm. He had a powerful grip, and I felt like I needed a trainer just to protect myself from Sebastian's masculine way of showing affection.

"I haven't joined a gym yet, but there's a pretty nice workout area at the apartment I'm living. I've been waiting to join one until I decide where I'm going to finally settle down," I said as I looked at my watch. It wasn't that I had to go anywhere, but my stomach was growling and I wanted to eat.

Sebastian saw me look at my watch and put down his beer and said, "I'm sorry, Raymond. I'm holding you. I 'preciate you taking the time to see me. Good lookin' out."

"No problem. Kirby said you were like a brother to him, so I want to do what I can to help you. Let's talk in the next day or two and set up a time to get together," I said as I took out a card from my wallet and pulled the pen from my suit jacket. I wrote down my address and my cell number and handed it to Sebastian.

"Here are all my numbers. Somehow you'll be able to get me," I said.

"Cool," Sebastian said as he inspected the card closely.

"So, are you heading to the train station?" I asked as I grabbed my briefcase.

"Naw, naw. I'm going to hang out here for a minute and see what might come through," Sebastian said as he looked around the restaurant.

"I'm heading home," I said.

"Thanks, Raymond. I needed to meet somebody like you," Sebastian said as he gave me another tight hug. This time I was prepared for his powerful embrace.

19

I don't care how many stories I read about celebrities, I'm still surprised by how people who swear they love them will turn over the goods on famous people in a heartbeat. I was reading the final rewrite on the cover story we were finally running on Yancey B. After the story was delayed and all the commotion her publicist had caused, I was ready to put this story to bed. Two days before the magazine was being put to bed, Kirsten called and said she had some explosive information that must be added to the story.

The next morning she turned in a story with supporting information on tape and documents revealing that Yancey B., after receiving the MAC (Mothers Against Crack) Entertainer of the Year award, had entered a forty-five-day rehab for crack and alcohol addiction.

Kirsten had come in at the request of our lawyers to review the story and new information. Before she was to meet with one of our attorneys, I sat with her at my conference table over tea and toasted bagels.

"This is powerful stuff, Kirsten. Tell me again how you got the infor-mation," I said.

"It was the strangest thing. Some lady called me on my cell and said 'I understand you're doing an article on Yancey B. I have some dirt that no one in the music industry is aware of.' She told me she worked at the Montana clinic that Yancey B. had gone to, and that for a price she could get me the medical records and insurance forms," Kirsten said.

"How much did you have to pay?"

"It wasn't much. I put it on my expense report. I mean, how much money could you spend in a place like Montana?" Kirsten said, laughing.

"So you sent her the money and she sent you the records? Aren't you concerned the records might be fake?"

"Yeah, I was at first, but the papers had her social security number and next of kin. I called the insurance company pretending to be Yancey Braxton and questioned when certain invoices were going to be paid, and after I had given them her social security number and date of birth, someone gave me the date the rehab had been paid," Kirsten said as she paused and took a sip of her tea. I spread some chive-flavored cream cheese over my bagel and nodded as Kirsten continued to talk.

"There's more. I contacted Yancey B.'s mother, Madame Ava, and with a little hesitation she was more than willing to talk because she said she felt it would help other young women dealing with substance-abuse problems. She agreed to an interview, which was taped, and I even got her to sign an affidavit supporting the tape. What I couldn't believe was I offered to come to California to do the interview, but Yancey B.'s mother is loaded and offered to fly up to New York to meet me," Kirsten said.

"I can't believe her mother would give you all this personal informa-tion," I said, looking at the words typed on the white paper and shaking my head.

"Yeah, I was surprised as well. I mean, I had the background information about Yancey B. giving up a child she had when she was young, but that had already been covered in *Essence* and I understood her plight. I didn't want to rehash that. I was leaning toward doing a fluff piece about how hot her career is with the music, stage, and movies. I mean, the diva is a legitimate triple threat," Kirsten said.

"Yeah, she is, and Yancey B. knows it," I said, recalling how she had behaved during the photo shoot.

"Her mother was in entertainment as well, and there might be a little rivalry between them."

"Did you ask why she was willing to cooperate?"

"Of course."

"What'd she say?"

"Ava said the family had tried to keep it a secret, but when she saw Yancey accepting the award from MAC, she couldn't remain silent. She showed me some of the receipts she had from paying some of the initial costs and plane tickets she had purchased to go to Montana to visit Yancey. I made copies of them and included them in your packet," Kirsten said as she patted the large manila envelope she had prepared for me.

"Boy, this is going to make big news. Are you prepared to go on the talk shows when all of this is exposed? I know the entertainment shows will pick up on this. I mean, with the entire baby-mama drama and divas in distress, this is going to make that stuff look trivial," I said, thinking how this story might bring the respect I'd been looking for when it came to my magazine.

"Yeah, I'm ready. Already hired a trainer to work off the ten television pounds I need to lose. I can't believe how this fell in my lap, but I am not going to turn away from a gift," Kirsten said.

On the tape Yancey's mother talked about how Yancey had done drugs in high school, even working part-time as a call girl to support her habit. Yancey had kicked the habit and had been clean for more than seven years, until she fell in love with a bisexual football star who had called off their wedding the morning they were set to be married. Ava told Kirsten how Yancey and she had gone on vacation to help pull Yancey together, and she had relapsed but had managed to keep it from wrecking her record and movie deals by telling the record company she was making a movie and telling potential producers that she was working on a new album. Yancey's mother had said she had warned Yancey about going to high schools and colleges speaking out against drugs and lying about never doing drugs when quizzed by students.

"I don't think we can or should use the information about her working as a hooker. I mean, it's old news and there's no way of verifying that kind of information," I said.

"Well, Ava told me she could put me in contact with the lady Yancey worked for, but I don't really think we need it," Kirsten said.

"Still, I'd like to stay away from that. Did you try to get Yancey's side of the story?" I asked.

"I did. I called her and told her I needed about an hour to clear up some facts and some new information I wanted to include in the article, and she told me she was preparing for a world tour and didn't have time. I called her publicist and manager, encouraging them to have Yancey speak with me, and neither one of them returned my calls," Kirsten said.

"Okay, if the lawyers approve this, we've got a real exclusive. Great work, Kirsten," I said as I stood in front of the conference table.

"I'm just glad you didn't run the story when you had intended. Maybe some other writer or television person could have gotten the story. This might be my Pulitzer," Kirsten said as she put a copy of the story and the packet in her plaid bag.

While Kirsten was putting on her jacket, I walked to the outer office and gave the packet of information and the story to my assistant. I told her to tell the legal staff that I needed a response right away.

Veronica had a request Davis didn't know how to handle. She wanted media mogulette Oprah Winfrey at her next dinner party. When Davis suggested Diana Ross, who he knew personally, Veronica told him it had to be Oprah since one of her good girlfriends had recently dined with Oprah in Palm Springs. Besides, Veronica said we have more money than Oprah and she should be grateful to meet the McClintons.

Davis knew Zola had recently been on a committee with Oprah at their alma mater, Tennessee State, so he asked Zola what she thought would be the best way to get Oprah's attention. Zola suggested that Davis donate a large sum of money to one of her favorite charities, like A Better Chance (ABC), an organization that took deserving minority students from the inner city and small towns and sent them tuition-free to exclusive prep schools on the East Coast.

Davis told Zola he would have no part of an organization that would put minorities in such a fish out of water environment and would rather give money to an organization that helped minorities to make better use of what they already had in their own neighborhoods.

Zola was shocked and disappointed and told Davis he already did that every time he paid taxes, and she would be more than happy to take him to some of the schools she'd seen in New York and show him how his money was being wasted.

Veronica's request was denied.

20

Before my day got started, I gave Basil a call at his office. I wanted to tell him about Sebastian and see when he could meet with him.

"'Sup, Raymond Tyler? What did I do to start my day off so good?" Basil said.

"I guess you're living right," I said.

"What can I do for you? Or what can I do to you?" Basil asked with sex dripping off every word.

"I got somebody I want you to meet," I said.

"Who?"

"Actually it's somebody you already know, or at least you've met."

"So you don't want to have nothing to do with a playa so you giving me to somebody else. Does he look as great as you?" Basil asked.

I was wondering how many conversations he had like this every day in his office, as I tried to keep my mind on the business at hand.

"It's not that kind of party. He's an ex–football player like yourself who just got cut by the Chargers. He's really good friends with my brother, Kirby, so be on your best behavior when you meet him," I said.

"Why do I need to meet him?"

"He's interested in becoming an agent. You might need somebody to help you with the young boyz. We aren't getting any younger," I said, laughing.

"Speak for yourself. Also, ain't every ex–football player trying to be an agent?"

"He remembers meeting you and had good things to say about you," I said.

"Where did he play?"

"Florida State."

"Then I know I don't want to meet him again. I spent a lot of time in that country-ass town, and most of the brothers down there end up signing with the white boys," Basil said.

"Will you at least meet him and talk with him about the business?"

"What am I gonna get out of it?"

"The satisfaction of helping out a young brother."

"I need more than that."

"I'll bring him by so you'll get a chance to see me," I said.

"Now we're talking. When and where?"

"You tell me," I said.

"I haven't been to the Shark Bar in a while. Let's meet there," Basil said.

"Cool. Is it still on Amsterdam?"

"Yeah, between Seventy-fourth and Seventy-fifth. Meet you guys around seven."

"Cool. Have a nice day."

"I'm sure I will. Look how it started."

❖   ❖   ❖

Davis called just before I was getting ready to leave the office to meet Basil and Sebastian. He wanted to talk about yet another company in

London he was trying to buy and one he wanted to sell. I was beginning to wonder when he ever just cooled out and relaxed.

I couldn't get a cab even in front of my office building, so I walked a few blocks and caught a train to the Seventy-second Street station. It never failed that when I walked out of this particular station I looked toward Columbus Avenue and the block where the Nickel Bar used to be. A bar where I had many fond memories during my stay in New York during the late eighties. I would think about my friends, many of whom were dead, the music, and the many Friday nights when I entered with hopeful anticipation that I was going to meet the man of my dreams.

A few minutes later I saw the dark blue awning with THE SHARK BAR emblazoned across it. I walked into the dimly lit small bar area and immediately my eyes met Basil's. He was smiling broadly, and I realized that he was already talking with Sebastian. I walked over toward them and Basil extended his hand and said, "Mr. Tyler, so good to see you again."

Sebastian turned around quickly with a pleasant smile and said, "'Sup, homes? Thought you'd forgotten 'bout a brotha."

"'Sup, Sebastian. Just got caught up with something at the last minute at the office. I see you two have reacquainted yourselves."

"Yo, dude is cool. I might be able to find something for him," Basil said.

"Great," I said as I looked toward the bartender. I ordered a cranberry juice because I was debating going back to the office to get a head start on the information Davis had given me about the companies he was buying in London.

I was taking a sip of my cranberry juice when Sebastian pulled out a white envelope and handed it to me.

"What's this?" I asked.

"Take a look," Sebastian said.

I opened the envelope and saw a contact sheet with several pictures of Sebastian in several stages of undress. I mean, he had on clothes, but the pictures showed what an incredible body Sebastian was hiding beneath his baggy jeans and jacket.

"What are these for?" I asked, making sure I wasn't staring too hard at the pictures.

"I'm going to use them in my ad for training," Sebastian said.

"Let me see," Basil said as he reached for the pictures.

"I wanted to ask you what magazines and newspapers I should run ads in. I'm also gonna get some cards made and leave them at gyms around the city," Sebastian said.

"These are tight, dude. Just make sure you don't run ads in some of those gay magazines. I mean, with these pictures, your phone's going to be ringing off the hook and those faggots won't be looking for training," Basil said, laughing but looking at me from the corner of his eye.

"I hear ya, 'cause I ain't looking for no faggot clientele," Sebastian said as he exchanged dap with Basil.

I felt my body become warm and I placed my drink on the bar and made eye contact with Basil and said, "You two seem to be getting along just fine. I'm leaving." I didn't say good-bye to either Sebastian or Basil.

I was halfway down the block, heading toward Seventy-second when I heard Basil call my name. I didn't stop but increased my pace. I could hear the sound of shoe soles running and a few seconds later Basil was standing in front of me, moving backward.

"Ray . . . man . . . stop and talk to me. What was that about?"

"What in the fuck are you talking about?"

"Why did you leave like that? Left me hanging with youngblood. Old dude doesn't know what to think," Basil said.

"Basil, I don't give a fuck what either one of you thinks," I said as I kept walking toward the subway station. I could see the bright lights of the hot dog stand made famous for still selling food for under a dollar, and people moving with care along the sidewalks. I was making eye contact with strangers rather than Basil.

"Ray, come on, man. Talk to me. I'm sorry."

I suddenly stopped and turned toward him and said, "That's the only truth you've probably spoken today. You are a sorry mutherfucker."

"Why you got to make everything about being correct? We're just boys hanging out. Playing the game."

"I'm too old for games."

"Come on back to the bar. I promise I won't use that word again."

"I got more important things to do," I said. I saw the light change to green and I darted across the street like I was running the hundred-yard dash, leaving Basil in the dust.

21

It was late and I thought I was the only one at the office until I heard a door shut. I got up from my desk and walked toward the outer office and saw Raymond reviewing some messages. What was he doing here so late? There was only one way to find out.

"Raymond, I thought you were gone for the day," I said.

Raymond seemed a little surprised to see me, but he looked up and said, "Oh, hi, Zola. Just thought I'd get a head start on tomorrow."

"Trying to impress the boss?" I asked.

"Not really. What are you doing here?" Raymond asked.

"Oh, an editor's work is never done," I said.

"Oh," Raymond said.

"Are you all right?" It was obvious his mind was on something besides me and my magazine.

"I've had better days," Raymond said.

"Is there anything I can do?"

"Do you have a magic wand that can get rid of all the world's seriously deranged people?" Raymond said. The wry smile on his face let me know he wasn't really serious.

"It's a good thing I don't have something like that, because I would have to zap some people I really love on most days," I said. I walked over toward the receptionist station where Raymond was standing and pressed my backside against the desk. Sounded like Raymond needed to talk.

"So who's been bothering you?" I asked as I playfully put my arms around Raymond's shoulders.

"How have you women put up with us men for so long?" Raymond asked.

"If I could answer that, I wouldn't have to look at another magazine layout or model comp card in my life. The one thing I know for sure about you men is that eventually you'll fuck up. You guys are consistent about that," I said, laughing.

Raymond shook his head and said, "You know, Zola, you're right."

"I wish it weren't true," I said. Raymond smiled at me and said, "I think I'm going to get my work and take it home. How long are you going to be here?"

"Maybe an hour or so," I said.

"Be careful. I don't like the idea of you being here by yourself," Raymond said.

"Trust me, I have been up here way past midnight."

"Thanks for listening," Raymond said.

"I wish I had that wand," I said.

"So do I," Raymond said as he walked down the hallway toward his office.

I went back to my office, still in search of the perfect man at least on the outside.

After hours of reviewing guys for the Sexiest Brothaman Alive contest, my eyes grew tired of good-looking half-dressed men with confident and sexy smiles and I decided to call it a night. I put on my white knee-length coat, grabbed my purse and briefcase, and headed toward the door. I turned off the lights and was walking toward the door when I heard the buzzer. It scared me. Who was buzzing so late? I looked down the hallway to see if any light was coming from Raymond's office, but I could see the lights were out from the clear glass panels on the side of the wood door.

I went over, pressed the intercom, and said, "Can I help you?"

"I'm looking for Raymond Tyler," a deep male voice said.

"I think he left," I said.

"Hey, you think I can use the phone?"

"Who are you?"

"I'm a good friend of Raymond's. My celly is dead. I promise you, I'm totally harmless."

"What's your name?" I asked.

"Basil Henderson," he said.

"Let me call Raymond and see if he knows you," I said.

"Cool," he said.

I waited a few minutes, pretending I was calling Raymond. The truth was I didn't have his home number, but I figured if this man was legit, then he would wait. I then pushed the intercom and asked, "Are you still there?"

"Yep. Did you talk with Raymond?"

"Sure did, said he never heard of you," I said, trying very hard to keep myself from laughing.

"Come on now, Miss Lady with the Beautiful Voice. I know my good friend didn't . . ."

I opened the door, and I don't know if my eyes bucked or my mouth dropped, but I know one of them happened as I stood face-to-face with one of the best-looking men I had seen in a long time. When he smiled I know my knees began to wiggle like a bowl of yogurt.

". . . say anything like that," Basil said.

"I was just kidding. I couldn't reach him," I said.

"Now, I hope you don't open the door like this for everybody," he said.

"I'm not worried. It takes a lot to scare me," I said.

"Please tell me the name that belongs to such a lovely lady," Basil said as his beautiful eyes scanned me from my own eyes to the toes of my black mules.

"Zola Norwood," I said.

"Nice meeting you, Zola. I wonder why Raymond hasn't told me about you."

"Does Raymond handle your social life?" I asked.

"Not at all, but he knows how much I appreciate a beautiful woman."

"Do you still need to use the phone? I really need to get home. It's been a long day," I said.

"Yeah, I do. But after I make my call, what would I have to do to convince you to have a drink with me?"

"Do it some other time. I'm going home."

"You're tough. Where's the phone?"

I pointed to the phone on the receptionist's desk and Basil walked over slowly to the area, turning his head every few seconds to see if I was looking at him. I was, but he couldn't tell. He was a handsome man, and I was wondering why Raymond hadn't introduced us.

Basil made his call and hung up after a few minutes. He turned toward me and smiled.

"You get in touch with Raymond?"

"Yeah, he's at home. He said he was tired too. You people must work hard here," Basil said.

"What do you do for a living?"

"What would you like me to do?"

"I would say model."

"Not hardly," Basil said.

"Now, I know someone has told you you could model if you wanted to," I said.

"People have told me I do a lot of things well."

"Would you be interested in doing some shots for me?"

"Are you a photographer?"

"No, but I have this issue I think you might be great for," I said.

"What's in it for me?"

"I would have that drink with you and you would have a whole lot of female fans all across the country," I said.

"Let me think about it," Basil said.

"I don't have much time," I said. I looked in my bag and pulled out one of my cards. I printed my cell number on the back and then handed it to Basil.

"So will I be naked in these pictures? You want to see me butt-ass naked?"

"That will be between you and the photographer," I said.

"Are you going to be at the shoot?"

"So you'll do it?"

"Not so fast. I still need to think about it," Basil said.

"That's fair. But I hope you'll call me soon," I said as I noticed it was almost ten o'clock.

"Damn, what am I thinking, the women of the world needs to see this jammin' body I got. I'll do it. Naked, half naked, whatever the pretty lady wants," Basil said.

"Thank you. I know you'll be great," I said.

"Can I offer you a ride home? Maybe I could give you a little preview of what your readers are going to feast on," Basil said.

"Thanks, but I have a car service," I said. "And I'll wait with my readers on that look."

"Oh, you're big-time. I guess they don't call the magazine *Bling Bling* for nothing. When you take a look at my pictures, you'll wish you'd taken me up on my offer," Basil said, smiling and licking his beautiful full lips.

"I don't mean to be rude, but I'm going to have to let you out. I need to go over a few things," I said.

"You want me to wait for you?"

"Thanks, but I do have something I need to do. It was nice meeting you, and I'll look forward to your call so we can set up your photo shoot," I said as I extended my hand toward Basil.

He took my hand and looked at my ring finger and said, "No wedding ring. That's what's up." He then very gently kissed my hand, nodded, opened the door, and vanished.

From *Bling Bling* Confidential

Davis often offered Zola unsolicited advice when it came to her life. He once told Zola she should get on as many charity boards as possible, with the exception of the ones Veronica was already on. When Zola told him how she served as principal for a day in one of Harlem's elementary schools and gave generously to the NAACP and United Negro College Fund, Davis told her no one of importance would notice.

22

When I walked into my apartment, the phone was ringing. It was Basil saying he needed to stop by and talk with me, so I told him to give me thirty minutes so that I could take a shower, and he agreed.

I finished my tension-relieving shower and decided to give Kirby a call. I wanted to tell him I had met Sebastian and let him know what a knucklehead I was beginning to think Sebastian was.

I dialed Kirby's number and he picked up the phone and said, "'Sup, big brotha."

"How's it going, Kirby?"

"Little tired from practice, and I promised this honey I would take her for something to eat. Man, you got to wine and dine these San Diego ladies before they ready to roll," Kirby said.

I ignored Kirby's last statement and said, "I met Sebastian."

"You did. He's a cool dude," Kirby said.

"If you say so. This evening I had set up a meeting to introduce him to Basil. They seemed to hit it off," I said.

"Thanks, Ray. Good looking out. I appreciate you doing this. Is Basil going to help him get a gig?"

"I don't know. Since they were getting along so well, I decided to leave the two of them alone," I said. I didn't know how to tell Kirby what happened. I didn't want to assume that he always told his friends that his big brother was gay. Maybe he was embarrassed by it.

"Are you all right?" Kirby asked.

"I'm cool. I'm a little concerned that Sebastian uses the word *faggot* with ease," I said.

"Dude, tell me he didn't come out of the box like that. I mean, he's my boy and all, but if he did that, then I'm going to be on a plane and jack a niggah up," Kirby said.

I started laughing at the thought of Kirby flying all the way to New York to defend my honor and said, "Naw, he wasn't crazy enough to do that. I just wondered if you had told him about me and whether it would make a difference. We've talked about him training me, and I don't want to be in a situation where I've got to watch what I say and talk about women, using terms like *bitch* and *whore* just to seem cool around some youngblood. You know I don't roll like that."

"I didn't tell him 'cause I didn't think it mattered. Sebastian is just frontin' for your boy Basil. You know that's locker room talk. You know when dudes are just one-on-one shootin' the breeze with each other they don't talk like that. But if you want me to say something to him, I will. I'll make sure the niggah will come correct around my peeps," Kirby said.

"Naw, I'll handle it," I said.

"You sure?"

"Yeah. So you think he's a good kid?"

"Trust me, Ray. Give Sebastian a chance and you'll see what I'm talking about," Kirby said.

"Okay, I'll give him another shot," I said.

"Thanks."

"Well, you better get your tired bones up and get ready for your date," I said.

"That's what's up. I need to take a shower, put on some smell-good, and see if I can find some new pussy," Kirby said, laughing.

"Don't forget your raincoats," I said.

"Never leave home without them," Kirby said.

"I love you, Kirby."

"And I love you back," Kirby said.

After I hung up the phone, I went to the refrigerator and poured me a glass of grapefruit juice. I wasn't wearing anything but a robe, and I remembered Basil was coming, so I went into the bedroom and put on some light blue pajama bottoms and a Northwestern football jersey Kirby had given me from his final season playing there.

I was walking back toward the kitchen to select one of the takeout menus I kept in the drawer above the dishwasher when the doorman's phone rang. I picked it up and he told me Basil was on his way up.

"Thanks," I said.

I decided I wasn't going to spend a lot of time rehashing the evening with Basil and I would wait until he left to order something. I was also thinking maybe I would just eat some microwave popcorn since it was so late. I was looking in the cabinet to see if I had any popcorn when the doorbell rang.

I opened the door and there was Basil with a huge smile on his face and he asked, "You in bed, dude?"

"I will be soon," I said as I walked back toward the kitchen. I heard Basil holler, "You got any brew in this place?"

"Yep, but there's a one-beer limit in this place after eight," I said.

"Cool."

I grabbed two beers from the vegetable crisper, flipped off the caps, and walked back into the living room, where Basil was sitting on the sofa with his legs spread suggestively open and his large hands covering his crotch.

"Ray, why haven't you introduced me to that honey in your office?"

"Are you talking about Zola?"

"Yeah . . . yeah, Zola, that's her name. Man, she is a fox. She has that pretty brown skin and those lips look like jimmie-sucking lips if I ever saw them," Basil said.

"I'm not trying to have you sleep with the women I work with. Zola is off-limits," I said.

"I don't think Zola is going to go for that. She is already dreaming of seeing me naked," Basil said.

"What are you talking about?"

"Dude, she wants me to do a photo shoot for her magazine, and I'm going to be in those panties before the week's out," Basil said confidently as he took a swig of his beer.

"What did you come over here for?"

"Dude, I want to tell you how sorry I am for what happened earlier this evening."

"You already did that."

"But you're still mad at me."

"Basil, trust me, I've forgotten about your dumb ass," I said.

"Come on, Ray. Don't be so cruel. You know how the young playas talk. You got to speak their language," Basil said.

"Are you going to give him a job?"

"I need to talk with Brison, but he could help us out with some of the younger players we're trying to sign. He's from Florida, and there are three division-one schools down there. He could be a big asset."

"Cool, then you deal with Sebastian. Leave Zola alone."

"I can't promise that."

"Then we don't have nothing else to talk about," I said as I got up from the sofa.

"Raymond, why are you always trippin' like this? I can't get in the panties unless Zola wants me to. She seems like a lady who knows what she wants."

"You're just in it for the hunt. I'm not asking you, I'm telling you don't bring your playa-playa shit to my workplace," I said.

"What are you going to do if I just have to hit it?"

"I'll tell her you're a switch-hitter," I said boldly.

"You wouldn't do that," Basil said.

"Try me."

"Man, I come over trying to show you some love and you trippin' out on me. I'm outta here," Basil said.

"So you're going to leave because I want you to face the truth?" I asked.

"That's your truth, Raymond, as much you think you know me, you don't know jack," Basil said.

"You might be right, but I'm not going to let you bring your madness in my workplace," I said.

"Why not?"

"How would you like if I came into your office and tried to seduce your business partner, or better yet one of the players you were trying to sign?" I asked.

"You wouldn't do that."

"No, I wouldn't. Why don't you give me the same respect?"

Basil didn't answer. He finished the rest of his beer and then handed me the bottle and asked if I had another one.

"Sure," I said. I went into the kitchen and dropped the empty bottle into the wastebasket and then went to the bathroom. I came back to the kitchen and pulled two more beers out and walked back into the living room.

Basil was standing near the television with his face lit with a dazzling smile and his steel-gray eyes blazing with amusement. He had removed his clothing with the exception of black nylon underwear that left little to wonder about. I could even see a portion of the plump head of his sex between his powerfully built legs.

Basil had an awesome physique. About 215 pounds of ripping chest, ass, and abs layered to perfection on a lofty six-foot-two frame.

"I figured out what you need," Basil said as I moved toward him and gave him the beer. I remained silent as I gazed at his body like he was a nude model in an art class. Basil took a swallow of his beer and then set it on the coffee table.

"I still look damn good, don't I?" Basil asked.

"You don't need me to tell you that," I said.

"So you like what you see?"

"You know I'm not hatin'. You look good," I said.

"Don't you think this will make you feel better," Basil said as he gently touched his nipple, rubbed his abs and then his bulging sex.

"So you think you're what I need?"

"And you know that," Basil said confidently.

"What will we do in the morning?"

"What do you mean?"

"After you give me what I need, then what?"

"I don't understand," Basil said.

"That's the problem. You can give me what I need physically all night long, but I want the mental as well," I said.

"Raymond, why don't you just take what I'm offering? You do remember how good it is. Look what all that emotional shit got you with that nigga in Seattle. We're boyz. I'll always be here for you," Basil said.

"For sex only?"

"Whatever, whatever. You know I ain't gonna hook up with a dude 24-7," Basil said.

"Then I think I better pass. Besides, I don't know if I'm ready for the physical or the mental," I said.

Basil didn't say anything. He just put his clothes back on in silence. When he was dressed he took another swig of his beer and then headed toward the door.

I stood and watched him walk out. I felt disappointed, sad and alone.

BOOK TWO

Everything Must Change

OLETA ADAMS

1

I was sitting at my desk, reading the final version of the story on Yancey B. I knew we'd sell a lot of copies because of all the additional media coverage the magazine would get for breaking the story of Miss Yancey's crack problem. I couldn't wait to see what the public reaction would be to the juicy dish Yancey's own mother had turned over to Kirsten.

When I finished reading the article, I thought back to the night before, when Jabar had not only made love to me with his young-buck passion but had given me a deep-tissue massage, all while listening to Maxwell croon "This Woman's Work." My body was sore from pure, unblemished joy.

I knew I needed to get my mind back on work, when Raymond rushed into my office with a look of panic on his face.

"Raymond, what's wrong?" I asked.

"Turn on your television," he said.

I looked at him, puzzled, and asked, "Why?"

"You're not going to believe this."

I reached for the remote control and turned on the office television, which I rarely watched unless I was working late and didn't want to miss *Entertainment Tonight* or *E! News Daily*.

"What channel?" I asked.

"Any of them," Raymond said.

When the screen came on, I switched to Channel 2 and was a little surprised to see Bryant Gumbel and Jane Clayson still on. I knew it was a little past nine because Doug Banks and DeDe McGuire were no longer entertaining me on the radio.

"Can you believe it?" Raymond asked.

"What's happening?" I asked.

"Two planes hit the World Trade Center," Raymond said, looking at me disbelievingly.

"You're kidding," I said as I stared at the television. "Is it an accident?" I asked.

"They haven't said, but it doesn't sound like it. I mean, two planes hitting those buildings at the same time," Raymond said.

"That is bizarre," I said. A few minutes later, Cyndi walked into my office and asked if we had heard what happened.

"We're watching now. How did you find out?" Raymond asked her.

"My mother called to make sure I was all right," Cyndi said.

"Maybe we should close the office," Raymond said.

"You think so?"

"I think we should," Cyndi said. I looked at Raymond for an answer, as several employees starting gathering in my office. Melinda Turner, one of the staff writers, had tears streaming down her face.

"What's the matter?" I asked as I went over to console her.

"Zola, you know there have to be people on the floors where the planes hit," Melinda said.

"Melinda, you're right. I don't know what I was thinking. This just doesn't seem real. It's too crazy," I said.

"Davis isn't in yet. I called his office before I came here," Raymond said. "I think we should get ready to close the office."

"Cyndi, tell everyone we're closing for the day," I said.

"I will," Cyndi said as she dashed out of the room.

"I'll have Bristol tell everyone on my side of the building," Raymond said as he left my office, leaving me with Melinda, who was now sobbing like a baby.

Less than an hour later, the unthinkable happened, and we watched the towers crash to the ground. It looked like they were falling in slow motion. A security guard had stopped by and told us to evacuate the building immediately. I grabbed my purse and briefcase and headed out with Raymond, Cyndi and several staff members to the stairwell.

Pandemonium was barely contained as we descended from floor to floor in a half-dark stairwell. It was chaotic but unusually calm at the same time. I could hear the sound of shoes and heels hitting the concrete steps and people mumbling in disbelief.

Fifteen minutes later, when we all reached the ground floor, I breathed uneasily, thankful that I worked out. Some people were gasping. My body was drenched with perspiration as I walked through the door that led to the street. It was beautiful all day long, but after the events of the day, I wondered if the sun would ever really shine again.

I saw people hugging and holding one another while many of them were trembling like a leaf after the first fall rainstorm. My beeper went off, and I saw I had eight new messages. The first one was from Jabar, asking if I was all right. I sent him back a simple "OK" message. I responded the same way to messages from Justine, Kai, Hayden and Davis. I looked in my purse for my cell phone and realized I had left it in the office.

Raymond looked at me and asked how I was going to get home.

"I guess the subway."

"They've stopped the subway. I heard that on television right before I left my office," Raymond said.

"Well, I know catching a cab will be impossible," I said.

"So let's start walking," Raymond said.

As we hurried up Broadway, people on the streets walked briskly with a look of both shock and grief on their faces. Raymond and I moved in silence. I was thinking about the people in the towers and I felt so grateful to be able to walk a New York sidewalk. When we reached Fifty-seventh and Broadway, my eyes met the gaze of a somber-looking woman holding the hands of two small children. That's when I felt an intense sadness in my heart and I could no longer hold back my tears.

2
_____

"Let it go, Zola," I said as I held her tightly on the corner of a busy New York street. There were people everywhere, but it was unusually quiet. The city had a dreamlike quality, and all us residents were now extras in a low-budget horror film.

Zola pulled away, wiping tears from her face.

"I'm sorry. I just lost it," Zola said.

"I'm just glad I could be here with you. I think we're all going to shed some tears before this is over," I said, looking into her watery eyes.

"Don't you live near here?" Zola asked.

"Yeah, a couple of blocks up. Would you like to stop and wash your face?" I asked.

"Thank you, but I'll be fine. I think I'm going to keep walking. I have a lot to be thankful for and a lot to think about," Zola said.

"We all do. Do you mind if I walk with you?" I asked.

"You don't have to do that," Zola said.

"You'll be doing me a favor. To be honest, being alone in a quiet apartment is the last place I want to be right now," I said.

"Sure, I'd enjoy the company. But you know I live on 127th Street, don't you?"

"I knew you lived in Harlem. I'll just walk with you until you get tired of me," I said.

As Zola and I continued our walk up Broadway, stillness had settled over the city, which was ballooning with grief and love.

Perhaps for the first time ever in New York, people didn't react angrily when you bumped into them. Everyone was looking for a friendly face, and today it didn't seem to matter if that face was black, white or brown. New Yorkers weren't looking in store windows but into the eyes of one another. The gazes were comforting and nonthreatening.

When Zola and I crossed 100th Street I couldn't help but think about all the people who found themselves trapped in the two huge towers. Whenever I spotted people overcome with grief on the streets and crying, I wondered if they had lost a loved one and I wanted to reach out and hug them as I had hugged Zola.

I called Basil's office on my cell phone and was told that he wasn't in, but his assistant assured me he was safe. I called his apartment and got his answering machine. Even though I knew he was okay, I very much wanted to hear his voice.

"Well, this is where I live," Zola said as she pointed to a handsome carrot-colored brownstone an hour or so later.

"Beautiful building," I said.

"Would you like to come in?" Zola asked.

"Thanks, but not today. I don't know how long the subways are going to be out of service, and I want to get back to my apartment and turn on the TV and see if there's more information on what happened," I said.

"I understand," Zola said as she started up the steps. I had walked a few feet, when Zola called out my name. I turned and she moved swiftly toward me and kissed me on the cheek and whispered, "Thanks for being there."

"Thank you for letting me," I said.

3

After two hours in a soaking bath I was ready to return to the world. The walk from midtown to Harlem was more than a notion and my body was aching with stress. My phone had been ringing off the hook and I knew I needed to talk to my family.

After I put on my robe and turned on the television, the phone rang again. The caller ID displayed my folks' number.

"Hello, Mother," I said.

"Zola, baby, are you all right?" my mother asked, crying.

"Mother, please stop crying," I said.

"Zola, honey, I am so glad to hear your voice. I know you have meetings all over that city, and all I could think of was you being there in that burning building. I was shaking and screaming when I couldn't reach you . . . I mean, I have been praying all day. Thank God you're all right," Mother said. While my mother was rambling, my two-way pager went off. I looked at it and saw a message from Kirsten asking if I was okay. I paged her back with a simple "OK."

"Most of the cell phones were out most of the day and I had to walk home because the subways weren't running. But I'm fine, Mother," I said.

"What about your friends?"

"So far, so good. I have gone through my phone book, but I've heard from most of my friends," I said. My pager went off again, and it was Jabar, leaving a one-word message: *kwel.*

"How's the city?"

"It's strangely quiet. I mean, people are walking around in shock. It's so sad," I said as I fought back tears. The television was on mute, but the image of the day was being repeated almost every five minutes. I switched the channel to the E! network, where they were doing one of those true Hollywood stories on some female star I had never heard of.

"Your sister called, asking about you," Mother said.

"Asking what?"

"She just wanted to make sure you were okay. Do you want me to give her your number?"

"No!"

"Why don't you want to speak with her?"

"I have enough drama right here in New York. Tell her I'm safe, but right now I can't deal with her problems. Today taught me what real problems are," I said.

"Trust me, baby, I understand."

"Thanks, Mother. Is she still on that crack?" I asked.

"She say she's not."

"Give her my cell number," I said.

"Are you sure?"

"Yeah, I think I'm ready to speak with her."

"I'll give her the number. You know, I think you need to move back to Nashville," Mother said.

"Mother, I have a career here. I am not going to let these crazy fools run me out of the city I love," I said firmly. My call-waiting beep sounded and I looked at my caller ID and saw Jabar's cell number. I didn't click over, but I felt good he was reaching out. For a brief moment my thoughts went to imagining Jabar and his big, strong arms wrapped around me, protecting me from the dangers of the world.

I had never thought of him in that way before, and for a minute it threw me. Was it just an emotional reaction to the day's events?

"Then consider coming home for a couple of days, maybe even a week."

"I'll think about that, but I don't know when the airports will reopen, and to be real honest, I'm not too eager to get on a plane," I said. I hadn't been able to shake the image of the planes crashing into the World Trade Center. I thought of my mother sitting on the edge of her bed, braiding and greasing my hair when I was a little girl, and I smiled to myself at the memory.

"Your father and I aren't doing anything. We can drive up there and get you."

"Mother, you don't have to do that. I'll be fine and I'll come home soon. I need to go. I have some more calls to make. Please tell Daddy I'm fine. I love you," I said softly.

"I love you too. Please be careful. Please promise me you'll do that," Mother said.

"I promise I'll be careful. You get some rest," I said before I hung up.

It seemed that just as I hung up the phone, it rang again. It was Hayden.

"You okay, boyfriend?" I asked.

"Honey, I'm alive. Did you hear they think there might be over ten thousand people dead in those buildings?"

"I have the television on, but I have it on mute. I can't bear to listen to it. I mean, all those people with pictures of loved ones. Every time I think about it, I start crying all over. Can you believe this has happened?" I asked.

"No, I can't. You know it's a strange day when both my father and mother call. I guess my father really does love me," Hayden said sadly. I knew it had been several years since Hayden had spoken with his father. They'd had a big blowout when Hayden started accepting gifts from a much older and married man whom his father knew. Hayden had moved out of the house when the man left his wife and rented an apartment for Hayden. I guess the 9/11 tragedy was quickly having a positive effect on estranged family members. I mean, why else would I permit my mother to give Pamela my number?

"Have you talked with Kai?"

"Yeah, she's gone upstate to see her parents for a couple of days," Hayden said.

"Is she okay?"

"Kai said she was, but we both know that child is fragile enough without all this shit happening," Hayden said.

"At least she won't be alone," I said as I looked at my empty carved four-poster bed. I was thinking about calling Jabar, but I didn't know if this was sending out a signal that I wanted to change our arrangement.

"I've been going through my phone book, trying to find a warm body to come over here and hold me tonight. I guess this is what I get for dating only men with females," Hayden said.

"You want to come over here?" I asked.

"You're not going to try nothing are you?" Hayden asked, laughing.

"No, Fool," I said. The phone beeped, and I saw Justine's number flash across the phone.

"Baby, this is Justine. Call me if you need to talk," I said.

"I will. I love you, Zola Mae," Hayden said. I loved it when he called me Zola Mae because he said he didn't want me to ever forget I was a Southern girl.

"I love you, Hayden. Good night."

I clicked over the line and greeted Justine.

"How are you doing, darling?" Justine asked.

"Glad to be alive," I said.

"Me too."

"I don't know why, but I feel the need to call everyone I've ever known," I said.

"Even Wilson?" Justine asked.

"I'm not delusional. Did you forget what you promised?"

"I'm sorry. I know I promised not to ever say his name."

"Are you alone?" I asked, trying to move on.

"Actually, I'm not," Justine said.

"Aren't you lucky? I should have known you'd find a man to keep you company," I said, laughing.

"It's not a man," Justine said softly.

"What? Justine, stop tripping," I said.

"Zola, please. I'm here with my neighbor Rhonda. She stopped by and invited me to go to church with her tonight. They're having a midnight prayer service. I called to see if you wanted to go," Justine said.

"This is some day. You just make sure Rhonda knows how long it's been since you've been in a church," I said.

"I told her and I was embarrassed. Tonight I think I need to feel the warmth of several people and not just one."

"I hear you. Say a little prayer for me, but I am ready for bed, so I'll pass," I said. I knew sleep wasn't going to be easy, and I couldn't bear watching the news, seeing those planes, the smoke and fire over and over. It would give me nightmares for months to come.

"If God still hears my prayers, then I will certainly pray for you. I love you, Zola. I'm happy you're all right," Justine said.

"I love you too. Please be careful," I said as I hung up the phone, still slightly stressed and tired from a most eventful day. Still, I had never been happier to be alive.

4

Dusk arrived as I sat at my home desk and watched the television's constant replay of the day's horror. I pushed the mute button and decided to call my parents.

My mom answered the phone after a couple of rings.

"Hey, Mama. How are you and Pops doing?" I asked softly.

"We're fine, baby. How are you doing? I've been calling you all day, but there was a recording saying that the circuits were busy. I called your cell phone and couldn't get through on that either. Is everything all right? Where are you calling from? The caller ID came up with a 212 area code," my mother said. I suddenly felt sad that I hadn't told my parents about my move to New York and breakup with Trent. It was like I was telling a silent lie. Yet I knew today wasn't the day to spread the news of Trent's new life.

"I'm in New York."

"What are you doing in New York? Oh, baby, are you sure you're all right? You're not near that area, are you?" my mother asked, her voice filled with concern.

"I'm working and I'm fine. But it's really been a crazy day up here. I just wanted to call you guys and let you know I'm doing okay."

"How is Trent? Is he up there too?"

"No, and Trent is fine," I said. I assumed he was fine and was suddenly debating if I should call him after I finished the phone call with my parents.

"When did you get to New York?"

"I've been here a couple of months, working on a big project," I said. I knew that I should tell her that I had moved permanently, but I thought enough had happened today.

"Where are you staying and why didn't you tell us?"

"I'm staying in a corporate apartment, and I've just been really busy. I'm sorry. Where's Pops?" I asked. I felt I needed to get my mother off the phone before her probe into my personal life continued and I could no longer tell half-truths.

"He's sitting over there in his chair, watching the news. They aren't showing anything but the World Trade Center. It's horrible and just makes me sick to my stomach."

"Can I speak to Pops?"

"Hold on, baby," my mother said. Before she gave my father the phone, I called out her name. "Mom, I love you. I really love you," I said softly.

"And I love you too, baby. Here's your daddy."

"Hey, son. How's Seattle?"

"I'm not in Seattle, Pops. I'm in New York. I'm working with Davis McClinton. You've heard of him, right? He's one of the richest black men in the world," I said. I knew I could steer my father into talking about something other than the day's events or my relocation. I was glad Kirby kept his little-brother pact and hadn't revealed my move.

"Can you believe what those crazy religious fools did? I don't want any part of that kind of religion. You're safe and I'm glad. What about Jared and his family?"

"They're doing great. I forgot to tell you. Jared moved his family down to Atlanta this summer," I said.

"I'm glad to hear that. Atlanta is a wonderful city. Maybe you and Trent should consider moving there. Have you talked to your little brother?"

"No. I'm going to call him a little later on. Have you heard from him?"

"Yeah, I talked to him before he left for practice," Pops said.

"I'm sure he tried to reach me but my cell phone isn't working and it's hard to receive calls in New York. But I'll call him next," I said.

"I'll call Kirby and tell him you're okay. How's Trent?"

"He's fine, back in Seattle," I said.

"Tell him I said hello."

"I will. I love you, Pops. I've got to run. I've got to make sure all my employees and friends are okay."

"Listen to you."

"What?" I quizzed.

"Your employees? What are you doing for this Davis McClinton guy? I've heard of him. I remember reading some articles on him," he said.

"He's been on the cover of *Fortune* and *Business Week*. I'm the CEO of one of his publications," I said.

"Are you enjoying it?"

"It's challenging, but I love the responsibility," I said.

"That's great, son. I'm proud of you."

"And I'm proud of you, Pops," I said before I hung up the phone.

I got up from my desk and walked over toward the window, thinking about the traumatic day and who I was going to call next. I noticed lines of white clouds going in different directions like they were readying the release of another great disaster.

I looked down on the near-empty streets. Everything seemed to be moving in slow motion.

I went back to my desk and made a series of phone calls, but I got no human voice, only several cheery voices on answering machines unaware of what sorrow the day had brought. I left a message for Kirby. I called and spoke with Jared and Nicole, who were relieved I was safe. Nicole told me she had been on her knees, praying for hours for all the victims and hoping that she wouldn't receive a call with bad news about people she knew.

Before I picked up the phone again, I slowly walked barefoot into the kitchen and pulled out a bottle of water. I wanted a glass of wine, but I felt it would only heighten my sorrow.

I slowly dialed Trent's cell phone, planning just to leave a message telling him I was all right. Damn, I didn't even know if I still mattered to him. No, that wasn't true. I knew he would be concerned.

"Hello," Trent said, his voice low and subdued.

"Trent," I said.

"Ray. Man, I'm so glad you called. I was so worried about you, but I didn't know if I should call. Can you believe that shit? Man, I've been going crazy with worry. How are you? Were you anywhere near the World Trade? Where were you when it happened?"

"I was at the office, preparing for a trip to London," I said.

"Oh, Ray, you need to stay off those planes for a while. Let them figure this shit out. Promise me you'll do that."

"I'll be fine. How are you?"

"I'm doing okay. The babies keep me up," Trent said.

Babies? Did I hear Trent correctly? I wondered. Maybe he was talking about his newborn and his son, Trent Junior, who spent a great deal of time in Seattle. I didn't want to delve into his personal life.

"Today was a crazy day. Even more frightening than the earthquake in Seattle last year," I said.

"Man, I thought the same thing. Remember the phones were out all over the city, and I was going crazy trying to locate you," Trent said.

"Yeah, I remember," I said softly. I suddenly recalled that day of madness, which ended with Trent and me throwing lunch meat on the grill because the electricity in the house was out for close to forty-eight hours. It actually turned out to be a romantic night, as Trent and I had our own picnic by starlight and then held hands as we maneuvered ourselves into our bedroom in the darkness. I missed Seattle and Trent. I missed the rain, I wanted to hear it coming down fast and furious, or feel the mist on my face like a protective cover.

"It's so good hearing your voice," Trent said softly. It's what I wanted to hear, but he had another life now, and what we had had was over.

"Did you say babies a couple of minutes ago?" I asked.

"Yeah, Ray, we had twins. A boy and a girl. Brandon and Bailey. They're beautiful, Ray. I wanted to send you a picture," Trent said. His voice was no longer low, but booming with pride. A thin ringing silence followed before I said, "That would be nice. Do that. Trent, I've got to run. I'm going to meet a friend for dinner," I lied. I just wanted to hang up and have a drink to ease the pain I was feeling. The silence returned thicker than before and was broken only by Trent's voice.

"You take care of yourself, Ray," Trent said.

"You too," I said as I hung up. The silence and loneliness of my apartment saddened me, and I picked up the phone and dialed Basil's number. I was expecting to get his answering machine, but instead Basil picked up, his voice a whisper.

"Basil?"

"Ray. What's going on?"

"Did you get my messages?"

"Yeah, I did, dude, but like everyone else, I've been running around like a crazy man. Can you believe this dumb-ass shit? I guess those crazy mofos really hate us," Basil said.

"Yeah, I guess they do. What are you doing?"

"Sitting here, holding my baby girl. Talley is asleep. Man, this girl has stolen my whole heart," Basil said.

"Is Rosa all right?" I asked. I felt a pang of jealousy that Basil and Trent had children to provide them comfort.

"She's fine. The first thing I thought when I heard what happened was where was Talley and where was Rosa? Was she on a flight? Man, I almost broke down when I went to her apartment and found Rosa and Talley there safe," Basil said.

"Well, I won't keep you. I just wanted to make sure you're okay," I said.

"I 'preciate that, man. I didn't call because when I got your message I knew you were all right. But brothas like you and me gonna always be cool." Basil's voice was smooth and steady.

"You think so?"

"No doubt, my brotha. Hey, I need to go and put my little girl in the bed. Take care of yourself," Basil said.

"You too."

From *Bling Bling* Confidential

In support of the victims and families touched by 9/11, *Bling Bling* Confidential will be discontinued until further notice.

5

I guess it wasn't hard to understand why choosing the sexiest brothaman and exposing a lying diva didn't excite me as much as it did just a few days ago. But I had a job to do and it seemed like everyone in the city and on the staff was trying to get back to normal, although I knew normal left on September 11.

I spent the afternoon going over photos, first the ones submitted by modeling agencies, then the ones readers sent in. Obviously some of these people didn't really know what sexy meant. I had a lot to consider in making the final selections. I couldn't have too many curly-headed, light-skinned guys with light eyes, and I had to have at least one brother with dreads, a bald-headed brother and at least a couple who looked like their chiseled bodies had been dipped in Godiva chocolate.

During the days the office was closed, I had spent time writing in my journal and playing the piano and trying out recipes from *O* and *Martha Stewart Living* magazines. I made some of my favorite childhood delicacies like Spam on white bread with mustard and pickles. I called several people I hadn't talked to in years, especially the ones who lived in New York City, and apologized for not following up on promised lunch dates.

One of those calls was to a friend, Megan Norman, whom I met when we both did summer internships at *Vanity Fair*. Megan was a cool white girl from St. Louis who loved rap music, Broadway show tunes and classical piano. We had shared an apartment and for years afterward often ran into each other at functions and always promised to visit some of our old haunts. Megan was now an executive editor at *Town & County*, and she broke into tears when she heard my voice. I followed suit.

I had already decided to postpone the Yancey B. cover story, because once again I didn't think people were ready to read the trials and tribulations of such a tortured mother-daughter relationship. It seemed like every time we were ready to run the story, trouble and tragedy followed. Maybe this girl was bad news.

Cyndi stepped inside my office and told me Hayden was on line two.

"What's going on, Hay-den?" I asked.

"My feet are killing me," he said.

"Where are you?"

"At rehearsals for the *Dreamgirls* benefit," Hayden said.

"Are they still doing that?"

"Oh, yes, honey. The show must go on. They don't call us troopers for nothing," Hayden said.

"I guess you're right. When am I going to see you?"

"Hopefully soon. I just called to share some good news," Hayden said.

"What?"

"Looks like I got a job."

"In a show?"

"The biggest show," Hayden said.

"*The Lion King*? Did you get the part?"

"I sure did."

"That's great. When did you find out?"

"My agent called me a couple hours ago. I got it by default."

"What do you mean?"

"They were going to give it to this guy from Los Angeles who had flown in for the audition, but when they offered him the part, he said he wasn't flying or living in New York," Hayden said.

"Oh, that's sad for him but good for you," I said.

"You got that right. Hey, I got to go; we're getting ready to start back."

"Bye Hayden."

After I got off the phone, I checked my e-mails. The first one was from the corporate office, about how Davis and Veronica had given five million dollars to the 9/11 relief fund. I was impressed, but I thought both Davis and Veronica probably spent just as large a sum of money on a stylist to pick out the right outfit when they posed for the cameras. There was an e-mail from Jabar, which I didn't read because they always required a thug-boy interpreter. He always used words like *kwel* and *U* and a bunch of other words and phases I didn't understand, like *I think I will parlay at your crib dis evening.* I once asked him what did he think the word *parlay* meant, and Jabar explained it meant to chill at the highest level. Whatever.

A couple hours later I was looking forward to the bus ride home. I had given up on the subway. I didn't want to be stuck underground if there was another terrorist attack.

I kicked off my flats and was reaching for my tennis shoes, when my cell phone rang. The caller ID read *Private.*

"Hello. This is Zola Norwood," I said.

"I guess it is," Pamela said. I recognized her slow, weighty voice immediately, even though we hadn't spoken for over five years. Was she calling to find out how I was after 9/11?

"Pamela, how are you?"

"There you go, forever the little polite debutante. You know I ain't doing good. I know Mama told you I was still hittin' the pipe," Pamela said.

"So you called up here to ruin my day," I said.

"Mama said you wanted me to call you," Pamela said.

"I did not. She said you wanted my phone number."

"That was a while ago. I wanted to see if you'd pay for me to go back into rehab, but I figured you'd try and send the check straight to a clinic I wasn't going to. I know how you think you're smarter and better than everybody," Pamela said.

"If you called up here to start something, then this is the wrong time. I have work to do. . . ."

"I know, and people to meet. Little Miss Zola, who always could talk the stank out of shit," Pamela said.

I didn't respond. Instead, I clicked the end button on my phone and turned the power off.

6

_____

There was a handsome leather binder on my desk with a note from Davis instructing me to review the contents and call him to discuss. Inside the binder was a three-day itinerary for London.

Still, the thought of getting on a plane of any kind caused a sudden surge of panic to pulse through every part of my body. I was trying to think of some reason I could give Davis as to why I couldn't make the trip, when I noticed an airplane in the sky from my office window.

It looked strange and scary, like a flying tube vulnerable in the vastness of a pale blue sky. I picked up the phone, put it back in the cradle and fumbled with my keys resting on the edge of my desk. I thought about the mayor and the police chief on television all day on 9/11 encouraging New Yorkers to get back to life, to take their business trips, go to restaurants and Broadway shows, and in my heart I knew they were right.

The day before, I had gone to a Broadway show I never would have attended before 9/11. Members of the Broadway community were encouraging New Yorkers to attend a show, since the city seemed tourist free. There was a list of shows in trouble and I decided to go to the Neil Simon Theatre, where *The Music Man* was playing, and buy a couple of tickets. I wasn't really interested in seeing the show, but I thought my ticket money would give the community some hope.

I often did this during the opening weekend for black movies when I didn't actually have the time or any interest in seeing the film, because I felt it was sending a message to Hollywood to keep making black movies.

The second Sunday after 9/11 was a gloomy, rainy day, like the city was still shedding tears. When I got to the theater I was happy to see the lobby packed. I walked up to the ticket window and asked what was available. A friendly white lady with gray hair told me she had only one single seat left, in Row T, center, the last one. "I'll take it," I said as I slipped my credit card through the tiny opening.

After I had signed the receipt and was deciding what I wanted to eat for a late brunch, I decided I would at least check out the first act of the show. I realized I didn't want to spend a rainy Sunday alone, so I entered the theater and gave the usher my ticket.

The theater was packed and buzzing with excitement. I was in the middle of a row and thought if the show was just too corny, it was going to be tough getting up and heading for the exit. But soon after the curtain rose and after a few songs, I found myself actually enjoying the show, whose cast included several African Americans in ensemble roles.

I didn't even get up during intermission; instead, I spent the time reading the biographies of the actors and a list of songs still to come in the second act. At the end of the show, the audience gave the cast a rousing standing ovation, and I was among the first to my feet. Then something happened that surprised me. During the curtain call, all of the actors played instruments like a real-life marching band and a huge American flag unfurled on the stage. I didn't know if this was a part of the show or something special the cast had decided to do in support of the city and the country. All I knew was that it took everything I had to blink back the tears forming in my eyes as I cheered loudly. It was like I was at the Super Bowl and my team had just won in overtime. I realized how much the city, the nation and I had endured since 9/11, and the tears somehow released feelings about my country that I had ignored. I felt pride in being an American. It didn't matter one bit that the people cheering alongside me and those in front of me didn't share my color or anything else about me. We were one.

But now this. Was I ready to get on an airplane, or would the fear the terrorists had intended become a reality? My reality. I picked up the phone again and this time I dialed Davis's private line. He picked up after a couple of rings.

"Davis here."

"Davis, this is Raymond."

"Did you get the schedule?" he asked.

"Yes, I did. I haven't heard of the airline listed," I said as I scanned the information closely. "Is it a foreign carrier?" I asked.

"Only if you consider a black man owning his own jet foreign," Davis said, laughing.

"Oh, I'm sorry. Are they allowing private planes back in the air? I thought there were some restrictions," I said.

"Restrictions for those who don't have the money to make things happen," Davis said.

"So you're ready to get back in the air?" I wanted to ask him how long his pilot had been flying, but I didn't want him to know that I was still holding on to my keys to keep my hands from shaking. I was trying to remember the very first time I had flown and if I'd had any fear. Probably not, since my first flight most likely occurred when I was a fearless little boy.

"Of course I'm ready to fly. We've got a deal to close. People in Europe are supporting us, but they're also conducting business. We need to close this deal before somebody else realizes what a steal it is and slips in and buys the company while Americans are over here, acting like punks."

"I hear you. So we'll be gone three days?" I asked.

"That's the plan, but I would pack for at least a week. I'll attend the first couple of meetings, but then I'm coming back and allowing you to handle all the business matters. It's up to you when you come back. All I expect is for you to come back with signed contracts." It was business as usual for Davis; it seemed that 9/11 didn't cause a blip on his radar for buying and selling companies.

"So will I fly back commercial?"

"You can. Is that a problem?"

Again I didn't want to sound like a punk, so I quickly said, "That's fine."

"Good. I'll see you in the morning. My driver will pick you up around seven."

"I'll see you tomorrow," I said before I hung up the phone. I loosened my tie and the top button on my shirt so I could wipe away the film of sweat that was surrounding my neck. I made a mental note to pick up a turtleneck for the trip just in case the same thing occurred on the plane. The last thing I wanted was to have Davis see me sweat.

7

It had been about three days since I'd talked to Justine, and we had been engaged in a serious game of telephone tag. I had decided against asking Jabar to *Dreamgirls* because I was really scared he might show up in sagging jeans and combat boots.

I finished looking over a story I had asked one of my staff members to rewrite, and I was going to make some herbal tea but decided to call Justine and see if she wanted to attend the performance with me.

I hit speed dial number three and a voice that sounded like Justine's answered quickly, "Praise the Lord in the name of Jesus."

I was taken aback for a moment, but I said, "Justine. What are you doing, girl? And what's with that greeting?"

"Oh, hello, sister Zola. How is the Lord blessing you today?" Justine asked. I looked at the phone like I wasn't hearing her correctly. She had called me sister, not sistah.

"Come on, girl. Why are you using the Lord's name in vain? What kind of joke are you playing?"

"Sister Zola, I would never use the Lord's name in vain. I have been born again in the blood of Jesus: Thank you Jesus," Justine said sternly.

"Come on now. Stop playing."

"Zola, I am not playing. Sunday I was baptized in the blood of Jesus and I was reborn. The old Justine is gone, praise the Lord. Thank you, Jesus. I need to take you to this wonderful church on Ninety-third and Broadway, where I found Jesus."

"What was he doing?" I joked.

"Now, Zola, I can't have you using the Lord's name in vain. I will pray for you."

"You're serious, aren't you?"

"Devoting your life to Jesus is serious, Zola. I just wish you understood how I feel."

"How do you feel?"

"Wonderfully blessed."

"Then I'm happy for you."

"Thank you, sister," Justine said. The voice sounded like Justine's, but the words coming out didn't sound like my childhood friend's. This was not the woman who said she didn't want anything to do with church unless she was certain that it was filled with good-looking, well-hung single men.

"I called to see if you wanted to go to this special concert performance of *Dreamgirls*. Hayden is in the chorus and he gave me his comp tickets. It should be big fun, girl. Tickets are going as high as twenty-five hundred dollars," I said.

"I can't go. I will be at church," Justine said quickly.

"I didn't even say when it was."

"Doesn't matter. I will be at church, praising the Lord, every evening. I have so much prayer to catch up on," Justine said, her voice now sounding distant.

"Okay, maybe I should ask Jabar or maybe Davis, but he probably can't go out in public with something like that. Do you want to get something to eat tomorrow? It's been a while since I've seen you, and I haven't seen you since you've been reborn. Do you still look the same?" I joked, trying to switch the heavy conversation into something light.

"I look the same, but I will never be the same. Thank you, Jesus."

"What about dinner?"

"Not this week. I'm fasting. Maybe when it's over."

"Are you trying to lose some weight for the Lord?"

"I am cleansing my soul."

"Okay, well, I guess I'm happy for you," I said softly.

"Be very happy for me. God is so amazing."

"I guess so. Well, you take care of yourself."

"I will and I will pray for you, sister Zola."

"You do that. Good night, Justine."

"With Jesus every night is a good night."

I wanted to say whatever, but instead I ended the conversation with another good night.

I didn't even hang up the phone but dialed Kai's number. She picked up after a couple of rings.

"Hello, Zola."

I hated caller ID, because it took all the surprise out of calling your friends.

"Hey, girl. What are you doing?"

"Sipping on a little champagne, thinking about all the men that got away. What are you doing?"

"I'm getting ready for bed. Have you talked to Justine lately?"

"Yeah, I talked to Sister Jesus. Isn't that the craziest shit that has happened since 9/11?" Kai let out a loud, exotic laugh.

"I think she's serious. But I guess I need to see what the minister and the deacons look like at that church. It sounds like somebody has taken over her body. Justine didn't even sound like herself. I kept looking at the phone and around my bedroom to make sure I wasn't in some crazy dream."

"It's some strange shit. I was going to call you and warn you. I had talked to her just after she had walked on the water or whatever they do when they get saved. You want to go out and have some drinks and see if there are any new men on the scene?"

"I can't do that, honey. I wish I could, but I have a busy day tomorrow. I can't believe you want to go out on a Sunday night."

"Zola, I am going out every night until I meet somebody I can bring home. I have had enough of this being-alone shit. Girl, I was so lonesome the other night, I almost called that good-for-nothing ex of mine. He was always good for holding me tight after I gave him some, and, honey, your sister needs to be held on a regular basis."

"I heard that, but I don't think you should tell Justine that. She's busy praying for my soul now. I don't think she's got time for the both of us. You know, since she's Jesus' new best friend." I laughed nervously. I believed in God but wasn't convinced Justine was now dealing with a full deck—I couldn't really be sure until I was face-to-face with her.

"Don't worry about her, honey. Justine is just tripping. She will be back to her old ways in no time. Give this religion shit about a month. So I can't talk you into going out?"

"Not tonight, but maybe this weekend if you haven't found your prince."

"Honey, you should see this outfit I am going to wear tonight. If I don't find him tonight, this is going to be much harder than I expected," Kai said.

"What are you wearing?"

"Let's just say it involves a mini, something sheer and something leather."

"Sounds hot! Good luck, hon."

"I got a question to ask you," Kai said.

"I'm listening."

"Can women buy condoms, or is that like men trying to buy sanitary napkins?" Kai asked. Here I was, thinking what a normal conversation we were having, so I decided to ignore her question.

"Talk to you soon. Love you."

"I love you too," Kai said.

❖   ❖   ❖

When I walked into the elevator at work the next morning, fine-ass Raymond Tyler was there with a smile on his face. I wondered how long he had had to wear braces, since his teeth looked perfect. He had on a well-tailored blue pin-striped suit with an off-white shirt and matching silk tie, and he smelled good.

"Good morning, Zola. Going up?"

"Good morning. I think I'd better, since it's such a beautiful day. I might be tempted to play hooky if I stay in this lobby a second longer," I said.

"I feel you. I've been on a plane all night," Raymond said.

"Oh, that's right. You were in London. How did it go?" I asked.

"Great. Now, Davis owns a part of the media in London," Raymond said.

"That Davis, even a national tragedy doesn't stop him from making money," I said.

When we reached our floor, Raymond, ever the gentleman, motioned with a slight nod of his head and hand for me to go first. I thought about the times when I was on the elevator with Jabar and men like him and how they didn't think anything about walking out before me. Davis did the same thing when we were alone, but never when there were other men present. He always strutted out front like he was the king of the world leading a parade in his honor.

When he opened the door for me, I decided I loved this kind of treatment, so I turned to Raymond and asked him, "What are you doing this evening?"

"I don't have any plans. Maybe a little workout and some dinner," Raymond said.

"How would you like to attend a performance of *Dreamgirls*?" I asked.

"*Dreamgirls?* I didn't know it was in town," Raymond said.

"It's only one night. It's the twentieth anniversary of the show and they're doing a benefit," I said.

"I can't believe it's been twenty years since that show came to Broadway. It's a wonderful show. Sure, I would love to go. Are any of the original stars going to be in it?" Raymond asked.

"I don't think so. Audra MacDonald, Lillias White, Heather Headley and Tamara Tunie are the headliners. One of my best friends is in the cast," I said proudly.

"I love all those ladies. Hey, we all need a show like *Dreamgirls* to cheer us up. Thanks for asking, Zola." Raymond smiled.

"There is a cast party afterward. You think you'll be up for that? You would get a chance to meet my friend," I said. I knew Hayden didn't really like polished guys, but maybe he would make an exception for someone as handsome as Raymond.

"Sure, I'm getting old, but I like to hang out every once in a while. Thanks again."

"Just glad you can make it," I said as both Raymond and I walked into our respective offices.

8

I went home a little early to get ready for the *Dreamgirls* big event.

Zola and I reached the new Ford Theatre on Forty-second Street and joined a well-dressed crowd crackling with excitement. It seemed like New York City was slowly returning to life as I looked at a crowd of all different types of people who seemed excited to be out. Zola and I located our orchestra seats right before the opening cowbell, which signaled the start of the show, and I, along with a packed house, let out a roar that sounded more appropriate for a sporting event than a Broadway show.

Zola looked beautiful in a royal blue strapless, short, sequined dress and her hair was up in a French roll instead of down like she normally wore it. I was glad I had worn my black tuxedo with an ivory shirt and matching tie, like I had seen Will Smith wear to some awards show. I used my hand to press down the back of my hair, hoping Zola and others looking at me wouldn't notice that I needed a haircut.

"Thanks again for inviting me," I whispered as the curtain began to rise.

"Glad you could make it," Zola said as she leaned toward me and touched my hand gently.

The performance of *Dreamgirls* was amazing. Audra, Heather, Lillias and Tamara turned it out. Performing one of the male leads was one of my favorite singers, Billy Porter, who had recorded one of my favorite songs, "Love Is on the Way," a couple of years ago and wished the song were true. There was also a very handsome brown-skinned man playing the lead role of Curtis Taylor Jr., and he had an incredible voice. I was hoping I would have the chance to meet him at the after party.

When Zola's friend Hayden made his first appearance in the chorus, Zola started clapping and hollering his name. "That's my friend Hayden, the third guy from the left. Isn't he nice-looking?" she said to me.

I nodded slightly and smiled.

For me, hearing the songs took me back to the eighties, when I lived in New York right after law school. I thought about Nicole and how I loved seeing her play one of the female leads, Deena Jones, when we were dating. I thought of how simple and easy life had been dating women and wondered if I could enjoy dating again if I met the right woman, someone as beautiful and talented as the ladies gracing the stage. But as the image of a woman and me lingered in my mind, I realized that it was just a dream whose time had passed.

❖   ❖   ❖

After the show, Zola and I walked a few blocks to an after party at a restaurant that had been closed for the affair. When we got there, several photographers and fans were standing behind a police blockade, screaming as stars of the show entered the restaurant. When we got a few feet from the entrance, we noticed a beautiful young lady and handsome man standing on the red carpet as photographers snapped pictures and young girls and a few boys screamed at the top of their lungs.

"Must be one of the boy bands," I said.

"I wish. That's Yancey B.," Zola said.

"The singer?" I asked as I peered over the crowd to get a look at the woman who had broken Basil's heart. She was stunningly beautiful and seemed to be enjoying her moment in the spotlight.

"Let's get in before she sees me," Zola said as she grabbed my hand.

"Do you know her?"

"Let's just say I know of her. I had to bump her off the cover of the magazine when Aaliyah died, and I don't think she's real happy with me now. Maybe tonight she's in a good mood and I can clear up our little misunderstanding," Zola said.

I followed Zola into the swank restaurant and she gave her name to a gentleman guarding the entrance. Zola checked her jacket and I enjoyed the view of all the good-looking men and women walking into the party, everyone seemed to be in a festive mood.

"Are you ready?" Zola asked, breaking the trance I had fallen into.

"Ready when you are. Lead the way," I said.

Zola walked up a flight of stairs like she owned the place, smiling at several people and giving pecks on the cheeks before we went through a large double door and into a large dining room covered in a low, buttery light. There were several dining tables, chairs, booths and a large circular bar.

"Let's see if we can find a table in the back. I need to make sure I spot Hayden. I can't wait for you two to meet," Zola said.

"You want me to get you something to drink?" I asked.

"Sure, white wine," Zola said as she surveyed the room.

I walked over toward the middle of the bar and found a spot where I could fit. After I ordered the drinks I heard a deep voice, so I turned around and realized that I was standing next to the male lead of *Dreamgirls*, a handsome man with near-perfect teeth whose face lit up with a dazzling smile. I felt my legs buckle. It was time to get back into circulation, I thought, as I started to hum "Love Is on the Way" to myself.

"How are you doing?" he asked as he shook my hand firmly.

"I'm doing fine. I'm Raymond Tyler," I said.

"I'm Merv Lewis," he said.

"You were great tonight," I said, trying not to sound like I was gushing.

"Thank you, Raymond."

"Yeah, Raymond Tyler," I repeated. Just as I was trying to think of what to say next, I heard a lady's voice say, "I thought that was you, Raymond Tyler." I turned in the direction of the voice and was greeted with a sudden kiss on both cheeks by a woman who had on a large black hat with a huge brim and sunglasses. She was wearing a lot of jewelry, including a duo of diamonds the size of popcorn kernels in the center of each earlobe, letting the world know she had money or a sugar daddy, since she wasn't wearing a wedding ring.

"Yes, I'm Raymond Tyler. Do we know each other?"

"We met at Nicole Springer's wedding," she said.

"How do you know Nicole?" I asked.

"We go way back."

"Oh," I said as I looked around the room to see where Merv had disappeared to.

"We have someone else in common too," she said.

"Who?"

"John Basil Henderson," she said with a bright smile.

"How do you know Basil?" I asked. This lady didn't look like Basil's type, but with him you never knew.

"My husband played pro football with him."

"Oh, yeah, who's your husband?"

"Well, he was husband number two. I try never to mention his name. Is that fine-ass Basil married?"

"No, but he has the most beautiful little girl," I said. I suddenly wondered why I was telling Basil's business to a woman I didn't know.

"Say . . . what? Basil's a daddy? How sweet. What's his little girl's name?"

"Talley," I said. I did it again, telling somebody else's business.

"Talley. What a beautiful name. I bet she's beautiful."

"Yeah, she is. I'm sorry, but I didn't catch your name."

"I didn't throw it." She laughed as she playfully hit me on the shoulder.

"My bad," I said.

"I'm kidding. My name is . . . oh, wait a minute. I think I see Yancey B. I need to get her autograph. Nice seeing you again, Raymond. Tell Basil and Nicole I said hello," she said as she kissed me again and then dashed off into the crowd.

I yelled, "Who should I tell them sends her regards?" But she had disappeared into the crowd. I grabbed my drinks and started looking for Zola and hoped to bump into Merv.

I walked around the room and didn't spot Merv, but I saw Zola in the corner booth with a man. My eyes met hers and she motioned for me to come over. I placed one of the drinks in front of Zola and took a seat next to her.

"Raymond, thanks for the drink. This is my friend Hayden."

"Nice meeting you, Hayden," I said.

"Same here. Did you enjoy the show?"

"Bet. Everything was tight and *Dreamgirls* is my favorite Broadway show. Tonight was just magical. How was it being in the show?"

"It was off the chain. I know there was a lot of drama onstage, but there was much more backstage," Hayden said.

"What happened?" Zola asked after taking a small sip of her wine.

"Oh, baby. Well, you know all the divas in town wanted to be a part of the show. I mean, do you know how many Deena Joneses, Effies and Lorrells there have been? It didn't matter if they had gained weight or hadn't been on a stage since the last time they did a bus-and-truck production of *Dreamgirls*," Hayden said.

"One of my good friends used to play Deena," I said.

"Who?" Hayden asked.

"Nicole Springer."

"Oh, I know Nicole. She's a smart and pretty girl. A great Deena. She might be one of the few who turned the producers down. I heard they offered her a chance at directing because she's a smart cookie. She knows there are new young divas getting off the Greyhound bus every day trying to get where she's been. I heard she moved back to Atlanta and is directing a lot of shows, and I am not just talking black shows," Hayden said.

"Yeah, Nicole and her family are back in ATL," I said. I was thinking maybe that's where I should have moved instead of New York, but I knew now was not the time to bail out of the city.

"So what was the drama?" Zola asked.

"Y'all heard of Yancey B., right? She had a hit song and album last year. Anyway, she played Deena in the last Broadway production of the show. Now, Miss Girl is big-time with records and movies and was all set to play one of the lead roles, but she had so many requirements, like special kinds of water, and chocolate-covered fruit, so the producers told her thanks but no thanks. Anyway, right when the stars of the show came from the stage door, who was there trying to upstage them but none other than Miss Yancey B., with her fine-ass boyfriend or whatever. The ladies from tonight were pure class, just smiling, waving and getting into their cars."

"Sounds salty," Zola said.

"Oh, it gets better. Miss Yancey must be riding in a spaceship, because not only did she stay at the theater for photo opportunities, she hightailed it over to the party and upstaged the girls again as they were getting ready to come into the party. I caught only a tiny glimpse of her, but it looked like girlfriend had changed her dress." Hayden laughed.

"Where is she? I need to see what Yancey B. is looking like tonight. My work is never done," Zola said.

"Over there somewhere," Hayden said as he pointed into a crowded area of the room.

"Excuse me, Raymond. Looks like duty calls. You and Hayden talk amongst yourselves," Zola said as she scooted out of the booth and disappeared into the crowd.

A few moments of silence passed as Hayden and I both looked around the room. I was still hoping to spot Merv, and Hayden seemed to be just people-watching. Suddenly we were both looking at each other and Hayden said, "Miss Zola thinks she's slick. Talking about trying to get some information for her magazine. Those divas know she's press, and if there's anything going on, then they'll either move it to over-the-top drama or close their mouths."

"So what is she doing?" I asked.

"Trying to play matchmaker with us," Hayden said in a nonchalant tone, like he wasn't interested, and I guess the same thing could be said for me. He was attractive, but in the few minutes I was in his company I could tell Hayden wasn't my type, a bit too theatrical, although I hadn't ruled him out as a friend.

"I guess you're saying I'm not your type," I said, deciding I was much too old to be playing games and letting ole boy know I felt the same way.

"Now, don't get me wrong. Zola was right. You are fine with those faded green-apple eyes. And for an older guy, it looks like you're still holding it together," Hayden said as he paused and reached into his jacket pocket and pulled out a package of cigarettes. Now he was definitely eliminated. I didn't do guys who smoked.

"I guess I should say thank you."

"I'm just speaking the truth. You look good, but I don't really date guys who identify themselves as gay or bi," Hayden said as he lit up a cigarette, took a puff and blew the smoke in the direction of some man's back.

"It's been a while since I've been out here on the prowl. What do you mean you don't date men who are bi or gay?" I asked.

"I just don't. Give me a man with a girlfriend or a wife. I don't want a full-fledged, card-carrying homosexual. I won't even date an *HS*."

"What's an HS?" I asked.

"You know, a heterosexual sissy. A man who is really and truly straight but acts gay because he just can't help himself," Hayden said.

"Oh, that's the first time I've heard the term. So you're looking for sex, not love?" I asked.

"Don't tell me you're looking for both?" Hayden asked.

"I'm not really looking for anything," I lied. I took another glance around the room in search of Merv. Just as I decided this conversation with Hayden wasn't going anywhere, I realized he probably knew Merv and could maybe arrange an introduction.

"If you change your mind, then there is plenty of anything in here. Thank God the kids know to leave me alone," Hayden said.

"Do you know this guy Merv? The one who played Curtis?" I asked.

"Oh, so that's your style. I feel you. The boy is blessed in many ways, but I am sorry to tell you he's strictly for the dames. Believe me when I say almost every sissy in that chorus has tried to change his religion," Hayden said, laughing.

"That's cool," I said, trying to make sure I didn't sound disappointed.

"I'm going to the bar and get me a drink, say some hellos and good-byes and then hope something is waiting at home for me," Hayden said as he got up from the booth.

"Nice meeting you," I said.

"Great meeting you as well. Maybe we can get together soon. I can take you to some places where they will have plenty of your type."

"Give me a call," I said.

"Will do."

I finished my drink and was going to look for Zola to tell her I was getting ready to leave, when the woman with no name suddenly reappeared.

"Do you have a card?" she asked.

"No, I don't," I said. I wasn't about to give my information to someone so cagey.

"Then how am I going to invite you to my next big party?"

"Just call the offices of *Bling Bling*. So, is the party going to be in New York?"

"They're not parties. I produce events that would make this little party seem like a kiddie's birthday. As I look around here tonight, the only thing missing are the animals. Although there are plenty of heifers and cows in too-tight dresses and jackasses who don't know what black tie means," she said as she looked over the crowd with a mock disgust.

"So, do you live in New York?"

"No, darling, I'm a resident of the world," she said as she once again disappeared into the crowd.

9

Everything seemed to be slowly getting back to normal with my friends and me. It was a cool fall evening with a full moon floating brightly in the sky. I had invited Justine, Hayden and Kai for a potluck supper, cards and conversation. I had fried some chicken legs and thighs and made potato salad with hard-boiled eggs garnishing the top. Justine brought over some collard greens and rice pilaf, while Kai brought the wine. Hayden contributed a deep-dish apple pie from the Little Pie Company, a bakery in the theater district, and Ben and Jerry's ice cream. The scents of the food blended in well with the raspberry- and clove-scented candles I had placed on several of the tables on the main floor of my brownstone. A wooden box of colorful roses sat on the center of the table. I had even pulled out the wedding-white linen tablecloth my mother had given me one Christmas. Everything felt and looked like an evening in celebration of life and friendship.

We all exchanged hugs and kisses, and everybody seemed to be having a good time, especially Kai, who had gulped down two glasses of wine before anyone else had a chance to finish one. Justine wasn't drinking and had brought her own concoction of cranberry and lemon juice. After I placed the food out on my dining room table, I clapped my hands and asked everyone to gather around the table, and I began to pass out the plates. I noticed that Kai was wearing her hair differently, letting it flow down her back in waves of curls. I couldn't help but stare at the low-cut sheer blouse she was wearing and realized she had honey-brown freckles on her cleavage.

"Everything looks great," Hayden said.

"It sure does. That chicken looks golden brown, like this man I fucked the other night," Kai said. Justine clutched her chest in horror. We had seen her do this before in a playful manner, but tonight she looked dead serious.

"Who was he, honey, and does he have a brother?" Hayden asked.

"I don't know, but you can have him, darling. There are many men out there, and I intend to get to as many of them as possible," Kai said, laughing.

"You guys need to chill," I said as I pulled some wine goblets from the cabinet.

"We need some music up in here," Hayden said as he went to look through my CD collection.

"Put on India Arie," Kai suggested.

"Oh, I do love her. What's that song, 'Brown Skin'? That's the truth," Hayden said.

"Justine, is there anything you want to hear?" I asked when I noticed her rolling her eyes at both Hayden and Kai.

"You probably don't have what I want to hear," she said softly. Justine suddenly looked sad.

"Whatever," I said. "Come on, let's eat before the food gets cold."

Hayden quickly put in the India Arie CD, and when he returned to the table, he and Kai started piling food on their plates. When Hayden took a bite of chicken, Justine suddenly screamed, "We need to say grace, Hayden, before we start eating."

"Well, excuse me. I forgot my home training," he said as he placed the chicken back on his plate. Suddenly the temperature in the room was dropping.

"Justine, would you like to say grace?" I asked.

"Yes I would," Justine said.

"Okay, let's all hold hands," I suggested.

The four of us closed our eyes and Justine started her prayer.

"Lord, we thank You in the name of Your son, Jesus, for bringing us here tonight. We thank You for the food our bodies are about to receive and for the hands that prepared it. Lord, we thank You for the families that are represented here tonight and we thank You for waking us this morning. Lord, we ask You to forgive us for our sins and thank You for dying on the cross so that we might be forgiven. I ask You to forgive me for my many evil ways I had before I met You. Lord, I ask that You take the demons that hover in this place and these people," Justine said, and paused. Her voice had the righteous sound of a Southern minister, and I was thinking she was getting to the end of her prayer, but instead she continued and the volume of her voice seemed loud and self-assured.

"Lord, I ask that You take the demons of homosexuality from Hayden. Make him new and whole. Save him, dear Lord, with the blood of Jesus."

Hayden suddenly squeezed my hand harder, and I could hear Kai coughing. I opened one eye and noticed that Justine was the only one with a calm look on her face as she continued praying. "Lord, please take away the drunkenness and the loss of moral values that hang over this room. Teach us that in times like these we can't fall prey to the demons of sex, and remind us that You said in Your word that marriage between a man and woman is the only true love. Show us the way, dear Lord, and please teach my sister and good friend Zola that You love her and that she doesn't need the love and lust from men who can never be her own."

Well, I had heard enough, so I said, "Amen," and released Hayden's and Kai's hands.

"Bitch, what is wrong with you?" Hayden asked as we all glanced at Justine like she was smoking crack.

"Hayden, please, my brother, don't refer to me with that evil name," Justine said.

"Justine, what's wrong with you?" I asked.

"Wrong with me? Nothing. Just because I prayed for God to save you doesn't mean there has to be something wrong with me," Justine said.

"I tell you what, Sister Jesus. That was foul. I mean, calling us all out here like you got a direct line to Jesus. I don't appreciate that shit one bit," Kai said.

"I was just praying for you," Justine said defensively.

"Justine, we all appreciate what you're trying to do, but I don't think this was the place or the time. I wanted an evening for us to get together and have fun like old times. Now you've ruined the evening for everyone," I said.

"And no need for you praying for the demon of homosexuality for me, sweetheart, because I ain't no homosexual, I just like sleeping with men," Hayden said as he smirked at Justine.

"Hayden, I will continue to pray for you. You can be released from that demon," Justine said.

"What part of I-don't-want-to-be-released-from-any-demons don't you understand?" Hayden asked.

"Where is my purse? I am going home and change clothes and go and see who's out looking for a little lust. This shit is making my brain scream," Kai said as she looked around the room for her jacket and purse.

"Kai, don't leave. We need to talk about this. Justine, I think you owe us an apology," I said.

"An apology? I am trying to help you, Zola. I love you, but you're living your life in sin, and if another attack comes upon this earth, then we might not be so lucky. I want you to come to heaven with me. I have been released from the demons of the world," Justine said.

"How lucky God chose you to save all us sinners," Hayden said sarcastically.

"This child is crazy, and, Zola, if you want to do your friend and the city a public service, then you need to investigate this church sistah girl is going to, and I would most definitely check what kinda wine and crackers they're serving at communion. I am willing to bet it includes a little crack," Kai said as she put on her coat.

"Justine, are you going to apologize to Kai before she leaves?" I asked with my arms folded tightly across my chest.

"I am going to pray for her. I am going to pray for all of you," Justine said calmly.

"That's it, I'm out. Y'all holla when sister Justine comes to her senses," Hayden said as he grabbed his oxford-red leather bag. He came over and kissed me on the cheek and whispered, "Check your knives in the kitchen. I would suggest locking them up."

I patted him on the back and whispered, "Everything will be just fine."

After Kai and Hayden left, I walked over to the table, where Justine was finishing up a plate of food like nothing had happened.

"Will you please explain what that was about? I have never seen you act like this, even when you were drunk," I said.

"Are you reminding me of my past so that you can feel better about the life you're leading?" Justine said. It was like her words were slicing through the room, cutting anybody who got in her way.

"I am just trying to understand what has happened to my friend," I said as I grabbed her hand and looked directly into her eyes.

"You should be happy for me. I want you to find the peace and joy I've found, Zola, and you can't have that if you continue to sleep with a married man and someone you're not married to. If you turn your life over to Jesus, He will release you from the burden of lust," Justine said, her voice rising again to a religious fervor.

Again I took Justine's hand in mine and said, "Please help me understand what's happening to you."

"Zola, that's Satan using you against me and God," Justine said firmly. I gazed into her eyes, expecting them to be blank, but they were filled with intensity.

"I think you should leave and we'll talk later," I said. I could feel my eyes brimming with tears.

"Zola, I'm sorry you can't accept the wonderful change that has come over me. But I still love you, and I will continue to pray for you," Justine said.

"You do that, and if you find my friend, please tell her I miss her dearly."

10

It had been a long day at the office and I was running late for my appointment with Dr. Few, so I ran the last two blocks. I felt like I needed a shower when she opened the door.

"Sorry, Dr. Few, had a hard time catching a cab," I said as I wiped a film of sweat from my forehead.

"No problem. I was a getting a little concerned," Dr. Few said.

I followed her into her office, took my regular spot on the left end of the sofa and was ready to talk.

"I went out for a night on the town. To see what the dating scene was like. I don't think I want to do the on-line dating thing that gay men are into heavy these days," I said.

"What made you do that?"

"I was bored, tired of taking things into my own hands, so to speak. Zola's friend Hayden called me and invited me to hang out with him. At first I said no, but doesn't shit come on television on Friday night, so I said sure."

"Where did you go?"

"We caught the subway down to the Village and went to several bars. Hayden kept telling me how he visits the Village only a couple of times during the year and last weekend was one of those times," I said.

"Did he say why?"

"Something about if the moon and wind were right he would usually meet some married or stray guy who had wandered into the bars with curious wonderment," I said.

"I'm not quite sure I understand, but did you have a good time?"

"It was cool. I got a lot of attention, but just when I was getting ready to make some progress, Hayden would be ready to leave. After bar three I got tired of that and so I decided to settle in. I told Hayden I would talk to him later," I said.

"Go on."

"I was standing at the bar, having my third glass of wine, starting to feel a little numb and adventurous, when this really good-looking guy came over and stood next to me, smiling. He didn't have a drink in his hand, so I had the bartender ask him what he was drinking. I felt stupid there for a minute because I didn't know if people still did that," I said.

"Did what?"

"You know, seeing someone you're interested in talking to and instead of facing rejection have the bartender ask what they're drinking and then telling them that someone wants to buy them a drink. If they accept the drink, then you move to the next step. If they say no, then you move to the other side of the bar or you leave," I said.

Dr. Few nodded and I took a moment to pull a bottle of water from my gym bag. The water was warm, but my mouth felt dry. I took a couple of swigs and then continued.

"So I go over and introduce myself to the guy, whose name is Damon. He was really friendly. We talked about sports. I am always surprised to find gay men who enjoy sports as much as I do. Damon was from the South, New Orleans, and he had that Creole look, you know, curly hair and custard-colored skin. I mean, I could tell he was mixed when I saw him, but I thought he might be from the Caribbean. Anyway, we talked and were really enjoying each other's company, when all of a sudden he asked me if I wanted to go home with him."

"What did you do?"

"I thought about it for a few minutes, looked at him and said let's go."

"So you went home with him?"

"Yeah, he told me he didn't live that far. We were walking, and I was feeling like I was going to wake up the next morning feeling wonderful. Damon couldn't believe it when I told him I was forty, and I knew I was feelin' him when he said I looked like I was in my late twenties. I told him flattery would get him everywhere. That's when he—" I paused for a few seconds, recalling the moment.

"He what?" Dr. Few asked as though she couldn't wait to hear what had happened.

"He took my hand and gently kissed me on the lips. It felt nice, and I couldn't wipe the smile off my face," I said.

"Are you going to see him again?"

"Oh, no!"

"Why not? Didn't you have a good time?"

"I didn't finish the story. We got to Damon's apartment and he turns on the music. Angie Stone. He gives me a glass of wine and then he excuses himself for a few minutes. I kick my shoes off and take off my sweater, making myself comfortable even though Damon hadn't really told me to. But I figure I was going to be spending some time there."

"What happened?"

"I heard these voices coming from the bedroom. At first I thought it was a part of the CD, but I listen to Angie so much that I realized it wasn't coming from her. I was starting to slip my feet back into my shoes, when Damon walked out with this man. A great-looking dude. A little taller and thicker than Damon, and he had this beautiful skin and white teeth that reminded me of the contrast of piano keys. Damon introduced him as Jonathan, his life partner."

I looked at Dr. Few to see if she seemed shocked or surprise. She didn't, just the same passive look, so I continued.

"When I asked Damon what was going on, he explained that they, he and Jonathan, were interested in a three-way with me. I became a little nervous, but I think I am a pretty good judge of character, most times, so I wasn't scared. Besides, I was close to the door and I had my shoes on."

"What did you say?"

"I asked them what was involved and they said why don't we go to the bedroom and see what happens. I was actually thinking about doing it. I figured wasn't anybody going to know about it but Jonathan, Damon, God and you," I said as I looked directly at Dr. Few.

"So you didn't join them?"

"No."

"Why not?"

"Too many rules," I said, laughing.

"Rules? I don't quite understand," Dr. Few said.

"Before we were getting ready to retire to the bedroom, Jonathan told me he or maybe the both of them, I don't quite remember, had a few rules. When I asked him what he was talking about, he told me."

"What rules did he have?"

"It was so crazy. It sounded like I was getting ready to join some secret club. The Three-Way Club. Anyway, Jonathan tells me: if I want to do this again, because they were both awesome in bed, it must always be together. That there would be no kissing on the lips. The sex would be safe. He also mentioned that one of them was HIV positive and the other negative. Jonathan also said there would be no exchanging of phone numbers but we could share e-mail addresses. He had some other rules, but by then I was in that I-don't-believe-this-is-happening zone and I didn't hear him," I said, taking another swallow of my water.

"So you declined?"

"Politely," I said. "I started to tell Jonathan that I couldn't join the club because I had already broken one of the rules by kissing Damon on the lips."

"Were you disappointed?"

"Not really," I said.

"Why not?"

"Maybe a tiny bit," I said, using my fingers to show what my mother used to do when she was describing a pinch. "The time I spent with them, and it was short, I got the feeling they really cared about each other and wanted to ask them why they felt the need to include others in their relationship."

"Why didn't you?"

"I felt the explanation would take too long."

"Why did you even consider their arrangement?"

"Because I was horny, that's why. Look, I knew if I was going home with some guy and getting ready to kick it with him, that the best I could hope for was a fuck buddy. I know one-night stands never become a love connection. It was just the dumb rules. It really seemed like there was some type of secret society within the gay community. I was talking with Hayden when we went to the first bar, and he was telling me about these groups of guys who were having unprotected sex, group sex. He told me they met at HIV support group meetings, so you had to be HIV positive to get invited to the private parties they had. It's still a crazy world," I said as I looked at my watch and realized that Dr. Few had allowed me to go over by five minutes. She must have enjoyed my story.

11

I was excited and surprised when Justine called and invited me to lunch. It had been two weeks since I had seen her, but I knew our friendship would return. We met on a splendid and tranquil day that felt more like spring than fall, at Cafe Fiorello on Broadway between Sixty-third and Sixty-fourth.

Justine seemed happy to see me as she gave me a warm hug and kiss on the cheek. She looked good, happy and content, although I detected something unreadable in her eyes.

"God bless you, Zola. It's good seeing you," she said.

"It's great seeing you," I said as I squeezed her hands once she'd released me from our embrace.

The waiter showed us to a table in the corner of the patio, and for a few minutes we just stared at New Yorkers who walked swiftly past the restaurant, getting on with their business, looking and acting more like New Yorkers than in the months before.

Justine ordered a sirloin steak salad and I decided on the fresh peppered tuna niçoise with iced tea. After the waiter left, I wanted to make sure I didn't get Justine upset, so I casually asked what the rules were.

"Rules? Zola, you and me go way back. There are no rules."

"So you've given up that Jesus thing? Girl, I knew you'd come back to your senses," I said.

The smile on Justine's face faded and she replied quickly, "Zola, I am still in the church, living by the word. I am a child of God. I didn't think I needed to tell you how not to make yourself look silly in the eyes of the Lord. I came to share some good news with you."

"Oh. What's the news?" I asked. I felt like a child who had just been chastised by her parents. I didn't feel the warmth and love of friendship I had felt with Justine almost twenty years of my life.

Justine held out her left hand and I noticed a small silver ring with a small stone, and before I could manage a sound, Justine beamed, "I'm getting married. The Lord has sent me a husband." There was an awkward pause.

"You're getting what?" It was a good thing I hadn't eaten any of the bread and olive oil, because I most certainly would be choking to death.

"I'm getting married. Aren't you happy for me?"

"Who are you marrying?"

"His name is Deacon Dexter Fisher," Justine said proudly.

"Is his name Deacon or is he a deacon?" I asked.

"His first name is Deacon and he is the associate minister at my church. I'm going to be a preacher's wife."

I needed something stronger than iced tea, so I motioned for our waiter and ordered a glass of Merlot.

I touched Justine's ring finger and said, "Justine, please tell me you're joking. How long have you known this man?"

"I feel like I've known him all my life. This is who God has planned for me to marry," Justine said calmly.

"You can't do this! Have you told your mother? What does she think?"

"It's not important what anybody thinks. I'm in love and it feels right."

"How long in real-people days have you known him? I can't deal with church people days. A week? A month? How long?"

"I've know him long enough," Justine said.

"This is just crazy. Crazy . . . crazy," I mumbled as I broke off a piece of a bread stick.

"Why is it crazy, Zola?"

I just shook my head in disgust, wondering what had happened to my friend. The girl who I had shared every secret with when I was in high school, and who always made me feel cherished every time I was in her presence. What had happened to that Justine?

"Answer me, Zola! Is it crazy because I finally have something you don't?"

"What are you talking about?"

"I have the Lord in my life. Very soon I will have a husband. I finally have something you don't have," Justine said.

"What are you talking about? I don't believe this shit," I said.

"Zola, please don't use that word," Justine said. "And we both know why my getting married makes you so angry."

"Don't tell me what words to use," I said as I sulked in the iron chair. I wanted to get my food in a takeout container and carry my behind back to my office.

"I am so sorry you feel this way. But think about it. All our lives you've had everything, the nice house, nice clothes, two loving parents. People loved you because you were beautiful and smart. Everything you've wanted you've gotten. You have the perfect job and in your sick mind you think you've got the best love life in the world. You don't. One day you will realize that. But most important, Zola, you don't have Jesus in your life, and if you don't repent, all these earthly things will mean nothing when your time on Earth is over," Justine said.

I reached into my purse, pulled out a couple of twenties and placed them on the table as I stood. "Enjoy your lunch, since you seem so happy destroying mine," I said as I exited the patio area and headed down Broadway with warm tears rushing down my face.

12

The thought of spending another evening alone broke me down. I got home, popped in my Janet Jackson CD, uncorked a bottle of Chardonnay and started thinking how wonderful it would be to spend the night with someone next to me. It was the one thing I missed the most about Trent and not being in a relationship, holding and enjoying the smell and feel of another human being. There was only one person in New York who I had shared time wrapped together like a human pretzel—Basil Henderson. The problems with Basil were many, from not knowing what to expect after he'd gotten his sex off to knowing he would spend half the time with an I-told-you-so grin on his face. Still, his was a handsome face with a body to match, so I picked up the phone and dialed his number. I was hoping to leave a message and then it would be up to Basil to get back to me, but after a couple of rings he picked up the phone.

"'Sup, playa," Basil said.

"How did you know it was me?" I asked.

"Dawg, I told you, I got a special ring to let me know when you're calling," Basil said, laughing.

"So, what are you doing?"

"At this moment?" Basil asked.

"Yeah."

"Sitting here at my desk, looking at a blank computer screen, with my drawers down and my jimmie on hard," Basil said.

"What you gonna do about that?" I asked. I could see his fine ass, and I knew this was just what I needed if I could stand the consequences of feeling guilty once I had released some tension.

"I was just wondering about that. I know what I'd like to do," Basil said with sex dripping through the phone.

"So are you gonna put on some clothes?" I asked.

"Now, why would I want to do that?" Basil asked.

"Might be kinda hard, pun intended, if you had to get in a taxi to come see me with just your drawers on," I said. Maybe Basil would realize I wasn't as square as he thought I was when it came to sex, but it had to be on my terms and on my court.

"So you want a brotha to leave his comfortable pad with this big ole bed and big ole hard-on to come uptown to see you?"

"I promise you it will be worth it. Remember, it's been a long time for me," I said.

"Now you talkin', dawg. Two days is a long time for anybody," Basil said, laughing.

"So, what's it gonna be?" I asked.

"Give me thirty minutes," Basil said.

"I'll give you an hour, and not a minute more," I said.

"I'm on my way. Holla!"

I smiled a satisfied smile to myself and headed to my bathroom to see how my skin and body were looking. I had a five o'clock shadow, so I decided to shave and give myself a quick facial. I was feeling a little buzz from the wine and swaying to Janet's sensual voice.

I turned on the shower, and when steam covered the door, I stepped in and enjoyed the pulse as I soaped up my sex with the vision of naked Basil in my head. I tried to remember the last time I had seen Basil totally naked, and when I couldn't, I knew it had been too long. Suddenly I realized I didn't have any condoms or lube, since I had thought I would abstain until I found love. A pledge that I was beginning to realize was going to be hard to keep, and nobody really gave a damn.

I jumped out of the shower, put on my jeans without drawers, pulled a sweater over my head and slipped on my loafers. I was thankful there was a drugstore a block and a half away.

The night air was cool and crisp and I started to go back inside to get a jacket, but time was moving fast, so I jogged down the sidewalk until I reached the stoplight. It was flashing DON'T WALK, but I didn't see any cars coming so I raced across the street and moments later into the drugstore. I immediately spotted the condoms at the register and I felt like a horny high school boy purchasing his first package of rubbers, as we called them back in the day.

"Can I have a three-pack of the Magnums?" I said nervously to a wiry girl with braces and fire-red hair. She didn't look old enough to be selling condoms, but I didn't care.

"We have a twelve-pack too. Would you like to see them?" she asked.

"I'll take them," I said as I stuck my hands into my front pockets, but all I felt were my keys. I tapped the back of my jeans and let out a sigh of relief when I discovered my wallet. I opened it and didn't see any money, but I did have my credit cards.

I pulled one out and placed it on the counter. The young girl picked it up and then said, "I'll need to see some ID."

I was about to go off and tell her that what she was asking was against the law but decided that would only cause more frustration. I laid my driver's license down on the counter and mumbled, "All this for some condoms."

The young girl compared my license with my credit card and then passed them both back to me along with a small bag containing the condoms. I raced back to my apartment, and when I got back upstairs I felt sweaty and decided I needed another shower. This way I could lotion up and make sure I had on the right pair of come-and-get-to-this underwear.

After my shower I located the perfect pair of navy blue nylon boxers and I finally felt ready for John Basil Henderson and his substantial body. I was feeling so sexual that I thought maybe this time I could teach him a trick or two. I reminded myself that I was looking for lust, not love.

Two hours and three glasses of wine later, and after being caressed by the sounds of Angie Stone, Janet and Maxwell, I decided to carry my tired ass to bed. I started to call Basil and see if he was all right, but I thought maybe he'd gotten a better offer and that Basil, the original down-low brotha, hadn't changed. Never could, never would.

13

Kai moved through the lobby of the Lowell Hotel like she was walking the runway—unhurried, despite being thirty minutes late. She looked like a model, with her long auburn hair worn in loose waves and wearing a rayon jersey dress with a suede belt.

"Zola, I'm sorry, hon. I don't know what happened to the day," she said when she saw me shaking my head and looking at my watch.

"Time is money, but you wouldn't know that since you don't have a job," I said as I leaned over and kissed her on the cheek.

"Now, darling, you know what Mary J. Blige says, 'We don't need no hateration,'" Kai said, laughing.

"Is that even a word? Hateration?" I asked as we took the elevator up to the second floor. At least once a month, usually on Fridays, Kai, Justine and I tried to get together for high tea at different hotels in the city. I had no idea what the church said about high tea.

"Hateration is a word now. Mary sang it, so it's become a part of our language," Kai said.

"Sorry to say, you're probably right," I said.

"Did you make a reservation?"

"I did, but not for four-thirty," I said. I looked in toward the area where the hotel served tea and saw that it was only three-fourths filled and hoped there wouldn't be a problem getting seating.

"Is Justine going to join us?" Kai asked.

"I doubt it. I left her an e-mail. I didn't feel like hearing that having tea might fall under worshiping the devil too," I said.

"What are we going to do with her?"

"I'm through. Until she comes to her senses, I'm going to keep my distance," I said.

The hostess told us they had plenty of room and seated us at a marvelous corner table. The room was cozy and beautifully appointed.

"Where did you get those earrings?" I asked as I admired a pair of sterling-silver clover studs adorning Kai's ears. The girl had great taste when it came to jewelry.

"Let's just say they came in an aqua box," Kai said, smiling.

"A gift from one of your new beaus?"

"No, darling. Thanks to my ex, I don't need the new men to buy me anything," Kai said proudly.

"So, have you talked to Justine?" I asked.

"No. I left her a couple of messages. To tell you the truth, after the way you said she carried on at the lunch you two had, I made sure to call when I knew she wouldn't be there. From what I can tell, she's at church almost every evening. I mean, I'm happy she's happy being a Christian, but this is just weird," Kai said.

"They say there are two kinds of Christians, real Christians and crazy Christians," I said.

"I still can't believe Justine came out of her face saying you were envious of her because she had something you didn't," Kai said.

"Me either," I said as I picked up the menu in the middle of the table. The waiter came over and we ordered high tea.

"I guess you shouldn't be surprised," Kai said.

"Surprised about what?"

"That Justine was jealous of the life you lead. Are you sure she never showed any of that when you two were growing up?"

"Not at all," I said firmly.

"Maybe she was keeping it to herself. Now, I'm not saying she wasn't a true friend, because you know I love the girl. But when I was in high school there was a girl named Tiffany who pretended to be my friend because my family had a little something and I was in the A group, you know, the popular girls. By the time we were seniors, Ms. Tiffany didn't feel like she needed me as her friend because her once-single nurse mother got lucky and married a doctor. Miss. T. carried on like she was the princess of a small country. She suddenly became too grand for me," Kai said.

"Thankfully I never had that problem until now. I can tell you, it hurts deep that it's Justine. But I'll survive," I said.

The waiter served our tea and placed a tower of scones and finger sandwiches in the middle of the table. I picked up a scone, broke it open and spread a little dab of clotted cream. I told myself to eat only half, since I hadn't been to the gym all week.

"So what exciting thing did you do today?"

"Oh, we had a staff meeting about the sexiest man contest. We've already put it up on the Web site. We're going to choose fifteen semi-finalists and then narrow it down to four winners. We'll give each guy three months, you know, like giving them each a different season. I talked to our marketing department and they are going to do giveaways on radio stations of posters of the men and maybe even a calendar. We're going to bring the final four to New York for photo sessions with a couple of big-name photographers and just let the winners run wild in the city for a weekend. It's going to be so much fun," I said.

"Just make sure I get a first look so I can tell you which three I want to spend some time with," Kai said.

"By the time we get to the end of the contest, you might have already found Mr. Right," I said.

"Zola, I ain't looking for Mr. Right. Matter of fact, I'm not interested in anybody that's serious. Life is too short for that," Kai said.

"Then what are you looking for?"

"Two kinds of sex," Kai said quickly.

"Two kinds?" I repeated.

"Yes, love. Great and greater," Kai said.

"I've been thinking about cutting Jabar loose," I said.

"Why are you going to do that?" Kai asked.

"It's not going anywhere, and I think maybe it's time for the two of us to stop using each other," I said.

"I thought you said the sheets were sweet," Kai said.

"They are. Amazing sex, but when we finish we just sit there, making small talk," I said as I picked up the teacup and sipped some of the steaming brew. It was just right.

"If you ask me, that's more than enough. I don't want to hear what no man got to say, because nine times out of ten it's a lie. 'I love you. You're the only woman in my life. I want to take care of you,' and on and on. I don't want to hear a bunch of empty promises."

"I think you're setting yourself up," I said.

"For what?"

"For love," I said, smiling.

Kai leaned over, peered into my teacup and asked, "What did you put in that tea besides cream?"

"Wisdom, sweetheart. A little bit of wisdom."

❖   ❖   ❖

All I could do was shake my head and smile when I saw Kai step out of the back seat of a black town car on Harlem's edge at Ninety-third and Broadway. When she walked over to where Hayden and I were standing, I pulled her close to me and said, "We're supposed to be incognegro, girl. You look like you just leaped off the pages of *Bling Bling*."

"If that's supposed to be a compliment, I'll take it," Kai said, pulling the sheer black veil of her pillbox hat over her face. "I was raised to dress for church, and there's got to be a few sinner men here," she said, tugging at the bottom of her black silk bolero jacket.

"Some of these folks look like they're going to a Prince concert with cheap tickets," Hayden said. He was dressed down in tight jeans, a white collarless pullover and a chocolate-brown leather jacket. A tiny gold cross dangled at his neck. It looked beautiful, and so I moved toward him for a closer inspection.

"Where did you get this?" I asked.

"I always had it. Got it when I was high school and I was trying to have this boy who was really into the church and God. It didn't get me anywhere, but I feel if there are any demons in this church, this will save me," Hayden said.

"Let's go in and see what's going on," I said as I hooked elbows with Kai and Hayden and we made our way into the gothic-style sanctuary arm in arm. Most of the congregation were searching for seating as close to the front as they could, while we headed directly for the very last row of pews, as close to the polished wood double doors as we could get.

"Zola," Kai said, looking at the rows and rows of churchgoers who had completely filled the church, "do you see Justine anywhere?"

"The question, Kai," Hayden said, "is can Justine see us?" We looked at one another, pulled out our sunglasses and put them on.

"Oh, that's great! Now we look like a cross between three blind mice and the FBI," I said.

"Honey, it's a good thing we got these glasses on. Do you see some of the dresses these sisters are wearing? When did Stevie Wonder start designing dresses?" Hayden asked, laughing.

A middle-aged lady in a black usher's outfit with a starched white collar was at the end of a pew, looking at us like an angry librarian. I knew she would be watching us the rest of the service.

A five-piece combo at the right of the stage started to play a rousing, jazzed-up rendition of "Lift Him Up," complete with a thigh-slapping tambourine. The back doors opened and in marched a choir, bringing most of the members of the congregation to their feet, swaying and clapping to the beat. Hayden jumped up and began singing along with the choir, until Kai pulled him back down by his jacket.

"Sit down!" she commanded. "Do you want Justine to spot us?"

"How's she gonna see us all the way back here? You know her man is an associate minister, so they've got to be sittin' up front with the other hoity-toity of the church," Hayden protested.

Kai just looked at him like he had no sense at all. "Hayden, she doesn't have to see you; she will hear your off-key ass demolishing this song!"

"Kai, I will slap you through that stained-glass window for hatin' my singing. I was in both the junior and adult choir at my church back home. I am a member of AFTRA and SAG. I get paid to sing," Hayden said.

"Stop it, you two," I said as I noticed our usher friend looking in our direction with a frown.

When the music stopped and people settled back down in their seats, Hayden spotted Justine in the center of the second pew from the front. She was sitting next to a thin man who had his left arm around her broad back, the other resting on the back of the pew. Even from where we sat, we could see that his wristwatch looked like a faux Rolex and the gold chain-link bracelet on the arm around Justine was way too shiny. We couldn't tell, however, if the diamond-studded ring on his left pinkie was real or Memorex.

I looked around and saw that most of the women were wearing jewelry. If this was a cult, it was dumb to let its members keep all this bling.

I also noticed that this wasn't an all-black church, as I had expected.

I saw people of all different colors. There were two middle-aged white women seated next to me. I saw some Asians intermingled with Mexicans. It was truly a mixed bag, and everyone seemed comfortable. This wasn't a church the cast of *Friends* had discovered.

"Welcome, everybody! Do you love the Lord?" a large black man asked, his arms outstretched toward the congregation. "One love!" He wore a kente dashiki, and I guess he was either the minister or the leader of the alleged cult, because everyone clapped when he stepped up to the microphone.

"Stand up and show the Lord you love Him," he said. All of a sudden everyone stood and just started clapping like they were giving Jessye Norman an ovation for a diva performance. It made the tiny hair on my arms lift and separate, and I felt cold.

"Greet your neighbors, show 'em some love now," the leader called out. Then everyone turned to the person seated next to them and hugged like they were at a family reunion. I hugged the two white women and they both whispered, "Jesus loves you and so do I."

All I could say is "That's nice. Bless you, or whatever."

Some of the people in the front rows were making their way to the back, kissing and hugging one another. I noticed Justine and Deacon stayed close to the front of the church, spending time chatting with each person they hugged. Kai and Hayden were doing selective greeting. I wanted to tell them they weren't at the club.

When the meet-and-greet ended, a thin black woman walked up to the pulpit and said, "We will now ask that Mother Lurline Lacy, a member in good standing and chairwoman of our fine prison outreach program, come forward and read the announcements from this week's church program. Mother Lurline."

Hayden leaned over and whispered, "Where do I sign up for the prison program? Maybe they'll leave me there for a few days."

I playfully slapped him on his arm.

"Why does the good mother have to read the announcements? Here they are on the back of the program," Kai said.

I looked at her and rolled my eyes.

While the announcements were being read I looked around the beautiful old church. There were four magnificent arched windows on each side of the sanctuary. It looked as though each stained-glass piece was clearly created by different artists. One looked like it could have been somebody's twisted perception of Jesus Christ smiling while being nailed to the cross. I guess that was one point for the cult theory.

"Did you hear that?" Hayden asked excitedly. "Did you hear what Mother just said?"

"No. What did she say?" I asked, coming out of the trance the amazing building had taken me into.

"She just announced the forthcoming nuptials of Deacon Fisher and Justine."

I looked up, and there was Justine, Deacon, who looked at least fifty, and two other couples who were asking the church's blessing on their marriage. There was a young black couple on the end and a heavyset white lady who was engaged to a dark-olive-colored man who looked Polynesian.

Justine looked happy even though she was dressed a bit matronly. I wondered what she had done with all her attention-grabbing black dresses. Deacon looked frail and could have used a fashion consultant. His skin was the color of Jamaican Rub and he had one of those cul-de-sac hairstyles, bald at the top with a salt-and-pepper mix on half his head.

Hayden leaned over to me and said, "I know what I would get the young girl on the end for a wedding present."

"What?" I asked foolishly.

"A heterosexual husband," he said, laughing. "That husband to be used to close up the club."

"You know you ain't right," I said.

After the couples received the church's blessings and returned to their seats, I thought maybe Justine had really experienced some type of religious conversion and maybe God had sent her Deacon.

The minister preached a rousing sermon about brotherly and sisterly love as a key to world peace that was really quite moving. I was used to a call-and-response type of church, but here everyone stood and clapped at the end of the sermon, applauding again like they were happy to be there. To be alive. From the smiles on the many faces I saw, maybe they were right.

"It's time to go," Hayden said. "Here come the toll takers! I knew this show wasn't free."

I saw ushers with silver buckets spilling into the aisles, where the buckets were passed from one end to the other of each pew. There was no begging by the minister, just a request to give what your heart told you.

The congregation stood and started singing again. When the bucket reached us, Hayden quickly passed it to Kai, who dropped in a check. I pulled a twenty from my purse and placed it in the bucket.

The entire church was holding hands and singing together and it felt nice. I saw tears form in Kai's eyes, and I felt tears coming as well. The three of us looked at one another, and without a word we slipped quietly out of the double doors into the bright sunshine of a chilly October morning. We'd got what we came for. Justine was going to be all right, and hopefully so would we.

14

I was on my way to the subway when my cell phone rang. It was Basil saying he had a big problem and needed to see me right away. I couldn't believe I was now in a taxi headed downtown to once again rescue him after he had stood me up, but his voice held such panic and sorrow that I had to find out what was going on.

When I arrived at his building, his doorman asked me if I was Mr. Tyler, and when I nodded he told me to go right up. I took the elevator, wondering what condition I would find Basil in and what his latest crisis was. When I arrived at his door and rang the bell, Basil swung open the door. The whites of his gray eyes were pink, like he had been crying.

"Basil, what's going on?" I asked as I walked into his apartment.

"Raymond, the bitch has taken my baby," Basil said.

"What are you talking about? Who has taken Talley?" I asked.

Basil didn't answer. He just paced across the living room toward his bedroom and then he quickly turned and headed back toward me with this wide-eyed look of panic on his face.

"Basil, come on. Let's sit on the sofa and tell me what's going on," I said as I walked toward the caramel-brown leather sofa. Basil just kept pacing and mumbling, "I can't believe that bitch. She is going to pay for this. Nobody messes with my baby."

"Basil, bring your ass over here and tell me what's going on," I yelled.

Basil didn't look in my direction and my tone didn't seem to have the desired effect. Now he was rubbing his head with both of his large hands.

I stood and said, "Okay, it looks like you don't need me. I'm going home."

I picked up my briefcase and was heading toward the door, when I heard Basil say, "Wait. I'm sorry. I'm just freakin' out here. Let me tell you what happened."

I walked back over to the sofa, and I could feel Basil following me. I took a seat on the sofa and Basil sat on its arm and handed me a piece of paper.

"What's this?"

"Read it," Basil instructed.

I opened the ivory note card and read: *Basil, Don't try to find me. I can't take this anymore. Don't worry, I will take care of Talley, but I can't have her growing up in this type of environment. Why didn't you tell me? Didn't I have the right to know? Don't try and find us, and we no longer need your money. Rosa*

"Can you believe that shit?" Basil mumbled.

"What happened? I thought you two were cool."

"I did too, dude. I went over to Rosa's place to pick up Talley for our regular visit. Man, Rosa had blazed. The apartment was empty. It was like she and Talley had never lived there," Basil said.

"Where did you get the note from?"

"It was taped to her door with my name on it."

"What does she mean by 'why didn't you tell me'?" I asked.

"Man, you know what she's talking about." Basil glanced at me with a get-real look on his face.

"Does she mean because you're bisexual?"

"What else could it be? Maybe she thinks I can't be a great father," Basil said mournfully.

"Did you tell her?"

"Fuck no! Are you crazy?"

"Then who told her?"

"Raymond, I got so many mofos out there who would want to put my shit in the street. I mean, do I need to have a roll call? Bart, Ava, Nico and Yancey," Basil said, naming people from his checkered past.

"I thought you and Yancey had reconciled. You told me you guys were cool," I said.

"I thought we were too, but you know women. They wake one morning and think about the fact they ain't got no man lying there beside them and some of them just snap and start thinking about how they can fuck with a brother," Basil said as he stood and walked toward the window.

The room was silent as I debated whether I should start preaching to Basil about how honesty was the best policy, but I knew he didn't want to hear that tune.

"What are you going to do?"

"Man, I got to find that bitch!"

"Where does her mother live?" I asked.

"In Jersey."

"Have you called her?"

"Yeah. That's the first place I called, and there was a message saying the phone number had been changed to an unlisted one," Basil said.

"You can find out a private number," I said confidently.

"Can you do that?" Basil asked.

"I'll see what I can do. Give me her name," I said. I spotted a sofa table covered with silver-plated frames containing pictures of Basil's little girl. Several of the photos were of Basil planting kisses on her chubby cheeks, and Talley's smile expressed pure joy the way only a child could.

Basil went over to his desk and scribbled a name down on a notepad. He came back and passed it to me and then with a sad look he asked, "What if she doesn't know anything?"

"We need to find that out. Do you have any kind of joint-custody agreement with Rosa?"

"You mean like papers? Some type of legal agreement?"

"Yes."

"We never needed one. She was always cool with me being close to Talley."

"Did you call her job?"

"Didn't I tell you?"

"Tell me what?"

"Dude, Rosa quit that gig about two weeks after 9/11. She said being a mother, she didn't want to take risks by being on a plane every day. I supported her decision and told her I would even increase the check I gave her, plus, she was going to save money by not having to pay a live-in baby-sitter," Basil said.

"Have you called any of the people who might have told Rosa about your other side?"

"Hell no, 'cause I might kill the mofo who did. But don't think I ain't going to check this shit out. But the first thing is finding my baby," Basil said.

"What do you want me to do?" I asked.

"You can start by helping me to get in contact with Rosa's mother. I'll worry about the other mofos later," Basil said.

"Promise me you're not going to do something crazy and make this thing worse," I pleaded.

"How can it get any worse? I don't know where my baby girl is," Basil said sadly as two large tears dropped from the corners of his beautiful gray eyes.

I felt so sorry for him that I walked over and put my arms around his massive shoulders and whispered, "Don't worry. Everything will be fine."

Basil put his arms around me tightly and said, "Stay with me, Raymond."

How could I say no?

15

I was looking over some suggestions for possible cover subjects from the morning staff meeting, when I heard a knock on my door. I assumed it was Cyndi, so I said, "Come in."

"Hey, Zola! Got time for your best friend?" Kai asked as she walked into my office. She was wearing a short indigo-blue dress that accentuated her figure, a light blue shawl, and she was carrying a large, plush leather bag.

"Kai, what are you doing here?" I asked as I got up from my desk and walked over and gave her a kiss on the cheek. She had on too much perfume, but it was early evening.

"I'm going to a bar a couple of blocks from here and I just thought I'd drop by and see if you wanted to join me. I heard there are a lot of good-looking men who hang out there," Kai said as she took a seat in one of the brown leather chairs that faced my desk.

"I wish I could, but I've got work to do," I said.

"That's why you've got all these people around you. Let them do it."

"I wish I could. I got people who can do a lot of things for me, but when it comes to making decisions and coming up with new ideas, well, that's my job," I said as I pushed my notes and some competing magazines to the side. I couldn't believe what had happened to my two best friends. One had turned to Jesus and one to any old Jim Dandy will do. Justine didn't have time for anything but church, and Kai seemed interested only in the relentless pursuit of a social, or, should I say, sex life.

"Just come for one drink," Kai pleaded.

"I wish I could, but I'm just trying to figure out what I'm going to do for the first few issues of the new year. Should I change what I'd planned because of 9/11, or should I go on with my original plans? I don't want to do any more sad 9/11-type stuff. It's a new year, time to live again," I said.

"I hear you, girl. But I'm talking about let's start living tonight. Can I ask you something?"

"Sure," I said, fully expecting one of Kai's senseless statements.

"Have you ever been with two men?"

"Kai, you know I've been with more than two men," I said.

"I mean at the same time," Kai said.

"Are you kidding? No," I said. I felt like I was sounding like a prude or something.

"Have you ever thought about it?"

"Kai, why are you asking me a question like that?"

"I met this handsome man who has a dick the size of an ear of corn, and he was wonderful in bed. Just as he had me screaming his name, he stopped and looked into my eyes and said, 'Tell me your fantasies.' When I told him I didn't have any, he looked at me like I was lying. But you know me, I didn't have any," Kai said.

"So what did you do?"

"I just started giggling like a teenage girl."

"Then what?"

"I asked him if he had any."

"What did he say?"

"Zola, he had some wild ones. Shit I had never thought about. Of course he wanted to see two beautiful ladies make out, but I told him I wasn't into freaky shit. I told him I was strictly dickly," Kai said, laughing.

I moved over to the end of my desk, engrossed in Kai's new life. "So what did he say?"

"He asked me if I ever thought about being with two men, and I told him yes, since I didn't have anything to say. Zola, you will never guess what he said," Kai said.

"What?"

"He told me he had an identical twin and that they sometimes make love to the same girl at the same time. He asked me if I was game," Kai said.

"What did you say?"

"I told him I would think about it," Kai said as she crossed her legs and rested one of her arms on her knees and her chin on her fist. She had a mischievous smile.

"You're not serious, are you?"

"Let's just say I'm thinking about it, and if they're identical twins, I figure it would be like making love and looking at yourself in the mirror," Kai said.

"It's a little bit more than that," I said.

"You should see him. Just so handsome with these beautiful lips, smooth hands and his skin looks soft, but it's so very hard, all over. And I told you about the equipment. I think it's something I should try. We know tomorrow isn't promised, Zola."

"Kai, you've got to get hold of yourself. Please tell me you'll tell this man where he can go with his freaky ass," I said.

"Wait till you see a picture of him or meet him. And if you still feel that way, then maybe I will. Girl, you need to put him, his brother and a couple of my dates from last week on the cover of your magazine or in that calendar," Kai said as she stood and walked over to the window.

"Kai, are you really happy?" I asked.

Kai turned around with the twirl of a majorette and said, "Of course I'm happy. Why wouldn't I be? I'm alive. I got a little money in the bank and I have finally taken control of my sex life."

"You didn't feel like you had that when you were married?"

"Zola, please. When you're married you don't have a say in your sex life," Kai said.

"Maybe that's why I'm not married," I said.

"You know you want to get married one day," Kai asked.

"No, I don't," I said quickly.

"Come on now, don't tell me you didn't think about a beautiful dress and all your girlfriends in ugly dresses," Kai said, laughing.

"Marriage is not an institution I have a lot of faith in," I said.

"Don't your parents have a good marriage?"

"As far as I know."

"I do think you ought to be able to have some kind of trial marriage first, and if it doesn't work, you just leave your partner a note or a standard letter saying *This isn't working. I'm outta here*," Kai said.

"I am sick of talking about marriage and men. I do have a job. I got work to do," I said.

"Now, I know you're not trying to crack on me. Charity work isn't always easy. You'd be surprised at some of the things I've done to help others."

"No, Kai, I'm not cracking on you. There are times when I wish I could just spend my time helping people too. But I have a house note to pay and I still dream of buying my folks a little vacation place," I said.

"Have you decided what we should do about Justine?"

"I thought about writing her a letter," I said.

"What are you going to do if she sends you one back filled with scriptures highlighting the errors of your ways?" Kai said.

"I can accept that. Now that we've been to her church, at least we know Justine is not in some cult," I said.

"Suit yourself. I say she comes back to her senses on her wedding night. You know how Justine likes to get down. Deacon doesn't look like he's up to the task," Kai said.

"Sweetheart, I hate to run you out, but I've got to get back to work," I said as I looked at my watch.

"What do you have to do? Can I help?"

"You got any good, juicy story ideas that haven't been in other magazines?"

"If I come up with one, will you go out and have at least one drink with me?"

I quickly said yes, knowing full well Kai wouldn't be able to deliver.

Kai moved the chair closer to my desk and said, "I met this guy and I think he might have an interesting story."

"Kai, I'm not running a story about your sex life," I said.

"But maybe you would like to write one about his," Kai said with a twinkle in her eye.

Kai told me a story of a great-looking guy she had met named Parson, who made his living by pretending to be gay. He sought out gay men by joining a support group for men who had recently lost lovers.

Kai said he tells his potential victims that he lost his lover either to AIDS or to 9/11 and he would go on dates but refuse to have sex because he was still in mourning, and looking for true love.

"He goes all over the country doing the same thing. I've been to his apartment here in New York, and Parson is doing quite well."

"How do you know he's telling the truth? I bet he's gay," I said.

"No, Zola, he's not gay or bi. Trust me, sister."

"Kai, you need to get out more. Because he slept with you doesn't mean he isn't."

"Zola, just talk with him. He's already talked to a couple of publishers about his story and they were interested. It would be great if you got the story first."

I thought for a moment and decided maybe I should look into this guy. I already had the title for the story if it checks out: *The Great Pretender.*

"Come on, Kai, let's go get a drink," I said as I scribbled the title on my writing pad.

16

I called Chris Thomas, the lawyer I'd met at Davis's apartment, and invited him to dinner. I told him I had a project I wanted to talk with him about and he quickly agreed to get together. When I asked Chris where we should meet, he suggested the Gotham Bar and Grill, a restaurant on Twelfth near Fifth Avenue.

I wanted to meet Chris for a couple of reasons. During our brief meeting at Davis's party I liked him and thought he might offer direction to something I had been thinking about for a couple of days. After September 11, I, like a lot of people, took a closer look at my life. I felt as though I should be doing more for other people. Normally for me, the fall was my favorite time of the year, but now it was a sad yet still lovely time, when I was reminded of the fragility of human life, how it could all end suddenly.

The first time I had come face-to-face with that fact was during the late eighties and early nineties, when the AIDS epidemic was in full force. Almost every day word spread of someone else dying or being inflicted with the disease. Most times it was people whom I knew in passing from the bars or Sunday walks through the Village, but when it finally hit home with the death of my best friend, Kyle, I was devastated with grief and loss. I promised to do something about it, and after Kyle's death I did by starting a foundation in his memory. Still, 9/11 reminded me that there was so much more to do.

Even though it was the beginning of November, I felt the soft air of summer when I got out of the taxi and walked into the dimly lit restaurant. Chris was already sitting at a table close to the bar and door. I walked into the large dining room with polished teak floors and large, tasteful bouquets of flowers strategically placed throughout.

Chris spotted me and got up from his chair and greeted me with a firm handshake and smile. He looked taller and broader than I remembered from our first meeting at Davis's apartment.

"Chris, great seeing you again," I said as I shook his hand and patted him on his left shoulder.

"Good seeing you as well. Have a seat," Chris said. It was early evening and the restaurant was almost empty. It felt like I was meeting Chris in his own private dining room. Several waiters dressed in white shirts, black pants and long white aprons loomed around the empty tables.

"Thanks for agreeing to see me," I said.

"I was glad to hear from you. How have you been? You didn't lose anyone in the World Trade Center tragedy, did you?"

"I've been okay. And no, I didn't lose anyone that I knew personally. What about yourself?"

"Thank God, Debi and I were blessed and didn't lose anyone we knew. But I tell you, man, when I read some of the stories in the newspapers and watched some of the news programs, I felt like I knew some of those people, or at the very least wanted to know them. It was such a sad thing for our country, but I tell you, it woke up a lot of people and reminded us what's important," Chris said.

"I hear you. How is your wife and when will I get a chance to meet her?"

"Oh, Debi's fine. I hope you'll meet her soon. I told her about you after our meeting. My wife, God love her, but she is so dang busy. I mean, she is a wonderful mother to my son, Luc, and wife to me, but I just don't feel like I spend as much time with her as I'd like to. We're both so busy with our careers. One of the things we both talked about after 9/11 was spending more quality time with each other."

"You know you've got to make time for that, don't you?"

"I'm going to," Chris said as he picked up a menu the size of a legal pad. I looked to my left and spotted another menu and picked it up as I saw a waiter approaching us from the corner of my eye.

"What do you recommend?" I asked Chris without looking up.

"Everything is great here, especially the beef dishes. They cook up an awesome piece of beef," Chris said.

A bespectacled waiter asked if he could offer us a drink. I ordered a glass of Merlot and Chris a draft beer. A few seconds later Chris laid down his menu and asked me if I was married.

"No. I just got out of a long-term relationship," I said. I wondered for a moment if it was important to tell Chris that I was gay but decided another opportunity would present itself soon. I thought maybe people in New York were able to read between the lines with terms like "part-ner" and "long-term relationship," but maybe not.

"Are you happy about it?"

"Breakups are never easy and it's still rather new for me. I don't have anything against relationships. They're fine, but right now I'm concen-trating on getting used to my new city and job," I said.

"How do you like working for Davis?"

"It's cool," I said quickly. I didn't know the extent of Chris's relationship with Davis and wasn't going to go into detail about my boss with a virtual stranger.

"Davis is an interesting man. Very complex and at times very mysterious," Chris said.

"How so?"

"I can't put my finger on it. Davis was like that when I first met him at Harvard. He's a brilliant businessman and he gives a lot of his money to charities. I just get the feeling he's hiding something. I can be wrong. I have been on numerous occasions. Just ask my wife," Chris said, laughing.

"How long have you been married?"

"More than ten years."

"Did you meet at Harvard?" I asked.

"No. We met in an airport of all places. Debi did attend Harvard, and I knew who she was because she had the reputation of being one of the most beautiful women on campus and one of the smartest. But we didn't meet until a snowstorm closed down Logan Airport in Boston and we ended up spending the entire night talking as we sat on a hard, cold floor. People always look at me strangely when I say I spent the night with my wife the first time we met," Chris said.

"Sounds like a wonderful love story," I said.

"I think so," Chris said as a broad yet private smile crossed his face. The waiter brought our drinks and we ordered dinner. Chris continued to talk about his wife and son. There was a boundless pride and love in his voice, and I thought this man had everything, success and love in his life. Maybe white men were the only ones who could have it all. I thought about Davis and all that he had in terms of material things but figured his marriage must not be perfect because he was sleeping with Zola.

"So what can I do for you?" Chris asked as he looked at his watch. Maybe talking about his wife had him eager to get home, and I thought I needed to get down to business.

"I wanted to bounce a few things off you," I said.

"I'm listening," Chris said.

"Remember when we met, you mentioned that you and Debi contribute to a lot of AIDS charities?" I asked.

"Yes, I do. You mentioned you had a foundation," Chris said.

"More Than Friends," I said.

"Is that what you wanted to talk to me about?" Chris asked.

"Yeah. I'm beginning to think I should be doing more with my life and for other people. I think expanding the foundation might be a start," I said.

"Tell me a little more about the foundation," Chris said.

I told him how some of Kyle's close friends and I had set up the foundation to aid patients with cards, gifts and little tokens to let them know that people they didn't know cared about them during difficult times.

"That sounds like a great idea," Chris said.

"I want to do more. I read all the statistics in the paper about new AIDS cases, how young black men and women still disproportionately represent new cases, and I feel like maybe the message still isn't getting out," I said.

"Do you have some more plans?"

"Right now More Than Friends is very small. We don't have a lot of money because I have mostly bankrolled the foundation. I think we could do more if we had a full-time administrator and a staff to put on fund-raisers," I said.

"So how can I help besides writing a check?" Chris asked.

"A check would help, but if you could show me how to go to the next level or maybe merge with another organization committed to helping people with AIDS, that would be great," I said.

"I could do that. I tell you what. Let me talk with Debi and Lillian, the young lady who heads my foundation. Maybe we should set up a meeting with the four of us and see what the best solution is," Chris said.

"Thanks, Chris. That would be great. Any help you can offer," I said.
"We're all in this together," Chris said.

The waiter placed our meals down in front of us, and I said, "Now more than ever."

17

It was Wednesday and a springlike rain had cleansed the city, even though it was still autumn. Wednesday was usually my evening for eating fattening food like nachos and chicken fingers while watching *Soul Food* on Showtime with Justine and Kai, but I hadn't talked to Justine since our aborted lunch date.

I thought about catching a cab over to Sylvia's, the soul-food restaurant, for some smothered chicken and then walking back home so I wouldn't feel so guilty. I pulled out a bright yellow warm-up suit and put my hair in a ponytail. Maybe I would jog instead of walking. Just as I put on the bottoms over a light blue unitard, the doorbell rang. My heart started beating rapidly, because I was hoping that it was Justine and Kai coming to surprise me with food and hugs.

I was puzzled when I saw Jabar standing at the door with a black plastic shopping bag and a large smile. I realized I hadn't seen him since the night before 9/11.

"Jabar, what are you doing here?" I asked.

"Are you going to let me in?" Jabar asked.

I unlocked the glass door that protected the oak door and Jabar walked in slowly. He wasn't dressed in his usual warm-up suit but was wearing a beige turtleneck sweater and billowy khakis with Timberland boots.

"What's in the bag?" I asked.

"I brought you a little surprise," Jabar said as he headed toward the kitchen, and I followed.

"You still haven't told me what's going on," I said. Jabar put the bag on the table and then looked at me and said, "Yo, Z, I just wanted to see you. Is that cool?"

I looked at Jabar suspiciously. He was hard to resist, and the rich scent of his masculinity was inviting. When he smiled at me, I couldn't help but notice his deep dimples, and his captivating eyes had the warm glow of brandy.

"What are you doing, just dropping over? What if I had company? You know the rules," I said.

"Then yo, somebody would have to leave early, and I don't think it would be me," Jabar said as he leaned over and kissed me. The kiss was longer than usual and his tongue felt like it was dancing a tango in my mouth. When he finally pulled his tongue out, I had to catch my breath.

"So I guess me and my food can stay?" Jabar asked.

"Food, you brought food?"

"Sure did."

"Did you cook it?"

"I could lie and say yeah, but naw, I can cook breakfast dishes but I leave the suppertime grub for my moms," Jabar said.

"So your mother is a good cook?" I asked.

"She betta be, since that's the way ole girl makes a living," Jabar said as he pulled an aluminum pan from the bag.

"So your mother's a cook?" I asked, embarrassed by how little I knew about Jabar's family.

"Moms is a caterer. She have people who cook for her. Moms only cooks for the men in her life," Jabar said as he walked over to the kitchen cabinet and pulled out two plates.

"So what did your mother cook?"

"Some of the stuff I love, fried chicken, tomato and cucumber salad, fried corn and homemade biscuits plumper than that azz of yours," Jabar said as he looked at my behind with a mischievous gaze. I felt self-conscious and so I put my hands on one cheek like I was protecting it from viewing.

Jabar and I spent the next hour at the kitchen table, eating and talking. I learned that he had two younger sisters and that both his mother and father owned businesses in Newark. His mother had a catering business and his father a car detailing company, where Jabar still worked on weekends.

"So you plan to be a trainer the rest of your life?" I asked as I enjoyed the crustiness of a golden brown chicken leg.

"Yo, I'm always gonna keep the body type and I really dig helping people change the shape of the bodies, but lately I've been thinking about making a change. That's one of the reasons I wanted to see you today," Jabar said. He took the last bite of a biscuit that he had lathered with butter and grape jelly.

"I thought I knew why you came to see me," I said as I took my leg and playfully placed it between Jabar's thighs. I figured something more than my stomach could be satisfied tonight.

Jabar gently pushed my leg away and said, "Z, you know I love the punanny anytime I get within the sniffing zone, but tonight I just want to get in your bed and hold you."

Was I hearing Jabar correctly? Was he trying to change our fuck-buddy status? I knew that if I became involved in Jabar's life for anything other than sex, then he would start to chip away at the dark and guarded corner of my heart. I didn't want to admit it, but ever since 9/11 I found myself emotionally vulnerable, crying at the mention of both sadness and hope. I had stopped reading *The New York Times* because they were running a special section with profiles of victims.

It seemed all the people killed that day had such full lives, love, family and successful careers. The first couple of days the articles had become addictive. I would find myself reading the stories next to black faces first but wouldn't stop reading until I had finished every story on the tear-stained pages. Some days I really thought I was going to damage my tear ducts.

"So what do you want to talk to me about?" I asked Jabar.

"I'm thinking about joining the police force or becoming a firefighter. I haven't decided which one," Jabar said. I noticed he sounded serious, and the street lingo he always used was absent.

"Don't you know you have to take a civil service exam for those jobs?"

"Yeah, and I test well," Jabar said.

"You do?"

"You think muscles everywhere takes away from the brain?"

"Did you finish high school?"

"Better than that. I guess I didn't tell you I have an associate's degree from Trenton Junior College," Jabar said.

"You do?"

"Don't sound so surprised, Z. I got skills you don't have a clue 'bout," Jabar said.

"I guess so. Do you know how dangerous those jobs are?"

Jabar grabbed my hands and looked at me and said, "Don't worry. I will be careful. Always."

I felt myself losing control, so I stood and said, "Let's talk about this in the morning. I'm tired. You still want to spend the night?"

"Yeah, but I left my raincoats at home on purpose."

"Then you really are going to have to hold me all night."

"That's what's up."

18

Basil made it to my apartment in record time. Fifteen minutes after I called him and told him I had some great news for him, he was knocking on my door, sweating like he had just finished a grueling workout.

"Come on in, Basil," I said as I opened the door.

"Ray, what's going on? Did you find my baby girl?"

"Calm down, Basil. I just wanted to give you the information in person. Davis located Rosa and Talley in Atlanta. They're both fine from the looks of the pictures," I said as I walked over to my desk and picked up the envelope Davis had sent to my office.

I handed the package to Basil. I'd mentioned Basil's problem to Davis and he mumbled, "Women can be so damn stupid," and then asked if he could do anything. I gave him the information on Rosa that Basil had given me and Davis said he would take care of it. He said it with such confidence that I had no doubt he would find Rosa and Talley even if they left the country. Still, I didn't mention it to Basil because I didn't want him to get his hopes up.

"What's this?"

"Look inside."

Basil pulled the materials out of the envelope, and I didn't know if he was going to break down crying or do one of those silly end-zone dances football players used to do with too much frequency. It was hard to read his face. I couldn't tell if he was happy or still angry at Rosa for taking Talley.

"There's my little girl. She's safe," Basil said. I could tell he was fighting back tears.

"Are you all right?"

"I'm cool. I am heading to Atlanta first thing. What time is it?" Basil asked as he looked at his watch. It was a little after nine.

"I think it might be too late tonight," I said.

"Not if I start driving right now," Basil said.

"Are you serious?"

Basil grabbed me by the shoulders and said, "You don't understand. I've got to hold my little girl in my arms. I haven't been able to sleep since she left."

"Then that's reason enough for you to wait until morning. You might fall asleep behind the wheel," I said.

"Then come with me," Basil pleaded.

"Man, I want to help out, but I have a job," I said.

"I know I'm talking crazy. But I just can't sit around doing nothing," Basil said.

"Go home and get some sleep and then get up and catch the first flight to Atlanta. Inside the envelope there is also the name of an attorney Davis recommended who will help you with getting some type of joint-custody agreement. She's supposed to be the best in the business. Make sure you tell her Davis McClinton suggested you call, or else you won't have a chance in hell of her taking your case," I said.

"Ray, I'll never be able to thank you," Basil said.

"Yes, you can," I said.

"How?"

"Think everything out. Don't go down there half-cocked. Be safe."

"That's important to you?"

"You're important to me, Basil. So can you make me that promise?"

"I promise," Basil said. Before I could say anything, Basil moved closer to me and wrapped his large arms around my shoulders. We were so close that I felt his sweet breath blowing against my face like a fine mist, and then Basil kissed me. I mean, he really kissed me, like he had never done before. I was still silent when he walked toward the door, opened it and winked at me and said, "Ray, if I could ever totally love another man, it would be you. And that's the truth. You feel me?"

I blinked my eyes and said, "I feel you."

19

When I looked out of my window and down onto the streets, it looked as though New York was moving fast again. Shadows of its old self. It had been a gloomy day, but now a thread of sunlight broke through the sky.

"Looks like somebody has been real good," Cyndi said as she walked into my office carrying a vase of beautiful and exotic blooms.

I turned, smiled and said, "Put them on the coffee table."

"Do you want me to read the card?" Cyndi asked.

"No, I know who they're from." I gazed at the flowers and knew the arrangement was from Davis, sent from my favorite florist, the Daily Blossom.

"Do you need anything else?" Cyndi asked.

"Can you have travel check flights from New York to Nashville on Thanksgiving Day?"

"You're going home?"

"I'm thinking about it," I said.

"I want to, but I'm still scared to get on a plane," Cyndi said.

"I haven't made up my mind. See what's available in the morning with a return for Saturday," I said.

"I'll check on it. Oh, yeah, Kai called."

"Did she say where she was?"

"No. She said reach her on her celly," Cyndi said.

I walked to my desk, picked up the phone and dialed Kai's number. She answered after a couple of rings.

"Hello."

"Kai, this is Zola. What's going on?"

"Hey, Zola. I'm up on the East Side, looking at some fabric and wall coverings. I decided to redo my guest bedroom."

"That sounds like fun. Cyndi said you called."

"Yeah, I wanted to know if you had plans for Thanksgiving. My parents are coming down and I invited Hayden," Kai said.

"Funny you should ask. I was just thinking about going home for Thanksgiving," I said.

"Oh, that sounds like fun. I bet your mother and father are excited," Kai said.

"I haven't mentioned it to them. If I go, I want to surprise them," I said.

"I know they'll be so happy. Let me know if you decide to hang around. I'm even thinking about trying to roast the turkey myself instead of ordering one."

"Now, that's tempting, just to see you in the kitchen," I said, laughing.

"Do you think I should invite Justine?"

"Why not? She probably won't come," I said.

"Maybe Hayden and I will go over and kidnap her."

"Girl, you're crazy. What are you doing tonight?"

"I might have a date."

"Might?"

"Yeah, I met this rapper last night, but I don't think he's wrapped too tight," Kai said.

"Oh," I said.

"Here comes the salesperson. Talk with you later," Kai said.

"Good-bye."

Thanksgiving was a week away, and this year I felt I had a lot to be thankful for. My life, family and good friends. I thought about Justine, and an unexpected loneliness gathered inside me. I found myself picking up the phone and dialing her number.

After a couple of rings the answering machine clicked on and I heard Justine's voice say, "For in the time of trouble He shall hide me in his pavilion; in the secret of His tabernacle shall He hide me; He shall set me upon a rock." When the machine beeped for me to leave a message, I hung up.

I realized I needed to go home and get away from New York. I missed my parents and Nashville. I wanted to feel my mother's powder-soft hands and see the loving smile on her beautiful, finely wrinkled face. I longed to hear my father's laughter and smell the combination of his cologne and hair.

I wanted to visit the campus at Tennessee State and see golden and crimson leaves being swept across the student union by a brisk wind. I wanted to get a fish sandwich from Ed's Fish and have a miniature cheeseburger from Krystal's.

As I thought about what I needed, I felt tears forming in my eyes again. I tried to blink the wetness away, but I realized that tears were like memories, and I was ready to face the ones I'd left behind, the good and the bad. I needed to feel like I belonged, that I was truly loved. So even if it meant dealing with Pamela and my other secret demons, I had to go home.

20

Zola walked into my office with a huge smile on her face, carrying some large photographs, looking like a fashionista dressed in a fire-engine-red sleeveless dress that looked beautiful against her skin, which was the darkest shade of cinnamon brown. Her hair was pulled back in a tight bun and she was wearing gold hoop earrings.

"Raymond, you got a minute? I've got something I want you to see," Zola said.

"Sure," I said as I stood and met her in front of my desk.

"Look at this. I think this will sell a few magazines and calendars," Zola said as she handed me some beautiful four-color photographs of one John Basil Henderson.

In one picture he was completely nude with the exception of some strategically placed black underwear he was holding in front of his jim-mie. He had a sexy and provocative grin, a Basil trademark.

In another he was wearing a white dress shirt open to his navel, and his body looked like it was glistening with a golden sweat. A slight

uncontrollable smile came over my face, and Zola noticed. I was thinking how I missed Basil and wondering if he would ever return to New
York. In the pictures he looked like he didn't have a care in the world,
no concern about his little girl or his health. I wondered if I had made
the right decision by not mentioning the strange phone call I had
received from some woman implying that Basil was HIV positive.

"I guess you like them," she said.

"They look all right . . . I'm lying, they look great. What are you going
to do with these?" I asked.

"They're for *Bling Bling*'s Sexiest Brothaman Alive contest. I know
Basil will make the finals. He might even win. What's he like?"

"Who?"

"Basil Henderson. You've known him for some time, right?"

"Yes, we've been friends for a long time. Basil's a great guy," I said as
I tried to keep from glancing back at the photos. While Zola was talking
about all the excitement and interest the contest was generating for the
magazine, I was thinking about Basil and his body. I remembered every
nuance of it, the broad shoulders, the ripples on his stomach and that
magnificent ass, still the best one I've ever seen in my life.

"Is he married?"

"Who?"

"Basil."

"No. He's got a little girl," I said.

"Oh, so he really is a baby daddy," Zola said, laughing.

"How are ad sales going? I haven't seen this month's advertising revenues," I said.

"I'm really pleased; we're actually up five percent. That's great,
because some of the magazines with large circulations are having big
loss problems. I even heard that *Talk* magazine might be going under. I
think this contest is really going to help not only with circulation but by
bringing in companies that might want to clothe our winner," Zola said.

"So who's going to decide who wins the contest?" I asked.

"We're going to let the readers think they're picking the winner, but if truth be told, I plan to do a little informal poll around the office and pick the winner that way," Zola said.

"I would think about that," I said.

"Why?"

"You can't advertise voting procedures one way in a magazine and then do it another way. That's deceptive advertising, and if anybody found out about it, *Bling Bling* could be in big trouble," I said.

"Oh, I didn't think of that," Zola said as she used her index finger and touched her full lips that were covered in a dark wine-colored lipstick.

"That's why you have me around," I said.

Zola glanced at me and smiled as she picked up Basil's photos and headed toward the door. Before she walked out, she turned and said, "Thanks for the legal advice and the baby daddy."

"No problem. Hey, Zola," I said.

She stopped her stride and turned around and said, "Yes."

"What are you doing for Thanksgiving?" I asked.

"I'm going home to Nashville," Zola said.

"That's great."

"What are you doing?"

"I don't know. My little bro is playing football; my parents are going on a cruise. It looks like I'm going to be solo," I said, trying not to sound like I felt sorry for myself even though I did.

"What's Basil doing?" Zola asked.

I thought the question was strange, but I told her he was in Atlanta.

"Then that's why we haven't gotten the signed release from him. Will you mention it to him if you speak with him?" Zola asked.

"Sure."

"You know, Raymond, one of my girlfriends is cooking a big dinner and having some family and friends over. Hayden will be there, and if you'd like, I could get you an invitation," Zola said.

"Thanks, Zola, but I don't want to intrude," I said.

"Kai would love to have you," Zola assured me.

"I'll think about it, then let you know. When are you leaving?"

"Thanksgiving morning," Zola said.

"I'll let you know by Tuesday," I said.

"Please think about it, because I don't want you to spend the holidays alone."

"Thanks, Zola. I will."

21

Thanksgiving morning was one of those clear and cool days between fall and winter that made me happy I was going home. I couldn't wait to walk in the rambling Victorian house I grew up in and smell my mother's cornbread dressing and sweet potato pies. I could see the large smile on her face when she saw me, and the tears that would fall while she scolded me for not telling her I was coming home.

The airport wasn't the madhouse I'd expected. When I reached the ticket counter the agent with a pleasant smile looked at me and asked, "Are you the Zola Norwood who runs *Bling Bling* magazine?"

"Yes, that's me," I said proudly.

"Girl, I love that magazine. Every month I can't wait till it hits the newsstands," she said.

"You don't have a subscription, Trulissa?" I asked as I noticed her name tag and thought if Trulissa and I made a sister-girl connection, I might get an upgrade to first class and Trulissa might get a year's subscription to the magazine.

"Naw. I still live at home and my younger brother always steals my magazines so he can use them for his little private bathroom visits. He just learned what he can do with his hands, his thang and a magazine with pretty girls in it," she said, laughing.

I tried to manage a smile, although I didn't know what the young man could be doing with *Bling Bling*, unless it was our annual swimsuit issue.

"Do you have a card, Trulissa? I'd like to send you a free subscription," I said.

"Oh, that's so nice of you!"

"How does first class look for upgrades?" I asked without missing a beat.

"Zola, girl, you're reading my mind. I'm trying to see what I can do."

"Thank you," I said.

"So, are you from Nashville?" Trulissa asked as she rapidly hit the computer keys.

"Yeah, I am."

"I almost went to Fisk University."

"It's a great school. I went to Tennessee State myself."

"I ended up at City University," she said.

"That's a good school as well," I said.

"I guess so. Hey, who's going to win that contest you guys are having?"

"Are you talking about our Sexiest Brothaman Alive contest?"

"Yes. I started to enter my boyfriend because he sure is fine, but then he pissed me off," Trulissa said.

"It's not too late," I said, looking at my watch, hoping Trulissa would get the hint, but she didn't seem to notice as she continued to talk and type.

I had intended to carry my garment bag on board, but after being asked to show my ticket and identification three times before I went through security, I was told that I couldn't carry three bags on board no matter how small they were. All passengers were allowed two carry-ons, and that included my purse.

I didn't want to check my computer or my pocketbook, so I had to release my garment bag, which carried one good dress and a nice pantsuit just in case I ran into one of my girls from my college days who wanted to hang out during the short time I was going to be in town.

Trulissa wasn't able to upgrade my seat, but she did manage an empty row of three seats, so I took a blanket and pillow and slept for most of the three-hour flight.

After we landed, I pulled my purse from under the seat and checked my makeup in a small compact. I don't know why, but I started to think about Davis and the Thanksgiving he and Veronica were sharing, and I bet it would be reminiscent of an O magazine layout. I could see the long table filled with all kinds of delicacies and wondered if I would ever plan a holiday meal for a husband and children. It wasn't that I had ever expected those things from Davis. He had been quite clear when we met that he could never offer me marriage but he could give me a magazine. Since 9/11 I was beginning to realize that there was more to life than a career.

While I was waiting for my luggage I heard the murmur of a male voice saying, "You don't know how much I love you and missed you." I hoped for a minute that I was tripping. I knew I had been working hard, and the mind could be as tricky as a magic act. At least that's what I told myself.

I slowly turned around to see where the voice was coming from, and when I did, my worst fears were realized about returning home. My body suddenly felt tight with tension and I looked away before our eyes made contact. I saw my bag coming on the luggage carousel and quickly grabbed it and ran toward the automatic doors. When the wind hit me, I realized tears were rolling down my face, and I knew I couldn't go home that way. Layer upon layer of bad memories clouded my mind, and instead of getting in a taxi, I went back inside the airport to the ticket counter.

The lines were short and I found myself standing in front of a pretty Asian woman who asked if she could help me.

"What time is the next flight to New York?" I asked.

She hit a few keys on her computer keyboard and said, "There's a flight that leaves in about forty-five minutes. Are you going home for the holidays?"

"No, I mean yes," I said quickly as I passed her my round-trip ticket.

"Lucky you. I have to work all day," she said.

"Yeah, lucky me," I said as I wiped away fresh tears.

22

I woke up Thanksgiving morning not really feeling thankful for much. I know that sounds like I wanted to throw myself a pity party, but I did feel lonely. I thought about my parents enjoying each other on a cruise and Jared and his family enjoying their first Thanksgiving in their new Atlanta home. Jared and Nicole had pleaded with me to come down and visit them when they discovered I was spending the day alone, but I told them I had to work on Friday.

I thought about Trent and wondered how he was spending the day with his new family. I remembered our first Thanksgiving in Seattle. When we cut the turkey we'd cooked, we discovered that we'd left the gizzards and liver inside in a plastic bag! We laughed so hard that we ended up making love on the kitchen floor and had dinner later at the Four Seasons hotel downtown.

I made myself a cup of coffee and looked through the *TV Guide* to see if there were any movies on HBO or Showtime that I hadn't seen. I started to call Kirby but realized it was too early. I thought it was both

humorous and comforting that I depended on my little brother the
older I got. Instead of hitting Kirby's digits, I called Basil on his cell and
I was brought out of my holiday funk when he answered the phone.

"What's up, yo?" Basil asked.

"Just called to wish you a Happy Thanksgiving," I said.

"Same to you. Ray, I wish I could talk, but I'm on my way to pick
up Talley. I don't want to be late. Can you believe it? Ray! This is our
first Thanksgiving together, and I woke up this morning realizing how
much I have to be thankful for," Basil said.

"You're right. Have fun and I'll talk to you later," I said.

"Holla back when you can," Basil said as he clicked off his phone.

I took a shower and got dressed so I could go out and buy a newspaper. Just as I was headed out the door, my phone rang. Maybe it was
Basil calling back, or I suddenly feared it might be Trent wanting me to
say hello to the new wife.

"Hello," I said.

"Raymond?"

"Yes."

"Happy Thanksgiving, sir. This is Chris Thomas."

"Chris, good hearing from you. Happy Thanksgiving to you," I said,
thinking maybe I wouldn't have to spend the day alone after all.

"So what do you have planned today?"

"Sad to say, but I think I'm going to be working," I said.

"Does Davis know how lucky he is to have such a dedicated
employee like you? Man, I wish my people were like that," Chris said.

"Please don't tell anybody I'm working on the holiday," I said.

"I won't. We all should be thankful after the year the country has
had," Chris said.

"So true."

"Look, could I talk you out of working and doing something with
Debi, Luc and myself?"

"Sure. What are you guys doing?"

"We're going down to the AIDS youth center house that I told you both Debi and I support, and we're serving Thanksgiving dinner to the residents. We sure could use your help," Chris said.

I thought for a moment and said, "Sure. I'd like to help out."

"Great. We're on our way right now. A bunch of us cooked most of the food last night and we're going to have a feast," Chris said.

"Tell me where to meet you," I said.

Chris gave me the address and I changed from my jeans into some nice black slacks and a cranberry-red sweater and headed downstairs to catch a taxi. The city seemed like a ghost town and the cab zipped downtown into the Village area and stopped in front of a five-story solemn-looking building on the corner of Houston and Bleecker.

I walked into a building that looked like a combination office building and day care center. When I reached the elevator I saw a homemade sign on pink paper reading THANKSGIVING DINNER ON FOURTH FLOOR. I got on the elevator and pushed four. I reached the floor and walked into a large room full of teenagers and a few adults with small children. I looked around the room and after a couple of circles around I recognized Chris's bright smile.

"Raymond, over here," he said.

I walked over and greeted Chris with a firm handshake.

"Thanks for agreeing to help out. I wanted to let some of the people who stayed up all night get back with their families before the day was over. Here, let me get you an apron," Chris said.

A few minutes later Chris walked out with an attractive African American woman who was carrying a white chef's apron.

"Here you go. Try this on," Chris said.

I pulled the starched sugar-white apron over my head and tied it. At least I tried to tie it. When Chris and the woman saw me having trouble, the lady said, "Come here. Let me help you."

"Dang, I'm sorry. I forgot you two hadn't met. Raymond, this is my wife, Debi," Chris said.

"Hello, Raymond. It's so nice to meet you. Chris speaks so highly of you," Debi said.

For a moment I was speechless. I had no clue that Chris was married to a black woman. She was beautiful, with a head of tight curly auburn hair. Debi had a gentle angular face and skin the shade of Brazil nuts.

"Debi, it's nice meeting you. I've been looking forward to it," I said.

"Let me introduce you to Luc," Chris said as he looked around the room.

"I think he's in the kitchen, honey," Debi said.

Chris walked toward the kitchen and Debi gave me my assignment serving gravy on the dressing and mashed potatoes. While she was showing me how to ladle gravy and making sure I gave each guest at least one giblet, Debi looked at me and said, "I don't guess Chris told you I was black."

I was embarrassed, but I smiled and asked, "Was I that obvious?"

Debi started laughing and said, "Don't worry. It wasn't that bad. You know, when we're down south white people who do a double take. But in cities like New York, Philly and Boston, the black people give us *the look.*"

"I'm sorry. All Chris told me about you was that you were a great wife and mother, and a doctor doing a lot for AIDS," I said.

"I raised him right, didn't I?"

"I guess you did," I said as I placed my first spoonful of gravy on the plate of a tall Latina girl with multicolored hair and two nose rings.

Chris came back with a handsome little boy who was the same color as Debi. I knew this was Luc, and our meeting was not quite as surprising as my introduction to Debi. It was more like a second kiss, when you knew what to expect.

"This must be Luc," I said as I stooped down so that I was eye level with the little boy.

"Luc, say hello to Mr. Tyler," Chris said.

"Happy Thanksgiving, Mr. Tyler. So you came to help us serve food?"

"I sure did, Luc, and I am so happy your mom and dad invited me," I said.

"I'm the butter boy today. It's my job to put the butter on the rolls," Luc said, his moist brown eyes flashing innocently.

"It sounds like an important job," I said.

"Last year I was in charge of the cranberry sauce," Luc said.

"Luc, don't talk Mr. Tyler to death. Go back to your workstation," Debi said.

"Okay, Mommy," Luc said.

"He's something else," Chris said proudly.

Luc walked toward the end of the tables, where I saw a large tray of rolls, and then he suddenly turned back around and said, "You still love me, Mommy?"

"Of course I love you," Debi said.

"Good," Luc said with a huge smile.

When Luc had disappeared, Debi smiled and said, "Kids are God's gift that keeps on giving."

About three hours later I poured my last ladle of gravy onto some cornbread dressing for a young man who volunteered that his name was Dru Bolton and that he was HIV positive.

All I could say was "Happy Thanksgiving, Dru."

"What's your name?"

"Raymond," I said.

"Are you going to eat?"

"Yeah," I said.

"Do you mind if I join you?" Dru asked.

I looked over and saw Chris, Debi and Luc at a table, eating from paper plates, and decided to take Dru up on his offer. He was young, tall with a solid-looking body and big, widely spaced brown eyes.

"Sure, I'd like that," I said.

One of the volunteers made me a plate of turkey, ham, macaroni and cheese, string beans and a couple of rolls. The food smelled good and looked like what my mama makes on Thanksgiving. The only thing missing was her good china.

I sat down at a table with Dru. He'd already finished eating half of his food and started questioning me like we were on a date.

"How old are you?"

"How old do I look?" I asked.

"Like you're in your late twenties," Dru said.

I couldn't contain my smile, and I asked Dru how old he was. I was expecting him to say in his early twenties, but when he said eighteen I was surprised that he was so young.

"How long have you been living here?" I asked.

"Since I was sixteen," he said.

"Do you mind telling me how long you've been HIV positive?" I asked.

"For two years," he said.

I wanted to ask him why somebody didn't tell him about protection when he started having sex. Instead, I gazed at the shafts of evening sun filtering through the floor-to-ceiling windows.

"I guess you want to know how I got it," Dru said.

"Do you want me to know?"

"I was in love with this guy and he was the truth! He didn't like to use condoms, and he promised me he was HIV negative because he had a girlfriend. He was on the bi now, gay later plan," Dru said, laughing.

"What happened to him?" I asked.

"He married the girlfriend," Dru said, suddenly looking sad and lonely. I looked over at the table where Debi and Chris were sitting. They had finished eating and were gazing into each other's eyes as if they were sharing a wonderful secret. Maybe it was just the way love looked. It'd been a long time since I'd seen that look. I glanced back at Dru, and his expression hadn't changed.

"Are you okay?" I asked as I touched his hand.

"Oh, I'm so thankful for my life. I haven't been sick. I take my meds every day and I'm going to live long enough to fall in love again," he said confidently.

"You think you're old enough to know love?"

"Of course. Don't you?"

"Don't I what?"

"Know love when it comes," Dru said.

"I don't know, Dru. I just know I have a lot to be thankful for."

23

I was getting ready to leave my office, when my private line rang. I figured it was Davis and started not to answer. All I wanted to do was go home and crawl into my bed with a slice of pizza and a box of tissues for my tears. I was still upset over one of the worst Thanksgivings of my life.

"Zola Norwood," I said.

"Zola, are you ready for an evening of romance?" Davis asked.

"Davis, how are you?"

"I'll be better about an hour from now. I'm getting ready to send my driver to pick you up and deliver you to a perfect secret location I recently discovered."

I guess he found it with one of his other women. I took a deep breath, and when I released it, I heard Justine screaming, "You're going to hell!" and somehow it gave me strength for what I said next: "Davis, I can't."

"What?"

"I can't see you tonight," I said.

"You're not feeling well?"

"I feel okay. I just don't want to see you," I said.

"Have you lost your mind? Who do you think you're talking to?"

"Davis, I think we should end this relationship. I mean, if that's what you call it. I still want to work with you, but I'm looking for a love of my own," I said, realizing for the first time in a long while that I needed to change the way I viewed love and relationships. The evening of 9/11 flashed into my head, and I remembered how terribly lonely I felt sleeping in my bed. Neither Jabar nor Davis was available to comfort me and tell me everything would be all right. But these were rules I had set up, and it was time for me to acknowledge the life I'd created for myself based on one bad love affair.

"Like I said, my driver will be there in ten minutes. Make sure you're out front when he gets there," Davis demanded.

"Davis, did you hear what I said? Of course you didn't, but let me say it again. I don't want to see you tonight. I don't want to continue this arrangement."

"Hear me! Be downstairs and that's all I've got to say," Davis said.

"I won't be there," I said.

"You're a smart girl, Zola. You'll be outside, waiting," Davis said, and he hung up the phone.

I picked up my purse and briefcase and headed home.

❖   ❖   ❖

After two slices of sausage pizza I was ready for bed. I started to call my mother and tell her about my aborted trip home, when I heard the doorbell ring. I put on my robe, looked through the peephole and saw Davis standing outside my door. A light mist was falling and Davis's driver was holding an umbrella over his head.

"Davis, what are you doing here?" I asked.

"Zola, I need to talk to you," Davis said forcefully. Then he spoke to his driver. "Preston, I'll page you when I'm ready to go. I think you'll be safe here," he said as he looked around my neighborhood.

I opened the door all the way and he walked in.

"What kind of games are you playing, Zola?" Davis asked.

"I'm not playing games. What are you doing here? I thought my neighborhood wasn't good enough for you," I said.

"I'm not staying long. Pack yourself an overnight bag. Make sure you pack some nice sexy panties. I have a hotel and some nice things waiting," Davis said.

"What part of 'I'm not going' don't you understand?"

"Zola, are you on drugs? You know what our deal is."

"Our deal?" I asked as I raised my eyebrow at his statement.

"Yes, Zola, don't play dumb with me. You get to run your magazine and I get pussy on demand," Davis said without any emotion in his eyes or voice.

"You can't talk to me like that. I'm good at what I do. I don't want to sleep with you just because you demand it. I never looked at our relationship like it was some kind of job-for-sex arrangement," I said.

"Zola, please. What did you think this was? I told you when I met you I was never leaving my wife. Do you realize how much half of my total worth would be? I'll be with that bitch until the day I die," Davis said.

If I wasn't totally convinced I was doing the right thing by breaking up with Davis, his calling his wife, Veronica, a bitch was the sign I needed. My father had always told me never to give a man who referred to his wife as "that bitch" the time of day. I had been giving Davis much more of me than he deserved.

"Davis, please leave. I need to make some changes in my life and I need to reconsider some relationships, and I'm starting right now. With you," I said.

"While you're reconsidering these relationships, make sure you think about what you could lose," Davis said.

"Are you threatening me?"

"Figure it out," Davis said as he walked out the door.

24

I'd just closed my leather binder after a meeting with Davis and was getting ready to leave his office, when I heard him say calmly, "Oh, yeah, I need you to fire Zola," as the white barber removed a black cape from Davis's neck.

I stared at him for a moment and then asked, "You want me to do what?"

"Fire Zola. Get the locks changed and have security escort her out of the building," Davis said calmly. "Make it as embarrassing as you possibly can," he added.

"What's going on? What did she do?"

"Nothing. Fire her."

"Nothing?"

"Yeah, nothing. Get rid of her."

"What's the reason? What am I supposed to tell her?"

"You don't need a reason," Davis said without looking up from the papers on his desk. The barber was packing his equipment and didn't make eye contact with Davis or me.

"But, Davis, the magazine is doing great, even in a tough economy. Lots of magazines are hemorrhaging advertising and sales. I haven't seen that trend with *Bling Bling*," I said.

"I don't give a damn. The bitch isn't doing what she was hired to do, run a magazine and, more important, give me pussy when I need it. I don't have time to go out and look for new pussy," Davis said, looking at me calmly like I should understand his reasons.

"Doesn't she have an employment contract?"

"Yeah, she does. But I made sure it was to my advantage. We can give her some type of severance, but make sure you remind her of the non-compete clause. I don't want to see her starting a magazine or working at one for at least two years," Davis said.

"She has a noncompete clause? Did she have a lawyer look over her contract before she signed it?"

"Yeah, but it was somebody I recommended," Davis said proudly.

"Davis, this may be a problem," I advised.

"It's your job to make sure it's not. I want her out by week's end."

"Who's going to take her place?"

"I don't know. Call an executive search firm and find someone who can start right away. Have them check and see how much money we would need to offer Amy Barnett over at *Honey* magazine to come over here. I've been watching that magazine and I hear she's doing a great job over there," Davis said.

I couldn't believe that, as smart and brilliant as Davis was, he was acting like he was whipped. Davis thought this was going to be simple, but from what I knew about Zola, simple was the last thing firing her was going to be.

"Are you sure about this, Davis? Is there any way you can work this out?"

"Raymond, you didn't hear me stutter. Fire the bitch. Now, if you don't mind, I have some calls I need to make," Davis said as the barber handed him a mirror and he admired his cut. It was the tone he used when he dismissed people from his world. I'd witnessed Davis do this to several people before, but this was the first time he'd done it to me.

"You're the boss, Davis," I said as I headed out of his office. I heard Davis say, "Great job, Chester."

25

Jabar walked into my bedroom from the kitchen with chips in one of my treasured crystal bowls and salsa in one of my favorite caviar dishes. When I looked up abruptly from the article I was reading, he asked what he had done wrong.

"Nothing, Jabar. It's nothing," I said, even though I was a bit disgusted. I placed the article and my red pencil on the nightstand.

"Yo, Z, then why you lookin' at me like that? Do you want some chips and dip? I know you always watchin' what you eat, but there are some more chips in there," Jabar said as he sat on the edge of the bed in a pair of ice-blue boxers and white gym socks.

"Jabar, we need to talk," I said.

"I'm listening," Jabar said.

I moved closer to him, gently grabbed his arm and said, "I've been thinking about making some changes in my life, and I think maybe we should take some time apart."

"So whatcha saying? I can't get no more of the punanny? You ready to give it to Mr. Moneybags? Z, you act like that nigga pimpin' you or sumthin'. You know he can't please you like I can," Jabar said.

"What are you talking about?" I asked. I didn't know if Jabar knew of my relationship with Davis, but I was sure he knew I saw other people.

"Zola, yo don't play me for stupid. Mr. Moneybags let me know who was paying for your training. But I didn't give a damn. I don't care how much money he has, shorty ain't got shit on me when it comes to knowin' how to treat a woman," Jabar said.

"You talked with Davis?"

"He did all the talking. So is he the reason you trying to drop-kick my ass out of your life?"

"This has nothing to do with Davis. It's just that ever since I came back from Thanksgiving, I've been thinking I need some space to figure out what I'm going to do. I'll be thirty this year. You're not even twenty-five," I said.

"Age ain't got nuthin' to do with stuff. I don't know why you frontin' like this. You know I make you feel real good, Z. Let me remind you 'bout what you gonna be missing," Jabar said as he licked his lips sensu- ously. How I love those lips, but I was determined not to fall prey. I needed to end this so-called relationship, since it was headed down a one-way street.

"It's not about age. I think we're going in different directions," I said.

"Yo, so you saying I ain't good enough for you? Why sistas always think that about brothas? Is that why we always just meet here at your place?" Jabar asked.

"I thought that's what you wanted. I know you have other ladies in your life. This was never a serious thing."

"And I know about your sugar daddy. None of that shit ever got in our way. We're magical together. Look at me and tell me I'm lying, yo," Jabar said.

I looked toward the window and watched the thin silk curtains sway from the crackle of the fireplace.

"Yo, Z, look at me. Tell me whatcha thinking 'bout."

"Jabar, don't make this hard," I said.

"Yo, you always make me hard. I mean, just the sight of you. But if you give me my walking papers, you're going to have to go back to the end of the line when you start missin' my love," Jabar said.

"Jabar, this isn't love," I said.

"What's love for you? You want me buying you shit and writing poems for you? Is that what ole boy do? Do you like expensive gifts every day? Is that's what's up?"

"No," I said.

"Then you need to talk to a brotha. Z, you good people and I like you. I like you a lot, but if you don't want to roll, then that's chill," Jabar said.

"I hope you understand what I'm trying to say. It's not you. It's me," I said.

"Cool. I know I try and treat ya right, never disrespect you or nuthin' like that," Jabar said.

"I know that."

"Then I was right with it. Why don't you let me remind you what you going to be missin'," Jabar said as he used his index finger and lips to summon me close to him. I stared at Jabar and thought about what he was asking me to do. Slowly, I got out of my bed wearing a lilac teddy and matching robe. When I stood a few inches from Jabar, he pulled down his boxers and kicked them to the side and all I could see was that fabulous piece between powerful legs and I could feel the instant wetness between my thighs.

Jabar pulled me close. I couldn't resist his intoxicatingly masculine smell, and I dropped my robe.

"You look damn good, Z," Jabar whispered as his hands began exploring me slowly and tenderly until I was no longer wearing a single thread.

"Show me," I said as I kissed him. Kissing wasn't one of Jabar's favorite things, but he was so damn good at it.

"I want you to do sumthin' for me," Jabar said.

"I'm listening," I said.

"I want you to stand on that chair," Jabar said as he pointed to a leather-and-wood chair in the corner of my bedroom.

"You want me to do what?"

"I want you to stand on that chair," Jabar said.

"Boy, have you lost your mind?"

"Trust me, you'll love it."

"What if I fall?"

"Then I'll catch you," Jabar said.

I had mixed feelings. A part of me wanted just to put my clothes on and tell Jabar we were finished and I didn't want to make love to him, but a part of me was curious about what he wanted to do with me and the chair. The freak in me won out and I found myself standing on the chair like a circus performer. I was feeling a little shaky, but Jabar took his firm hands and held me in place until I felt safe. I glanced over at my curtains and I could see my shadow pour over Jabar's face as he knelt below the chair like he was praying to a female god. I felt powerful and in control.

Jabar reached his hands around me and placed them on my ass and firmly but gently drew me toward his mouth. He kissed the insides of my thighs sweetly and then Jabar's tongue found my most magical place and a thrill rushed through my entire body like I had never felt before.

26

After Davis told me to fire Zola, I couldn't sleep. I liked Zola and thought she was doing a great job with the magazine despite the tough economic climate. Instead of staring at the ceiling, I got up and spent a few more hours reviewing Zola's contract. As I read through each line, it was obvious that it was the work of one of Davis's attorneys. I wondered if Zola had even read the contract before she signed it. Still, it was going to be tough for Davis to fire Zola without a true business cause. I needed to make him realize that and how a lawsuit would soak up a lot of time and make the magazine look bad. Zola Norwood was *Bling Bling* just like Susan Taylor was *Essence* magazine.

I got to Davis's office around 7:15 A.M. and planned to wait in his outer office until he arrived. So I was a bit surprised when I got there and heard Davis's voice coming from his office. I guess that's why he was set to be America's latest black billionaire. I knocked gently and stuck my head through the slightly open door.

With a polite smile Davis motioned for me to come in. I stood in front of his desk as he finished his phone call. After a few minutes Davis hung up the phone and walked from around his desk. He gave me a firm handshake and said, "Good morning, Raymond. Have a seat. You're up early. Are you trying to keep up with me?" he said, laughing.

"That would take a lot," I said as I sat down in one of the two leather-and-steel chairs facing Davis's desk. Davis walked back behind his desk and sat down in a large high-back leather chair. I noticed how everything on his desk was lined up precisely.

"So, what can I do for you? Did you get the locks on Zola's office changed yet?"

"No, that's what I want to talk to you about. I think we should reconsider firing Zola," I said.

Davis's smile collapsed as he looked at me sternly and said, "What are you talking about? I want the bitch fired and I want it done today. I thought I made myself perfectly clear. Do I need to get one of my white boys to do it?" Davis asked.

I explained to Davis that while the contract was written in his favor, the company was still required to show just cause as to why Zola was being terminated. I very carefully and tactfully explained that discontinuing a sexual relationship with the boss could be a big problem in a court of law. I knew he was acting on emotion or sex, because Davis was much too savvy not to already know this.

"So how can I get rid of her?" Davis demanded.

"She would have to do something to breach the contract," I said.

"Damn, Raymond, give me an example. I don't have a whole lot of time to spend on this. If she caused the magazine to lose money or favor with the public, would that be reason enough?"

"I don't think I understand the question."

"What if I could prove she was stealing money?"

"Is she?"

"Zola wouldn't do that. But we could make it look that way," Davis said.

"*We?*" I was suddenly wondering how Davis had maintained his successful track record, since it appeared that he was willing to do anything to get revenge against someone who had done so much for the magazine.

"I don't need your help. I have a plan. We'll put it off for now, but I promise you within a week there will be a change at *Bling Bling* and the public will understand why. Zola will be so embarrassed, she wouldn't even think of suing. She'll just slink out of New York City and the magazine industry. Maybe she'll carry her country ass back to Hooterville and get married and make babies," Davis said confidently.

I didn't know what his plans were and I didn't want to. I simply looked at him with a sad and confused look. How did this man get where he is pulling tricks like this? Davis was acting like a rejected high school boy who got cut from the football team and his cheerleader girlfriend dumped him to boot.

"Have a good day," I said as I walked out of Davis's office.

"Yeah, you do the same," I heard Davis mumble as I reached the door.

❖   ❖   ❖

A few days later, Davis walked into my office looking quite pleased. He was carrying a magazine and what looked like legal documents. I was surprised to see Davis in my office, since he usually summoned me to his. I wondered what the big deal was.

"Davis, what are you doing here?" I asked as I stood up from my desk and walked over to shake his hand.

He slammed the magazine and documents on my desk and said, "I got just what I needed. Fire Zola today! Have the locks changed before noon."

"What's this?" I asked as I picked up the magazine and saw a beautiful young lady on the cover with the headline THE REAL DRAMA BEHIND YANCEY B. across the middle of the magazine.

"The bitch gave me the ammunition I needed. Zola published this damn article on this young lady that doesn't have an ounce of truth in it, according to Yancey B.'s lawyer and record company. They're suing *Bling Bling* and McClinton Enterprises for fifty million dollars, and if that isn't enough to fire her, I don't know what is," Davis said.

I picked up the document and started to read it as Davis continued to talk.

"I can't believe she was that stupid, running an article that sounds like it should be on the front of *The National Informer* rather than my magazine," Davis said.

I continued to read the legal document, and I guess it upset Davis that I wasn't paying more attention to him, so he came over and snatched the document from my hands and yelled, "Raymond, pay attention! You can read that shit later. We need to come up with the language to inform Zola Norwood of her dismissal. I want it delivered to her home this evening."

"What about the lawsuit? Don't you think I should look the documents over to make sure they even have a case? I mean, you will expect me to defend this, won't you?"

"No! I'll get one of my white boys to handle it. When you go into a court of law against the big boys, they want to see somebody who looks like them. Nothing against you and your skills, Raymond, but you understand, right?"

"I can't say that I do. If this is a valid case, then I'll defend Zola and your interests to the best of my abilities. I've handled cases like this in the past."

"I don't give a shit about defending Zola. She's the one who's gotten us in the mess. I hired you for a lot of things, and one of them is to oversee this magazine. There needs to be a change in the leadership. That's your job. Fire Zola and get someone to take over immediately," Davis said as he picked up the magazine and lawsuit.

"Davis, I think we should talk—"

"Raymond, there's nothing else to talk about. You have your orders," Davis said as he paraded out of my office like he was a general leading a war.

❖   ❖   ❖

When Bristol stepped into my office late that evening and told me the papers for Zola's termination had arrived from Davis, my initial thought was to look them over and then messenger them to her home.

While I was looking them over, I realized that Davis was serious about ruining Zola. Not only was she fired from her dream job, she was not allowed to seek employment with another magazine for at least two years. Zola also couldn't start her own magazine. The documents were as bitter as Davis was when he first mentioned firing Zola.

I wondered if she would be home alone when the papers arrived and how Zola might feel. Did she have somebody who would be there to hold her and tell her that everything was going to work out for the best? The thought of Zola learning about her termination from a bike-riding messenger who didn't give a damn didn't sit well with me. I could see the nameless messenger instructing Zola to "sign this" and then leaving her alone. I couldn't let that happen.

I pushed the intercom button and asked Bristol to come into my office. Moments later he was standing a few inches from my desk.

"You need something?"

"Yes, Bristol, call the car service and ask them to pick me up in front of the building in fifteen minutes," I said.

"Where should I tell them you're going?"

"Tell them I'm going to Harlem."

27

My oversize bathtub had become my newest boyfriend, and I was thoroughly enjoying my new beau after an exhausting day. When I stepped into the warm, perfumed bath, my body collapsed like a paper house hit by a fierce wind. I had candles burning and I was listening to Glenn Lewis, a new rhythm-and-blues singer from Canada who sounded just like Stevie Wonder. The record company had sent me an advance copy with hopes that we would do a feature on the handsome young singer.

About an hour later, the washcloth on my face felt ice cold and I figured it was time to curl up in front of the television with a bowl of raspberry sorbet and the remote control.

I brushed my hair, put it in a ponytail and grabbed my favorite light blue terry-cloth robe and headed toward the kitchen. I pulled out the sorbet, and just as I reached in the cabinet for a bowl, I heard my doorbell ring.

I was a bit surprised when I looked through the peephole and saw Raymond standing at my door.

"Raymond, what a surprise," I said after opening the door.

"Good evening, Zola. Is this a bad time?" Raymond asked.

"I was just getting ready to watch some television, but come in. Is everything all right?"

"Zola, I need to give you something and I decided it was important to do it in person," Raymond said as he walked into my foyer and then followed me into my living room. There was a look of concern on his face, and I wondered if something had happened to someone at the office.

"Is everything okay at the office?"

"Zola, I need to give you this," Raymond said as he handed me a manila envelope.

I opened the envelope and immediately noticed the letterhead from Davis's parent company, McClinton Enterprises. I began reading, and words like *terminated* and *effective immediately* felt like someone was throwing rocks at me. I read, *"Your contract prevents you from seeking employment in the industry for two years from the date of this letter."* I looked up at Raymond and he was still as a statue.

"Raymond, what is this about?" I asked.

"Zola, I'm so sorry. I tried to convince Davis that we should proceed with caution," Raymond said deliberately and gently. All I could think was I couldn't believe this was happening to me.

"Why is he doing this?" I asked.

"The magazine is being sued by Yancey B. and her record company. They believe the story you ran on her was written with a reckless disregard for the truth. Yancey and her people contend that almost eighty percent of the article is total fabrication. Davis feels that we must take a proactive stance, and he feels removing you from your position is the first step. Zola, you know how much I like you and I think you're doing a great job. Amazingly ad sales and circulation have gone up since 9/11, and I told Davis how the sexiest-man contest you're running is getting the magazine a lot of great publicity," Raymond said.

I just looked at Raymond and shook my head in disbelief. There was a long, pained silence and then I said, "He can't do this to me. Davis knows I am *Bling Bling*. He's doing this because I refused to sleep with him."

"What about the story? Did you fact-check?" Raymond asked.

"Of course I did. We always do. There is plenty of documentation. I have it in my office, and I can go down to the office right now and get the information that proves everything in the article is true," I said.

"You can't do that," Raymond said.

"Why not?"

"The locks on your office have been changed and security has removed your personal belongings from your office. You won't get past the security guards," Raymond said.

"Oh, I see. After all the years I worked for him, this is the way Davis is going to treat me. I am not going to just walk away. I will get a lawyer and sue Davis McClinton for everything he's worth," I said. My voice trembled with rage.

"Zola, you can certainly do that. I hope you understand the position I'm in. Are you going to be all right?" Raymond asked as he gently touched my shoulders.

"Oh, don't worry, Raymond, I'm a survivor and I'll be fine," I said. I tried to sound calm and in control. I was concentrating on not breaking down into tears. Not in front of Raymond and not after he left. I had to hold it together. I had to devise a battle plan to fight both Davis and Yancey B.

"Is there anything I can do?"

"Can you get the file I have backing up the story?" I asked.

"Where is it?"

"It's in my desk. At least it was," I said.

"What do you want me to do with it? I still work for Davis and this might be a conflict of interest," Raymond said.

"Don't worry about it. I am sure Kirsten still has her set," I said.

"Is she the writer?"

"Yes."

"I think that's what you should do. I'll find out what happened to it because we will need it in our defense," Raymond said.

"Thanks, Raymond. I guess it's better to hear this from you than showing up and getting my face cracked when I tried to enter my office. I'm sure that's what Davis wanted," I said. Raymond didn't answer, but his eyes told me I was right. I realized that this was hard for him and I didn't want to make it any more difficult. After a few moments of silence Raymond asked again if there was anything he could do.

"Get my job back," I said with a fake laugh.

"Zola, I know this is tough, but you're going to be fine," Raymond said.

"You got that right. I'll be more than fine. You might not know this about me, but my parents raised a fighter," I said, trying hard to sound calm and in control, hoping that my stoic refusal to cry could hold on for a few more minutes.

"I know that," Raymond said.

"Now, I just need to show Davis," I said. Raymond nodded and offered a polite smile and was out the door just moments before my dam of tears broke.

❖   ❖   ❖

I was exhausted, so I didn't get out of bed until a little after noon. I had tossed and turned so I couldn't even allow myself to think that last night was a bad dream. Besides, the letter and agreement Raymond and Davis wanted me to sign was on the edge of my bed. I had read it over ten times, hoping that it didn't say what I knew it said. I was out of a job and I couldn't look for one in the industry I loved.

I went into my bathroom and splashed cold water on my face and breathed deeply as I looked in the mirror and said to myself, "Wake up and live, girl! He can't do this to you."

I pulled a robe from the back of the door and slipped it on as I headed to the kitchen to make myself some tea. I needed to make a few phone calls, so I put a cup of water in the microwave and zapped it and then dropped in a tea bag.

I walked into the room adjoining my bedroom, which housed my piano. I sat down at the piano and pounded out Beethoven's "Pathetique" like I was in Carnegie Hall. The sonata was beautiful and expressed the pain I was feeling. But it wasn't helping; I needed to get busy clearing my name.

After two o'clock, I picked up my Palm, located Kirsten's home number and quickly dialed even though I thought it might be too early. I needed to make sure she still had a set of her notes and documentation, because I knew I would need it to get my job and most likely my reputation back.

After about four rings a groggy-sounding Kirsten picked up the phone.

"Hello."

"Kirsten. I hate to bother you so early, but I need to talk to you," I said.

"Who is this?"

"It's Zola."

"Zola from *Bling*?"

"Yes, Kirsten. Look, do you still have that set of notes and documentation from the story you did on Yancey B.?"

"Yancey B.? I think so."

"Kirsten, you can't think, honey. I need to know. I need a copy of those notes and the tapes," I said.

"What happened to your set?"

"It's a long story," I said.

"Yancey B. ain't trying to sue you, is she?"

"Have you heard something?"

"A couple of my girls told me they just heard Wendy Williams on WBLS talking about it on her show and there was some mention in the local rags today," Kirsten said.

"What?" I asked.

"I don't know, Zola. I didn't actually hear it. But you don't have to worry. I verified all of my stories and it's all true. Miss Girl is probably trying to save herself. I bet that organization MAC, Mothers Against Crack, is going to want their Entertainer of the Year award back," Kirsten said.

"Right now I'm not worried about Yancey B.'s award. She and her record company are saying our story is nothing but a bunch of lies," I said.

"Then let them prove it in court."

"When can you let me know if you have your information?"

"Let me get out of bed and get myself together. Do you want me to call you at the office?"

"No, call me at home. We should meet this afternoon and I can make another set. How does your day look?"

"I think it's pretty open. This is the day I reserve to work on my stories."

"Great. Call me in a couple of hours and we can figure out where we can meet," I said.

"Cool. Bye, Zola," Kirsten said.

"I'll see you later. Sorry again about waking you up," I said. Kirsten must have fallen back to sleep, because I didn't hear her say good-bye, only the dial tone.

I was feeling a little uneasy and I wanted to talk with someone who could reassure me that everything would be all right. I started to call Justine, who for so long had been a master at building up my confidence, but now I figured she would think that I was getting what I deserved for sleeping with a married man who was also my boss. I thought of my mother but didn't want her to worry. I was sure Hayden would cheer me up but knew he was in rehearsals for The Lion King.

After a few moments, I picked up the phone and dialed Kai's number. I needed to hear a friendly voice.

"Good afternoon, Zola," Kai said.

"Girl, what did we ever do without caller ID?" I said with a fake laugh.

"Talked to a lot of people we didn't want to," Kai said, laughing.

"What are you doing today?"

"I am working out with my trainer later, then depending on how I'm feeling I might take a yoga class or treat myself to a massage and facial," Kai said.

"Do you know any good lawyers who are reasonably priced?"

"My divorce lawyer, but since you're not married, I don't think he could help you. I'm assuming it's for you."

"It's for me, and I feel like I'm going through a divorce. Davis had Raymond fire me. Davis had him deliver some papers to me last night," I said.

"What happened? I guess he didn't take you dropping him too kindly," Kai said.

"I know that's what it's about, but Davis is saying he did it because we're being sued for a cover story I ran."

"What? Don't tell me one of those fine men you been putting in the magazine is really a woman or some type of terrorist?"

I shook my head and rolled my eyes and said, "No, Kai. It's the Yancey B. story."

"I wish I could help you out, Zola, but I don't know anyone right off the bat. I will ask around. Are you going to sue him?"

"Right now I don't know what I'm going to do, but I know I need to at least talk to an attorney."

"Why don't you come to the gym with me? I know you must be stressed."

"I wish I could, girl, but I got things to do. Maybe sometime later in the week. It looks like I'm going to have a little time on my hands," I said.

"Okay, but let me know if there is anything I can do. I'm here for you," Kai said.

"I appreciate that, Kai. It means more than you'll ever know."

❖   ❖   ❖

I spent my first day of unemployment updating my photo albums while listening to my favorite sista singers like Toni Braxton, Anita Baker and Faith Evans. Their voices and lyrics made me feel good about feeling so bad. When the songs became too much, I returned to the piano pretending I had chosen it as my career.

Before I knew it, evening was approaching. I looked at the clock and saw that it was almost five o'clock. I had been waiting for a call from Kirsten so I could meet her and get copies of the tapes of her interview and other documentation. I checked my answering machine to make sure I hadn't missed the ringing phone over my music. No calls from Kirsten.

I looked up her number and dialed it. Kirsten picked up after a couple of rings.

"Hello."

"Kirsten, this is Zola," I said.

"Zola, did you get the information?"

"No, that's why I'm calling. Did you send it to me? I thought we were going to meet," I said.

"I gave it to the messenger," Kirsten said calmly.

"What messenger?"

"The one you sent," she said.

"Kirsten, I have no clue as to what you're talking about. I didn't send a messenger to pick up anything," I said. I could feel my neck become moist with panic.

"Well, a messenger showed up at my apartment a couple of hours after we talked and said he was picking up the information for *Bling Bling* and I gave it to him," Kirsten said.

"How could you be so stupid?" I screamed. "Why didn't you call me?"

"Hold up, Zola. I thought it was for you, and I don't appreciate you calling me names. I was trying to help you out."

"I'm sorry. But I didn't get the information. Please tell me you have another copy," I begged. There was a long silence, and I knew I was in trouble.

"Kirsten, are you still there?"

"I have to go, Zola. I need to call my lawyer," Kirsten said as she hung up the phone.

28

When I walked into my office two days after firing Zola, Bristol greeted me with a cup of coffee, extra light, and told me Davis wanted to see me immediately. He had been in Paris the previous day, probably worried Zola might show up at the office and call him out about dismissing her.

"When did he call?" I asked.

"About fifteen minutes ago," Bristol said.

"Did he say what he wanted?" I asked. I knew he wanted to talk about Zola.

"Didn't mention anything to me, just told me to make sure you came right up," Bristol said.

With coffee in hand, I took the elevator to the top floor and Davis's office. His executive assistant wasn't at her usual post guarding Davis's office like it was Fort Knox, so I walked to his door and tapped gently. I didn't hear a response, so I just walked into his office.

"You wanted to see me?" I asked.

Davis had that dazed look of someone who had just glanced up from reading something important.

"Yeah, Raymond, come on in," Davis said.

I walked toward his huge desk and just stood until he told me to have a seat.

"How did the bitch take it?" Davis asked in a cold, impersonal tone.

"Are you talking about Zola?" I asked. I wondered how Davis knew, or if he knew that I had delivered the termination papers to Zola in person.

"I understand you took the papers to her," Davis said.

I didn't ask him how he knew. From what I learned about Davis since I started working for him, I wouldn't have been a bit surprised if he was having me followed, so I figured I should just give him the information I had.

"Yes, I took them to her. She didn't really have a strong reaction. I think everything was clear," I said.

"No tears?"

"No."

"You pointed out that she can't work for any other magazine, right?"

"I didn't, but I was there as she read the agreement."

"Did she ask you anything?"

"Like what?"

"Anything?"

"Zola did mention that she stood by her story and had documentation backing her up," I said.

"Zola might think she has documentation. It's clear she's forgotten who she's dealing with," Davis said with confidence.

"That information might be important when we go to trial," I said.

"There won't be a trial," Davis said.

"What do you mean?"

"We'll settle the case in the next couple of days."

"What if we have proof that the story is true?" I asked.

"Raymond, I don't have time to waste on a trial. I will instruct my lawyer to get the case settled."

"Why don't you let me handle this? I mean, that was one of the reasons you hired me, right?" I asked.

Davis looked at me sternly and said, "No offense, Raymond, but when you're dealing with black people, especially those idiots from the music industry, you need to show them right away that the record company would advise the singer to settle. The way to do that is with a white lawyer. You understand, don't you?"

"I have to be honest and say that I don't. It's reverse racism," I said.

"Call it what you want. But that's how I'm handling this. Your job is to keep in touch with Zola and make sure she goes away quietly. She needs that severance check if she's not going to be able to work for a couple of years."

"Who is going to run the magazine?" I asked.

"Bristol," Davis said quickly.

"Bristol?"

"You heard me! Bristol is a very talented young man. He'll be fine," Davis said.

"Do you think that's wise?"

"What are you talking about?"

"I mean, a white guy running a magazine geared toward the hip hop crowd. How long do you think that'll work?"

"It worked at *Vibe*. It can work here."

"What am I going to do for an assistant?"

"Call the executive search firm we used to find you. There are a lot of people out of a job," Davis said.

"I can't talk you out of this?"

"What's the problem, Raymond? I thought you liked Bristol."

"This doesn't have anything to do with Bristol. I just think if there is some way Zola can prove her story, then you're right back to firing her because of a failed relationship," I said boldly.

Davis leaped from his chair and started pounding his desk. I had never seen him lose his cool like this. Then he looked at me as though fire were about to beam from his eyes and yelled, "Don't you talk to me like that. Do you know who I am? I'm Davis McClinton, and when I want somebody out of my company, they're out. Do I make myself clear, Raymond? Have you forgotten who signs those big checks of yours? Zola just better get used to sitting on her ass for a couple of years. Now, unless there is something else we need to discuss, I think you should go downstairs and wish your assistant well in his new post."

I was stunned and felt like I had been stabbed with a verbal ice pick. I stood in silence then walked out of Davis's office.

❖   ❖   ❖

"I don't know how long I can keep working for *Bling Bling* and Davis," I said.

"Why, Raymond? I didn't know you were having problems at your job," Dr. Few said.

"It's not that I'm having problems. I just don't feel good about the way Davis does business," I said.

"How does he treat you?"

"He treats me okay, I guess."

"Then I don't understand your concern."

I spent about five minutes telling Dr. Few about how Davis had forced me to fire Zola because of the lawsuit. I also told her how I prevented him from firing her after she broke off their affair and how I was convinced that he had information that could help the company in the lawsuit filed by Yancey B. and her record company, but Davis was so full of revenge that he would rather lose in court and have a reason to fire Zola.

"That doesn't sound like a way to run a business," Dr. Few said.

"It goes deeper than that," I said.

"How so?"

"When I first started working for Davis, I felt a certain degree of pride. Here he was, a successful African American man making a difference in the world. Davis is one of the few black men who have both money and power, and whenever I mention to people I work for him, everyone, both black and white, is somewhat impressed. I guess it's another case of a man thinking with his jimmie rather than his brains," I said.

"Have you ever done that?"

"What?"

"Thought with your penis?" Dr. Few asked. I looked at her for a second with a slight smile tugging the corner of my mouth, when I realized she knew Basil's word for dick. This white lady was listening to me after all.

"I have in my personal life. Even now thinking about Basil, even though I know he would be the worst thing in the world for me," I said.

"Have you talked to him?"

"He calls every now and then, but I realize he's busy trying to get custody of his daughter, and even if he comes back to New York, I realize his daughter has his heart," I said.

"Is that a problem for you?"

"Oh, no. That's the way it should be. A father putting his children first. My parents did," I said.

"Did you have a personal relationship with the young lady you fired?"

"Yeah. I felt like her big brother. She was one of the few women who I felt like I didn't have to lie to. There is something very open about Zola. When I told her that I was gay, she was cool," I said.

"So you don't think she should have been fired?"

"No. Zola told me she had taped transcripts of the information she published in the magazine and supporting evidence. When I told Davis that some information that could help our case was missing, he just smiled and said very low, 'That will teach the bitch she can't just drop me because she suddenly develops morals.' When I asked him what he meant, he just stared at me like a gangster or a character out of a prime-time soap opera," I said.

"Couldn't she sue this Davis guy for sexual harassment?"

"It might be hard because from what I can gather, she entered into an intimate relationship with him before he hired her to run his magazine," I said.

"So, are you going to quit?"

"I don't know. I make a nice living. I mean, more money than I even dreamed of making."

"Is that important to you?"

"I want to do well," I said.

"You didn't answer the question," Dr. Few said.

"What would I do?"

"You mean with your career?"

"Yes, I'm not getting any younger and I wouldn't want to have Davis as an enemy. I know he doesn't play fair," I said.

"Have you thought about confronting him about your suspicions?"

"Davis would deny it. When I terminated Zola, I just wanted to give her a hug and tell her everything would be all right. I have this friend who is a great lawyer. I want Zola to speak with him, but he's a friend of Davis's as well. I don't know if he would take the case," I said.

"So you haven't thought of what you might do if you stopped working for Davis?"

"The only thing I think about is maybe working for a foundation, taking mine to the next level. Then there is always the opportunity of working for Basil if he ever returns to New York," I said. A picture of Basil leaving my apartment and coming back and kissing me on the lips caused a spontaneous smile to cross my face. Dr. Few noticed.

"You're smiling."

"Yeah, I was thinking about Basil. You know the last time I saw him."

"It looks like you had a good time."

"I did."

"Do you want to talk about it?"

"No. I think I'll keep the memory to myself."

Dr. Few looked at her watch and then said, "You have about ten minutes. Is there anything else you want to talk about?"

"Not really."

"Could I ask you something?"

"Sure."

"Does the fact that Davis is an African American man doing this to another African American bother you?"

I clapped and said, "Great question, Dr. Few. Great question!"

"Why is that?"

"It's just another way we separate ourselves," I said.

"I don't think I quite understand," Dr. Few said.

I thought maybe it was time Dr. Few got a brief message from the educating-white-folks foundation.

"Ever since I can remember, African Americans have had barriers that I think hold us back. Some call it the crabs-in-the-barrel theory. You know how when crabs are in a bucket and one tries to escape, there are always crabs pulling it back?"

"I get the picture. I think."

"In the African American community there is always something. For a long time it was color. The slave mentality of light-skinned versus dark-skinned, or people who grew up in the big house against those who worked the field. When I came to grips with my sexuality, I realized that was another barrier in keeping me from totally being accepted by my community. When I met Davis and some of his friends, I realized there was another trend happening within our community."

"What?"

"The haves and the have-nots. Those who have education and those who don't. Those who have money, and I'm talking big money, separating themselves from those who might not be as fortunate as they are. If you compared what I'm worth against Davis, I might as well be penniless," I said.

"You know other groups have the same issues," Dr. Few suggested.

"Maybe in terms of class. I'm sure wealthy white people don't have friends who live in trailer parks. I understand that people with blue eyes and blond hair may be treated better than brunettes with brown eyes. Still, this is the community I belong to, so I am more sensitive to what's going on with black people," I said.

"Do you think we will ever be a part of one community?"

"You mean a perfect world? You know, after 9/11 I thought there was a chance. I mean, for a few months I didn't think as much about being an African American as I did being an American. I thought we, and I mean everybody, treated one another with more kindness and on an equal level. But I think we've gone back to our old ways of separation. Out of that tragedy our country was presented with a tremendous opportunity," I said, looking at my watch.

"Do you think it's too late?"

"I hope not. It's one of the reasons I still thank God for waking me up each morning."

BOOK THREE

Ready for Love

INDIA.ARIE

1

Three days and nights passed, and one day was just like the next. I lay in the coziness of my bed, wishing for snow during an unnaturally warm winter. I watched a lot of talk shows, some good and a few so bad I couldn't believe they were on the air.

I drank a lot of water and tea and ate a lot of tuna fish with crunched-up potato chips, a delicacy from my youth. I don't know what I was thinking or hoping for, maybe that Davis would show up at my doorstep and tell me he couldn't run *Bling Bling* without me and beg me to come back on my terms.

I thought maybe my dream had come true when the doorbell rang just as dusk had begun to cover the neighborhood. I was so eager to see another human being who wasn't a television character that I raced from my bed and opened the door quickly.

"Miss Zola, have you lost your mind scaring me like this!" Hayden said as he walked into my house carrying a brown bag with handles.

"Did Kai call you and tell you what happened?" I asked.

"Yeah, she did, but she didn't have to. It's all over the radio and in the tabloids. Wendy Williams has been talking about it every day, calling it the Battle of the Tennessee Titans. Did you know that you and Miss Yancey B. are from the same area?"

"I think so. What have they been saying on the radio?" I asked as I followed Hayden into the kitchen.

"You haven't been listing to the radio? It's been on Tom Joyner and Doug Banks. I thought you didn't miss a day of listening to their shows," Hayden said as he pulled out several plastic containers of what smelled like good food.

"If it hasn't been on CNBC, *Regis and Kelly* or *The View*, then I haven't heard it," I said as I sat down at my little kitchen table.

"It seems that Miss Yancey has proof she was out of the country touring and promoting her CD when you guys said she was in rehab. The other day Wendy Williams said she had an interview with Yancey B. during the time *Bling* said she was drying out, and that's major 'cause Miss Wendy don't like Yancy B.," Hayden said.

"Tell me you're kidding," I said.

"I wish I could. Don't you have a lawyer or somebody helping you with this?"

"Not yet. I've been trying to figure out what I'm going to do next," I said.

"Might I suggest changing that old-lady nightgown," Hayden said as he let out a short, powerful laugh.

"What's that?" I asked as I pointed to one of the containers.

"I figured you weren't eating right, so I stopped and picked up some food. You can't be skin and bones when you're getting ready for battle. I brought a little tossed salad with ranch dressing, some tasty spinach ravioli, and if you're good, crème brûlée," Hayden said. He walked over to my cabinets and pulled out two plates and then turned and said, "I hope you got some liquor up in here."

"I have some wine, I think."

"Then that will have to do," Hayden said as he started dishing the food onto the plates.

"Hayden, aren't you supposed to be working tonight?"

"I called in sick. *The Lion King* is grueling, honey, and Hayden needs more than a couple of days of rest. Back problems, you know."

"That's why I didn't call you. I knew you'd be worried," I said.

"I'm not worried. I just need to get you ready for battle. You can't just let Davis take your job and then leave you out here to fight alone. If I were you, I would call one of them gossip columnists like LaVonya or Liz Smith and tell your side of the story," Hayden said.

"They don't want to talk to me," I said.

"You've got to talk to somebody even if you don't do nothing but tell them you thought the story was true. What's going on with the child who wrote the article, and did she even pass by a journalism school?"

"I think Davis has already gotten to her. She won't even return my calls," I said as I took a bite of the ravioli.

"You want me to get one of my men to rough her up?" Hayden asked.

"Hayden."

"I can't have everybody disrespecting my girl. Have you talked with Reverend Justine?"

"No."

"You want me to call her?"

"For what?"

"Zola, please. You girls need to stop this high school stuff. You two have been through so much. I know Justine would want to be here to support you. Shit, maybe you need to see how close she is to Jesus and let her pray and lay hands on you. I'm sure Jesus can get your job back," Hayden said.

I didn't say anything, but I felt the tears sting my eyes. I had carried the sadness of life without Justine in a private space in my heart that I refused to visit because it was so painful.

"What are you thinking about?"

I couldn't tell Hayden just how much Justine's friendship truly meant to me. I remained silent and clenched my eyes shut to fight back the tears and then opened them when I felt I could look at Hayden without crying. He moved his chair close to me and squeezed my hand lovingly. I could no longer contain my sadness, and the tears began pouring out of my eyes like water from a dam.

Hayden held me tight and whispered, "Everything's going to be all right, Zola. Everything. We all love you and we'll be there for you."

I cried for several minutes and then I pulled myself from Hayden's embrace. I was heading toward my bathroom to wash my face, but instead I just splashed some water on it from the kitchen sink. I used my nightgown to dry my face like I was a young child.

Hayden walked over toward the sink and took my hands and asked, "Do you want to talk about it?"

"What?"

"Whatever is making you so sad, Zola, I know you've had a lot happen the last couple of days, but those tears and moans sound like a deeper pain than losing your job," Hayden said.

"I was thinking maybe I've been wrong about a couple of things."

"Wrong about what?"

"Deserting Justine. Maybe this religion thing is real for her."

"Is that why you're crying so hard?"

"Sorta. I was thinking about a really painful time in my life and how Justine was there for me blow by blow whenever I needed her," I said.

"What happened?"

"Maybe you should sit down for this. I promised myself I would never tell this story, because telling it means reliving that night," I said.

"If it's causing you so much pain, then you should release it. Now, Zola, you know I love a good story and gossip, but whatever you tell me will remain right here," Hayden said as he patted his heart.

"His name was Wilson Montgomery III, and he was the man of my dreams even when he was in the seventh grade. He was smart and from one of Nashville's finest families. Wilson's grandfather owned a successful chain of rib joints from Nashville to Memphis. He had used his money to make sure Wilson's father got the best education available to black men during that time. Wilson Jr., my boyfriend's father, was the first black man to graduate from the law school at the University of Tennessee," I said as I paused and took a tiny sip of wine.

"I dated Wilson from the tenth grade, since my parents wouldn't let me go out with boys until I was in high school. Still, I felt like we started dating before then because he used to write me these wonderful love letters. The boy could write words of love, and he promised me he would write me a love letter at least every week for the rest of our lives. Wilson was smart and he was captain of both the golf and tennis teams."

"So you were really sprung?"

"Big-time. When I graduated from undergrad, as I was walking across the stage to get my degree, I was stunned when Wilson suddenly appeared from behind the president with a smile on his face. I was shocked to see him, because he was enrolled at the Air Force Academy, and had told me he couldn't come to my graduation. He looked so handsome dressed in military white. Wilson got down on one knee and—"

Hayden interrupted me and said, "Performed oral sex on you for the first time?"

"Fool, stop it or else the story will end there," I said.

"Okay. I promise," Hayden said.

"He proposed to me in front of the entire auditorium. When I said yes, everyone gave us a standing ovation. We made plans to get married that summer at the chapel at Vanderbilt University. Wilson had to fulfill his military commitment and I was headed to Chicago and Northwestern. Since the proposal had been so public, it seemed the entire city of Nashville was a part of our wedding. We were on the morning talk shows and in the newspaper. People were literally begging for an invitation. A local designer made my gown for free," I said as I paused for a moment and thought about the beautiful white lace gown with the long train I had planned to wear on my wedding day. I could see the dress in my head like I was looking at a photo in a scrapbook.

"Earth to Zola. Don't leave me hanging. What happened?" Hayden asked.

I continued. "The night before the wedding, we had the rehearsal. A lot of Wilson's classmates from the academy had come down to serve as groomsmen. I was so filled with joy I couldn't contain myself. I felt like a true princess. But during the rehearsal dinner at the Grand Ole Opry Hotel, Wilson disappeared. Several of his friends went looking for him, but no one could find him. I became upset because I thought something really bad had happened to him. I was crying just like I was tonight, so I went into the ladies' room to pull myself together. When I got in there I heard moaning and groaning like somebody was in a great deal of pain. I pushed open the stall door and realized the sounds weren't from pain but lust. Wilson, the love of my life, and my sister, Pamela, were having sex."

"No, she wasn't?" Hayden screamed.

"Yes, she was. My sister, with my intended. The man I had saved myself for couldn't wait for me. I started screaming like a madwoman, and of course it brought several members of the wedding party into the bathroom. Everybody saw them. Even if I had wanted to save face and go through with the wedding, I couldn't. Too many people saw them."

"What did you do?"

"I ran away from the hotel like a pack of wild dogs was chasing me. When I finally collapsed in the parking lot, I felt somebody's hand on my back, and when I turned around I saw Justine. She held my hand until I was ready to face the world, which took the rest of the summer. Justine's always been there for me," I said as the tears began to roll down my face.

"So now I understand why you and that tramp sister of yours aren't close. Whatever happened to Wilson?"

"I don't know. I don't want to know," I said firmly. I didn't tell Hayden I saw Wilson when I went home Thanksgiving.

"Aren't you a little bit curious?"

"No."

"So let me get this straight. You were the original runaway bride, not Julia Roberts," Hayden said with a huge smile on his face.

"I guess so."

"Zola, if I were you, I wouldn't be worried about your job at *Bling Bling*. I'd sit down at the computer and write a book about that shit."

"I could never write about that. I couldn't do that to my family. Besides, my crazy-ass sister would get a lot of joy out of more people knowing what she did to me," I said.

"What about helping Kai's friend Parson write his story?"

"I think he's going to do it himself. That would be an interesting story, but I still don't know if I believe him."

"Then write a book about my life. I've got some stories I've been saving," Hayden said.

"Nobody would believe *them*," I said.

"A lot of huz-bends would be running for cover. We'd both need twenty-four-hour bodyguards," Hayden said.

"At least we'd have each other," I said.

"Always," Hayden said as he hugged me tight.

2

"Mr. Raymond, a Basil Henderson is on line two," Jolie said over the intercom. She was the second temp that Personnel had sent me since Bristol had taken over *Bling Bling*. I started to correct her again and tell her that my first name was Raymond, but figured she wouldn't get it and decided to call Human Resources and get a real assistant.

I picked up the phone and said, "What's up, Mr. Henderson? How is ATL?"

"I'm getting used to it, but, man, I miss New York. What's going on up there? I heard on the Frank Ski show this morning that ole Yancey B. is suing you guys."

"Man, it's a big mess. We ran a story and it looks like the facts are wrong, but our editor has documentation. She's lost her job over it."

"You talkin' 'bout that fine sista you were protecting like she was a nuclear bomb site?"

"I was protecting the both of you from exploding," I said, laughing.

"Dawg, that's cold. I do have to say Yancey is a lot of things but a crackhead isn't one of them. I think you guys better get out your check-book, 'cause somebody is lying," Basil said.

"We had rehab reports and everything. Besides, her mother backed it up," I said.

"That's your problem, then. That Ava Middlebrooks is a lying, evil bitch from the bottom of hell. She'll do anything to keep whatever spot-light she can on Ava. She and Yancey don't get along, but this is like scraping the bottom of the Hudson River in search of attention. Be care-ful with Ava. Watch out!" Basil said.

"I started to call you about this, but I knew you were busy. How is the case coming with Rosa?"

"Just waiting for the tests to come back," Basil said.

"What kind of tests? Paternity?"

"We took another one for good measure, even though I have no doubt Talley is my baby girl. Rosa wanted me to take another HIV test," Basil said.

"Another one?"

"Yeah, dude. I haven't been talking to you as much as I'd like, but that was one of the reasons she up and left. She told me that someone from the health department had called her and told her I was HIV pos-itive. Can you believe that shit? I told her there must have been a mix-up at the hospital. She was off the chain with worry that she and Talley were HIV positive," Basil said.

As I listened to Basil I thought about the odd call I had gotten from that woman when I'd first moved back to New York. I thought the call was so silly that I hadn't mentioned it to Basil. Maybe the call I received and the one Rosa received were connected.

"Are you sure it was the health department who called Rosa?" I asked.

"That's what she said. Why do you ask?"

"I guess I should have said something before, but somebody called me and told me to be careful with you and led me to believe you might be HIV positive," I said.

"What? Get the fuck out of here," Basil said, laughing.

"I guess you still got some enemies out there, but this is low," I said.

"Why didn't you say anything to me about this before?" Basil asked.

"I figured if it was true, you'd tell me in your own time," I said.

"Was it a man or a woman who called you?"

"It was a woman."

"I guess that narrows it down a little, but Rosa told me it was a dude who called her. She said it was an effeminate man."

"Could have been the same woman trying to act like a man," I said.

"Yo, the more I try to do right, the more people want to fuck with a brotha," Basil said.

"So, did you take the test?"

"Damn yo, I have a complete physical every year. Of course, I take the test every year, and my shit is clean as a whistle. But Rosa's ass came with me to the doctor's office and then went back when the results came back."

"So, everything was cool?"

"Damn straight. Do you want to see the results?" Basil barked.

"That would be pertinent only if we were going to sleep together, and I think we both made the decision that that's not going to happen," I said.

"You made the decision," Basil said firmly.

"Do you think it was this Ava lady who's spreading these lies about Yancey?" I asked, switching the subject.

"I wouldn't put nothing past that bitch. I mean, that's what happens when people have money, they don't have shit else to do but try and ruin other people's lives. Even their own children's," Basil said.

"Maybe I should investigate Ava. Maybe she's the source of both of our problems," I said.

"I'd bet money on it. I'd kill that bitch if I thought I could get away with it," Basil said.

"If Ava created this mess, there are other ways to handle her," I said.

"The bitch in a coffin or an urn would still be the best solution," Basil said.

"Hey, B, you handle your business with your little girl and I'll take care of this end," I said.

"That's what's up. Holla," Basil said as he clicked off the phone.

3

My mother, like most mothers, thinks she's psychic when it comes to her children. So I wasn't surprised when she called with that certain tone and asked if I was doing okay. I knew my dismissal from *Bling* had been in some of the media outlets in New York, but it seems Mother got a little help from one of her former students who heard Sybil Wilkes and J. Anthony Brown talking about my face-off with Yancey B. on the Tom Joyner show, which I didn't know ran in Nashville.

"So, who is this Yancey B.?" Mother asked.

"A singer and actress," I said after I had assured her everything would work itself out.

"I can't believe she thinks my daughter would deliberately spread lies about her. Yancey needs to know you were raised right."

"Maybe I'll use that in court," I said, managing to summon a laugh.

"Now, Zola, don't take this lightly. Even if you don't have to pay her millions, hiring the right lawyer can still cost thousands of dollars. Your dad and I have gone through a lot of our retirement money trying to help Pamela."

"Don't worry, I can handle it."

"Did I tell you the latest about Pamela?"

I let out the loud sigh that I usually reserve for ridiculous men, dumb girlfriends or my annoying older sister.

"Zola? Are you still there?"

"I'm here, Mother," I said.

"Don't you want to know about Pamela?"

"Is she dead?"

"Zola! I can't believe you. Don't talk to me like I'm one of your girl-friends. We're talking about family."

"I'm sorry. What's going on?"

"She finally got into a clinic in Minnesota that your father and I think will help her, and we've been trying to get her in for years. Pamela came over about three days ago, drunk and high, wanting to borrow some money."

"I'm sure you gave it to her," I said.

"I did, but with conditions. I knew there was a spot for her in Minnesota, and so I told her I would lend her some money if she would come over the next day and help me with my garden. Unlike you, Pamela loves working in my garden. I knew she was going to go out and buy some drugs or liquor, but I felt if the good Lord could protect her one more night, I could have one of the intervention counselors from the clinic here in Nashville convince Pamela to go to Minnesota."

"So what happened?"

"Sure enough, Pamela showed up. She was late, but I was so happy my prayers had been answered. Donna, the counselor who Pamela really liked when she was in a rehab clinic here in Nashville, was at the house waiting for her. Donna is a gardener as well, and the two of them went out and worked in the garden. About two hours later, Pamela came into the house in tears, with Donna holding her tight. Pamela told me she was ready to change her life. I just threw my hands up in the air and cried, 'Thank you, sweet Jesus,'" Mother said.

"How long do you think she's going to stay?"

"I don't know, Zola, but I've got a feeling this is the place that can help her."

"I'm glad, if only for you," I said softly.

"Zola, you need to forgive Pamela for what she's done to you."

"I can't, Mother. I could have never done what she did to anyone," I said.

"It took two to tango. Wilson wasn't the saint you thought he was," Mother said.

"Mother, look, I can't expect you to understand how I feel."

"Zola, you've had just about all life has to offer. There are things about Pamela that you don't know."

I was silent for a moment, wondering what she was referring to, when Mother continued talking.

"I know I should have told you long ago, and I know the phone is not the place to share something like this, but I want you to stop carrying around all this anger in your heart."

"Tell me what, Mother?"

"I wish I could tell you this in person," Mother said.

I didn't know what to expect, so I asked her to hold on and I went to the kitchen and got a bottle of water. I opened it and sat on the edge of my bed and took a deep breath before I picked up the phone.

"I'm back."

"Zola," Mother said. Then there was a brief silence over the line.

"Are you still there, Mother?"

"Pamela isn't my natural birth daughter," she said calmly.

I wanted to jump for joy, but I wanted to make sure I'd heard correctly.

"She's not your natural daughter? What are you talking about?"

For the next fifteen minutes almost nonstop, my mother told me how my father had an affair with Pamela's birth mother and how she had given her up when Pamela was about three years old.

"Why did she do that?" I asked.

"She was on that stuff," Mother said.

"Crack?"

"I don't know. Back then they just called it dope or stuff," Mother said.

"What happened to her?"

"She was selling drugs for some man, and he killed her."

"Pamela's mother was a crack ho?" I asked.

"Zola! I didn't think I would live to see the day when my daughter would call another woman that word."

"But that sounds like what she was, Mother. Was she hooking?"

"Listen to me. Whatever she did, you can't talk about the dead with such disrespect."

"I'm sorry, Mother, but why didn't you tell me about this before?"

"It was grown folks' business. I should have told you when you were old enough to understand, but since you and Pamela were always fighting, I thought it might make the situation worse. "

"Were you and Daddy married?"

"No, we were just courting. He knew I didn't believe in premarital sex, but you know, baby, the rules are always different for men. But because he went against God's word didn't mean I was going to. Still, I loved him, and when he asked me to take Pamela in to prevent her from spending her life in some orphanage, I just couldn't say no. I prayed on it, and did what I thought God would want me to do, and then I loved her like she was my own. Pamela didn't ask to come into this world."

"Mother, that's a really sad story, but you and Daddy did all you could to raise her like me. At some point when Pamela became an adult, she also became responsible for her own life. Does Pamela know how her mother was killed?"

"She found out several years ago from one of those old drug addicts she was hanging out with, and then she confronted both your daddy and me. That was one of the times Pamela disappeared for more than a month," Mother said.

"Is this supposed to make me forgive her?"

"You've led a perfect life, Zola! Doesn't that make you happy?" Mother asked.

I thought about her question and I suddenly caught a glimpse of my face in the mirror on the wall. I had not led a perfect life. I had slept with a married man to advance my career. I had slept with men I didn't and couldn't love.

"I have not led a perfect life, Mother," I said.

"None of us have or will."

"I'm sorry, Mother. What can I do for Pamela?"

"Do whatever your heart tells you. If all that means is getting on your knees to ask God to support her on this journey, then that's fine. You might want to call, or even see her when she can receive visitors. I'm not making excuses for Pamela or for you for whatever sins you've committed, but I would have hoped that I raised compassionate children."

"You did, Mother. I love you," I said as I hung up and got on my knees and began to pray for the first time in a long while.

4

I started my session with Dr. Few with a question I hoped she could answer. How could I be forty and my life be such a mess? Just like most shrinks, Dr. Few answered with a question.

"What do you feel is wrong with your life?"

"I think moving to New York was a mistake," I said.

"Why?"

"I just feel really lonely here. My best friends Jared and Nicole moved before I even got here, and it looks like Basil is going to stay in Atlanta."

"How does that make you feel?"

"What? Jared and Nicole?"

"Let's talk about Basil."

"Let's not," I said with a faint laughter.

Dr. Few just looked at me for a few minutes and then I started to speak.

"I don't think I want to admit that I miss Basil. It's not like we spent a lot of time together, but I figured that might change. Then Rosa, the mother of Basil's child, dashed off with his daughter, and Basil was history."

"Have you told him how you feel?"

"What do you mean?"

"That you miss him."

"He'd just brush it off. Basil doesn't want to deal with his feelings about me, and I think that's best."

"Why?"

"I can't compete with the two ladies in his life. I mean, if that's what I wanted, I would have stayed in Seattle and fought for Trent."

"Why didn't you?"

I thought for a few minutes and then said, "I think deep in my heart Trent would have been unfaithful again. I know it sounds like a fairy tale, but I still want to believe that I can fall in love with someone who would love me only and that love would be enough to sustain the person when temptations appear. That's why I love women so much. They never give up on that dream."

"Then why should you?"

"I'm getting old. Maybe my time has passed."

"Forty isn't old," Dr. Few said.

"I certainly don't plan to bow out without a fight. Now that I'm working out on a regular basis, I think I might have four to five more years where men and women would find me attractive."

"So being attractive is important to you?"

"I know it sounds vain, but if I was totally honest with myself I would say yes. My father is a good-looking man, but I remember when he was forty he looked old to me. I know Kirby and I have been blessed with good genes. When I tell people I'm forty, they seem shocked. I still have the things in life people deem important. I'm smart and I have a little money. Being light-skinned with green eyes doesn't hurt. I know it's sad, but it doesn't seem to matter when people look at me as if I were an ax murderer, a woman beater, or an asshole like Davis. All I have to do is smile or blink and people are drawn to me, both men and women. Women, they know why they are attracted to me, but men, even straight men, are dumbfounded, but they still come. I know they don't all want to sleep with me, but they want something. I've had straight black men tell me they're attracted to me because I'm smart or they think I'm smart. I find myself wondering if black men bought in to the notion that black men are dumb and if you speak the King's English and are attractive that you're smart."

"So it's a mixed blessing."

"It is, but I'm not going to stop working out with Sebastian. I need him now more than ever," I said.

"Sebastian?" Dr. Few asked with a quizzical look.

"My brother's friend who I hired as a trainer. He's a good kid, but he really pushes me," I said, laughing as I thought of some of my workout sessions with Sebastian.

"What is the laughter about?"

"I was thinking about Sebastian. I think he's out to prove to me that he's not homophobic or just a free spirit," I said.

"What do you mean?"

"When I was growing up, especially in high school and college, if my boys thought somebody was gay or a little light in the shoes we would always keep our towels wrapped tight when they were around. Even though Sebastian knows I'm gay, he's the complete opposite. He doesn't wear underwear or a jock, and he's quick to rip his clothes off and shower with me after we work out."

"Does that bother you?"

"Hell no. Sebastian has a great body, and it's about as close to a sexual experience as I've come in a long time."

"So you're going to remain celibate?"

"I doubt it. I think it's just something I'm going through. The grief over a relationship ending. The 9/11 stuff still haunts me, but I know we all have to go on. I don't want to just have sex. I want to make love and be loved by one person," I said.

"You mentioned Davis, your boss, earlier. How is that going?"

"I can't figure Davis out. There are times when he seems to be totally in control, but I think he could use a session or two with a good therapist. Sometimes it seems like he's hiding something. I still don't understand how he thinks he can mess over Zola and not suffer some repercussions from it."

"Sometimes powerful men don't worry about consequences," Dr. Few said.

"Yeah, I think you're right."

Dr. Few put down her pad and pen and told me that this would have to be our last session of the year, since she wouldn't be back until the end of January 2002. Dr. Few asked how I'd been sleeping and I told her some nights were better than others. Again she asked if I wanted medication and I refused. I was going to do this my way. I started to ask her where she was going but then decided I wasn't really interested.

"So are you going to see your parents over the holidays?" Dr. Few asked.

"I hope so. I might even rent a car and drive down to Florida. It will give me some time to sort things out. I tell you, if I don't get my head together before I get down there, my mother will know something is wrong the moment I walk through the door," I said.

"I hope you have a Merry Christmas and Happy New Year. Why don't we schedule a session the first week of February?"

"That's cool. You travel safely," I said.

5

It was three weeks before Christmas, but Yancey B. decided to present me with a early little holiday cheer. Not only was the diva suing *Bling Bling* but me as well, to the tune of five million dollars. Yancey B.'s suit stated that my running the story showed malicious intent and that I knew full well that the drug accusation wasn't true.

Well, this little situation had gone far enough and I wasn't about to concede. I'd started working on an outline and proposal for a novel I was going to write about the magazine industry and had plans to call Raymond to make sure that wasn't a violation of my agreement with Davis.

Kirsten still wasn't returning my calls, but I figured if Yancey sued her as well, then I'd be hearing from her.

It was early afternoon and I went out to check my mail. I was greeted with a copy of *Architectural Digest* with guess who on the cover? Davis and Veronica in a six-page Christmas article. I couldn't drop the magazine in the trash fast enough. As I was walking back into my brownstone, I noticed a flicker of blue and quickly recognized it as one of my favorite things: a Tiffany's bag. I picked it up even though with the kind of day I was having, I wouldn't have been a bit surprised if it were a booby-trapped gift. Maybe from Davis, trying to work his way back into my life. But after what he did to me, there wasn't enough jewelry or magazine positions in the world for that to happen.

When I walked back into the house the phone was ringing. The caller ID displayed the number at *Bling Bling*, and I wondered for a moment if it was Raymond calling me.

I was curious so I picked up the phone.

"Hello," I said.

"Zola, is that you?" I heard a female voice whisper.

"Yeah, this is Zola. Who is this?"

"Don't you recognize my voice? This is Cyndi."

"Cyndi, why are you whispering?"

"My new boss, Master Bristol Barnes, is always popping out of his office surprising me."

"What's going on?" I asked. I had talked with Cyndi a couple of times since I'd been fired, but we usually talked in the evening. She'd call and let me know what was going on in the office and told me she was sure Bristol was going to get rid of her at the beginning of the year. Cyndi had encouraged me to go out and start my own magazine and was really heartbroken when I told her I couldn't do that for a while.

"Kirsten is coming to the office to see Bristol this afternoon. I know you can't come in, but there isn't anything that says you can't be in the neighborhood," Cyndi said.

"Cyndi, you're absolutely right. What time is she coming?"

"They are meeting at three," Cyndi said.

I looked at the clock and saw that it was 1:40. I had plenty of time to make it to midtown and try to intercept Kirsten before she met with Bristol. Since Kirsten always ran late, I wouldn't have any trouble running into her.

"Thanks, Cyndi. You don't know how much this means to me," I said.

"I'm glad to do it. I know Ms. Thang has been avoiding you," Cyndi said.

"Did you ever find out what happened to the documents?" I asked.

"No, it's like they just disappeared into thin air," Cyndi said.

"I can't worry about that. I want to know why Kirsten is tripping like she is. I'm going to make that heifer at least tell me to my face," I said.

"Carry your cell phone in case I need to reach you," Cyndi said.

"I will. Thanks, Cyndi," I said as I started to take off my sweatpants and head to the shower. I wasn't feeling my best, but I certainly knew I had to look my best.

❖   ❖   ❖

I arrived in the Times Square area about 2:45 P.M. I looked and felt like one of Charlie's Angels on a stakeout for Kirsten. I had on black leather boots and my deep-blue suede jacket, which was the color of the early-morning sky, over a cranberry cashmere sweater dress. I also wore a black floppy hat, a silk scarf and large dark glasses.

Waiting for Kirsten was frustrating, and almost every other second I scanned each corner, looking for her. I guess Kirsten was going to introduce Bristol to C.P. (colored people's) time.

I checked my cell phone to make sure it was working and started to call Cyndi to make sure I hadn't missed Kirsten, but decided to wait a few more minutes. I put my cell back into my purse and started to survey the corners again, when I heard someone call my name.

"Zola? Is that you?"

I turned. Raymond was standing a few inches from me.

"Raymond, how are you?" I asked as I kissed him on the cheek nervously.

"What are you doing here?"

"I'm waiting for someone," I said.

"How are you doing?"

"I'm doing just fine. I'm glad I ran into you. I have a question."

"Sure. What's your question?"

"Can I write a book? That damn contract I signed doesn't prevent me from writing a book, does it?"

"What kind of book? I think I can tell you without reservation that you can't write a book about Davis. That would break the confidentiality agreement."

"I'm talking about a novel. I've always wanted to write one," I said.

"I'm sure you could write a great novel, and I don't see a problem with that," Raymond said.

"Thanks, you saved me a call," I said. I heard my cell phone ringing so I asked Raymond to excuse me for a second.

"Hello. This is Zola," I said.

"Zola, this is Cyndi. Bad news. Kirsten canceled her appointment with Bristol. She just called a few minutes ago."

"Damn," I said. Raymond looked at me with concern.

"I'm sorry. If she reschedules it, I'll let you know," Cyndi said.

"Thanks for your help, Cyndi."

I clicked my phone off, and Raymond again asked me if I was okay. I wanted to break down and cry, but I had to remain strong and focused.

"I'm doing just fine, Raymond, but it looks like I'm going to have to find a damn good attorney," I said.

"Zola, you don't have to worry about that anymore. The lawsuit is the responsibility of *Bling,* and I'm pretty certain Davis is going to settle this thing out of court," Raymond said.

"I guess you haven't heard," I said.

"Heard what?"

"Yancey B. is suing me personally."

Raymond was silent, but he looked at me with the tenderness of a big brother. Then he started shaking his head and touched me on my shoulder.

"Zola, I'm sorry," Raymond said.

"It's not your fault. Yancey B. thinks that all I have to do with my life is to try and ruin hers," I said.

"Do you have anybody in mind for an attorney?" Raymond asked.

"No. If I knew any good lawyers, I certainly would have had them review the contract I signed with Davis," I said.

Raymond pulled a small leather notebook case out of his jacket pocket, tore out a piece of paper, and wrote something down. He handed me the paper and said, "Here's the name of a good attorney. Call this guy and tell him I referred you. I don't know if his firm handles your type of case, but he'll have some recommendations."

"Thanks, Raymond. I really appreciate this," I said.

"Zola, I looked over some of the notes from the case. Have you tried to get in touch with Yancey B.'s mother?"

"Why?"

"It seems she was the source of some of the information. I know I shouldn't be doing this since I work for Davis, but if I were your lawyer, I would certainly want to talk with Yancey's mother," Raymond said.

"Do you remember her last name?" I asked.

"I'm not certain, but I think it's Middlebrooks," Raymond said.

"That sounds familiar. Look, Raymond, I have to go. Thanks a million. I didn't connect with the person I wanted to see, but maybe you were the person I was supposed to meet," I said. Raymond looked at me with a puzzled look on his face, and I added, "I'll explain later." Then I leaned toward him and gave him a kiss on the cheek and headed toward the subway station.

When I got home I pulled out the piece of paper Raymond had given me and looked at the name *Chris Thomas—Partner* and a phone number, fax number and e-mail address. I picked up the phone and dialed the number.

"Chris Thomas's office," a female voice said.

"Is he in?"

"No. May I take a message?"

"This is Zora Norwood. Would you have him give me a call as soon as possible?"

"Can I tell him what this is regarding?"

"Just tell him Raymond Tyler suggested I call," I said.

"I will. Thank you."

"Thank you," I said as I hung up the phone. I went into my bedroom, sat on my bed and took off my boots. I was feeling optimistic, but I knew I still had to depend on Ava Middlebrooks sticking by her story. I was headed toward the kitchen for a glass of wine, when the phone rang. It was Hayden. How did we ever live without caller ID? I thought as I smiled to myself and picked up the phone.

"I need to hear a cheerful voice," I said.

"What's going on, Zola Mae?"

"Just trying to live my life, sweetheart," I said, laughing.

"What are you doing this evening?" Hayden asked.

"I'm going to take a long bath and have a couple of glasses of wine," I said.

"Sounds like you got some good news," Hayden said.

I told him about my conversation with Raymond and his suggestion that I contact Yancey B.'s mother. Hayden told me that everybody in his cast was talking about the case and that I was like a celebrity to some of them and he wanted to invite me to the show.

He also told me that some of his castmates had been in *Dreamgirls* with Yancey B. and that people were still talking about her *All About Eve* tactics and that her mother had once been in show business. He also said he heard that there was no love lost between mother and daughter.

"I need to talk to her, but I don't know how I can get her number," I said.

"Maybe I can help you," Hayden said.

"How are you going to do that?" I asked as I lifted my dress and pulled down my pantyhose.

"If Mother has a cell phone, I can get the number for a couple of hundred dollars," Hayden said.

"How?"

Hayden told me he was dating a guy who did consulting for a lot of the major cell phone companies and had access to all kinds of information, including unlisted numbers.

"Do you know where she lives?" Hayden asked.

"I think in California," I said.

"That's a big help and a start. Let me make a couple of calls and I'll get back to you. When all this stuff is finished, you've got to come to the theater and sign autographs," Hayden said.

"Hayden, baby boy, if you help me with this then I'll put on one of those beautiful costumes and sing and dance with you," I said, laughing.

"A simple autograph and photo will do."

"You saying I can't sing?"

"Don't make me use up a lie now so I can get this number for you later," Hayden said.

"Bye-bye, Hayden. I'm going to get my glass of wine."

6

I was getting ready to grab my gym bag and briefcase, when I heard a knock on my office door.

"Come in," I said.

Sebastian walked in with a smile and a masculine bounce I was getting used to.

"Yo, Raymond, are you ready to work out?" he asked.

"What are you doing here, dude? I thought I was going to meet you at the gym," I said.

"Yeah, I know, but I was in the neighborhood. I have a client over at MTV who I train in her office. We need to look at getting a setup for you like that. Since you got a shower and all, we could just get some weights and do our thang here. It's something to think about when winter gets here," Sebastian said.

"I'll look into that. It would sure save me some time," I said.

"So, you ready?" Sebastian asked.

"Yeah, I'll be ready in a few. Was there someone sitting out in the reception area?"

"Naw, that's why I knocked on the door."

I looked at the clock and it was fifteen minutes past five. I had told Jolie that I needed her to stay until at least six every day. I shook my head and went back and sat at my desk to make a note to talk with Personnel again about getting a qualified assistant. Just as I was finishing the note, Davis walked into my office.

"Raymond, I'm glad you're still here. I've got an exciting project I want you to get started on. Bristol has the magazine under control, and I want to make some moves with my radio business before Kathy Hughes buys up every station in the country," Davis said.

"Sure. When do you want to talk about it?"

"How does your schedule look tomorrow?" Davis asked.

I was looking at my calendar when I heard Sebastian clear his throat. I realized that both Davis and I were ignoring Sebastian.

"Davis, this is my personal trainer and a good friend of my younger brother," I said.

Davis looked toward Sebastian and then back at me without speaking or acknowledging Sebastian's presence. I had seen Davis be rude, but I didn't understand this.

"Check your calendar and get back with me first thing in the morning. This project will take your mind off *Bling Bling* and Zola," Davis said as he started walking toward the door.

When he was a few feet from the door, Sebastian yelled at the top of his lungs, "Yo, li'l short mutherfucker. You think you so bad you can just ignore a brotha? Man, I don't give a shit how much money you got. You need to show some respect to another black man in your company."

I looked at Sebastian like he was having an emotional meltdown in real time, but he didn't look my way. Davis turned around. His face was cold and angry, and he said, "Are you talking to me?"

"You the only rude mutherfucker in this office, so I gots to be talkin' to you, shorty," Sebastian said. His chest was sticking out like he was about to drop Davis to floor.

"Sebastian, I think you should head to the gym. I'll meet you there," I said.

"Naw, I came here to walk with you, and I'm not leaving until this asshole apologizes to me."

"Raymond, call Security," Davis ordered.

"Davis and Sebastian, come on, guys. Let's work this out," I said.

"If you don't call them, then I will," Davis said as he walked toward the end of my desk, where my phone sat.

"Sebastian, leave," I said firmly.

"Don't worry, Raymond. I'll take care of this young punk," Davis said.

"Like you took care of Scooter?" Sebastian asked.

Davis had picked up the phone, but he turned and faced Sebastian. "What did you say?"

"You heard me. Do you ever think about Scooter?"

"Who are you?" Davis asked as his eyes widened.

"You don't need to know who I am. I know who you are, and it ain't no Davis McClinton. I'm ashamed you're a McClinton, but you're one in name only," Sebastian said. His voice was scornful and impatient, and there was an eerie sound of embarrassment hanging in the air as Sebastian and Davis stared at each other as if they were professional fighters.

"Who are you?" Davis repeated as he moved closer to Sebastian. He was looking into Sebastian's eyes to see where his anger was coming from.

"Don't pull up on me, 'cause I will drop you," Sebastian said.

"How do you know about Scooter?"

"He's my uncle, and because of you I never knew him," Sebastian said.

"Who sent you here?"

"Ain't nobody sent me here. I came here on my own. I'm my own man. I just wanted to look into the eyes of a man who's frontin' to the world like he's all that and you ain't shit. Any man who would desert his family ain't nothing but a lying piece of shit. I'm glad you changed your fuckin' name. And for the record, Grandma and Papa know it's you that's been sending money to the house, but they don't want it. When you stopped sending those checks and started sending cash, they would just take it down to the church," Sebastian said as he continued with his one-sided conversation.

Davis looked like he was cornered, and I didn't know what to do, so I tilted my chair toward Sebastian and said, "Sebastian, I know you're upset, but I think we need to take this somewhere else."

"I done said my piece. I said it for Scooter, Grandma, Papa, Clinton, Adriana, Brenda, and my mother, Gail. You remember her, don't you?"

"Raymond, did you have something to do with this?" Davis asked as he looked at me. There was both fear and sadness in his eyes.

"Davis, I don't know what either one of you is talking about," I said.

"Get him out of here and make sure he doesn't set foot in the building again, or else I will have him arrested. Do you understand me?"

"I do. Sebastian, let's go," I said as I grabbed my jacket and briefcase. I left my gym bag because I had a feeling that after this Sebastian wasn't going to be in the mood to work out.

Davis headed toward the door and then turned back toward me. Sebastian was standing so close to me I could feel the heat from his body, and I swear I could hear his heartbeat.

"Raymond, I think we should talk about your future employment with McClinton Enterprises. I can't believe you have brought this kind of backwoods trash into my environment."

"If I'm backwoods trash, then I'm proud of it, but I'll make sure the whole world—" Davis stormed out of the office as Sebastian's voice became louder. "The whole world will know about fake-ass Davis McClinton. The whole fucking world," Sebastian shouted as he pointed his two fingers toward Davis.

❖   ❖   ❖

Sebastian and I walked through the maze of New York City, block after block, in silence. The evening wind was cool, blowing leaves and particles of trash in circles. I didn't know what Sebastian was thinking or what he was going to reveal about the chinks in Davis McClinton's powerful armor.

When we reached my apartment, the sun had dipped down and drenched the neighborhood in an apricot light. We walked through the lobby and onto the elevator in a silence that felt insulated by snowdrifts.

Once inside my apartment, Sebastian took off his jacket and plopped onto my sofa with a disgusted look on his face.

"Do you want something to drink?" I asked.

"You got any brew?" Sebastian asked.

"I'm pretty sure I do," I said as I went into the kitchen. The quiet was starting to bother me, and I thought about turning on the CD player or the television. But I wanted to be ready in case Sebastian decided to talk.

I took the beer and set it on the table in front of Sebastian. He drank almost half of it with one swallow. I sat next to Sebastian with a glass of wine, and just when I was getting ready to ask him if he wanted to talk, he posed a question.

"Is there anything Kirby could do that would make you disown him?"

I gazed at Sebastian for a moment and said, "No. I love Kirby unconditionally. He's my brother, my blood."

"Then tell me how a person can turn his back on his entire family. I mean, to go so far as to change his name," Sebastian said.

"Davis changed his name?"

"Yes. Grandma and Papa didn't name him Davis," Sebastian said calmly.

"What did they name him?"

"Norman."

"What happened? When did he leave the family?"

Sebastian finished his beer and then started to speak slowly, like his words were treasured drugs that could cure cancer.

"I've heard the stories from my mother. I pieced a little of it together. My family were sharecroppers on a peanut farm in Bainbridge, Georgia," Sebastian said.

I immediately thought about Davis and how he was adamant about me not offering my former student Sasha a job. Did he know Sasha or her family?

"My grandmother and Papa had four children who all worked on the farm, picking peanuts. Norman was the baby of the family, and he had two sisters, one of whom is my mother, and a brother, Jarvis, who was a year older. From what I've heard, Jarvis and Norman were very competitive, not only in picking peanuts but with their schoolwork and sports," Sebastian said.

For more than an hour Sebastian shared his family history with me. He told me how Davis's older brother was given a full scholarship to a New England prep school but didn't want to take it because he wanted to stay with his family. After his father and mother convinced him it was the right thing to do, everything was set.

Sebastian told me he thought Davis aka Norman was upset that he didn't get the scholarship and that he didn't like being the son of a sharecropper. About a month before Jarvis was supposed to leave, there was a terrible accident when Davis challenged his brother to a race across the dangerous Flint River. Never one to resist a dare, Jarvis accepted, even though Sebastian said his mother had told him Davis was the better swimmer of the two.

"What happened?" I asked when Sebastian paused. The intensity in his eyes had softened a little and he was carefully trying to control his voice.

"My uncle Jarvis drowned while Norman safely swam to the other side. I heard he didn't even try to save Uncle Jarvis."

"Are you sure?"

"Sure about what?"

"That Davis didn't try to help his brother?" I asked.

"I wasn't there, but that's what my mother told me," Sebastian said.

"What did your grandparents say?"

"They never talk about it. That stupid dare cost them two sons."

"Did Davis run away from home?"

"No. After my uncle died, Norman was given the scholarship to prep school, and he never, at least to my knowledge, returned to Bainbridge," Sebastian said.

"Didn't anyone from your family try to reach him?"

"Yes. My grandparents actually drove up to Rhode Island for his prep school graduation. That was the last time they saw him, and he was still Norman. They lost track of him when he went to college. He told my grandparents he was coming home for college," Sebastian said.

"Man, this sounds like a movie," I said.

"A real bad movie. My grandparents were heartbroken when they couldn't locate him through his prep school, and all the letters were returned. I think the fact that they lost one son and have another who doesn't want to have anything to do with them has been painful. When I was around ten, my grandparents, who had moved to Pensacola, Florida, started getting these checks, and when they didn't cash them, they used to get Federal Express packages with just cash in them."

"The money was from Davis?"

"Oh, yeah, it was from that sick asshole," Sebastian said confidently.

"How do you know?"

"When I got older and after a couple of years of college, I got tired of seeing the look on my grandparents' faces when my uncle Jarvis's birthday rolled around, so I started doing some investigating on my own. I took some of the money I got with my signing bonus and hired a private investigator. It took some time, but the P.I. finally turned up some information I could use. That's how I found out Davis McClinton was really my uncle Norman."

"Does your mother know that you've found him?" I asked. I wondered if there was more to the story and why a man like Davis would disown what sounded like a proud, hardworking family. It made his success seem even more impressive since it hadn't been handed to him from a wealthy and influential family.

"No, I haven't told anybody what I was up to. I really just wanted to talk to him and get his side of the story. But today, when he acted like I wasn't there, like my physical presence meant nothing to him, I just snapped. I can't tell you how bad I wanted to kick his ass for what he's done to my family."

"Are you going to the media?"

"Do you think I should?"

"Sebastian, only you can make that decision," I said. "But I think you should hear Davis's side of the story."

"He'd probably have me arrested if I went back to his office. Besides, I know what kind of people my mama and grandparents are, and they wouldn't lie," Sebastian said.

"Would you like me to talk to him?" I asked.

"Who?"

"Davis."

"I don't know. I need to think. I mean, I can't tell you how many times I've practiced what I would say to him or what I would do if I ever found him. Now that it's happened, I don't know if I even want him to be a part of my family."

"Why don't you sleep on it?" I asked as I looked at my watch and saw that it was almost two A.M.

"Damn!" Sebastian said. When I mentioned the time, he jumped up from the sofa.

"What's the matter?"

"I missed the last train to Jersey."

"You can crash here on the sofa," I said.

"Thanks, Raymond. Can I use your phone to call my boo and tell her I won't be home tonight?" Sebastian asked.

"Sure, use the phone in the kitchen," I said.

While Sebastian was talking on the phone, I was looking for another set of sheets and a blanket to drape over the sofa, but then I realized I didn't have a clean set. The apartment had come with only two sets, and I'd just sent the extras to the laundry. I thought about just staying up and cruising the Internet while Sebastian slept, but my body was tense and my muscles were telling me I needed to carry my ass to bed. The day and evening had been draining.

Ten minutes later, Sebastian hung up the phone and walked into my bedroom, rubbing his eyes. "Yo, Raymond, you got something I can put on the sofa?"

"Dude, I just realized I have only one set of sheets. But don't worry, I'll sleep on the sofa," I said as I kicked off my shoes.

"Yo, Ray, you don't have to do that. I can sleep in here with you."

"Are you sure?" I asked quickly.

"Unless you mind."

"If you're cool, then it's fine with me," I said.

Sebastian started to take off his clothes, and I went into the walk-in closet to see if I had any pajama bottoms. When I walked back into the bedroom, there stood Sebastian butt naked with his heavily muscled shoulders, chest and powerful thighs covered in milky brown skin.

"Yo, Ray, I hope it's not a problem, but I don't sleep in draws," Sebastian said.

I averted my eyes and headed toward the bathroom again, where I could talk to God privately and ask Him what was up and pray that it wouldn't be me.

7

After two days Hayden came through for me, locating not one but two phone numbers for Ava Middlebrooks. Hayden also discovered that Madame Ava had a Web site, and I pulled it up before making my call.

Ava Middlebrooks, or Madame Ava, as she called herself on her site, was a good-looking middle-aged diva. She had several photographs on her site with her wearing everything from mink coats with matching hats to her lying out on a yacht with a sun-yellow two-piece swimsuit. There was also a list of her cabaret dates, all of which were in places out of the country.

Madame Ava also presented a sample of her singing, which was okay, but I can safely say Whitney Houston and Mary J. Blige didn't have to worry.

For the first number I called, I got an answering machine, where a female voice I assumed was Madame Ava's was talking to someone whom she referred to as Josephine, her maid, telling her to get the phone and tell whoever was calling to speak with her agent for booking information. I hung up because I couldn't keep myself from laughing.

I regained my composure and then dialed the second number. After about three rings, a voice that sounded like the one on the answering machine said hello.

"May I please speak with Madame Ava?"

"This is Madame Ava. To whom am I speaking?"

"Should I call you Madame Ava or Mrs. Middlebrooks?"

"Please identify yourself and then I'll let you know," she said.

"This is Zola Norwood of *Bling Bling* magazine," I said.

"I bet you want to write my life story. Sorry, sister, but I'm going to write my own memoirs," Ava said.

"No, that's not why I'm calling. I'm sure you're more than capable of telling your own story, which, after visiting your site, I think should be very interesting," I said.

"Don't I look and sound fabulous?" Ava asked.

"I'm sure you've heard that before," I said, avoiding Ava's question.

"So what can I do you for you, Nola?"

"Zola. My name is Zola Norwood, and you spoke with one of the writers from my magazine who did a story on your daughter, Yancey B.," I said.

"Yancey B. is my daughter only because she came out of my womb. If there was any way I could stuff her somewhere, I would," Ava said, laughing. I hoped her laughter meant she was kidding.

"Are you aware that Yancey B. is denying most of the information in the story?"

"I'm not a bit surprised. She's a lying little bitch."

I had heard of mother-daughter conflicts, but this sounded like the mess that was going on in the Middle East. Nothing but venom and hate.

"Would you be willing to speak with my lawyer?" I asked.

"Will this be in the newspaper?"

I didn't know if it would, but I could already tell that Miss Ava loved publicity, so I decided to stretch the truth a bit. Any little-known cabaret singer with her own Web site loved publicity.

"I'm sure this will not only make the newspapers and magazines but television as well," I said.

"Then I am there," Ava said. "When do you need me?"

"I need to speak with my lawyer. May I get back to you?"

"Sure, let me give you the number to my residence in Palm Springs, but make it quick. I plan to leave the country before Christmas," Ava said.

After she gave me numbers to three residences, I thanked Ava for her help.

"Anything I can do to stop Yancey, I'll do. Somebody has to stop her before she becomes the cockroach of the entertainment industry," Ava said.

8

I wasn't a bit surprised when I saw a handwritten note on my desk from Davis, instructing me to come to his office immediately. I poured myself a cup of coffee, added a little milk and headed to Davis's office. This was not a meeting I was looking forward to, and I didn't think Davis was either.

Davis's assistant wasn't at her post, so I knocked on his door.

"Come in, Raymond," Davis said in his booming, authoritative voice.

I walked in slowly, avoiding eye contact with Davis, then I heard him say, "I guess you think you're better than me now?"

"Excuse me."

"That little episode yesterday in your office made you feel good, didn't it?"

"Davis, what are you talking about?" I said as I started to sit down.

"I didn't tell you to have a seat," Davis barked, and I jumped up.

"Davis, what do you want from me?" I asked.

"I want you to tell me how you met that little punk."

"If you're talking about Sebastian, then I told you. He's a friend of my younger brother's."

"Did he tell you he was related to me?"

"Before yesterday? No," I said.

"What did he say when he left? What does he want? Money? Find out how much money he wants and get him to sign an agreement saying he will never show up at this office again."

"Is that how you're going to settle this? With an agreement? Davis, Sebastian is a part of your family," I said.

"You don't know that," Davis said as he got up from his chair and started pacing behind his desk.

"I believe Sebastian," I said boldly.

"I don't give a damn who you believe. You work for me, Raymond Tyler. You'll believe what I tell you," Davis said as he continued pacing.

"Will your version be the truth?"

"It's my truth," Davis said as he punched his balled fist on his chest.

"Why don't you sit down and talk to Sebastian?" I suggested.

"For what?"

"To get to know him. He's really a great kid," I said.

"I can't do that. What did he tell you?"

"That's between Sebastian and me," I said. I couldn't believe I was still standing up.

"I know he wants money. That's got to be it. He doesn't even know me. If you're his friend, then you should warn him he's not dealing with one of his boys. I'll destroy him. I'm Davis McClinton, and no one fucks with me," he shouted.

"I think you've already destroyed him," I said.

"Don't talk to me like that. You think because you come from some upstanding family you can look down on me. You don't know my side of the story. What I went through. The pain and the guilt I've had all these years," Davis said.

"Then tell me. If not me, then tell somebody, Davis, before it destroys you," I said.

"He didn't ask you where I live, did he? Is he planning to show up on my doorstep?"

"No, Davis, he didn't ask me where you live."

Davis walked toward me and touched my shoulder and said, "Raymond, you've got to help me. Get him to leave the city. Tell him to forget whatever it is he thinks he knows. I'll give him whatever he wants. I just can't let my wife and children find out about this." His voice lacked its confidence and was laced with pleading.

"I don't think I can do that," I said calmly.

"You work for me. You have to. I don't care how much money it takes."

"Davis, listen to me. I won't do that. I think there is a way for you to have both families," I said.

"You don't know Veronica and her family," Davis said.

"Give her a chance. She might surprise you," I said.

"You're living in a fantasy world. If he doesn't want money, then maybe he still wants to play pro ball," Davis said.

"How did you know he played football?" I asked.

Davis didn't answer my question. Instead, he began thinking out loud. "Yeah, that's it. I can buy a football team or get some coach to promise him a tryout. That will get him out of New York. I have a good friend who knows Al Davis in Oakland. Yeah, that's what I will do. I can get him out of town."

"Davis, Sebastian is injured. I don't think he can still play football," I said.

"Help me, Raymond. Think of something."

"I can't, Davis."

"Then you need to start looking for another job."

"Suit yourself," I said as I turned toward the door.

"Don't forget you signed a confidentiality agreement. You can't tell a soul about this," Davis said.

I turned and looked toward him and said, "Don't worry. I would be too embarrassed to let anyone know I'd witnessed such a travesty."

9

The air was ice cold as I stopped at a traffic light on Sixty-third and Lexington. I looked up at the late-afternoon sun and motionless clouds that hung in the pale blue sky. I had just left Chris Thomas's law office, based on Raymond's recommendation, and Chris had agreed to take a serious look at my case or have one of his associates handle it.

I spent the majority of the time telling him about the Yancey B. story and how I had fact-checked it and had one of the lawyers at *Bling Bling* look it over. He seemed more than a little surprised that I'd been fired and that Yancey was suing me personally. When he asked about my employment history with *Bling Bling*, I decided to tell him about my personal relationship with Davis, and it made Chris a little uncomfortable.

"Do you think your ending the relationship had anything to do with your dismissal?"

I looked at Chris and said incredulously, "Duh. I'm sure it had everything to do with it."

"Well, that won't help you with the suit Ms. Braxton has brought against you."

"I know."

One of the things Chris was interested in was the role Kirsten played. He told me she would be a huge asset and that I should do whatever I could to get her back on my team. I got a good feeling from Chris. He seemed like a good white man, even though I was surprised when he greeted me. I don't know why, but I just figured he'd be black. When I was leaving his office he asked if he could ask me something. I had no clue of what he wanted to know, but I said, "Sure."

"I've been wanting to ask this for a long time and I know it might be a stupid question, but what does bling bling mean?"

"It's not a stupid question. In the Hip Hop world it means people who wear their wealth on their sleeves, mouth, ears, and fingers, anywhere they can show off their expensive items. It doesn't mean they have money, but they want to be ghetto fabulous," I said, laughing. Chris gave me a puzzled look and I thought I might need to explain ghetto fabulous, but he suddenly smiled and said, "Thank you."

When I walked out of Chris's office, I realized that I wasn't that far from Kirsten's apartment, so since she wasn't returning my calls I decided I would pay her a visit. After I crossed Third Avenue, I pulled out my Palm and located her address. When I walked into the high-ceilinged marble lobby and saw the doorman, I thought maybe I shouldn't use my real name.

"May I help you, miss?" the doorman asked.

"I'm here to see Kirsten Dawson," I said.

"Who may I tell her is calling?" the doorman asked.

"Lena Ford," I said. I figured if Yancey B.'s people hadn't gotten Kirsten to help Yancey's team, this was one way to find out.

The doorman picked up a phone and pushed a few buttons, and after a few moments he hung up and said, "No answer."

"Do you mind if I wait here?"

"Was she expecting you?"

"Yes," I said quickly.

"Sure, have a seat," he said as he pointed to a black leather bench.

While I was waiting for Kirsten I thought about my conversation with my mother about Pamela. I knew Mama wanted to have peace in the family and probably thought I was being selfish. I didn't know what it was like to be addicted to drugs, and maybe Pamela's birth mother being an addict had a lot to do with Pamela's problems.

I decided that I would write Pamela a short letter expressing my support and a promise for a new beginning. I was thinking about going home for Christmas, even though I didn't feel the holiday spirit. This time I wouldn't let anyone or anything keep me from my family.

I pulled a pad out of my bag and was getting ready to jot down some of the things I wanted to say to Pamela. We were still sisters, although the fact that we had different mothers explained why we were as different as sugar and salt.

I was looking for a pen when I heard the door open and laughter. I looked up and there was Kirsten with a big man with a thick neck and broad shoulders who resembled a pastry chef.

Kirsten saw me and the smile on her face was suddenly black with fear. She was wearing a turtleneck sweater the color of diluted watermelon, a long, flowing black skirt, and a leather jacket.

"There you are, Ms. Dawson," the doorman said as he looked toward me. "You have a visitor."

Kirsten rolled her eyes and then whispered something into the man's ear and handed him some keys.

"I'll see you in a minute, boo," he said as he walked through the lobby. When he disappeared past two double glass doors, Kirsten walked over to me, pulled my arm, and whispered, "What are you doing here?"

"I need to talk to you and you won't return my calls. Where are you taking me?"

"If you want to talk to me, then it's going to be outside."

Kirsten and I walked a few feet from the front door. I stopped and asked, "So, Kirsten, tell me what part of the game is this?" I kept my voice low but firm.

"What game? I'm not playing a game, and I shouldn't be talking to you."

"Is Yancey B. suing you?"

"For what?"

"You wrote the story," I said.

"She hasn't filed a lawsuit yet, not to my knowledge."

"Then why aren't you returning my calls?"

"I was warned not to," Kirsten said.

"By whom?"

Kirsten gazed impassively at me for a moment and then her eyes drifted toward the street.

"Kirsten, did you hear me?"

"I've got to go, Zola. I can't help you. I wish I could, but I can't. Please don't come back to my apartment, or else I'll be forced to call the police and tell them you're stalking me," she said.

"Kirsten, bitch, have you gone crazy?" I screamed.

"I'm gone. You can stay out here and make a fool of yourself. Maybe I'll call the press," Kirsten said as she walked swiftly to her door.

10

"Yo, Norman McClinton is the real brotha from another planet if he thinks he can just toss me a few coins and get rid of me," Sebastian said.

I had called Sebastian to tell him about my conversation with Davis. Sebastian laughed when I told him Davis had even mentioned buying a professional football team just to get Sebastian out of New York City.

"Tell him my skills got me in the league and that's the only way I'll go back," Sebastian said.

"So what are you going to do about money?" I asked.

"Do what every self-respecting brotha would. I'm gonna make a dollar any way I can. The personal training is picking up. Seems like people aren't going to sit around on their asses all winter. I guess the fact that it hasn't been that cold helps," Sebastian said.

"So what are you going to do about Davis?"

"You mean Norman?"

"Yeah."

"Just let him sit up in his big ivory tower and worry about what I'm gonna do," Sebastian said with a sinister laugh.

"Mind sharing your plans with me?"

"I trust you, Ray. I know you and Kirby come from good peoples. To be honest, I doubt I'll do jack. Just letting Norman know he can run but he can't hide, despite all his benjamins, was cool enough."

"So you're just going to let him slide?"

"That's the way I feel today. To be honest, he wouldn't fit in our family. We're too good for him."

"I hear you. Look, I think it's best we keep our workouts at the gym. I know Davis doesn't want to see you around the office."

"No doubt. You got time to work out today?"

"I'll make time."

"Cool. Hit me on the celly and let me know what time," Sebastian said.

"I will."

"Holla," Sebastian said.

I knew he was getting ready to hang up, but I felt I needed to say something else.

"Sebastian."

"Yo?"

"I think you're doing the right thing. I know your family must be very proud of you."

"Yo, that's what's up."

❖   ❖   ❖

The next morning I arrived at my office determined not to let Davis's behavior make me leave a high-paying job. I figured I needed to stay on for at least a year before exploring other opportunities, maybe even in Atlanta, since it looked like Basil would be there for a while.

Those feelings were tested very early in the day when Jolie walked into my office. She laid a folder on my desk and said, "I think these checks are for you. Sign them and I'll take them back to accounts payable."

I wasn't expecting any checks, but I opened up the folder and my eyes doubled in size. There were two checks, one made payable to Yancey H. Braxton for five million dollars and one payable to Kirsten Dawson for two million. No one but Davis could have approved these checks. I made two quick copies on my personal copier and stuffed the copies in my briefcase.

"Did you sign the checks?" Jolie asked as I sped by her desk. I didn't answer as I caught the elevator. When I reached the top floor, I didn't even make eye contact with Davis's assistant, who started shouting, "Where are you going? You can't go in there."

I opened the door and walked in on Davis and a woman sitting in the chair in front of his desk. Davis was caught off guard. When he called my name, the woman turned around and I recognized it was Kirsten from a photo I'd seen of her in the magazine.

"What are you doing, bursting into my office unannounced?" Davis asked in a condescending manner.

"I wanted to ask you what these checks were for, but I think I have my answer," I said as I looked at Kirsten.

"What checks?" Davis asked.

"Look in the folder. They were delivered to me by mistake," I said.

Davis looked at Kirsten with a knowing gaze and then asked her to excuse him for a few minutes. She picked up her briefcase and quickly left the office.

"Don't you ever embarrass me like that again. How did you get these checks?"

"I told you, by mistake. What's going on, Davis? Why are you paying Kirsten two million dollars? If you're paying Yancey B. a settlement, why is she still suing Zola?"

"None of your damn business," Davis said.

"Then I think I'm done. You'll have my resignation before the end of the day," I said as I walked out of the door.

"You're fired. Nobody resigns from this company. Hiring you has brought me nothing but trouble. Don't forget about your confidentiality agreement. You breathe a word of any of this and I will sue you for everything you've got!"

I stopped before I reached the door and turned back toward Davis and said, "You do what you have to do but expect the same from me."

❖   ❖   ❖

I left the office and stopped at the Hudson Hotel on Fifty-eighth between Eighth and Ninth avenues and had a couple of glasses of wine and tried to come up with a plan. I thought about moving to Atlanta. I wondered what Gilliam Battle, one of my former superiors, was doing and if she had any job leads. I didn't want to go back to practicing law full-time even though I was still a member of the bar in Georgia, Washington and New York.

I liked teaching and working in the business world. I didn't want to go back to a law firm and the politics of being a partner or having to start all over as an associate. Atlanta was still the black Mecca of the South, and there were several record companies and minority businesses that might be able to use my expertise.

When I walked into my apartment, I realized I had another major problem. I was staying in an apartment that belonged to McClinton Enterprises. Not only did I not have a job, I didn't have a place to stay. I could get a hotel room right next door, but I couldn't do that long-term.

I was thinking I should just buy a car, pack up my few personal items, and drive to Atlanta. I knew I could stay with Jared and Nicole, but I still had some loose ends in New York.

I wanted to find out why Davis was giving Yancey B. and Kirsten money, and help Zola any way I could. I also found myself thinking about Basil. It might be a good thing that he was in Atlanta. I remembered he had an apartment in New York City. Maybe I could crash there for a minute. If nothing else, it gave me a reason to call him.

I was walking toward the phone when it started to ring.

"Hello."

"Raymond. This is Chris Thomas. How are you doing?"

"I've done better. Good hearing from you."

Chris called to tell me that he'd met Zola and thought he could help her out if she got the information he needed. Chris also asked what I was doing for Christmas, and when I told him my plans were up in the air, he invited me back to the youth center and then to his home for a little holiday celebration.

I told him I would think about it. Chris also told me that Dru had been asking about me and Chris hoped next year I could spend more time at the center. He told me that since the majority of their clients were youth of color, he and Debi wanted a more diverse volunteer staff.

"I don't know if I'm going to be here next year," I said.

"What? Is Davis transferring you to another one of his companies?"

"I quit," I said calmly.

"Are you looking for a job?" Chris asked.

"I don't know what I'm going to do," I said.

"Then why don't you come by my office tomorrow? Let's kick around some ideas on how I can help out," Chris said.

"Thank you, Chris. I'll do that," I said.

11

Five days passed quickly and I felt like I was spinning in place instead of moving forward. I was spending a lot of time reading, playing the piano, and writing letters to Pamela, Justine and several friends I had lost contact with. My letter to Justine was part apology and part a show of support for her new life. I wrote and rewrote the letters, but I didn't mail them immediately.

I had gone to see Hayden in *The Lion King* and went to Joe Allen's for drinks after the show with a few of his castmates. Kai had talked me into a Pilates class, which left me stretched and sore, and was trying to talk me into going to Jamaica with her for the Christmas holidays. I told her I would think about it even though I was still leaning toward going home. I talked to Mama every day, checking on Pamela's progress in rehab, and she would say, "So far, so good. God is still in the miracle business."

I started my day with a bottle of apple juice and a toasted tomato bagel and cream cheese that I picked up at the deli near my subway stop. It was a beautiful morning pressing upon New York, with just a touch of winter in the air and wispy clouds floating in a blustery blue sky. I was on my way to the gym when my cell phone rang. It was Chris asking if I could come to his office right away. Even though I was wearing sweats, I told Chris I would be there. I had decided to go to different gyms because I had caught glimpses of Jabar working with his clients almost every time I worked out. I wondered if he had found someone to take up his Monday nights. I had managed to resist my occasional moments of temptation to call Jabar, but I thought it was best to switch gyms so I wouldn't feel so vulnerable.

When I got to the office, the receptionist told me Chris and Mr. Tyler were waiting for me in the conference room. What was Raymond Tyler doing here? I wondered as I walked down a long hallway with several numbered doors. At the end of the hallway, I finally located Conference Room D and opened the door.

"Come on in, Zola. I've got somebody who wants to talk to you," Chris said as I walked into a windowless maple-paneled room. There was a long polished table and only a couple of chairs.

"Zola," I heard a male voice say, and I gazed from Chris toward the voice and saw Raymond Tyler.

"Raymond, what are you doing here?" I asked, looking at him disbelievingly. He was dressed causally in a sweater and jeans, so I didn't feel so underdressed.

"I came to see if I can help," Raymond said as he walked toward me. He gave me a hug but I still didn't know what was going on.

"Are you here representing *Bling Bling*?" I asked.

"I don't work there anymore," Raymond said.

"What happened?" I asked.

"We can talk about that later," Raymond said.

"Zola, I'm not bailing on you, but I think you need to talk to Raymond and he will update me later. I have another meeting right now, but you know you're in good hands."

I looked at Chris and nodded.

When he left the conference room, Raymond told me how he resigned from *Bling Bling* and that Chris had offered him a position with his firm. He told me he hadn't decided if he was going to take Chris's offer but he wanted to help me with my lawsuit as a consultant. I was interested in what happened to make Raymond leave, but I was happy because he could now help me. I hadn't known him for long, but I already had a great deal of trust in Raymond.

"So what do we do?" I asked.

"The first thing is we're going to set up a deposition so we can find out what information Yancey B. has."

"I tried to talk to Kirsten," I said.

Raymond looked at me and said, "Forget about her. Kirsten's not trying to help you."

"What about Yancey's mother, Ava? I talked to her and she is more than willing to come to New York."

"We will definitely call her, but there are a couple of things I still need to check out. I'm going to get an investigator to help find out what was really going on at the clinic in Montana. Now, Zola, I want to tell you that I haven't done this type of case in a long time but I'm confident that we can win this thing or get it dismissed before it goes to trial," Raymond said.

"How quickly can you make this happen?" I asked.

"I don't know, but I'd at least like to have the deposition before Christmas," Raymond said. "It might be impossible, but we're certainly going to try."

"That would be great, because I think Madame Ava is leaving the country at the beginning of the year."

"We need Ava. I'm convinced she's crucial to this case, and it would be hard to enforce a court order in another country," Raymond said.

"Do you want me to call her? I have her number."

"No, let me handle it."

"Great."

"Zola, right now Chris is having one of his lawyers look over the con-fidentiality agreement I signed with Davis to make sure I can represent you or assist him. We think we're okay because Davis didn't hire me to be his attorney. Even if I can't represent you on the court record, I can assist. I have some information that I feel can help you, but I'll wait and share that with you later. I think you'll be pleased," Raymond said. He smiled, and I felt encouraged.

I wanted to rush up and hug Raymond, and I felt tears forming in the corners of my eyes. It seemed like someone had sent me a knight who could help me move on and not look back. I didn't really consider myself a damsel in distress, but I have to admit that sometimes knights come right on time.

12

"So tell me what will happen tomorrow, Raymond," Zola said as she sipped some of her hot coffee.

The two of us were having a drink at the newest trendy hotel in Times Square, the W. Somehow in record time I had managed, with the assistance of a great investigator, to get all the parties to agree to conduct the deposition before the holidays. I wanted it done quickly, because I was planning to join my family in Florida for Christmas and New Year's. Chris and I had even managed to get the nurse who swore that Yancey had been a patient at the clinic to come to New York and testify. This was major, since the lady, Gussie Armstrong, had never left the state of Montana or flown on a plane. Gussie told me she wanted to visit Ground Zero and make sure the mean and evil-spirited Yancey B. got what she deserved.

"First you will be sworn in by the plaintiff's counsel. It's just like you see on TV. They will ask you to hold your hand up and promise to tell the whole truth and nothing but the truth. There will be a court reporter who will record all of the questions and your responses. You can refuse to answer some of their questions, but it's not something that I would recommend. I can object on the record, but it's best to answer their questions."

"So all I have to do is go in there and tell the truth," Zola said.

"It's as simple as that."

"Have you met Yancey B. yet?"

"No, and I must say I'm looking forward to it," I said.

"Why? She's not all that. Pretty, but not Halle Berry/Vanessa Williams beautiful," Zola said.

"That's not why. You know she was engaged to my friend Basil," I said.

"So, was he the football player who left her at the altar?"

"Something like that," I said as I took a sip of the cognac I had ordered.

"Where is Mr. Sexy Basil these days?"

"He's living in Atlanta. I think he's going to stay. His little girl lives down there with her mother."

"So he really is the devoted daddy?"

"Yeah, he is. A good thing for me, because I might be staying in a place like this," I said as I looked around the dimly lit bar.

"Oh, I didn't even think of that. You were staying in one of Davis's corporate apartments. I did that when I first moved here. Have you heard from Davis?"

"I got a call and a hand-delivered letter reminding me of my confidentiality agreement and giving me two weeks' notice to vacate the apartment. That's where Basil comes in. He's letting me crash at his pad, and it's really nice. I could get used to it," I said.

"So you haven't made up your mind about staying?"

"Not really. I dig the hell out of Chris, but I just don't know if I want to practice law," I said.

"I still haven't decided what I'm going to do since I can't do something I love. I've been thinking about going back home and trying to get a teaching job at Tennessee State or Fisk and just chill."

"You'd be a great teacher."

"You think so?"

"Zola, you strike me as a woman who can do anything you set your mind to," I said.

Zola smiled at me and touched my wrist. "I can't thank you enough for helping me out. I mean, finding out all of that information to back my case. You've been such a blessing for me, and I don't know if I can ever thank you enough," she said.

"Don't worry, Zola. I'm doing what I think is right."

"You're not worried about the wrath of Davis McClinton?"

"He's not as tough as he wants people to think," I said.

"I agree. I know he doesn't like people to know that."

"When is the last time you talked to him?"

"Not since you showed up at my place with the bad news. But he's still trying to stay up in my mix," Zola said.

"What do you mean?"

"He's been sending me all these gifts. I get something almost every other day," Zola said.

"You're kidding, right?"

"I wish I was. I guess he thinks if he keeps sending me gifts that I'll come crawling back into his life. Sometimes I can't believe what I was thinking when I hooked up with Davis," Zola said, sighing.

"I guess I could say the same thing. We all make mistakes," I said as I looked at my watch. It was almost seven, and I still had to meet with Gussie Armstrong.

"Is it time for your next meeting?" Zola asked when she noticed me looking at my watch.

"Yeah, it is," I said.

"Then I'm outta here. Give me a kiss," Zola said as she stood and gave me a quick peck on the cheek.

"Sleep tight. Hopefully this will soon be over," I said.

"That would be the best Christmas present I've ever received," Zola said as she put on her full-length brown leather coat.

"I've never played Santa Claus, but let me see what I can do," I said as I stood and watched Zola walk toward the lobby of the busy hotel.

✿   ✿   ✿

I got to Basil's apartment, had a glass of wine and decided to take a bath and think about the deposition the next day. As I sat in the oversized marble whirlpool bath, I enjoyed the sound of water in the large bathroom swimming in golden light.

The next day I would meet the woman who had really gotten to Basil. I knew from our conversations that Basil really loved Yancey and most likely would have given up men entirely to please her.

As I continued to soak in the tub, I thought about how I would smile at Yancey and thank her for agreeing to do the deposition before the holidays and how I realized how important time was to such a major artist. Off the record, I might tell her how she was even more beautiful in person. No, I shouldn't do that.

I would start by asking Yancey why she had dropped her suit against *Bling Bling* and had chosen to sue Zola personally. Before she answered the question, I would remind her that she was under oath and that the conference room was just like a court of law. I was certain Davis and his money were behind her dropping the suit.

I hoped she would be truthful, because I hadn't figured out how I would let Zola and Yancey know that I was aware of the check Yancey had received from Davis. Depending on Yancey B.'s answer, I would start to inquire about her whereabouts during the time in question. I also needed to find out what her relationship with Kirsten Dawson was, and why she was not suing Kirsten.

Then I would make sure Gussie and Ava made their appearances and I would closely watch Yancey's reaction when the women entered.

That would be key. I felt like I was the director of a play and I was the only one who had a script. The actors would have to rely on the truth or think fast on their feet.

When I got tired of turning on the hot water to keep the water warm, I got out of the tub and rubbed baby oil over my body, dried off and then spread cocoa butter over some of my uneven blemishes.

Basil's bathroom was mirrored from floor to ceiling, which didn't surprise me at all, and I couldn't help but notice my own body. I was in great shape for a forty-year-old man, so working out with Sebastian had been a wise move. I put on a loose-fitting navy blue T-shirt and light brown pajama bottoms and searched for the remote in the bedroom. I located it under a couple of down pillows and clicked the on button.

I turned to *Biography* on A&E and then walked into the kitchen and poured myself another glass of wine. As I sipped the wine and savored the silence of Basil's living area, I found myself picking up and gazing at the pictures of Basil and Talley. They both looked so incredibly happy. I wondered if children were the only ones who could provide adults unconditional love.

I replaced the pictures and was preparing to pick out a suit and tie for tomorrow, when the phone rang. Even though I was a little uncomfortable answering his phone, Basil had insisted that I make myself at home.

"Basil Henderson's residence," I said.

"Yo, Raymond, you sound like a butler or something. My peeps are going to think I really have gone big-time," Basil said.

"Basil, you are big-time. How are you doing? I was just thinking about you," I said.

"That doesn't surprise me. I bet you think of me more than you'd ever admit," Basil said in a playful tone.

"You think so? You'd be the one who'd be surprised," I said confidently.

"Have you decided what you're going to do for Christmas?"

"I'm going to visit my parents. It looks like Kirby's season will be over and he's going to try and make it as well. I'm really looking forward to it," I said.

"Tell Kirby he needs me as an agent. I'd get him on a winning team," Basil said.

"So what's going on with your business? Are you going to be able to do your part from Atlanta?"

"Yeah, Brison has been great. We already have an office here and I'll just make it bigger. There are a lot of big football schools down south. It's actually a lot easier travelwise."

Basil and I talked for a few more minutes about sports and all the gifts he'd bought for Talley. He told me he'd even bought two camcorders to make sure he recorded every minute of Talley's first Christmas. He concluded by saying the greatest gift he was giving Talley she wouldn't be able to appreciate for several years and possibly not until she was an adult.

"Basil, please tell me you didn't buy her a car?"

"Nope."

"A horse?"

"Naw."

"Tell me what this great gift is," I said.

Basil was silent for a few moments, and then he said, "I'm going to marry Talley's mother. I've decided to ask Rosa to marry me on Christmas Eve."

"You're doing what?"

"I'm going to ask Rosa to marry me. I want to do it before the New Year."

Now I was speechless for a few moments.

"Ray, are you still there?"

"Yeah, I'm still here. When did you decide to do that?" I asked as I placed the wine I was drinking on the coffee table. I didn't want the effects of the alcohol to lead me to some wine-soaked confession of my feelings about Basil and his marrying Rosa.

"So aren't you going to congratulate me?"

"Are you in love?"

"As much as I can hope for," Basil said.

"What does that mean?"

"Come on, Ray. Don't go deep. You know me better than anyone and I care deeply for Rosa. She's the mother of my child. I can offer her and Talley a wonderful life. Love is just a word for romantics. I'm being practical," Basil said.

My silence returned and I found myself thinking about the intimate times I had spent with Basil. Some of the moments involved just sitting or lying in bed talking and gazing into each other's eyes. I remembered how we had made love in a pool under perfect moonlight in Atlanta many years ago. But it wasn't lust I was thinking about. I thought of how the heart recalled magic moments better than the head and how much I really loved Basil. I also realized I would never have Basil the way I wanted, and twinges of loneliness returned.

"Raymond, are you all right?"

"I'm fine, Basil. I'm happy for Talley, Rosa and you."

"Will you be there for me?"

"What do you mean?" I asked, praying that he wasn't going to ask me to be in his wedding.

"Just what I asked. Be there. I don't mean physically, because I want a private ceremony, but will you have my back even when we're not in the same room?"

"Like in spirit?"

"Yeah, that's what I mean," Basil said.

"Cool, I can do that. I got your back," I said quietly.

Basil and I talked a few minutes and promised to talk again on Christmas morning and then said good night. I lay out on the sofa, thinking about Basil, and eventually drifted into an uneasy sleep.

13

I walked into my lawyer's building under a tender blue sky with a banner of white clouds that made me feel hopeful about the day. When I reached the thirty-fifth floor, the receptionist told me Raymond, Chris and Gussie were waiting for me in Conference Room A.

The conference room was close to the reception area. When I opened the door, I noticed it was larger and nicer than the one in which I had met Raymond and Chris before. I noticed Raymond and Chris and a lady at the end of the room standing over a table loaded with bagels, smoked salmon, muffins, fresh fruit, juices and two large coffeepots.

"Good morning, everybody," I said as I walked toward the end of the conference room.

"Zola. Good morning," Chris said with a very gentle smile.

"Hey, Zola, are you ready?" Raymond asked. He looked very professional dressed in a proper navy suit with a white shirt and a silver and light blue tie.

"As ready as I can be," I said.

"I have someone I want you to meet," Raymond said.

"Hello, I'm Zola Norwood," I said as I extended my hand to a short white woman with dirty-brown hair styled in what looked like a page-boy.

"Hi, Zola, I'm Gussie Armstrong. So nice to meet you," she said.

"Thank you so much for agreeing to help," I said as I shook her hand.

"Glad to do it," Gussie said.

"Zola, can I speak with you for a moment?" Raymond said.

"Sure," I said as I placed my briefcase on one of the reddish-brown leather chairs.

Raymond and I moved into the middle of the conference room and I noticed concern in his eyes.

"Is everything all right?" I asked.

Raymond explained to me that he was trying to serve Kirsten with a subpoena but had been unsuccessful.

"It seems like she's just dropped out of sight," Raymond said.

"Do we really need her?"

"If this goes to trial, most definitely. She's the one who wrote the story," Raymond said.

"Yeah," I said. I thought, Why on earth didn't I hire Veronica Chambers to write the story? No way would I be in this mess now.

"Well, let's not worry about it right now. We have Gussie and Ava. Why don't you get yourself something to eat while I speak with Gussie again? I think Gussie is a little nervous. I don't know if it's New York or the process," Raymond said.

"Okay, I didn't have a chance to get anything to eat," I said.

I had a little plate of salmon, a bagel with cream cheese and a few strawberries. I poured myself a cup of coffee and added three sugars and milk instead of cream. I was enjoying my breakfast, when a tall black woman with long hair three different colors walked in. She looked too young to be Yancey B.'s mother, unless Madame Ava had found the fountain of youth and the world's best plastic surgeon.

"Good morning," I said.

"Hello. I'm Victoria Mills, the court reporter, but you can call me Vicki," she said.

"Nice meeting you. I'm Zola Norwood," I said as I picked up a napkin and wiped my mouth.

"Are you the plaintiff or the defendant?" Vicki asked.

"I think I'm the defendant," I said.

"So you're the one who's the editor of *Bling Bling*?" Vicki asked.

"I used to be," I said.

"I love that magazine. Who do you think is going to win the Sexiest Brothaman Alive contest?"

"I don't have a clue," I said as I took a sip of my coffee.

Vicki went over to the buffet, poured herself some apple juice, sat down and started to pull out something that looked like a computer.

A few minutes later, Raymond, Chris and Gussie walked back into the room. Raymond looked at his watch nervously and said he was ready to get this show on the road.

There was a knock on the door, and when Chris said to come in, the receptionist stuck her head in and announced that Yancey Braxton and her attorneys were here.

"Send them in," Chris instructed.

A few minutes later Yancey B. and three white men entered the conference room. The men followed Yancey B. like she was dropping priceless diamonds in her wake. Her face was beat and her long auburn hair was layered perfectly, looking very much like the diva/victim. She was wearing oversized sunglasses and a mink coat, and she was carrying a small leather clutch bag.

The way she strolled in, I was waiting for a band or at the very least a string quartet to provide her theme music. She nodded briefly in our direction, lowered her head and then stood as one of her attorneys pulled out a chair and removed her mink coat as though he were her personal man-in-waiting. Yancey B. was wearing an ankle-length peach pastel wraparound dress that looked like cashmere. She had on diamond drop earrings that must have cost a small fortune.

Raymond and Chris went over and greeted them, and I heard Raymond say he'd been looking forward to meeting her. Yancey B. asked him to repeat his name, and when he did, she put her finger on her lips and asked, "Where have I heard that name before?"

Gussie was looking at the group with confusion. She came over to me and asked, "Who is that beautiful woman?"

"Don't you know her?"

"No."

"That's Yancey B., the recording star and the one who was at the clinic," I said.

"That's not the woman at the clinic where I worked," Gussie said.

"Oh, shit. Please tell me you're kidding."

"No, the woman who said she was Yancey B. was kind of attractive and grand, but she wasn't that young or beautiful," Gussie said.

"Raymond," I said as I stood. Raymond looked toward me. I know my voice sounded loud and panic-stricken.

He walked away from Yancey's court and toward Gussie and me and asked, "What's the matter?"

I looked at Gussie and said, "Tell him."

Gussie coughed nervously and then whispered, "That's not the Yancey B. I know."

"What?"

"That's not her," Gussie repeated.

"Are you sure?"

"I've never seen that woman in my life."

"Gussie, did you call a writer representing *Bling Bling* telling them about Yancey B. being at your clinic?" I asked.

She looked at me with a puzzled look on her face and said, "I don't mean any disrespect, but I've never heard of *Bling* anything. The woman who said she was a famous recording star talked about how she needed some publicity to revive her career. She was on the phone all the time. She gave me a few dollars to allow her to use my cell phone when they took her phone privileges away for breaking the phone rule."

Raymond looked at Gussie and then turned and called Chris's name. When Chris walked over, Raymond told him what Gussie had said and Chris suggested we go to his office and talk.

Just as we were headed out of the room, the door opened and in walked a breathtaking burst of red worn by a middle-aged woman whose made-up face was pure Betty Davis drama. She slithered in with a sweet-smelling cloud of sophistication. She was dressed in red from head to three-inch trick-me, fuck-me pumps. Skintight sheath dress. Red. Embroidered jacket. Red. Stockings. Red. The oversized leather purse? Red. She was wearing a wide-brimmed crimson hat with a single feather tilted over one eye.

"That's her!" Gussie whispered to Raymond. "That's the woman who was at the clinic."

Raymond pulled Gussie by the arm and led her out of the conference room. I couldn't hold myself back; I had to introduce myself to the lady in red.

"Hello, I'm Zola Norwood. You must be Madame Ava."

"Zola, darling. It's so nice to meet you in the flesh," Ava said as she air-kissed me on both cheeks. She took off her hat, placed it on the conference table and suddenly cast a furtive glance in the direction of Yancey B., who was huddled on the opposite end of the table with her lawyers.

"Yancey! Did your phone get cut off? Again?" Ava yelled across the room.

She didn't respond to Ava, but her eyes glittered with surprise and hatred.

"The bitch is trying to be shady so early in the morning," Ava whispered to me. "Just wait until I finish with her ass."

Raymond, Gussie and Chris walked back into the room. Raymond and Chris introduced themselves to Ava and then Chris asked if he could speak with her privately. As Raymond walked over toward Yancey and her lawyers, I grabbed his arm and asked what was going on.

"I think we've got problems. I'm going to ask for more time," Raymond said.

"Why?"

Raymond told me that Gussie was convinced that it was Ava who had been at the clinic. When I asked him how that could be, he said Chris was going to try to find out Ava's side of the story without letting her know what Gussie had told them.

Raymond walked over to the end of the room and began talking with Yancey and her lawyers. I was beginning to feel like I was a character in some courtroom drama called *Law and Disorder.*

A few minutes later, Ava burst back into the conference room with Chris trailing.

"I don't care what that pale white girl said. I have never been to a drug clinic," Ava said in a very loud voice as she headed to the end of the table where Raymond and Yancey stood. She took a seat and announced, "I'm ready to testify. Where is the judge?"

Yancey pushed one of her lawyers aside and walked toward Ava, demanding to know what she was trying to pull.

"Yancey, whatever are you talking about, dearie? I'm just here to make sure you stop your lies against this lovely young lady," Ava said as she looked at me and smiled.

Yancey took a deep breath, rolled her eyes and just stared at Ava, demanding to be noticed.

Ava opened her bag, and with full diva flair she rummaged through the contents until she apparently put her hand on whatever she'd been searching for. A sly smile crossed her lips. She pulled out a mirrored compact with a silver-plated tube of lipstick and took her sweet time applying a splash of red to her lips. When she finished, she puckered her lips, admired her image for a second, then snapped the compact shut and looked over at me and said, "I wish I had a daughter as pretty and as smart as you. I mean, running a magazine requires real talent. Every little skinny bitch who wins a beauty contest thinks the world needs her to sing and act."

"I should have known you were behind this," Yancey said.

Ava looked at Gussie and said, "Sweetheart, could you pour me a little coffee? Two lumps of sugar and a smidgen of cream."

"Get it yourself," Gussie snapped. "We're not at the clinic anymore."

"You mean the clinic where Yancey dried out?" Ava asked, sounding amused and enjoying the fact that everyone in the room was looking at her.

Raymond turned his back and started speaking with Yancey and her lawyers. I couldn't hear what he was saying, but they were listening intently.

"When are we going to get started? I have a plane waiting for me," Ava said.

Raymond turned around, moved toward Ava and bent down and asked, "Mrs. Middlebrooks, are you okay? Can I get a doctor for you?"

"What are you talking about? I don't need a doctor. Do you need me to get a man for you? Maybe you need a little dick before we get started," Ava said as she exploded into a hearty laughter.

"Stop this shit, Ava! Just stop it! I told you I wanted you out of my life, and I meant it. Is this your little trick to get my attention? If it is, then it won't work. I want you out of here. Leave me alone. Forever. Please, for the love of God," Yancey begged.

"You ungrateful bitch," Ava screamed as she stood and reached over and slapped Yancey. The impact sounded like thunder. "I should have done that a long time ago," Ava said.

Yancey's lawyers rushed to her side, and as she rubbed her face, she pushed them back, moved over to Ava and slapped her back, then pulled her hair while shouting, "You evil bitch!"

One of her lawyers pulled Yancey back, and Raymond tried to move Ava away from her daughter.

Yancey started crying, and in a rapid tumble of words she continued screaming at Ava. "Just leave me alone. Leave me the fuck alone."

"I'll leave you alone all right," Ava said as she picked up her purse and started rummaging through it again. I looked at Raymond and I suddenly saw his eyes double in size. He grabbed Yancey and then in a flash I heard the sound of a gun. One shot. Then another. *Pow,* like the sound of a firecracker. Both Gussie and I screamed and Yancey's eyes were dazed with shock and then I saw Raymond fall to the floor.

"Someone call 911," Chris yelled.

I rushed over to Raymond, and it seemed all the color had faded from his face. His eyes were wide open, and blood gurgled from his mouth like it was coming from a boiling pot.

"Raymond, hold on. We're getting help," I said as I kneeled down beside him. Raymond's eyes closed and I feared the worst.

He didn't answer, and I heard people saying things like "Hold his head up. Call 911," and finally I heard Yancey scream, "Stop that bitch. She's trying to get away."

14

I felt a gentle touch and opened my eyes from a deep sleep and saw my mother's face, which looked both lovely and sad. I wanted to ask her where I was and why she was here, but I couldn't speak. There were tubes in my mouth and my body felt sore on the damp, cold sheets.

I looked around and realized I was in a hospital. My father sat close by and his deeply lined face was blank, and I thought I saw tears in the corners of his eyes.

"How are you feeling, baby?" my mother asked in a sweet, lullaby voice.

"You know he can't talk," my father said.

I closed my eyes and tried to remember what had happened. I remembered seeing the lady in red pointing a gun and thinking I should grab it, and then something that felt like fire entered my body and exploded. I felt like I was on fire and a liquid that moved slow as honey was traveling through me.

My head felt as if it had been disconnected from my body and was floating around like a single snowflake looking for a place to fall.

I remembered dreams that went on for days. I dreamed of my mother and how she would sneak me ice cream after Pops had said I could only have one scoop when I was nine years old.

I dreamed of being with my father after my first Peewee football game and the smile on his face when my team won and I scored a touchdown. I remembered the two of us stopping for corn dogs and how I got mustard all over my uniform and Pop's car.

I had visions of the people I had loved in my life; Sela, my high school love, smiling and cheering me on with two ponytails swaying back and forth. Then Nicole and I having a picnic by a huge lake and the happiness we felt when Jared joined us.

I had a memory of racing into a moonlit ocean and having Kelvin, the first man I had fallen in love with, chasing me and calling my name. The waves crashed over him, and when they died down, there was Trent, smiling and holding open his arms. When I moved toward him, another wave rose, and suddenly he was gone. I was swimming deeper in the ocean, looking for Kelvin and Trent, but I grew tired when I couldn't find them.

When I raced to the shore, exhausted, I bumped into Basil, wearing gold swimming trunks that had memorized every part of his body. He was smiling and he was holding a white beach towel. Basil walked toward me and wrapped my body in the towel and his massive arms. The two of us walked slowly down the shore and watched the moon disappear and be replaced by a beautiful morning sun. The depth of my dreams was like nothing I had ever experienced. I felt as if I could have dreamed forever if there hadn't been a strong force pulling me back to reality.

"When do you think he's going to be able to eat regular food?" I heard a female voice ask.

I opened my eyes and saw Aunt Mabel and Uncle James standing in the corner of the room. Aunt Mabel opened a plastic box and pulled out something that looked like meat and placed it in her mouth. Mabel is a pear-shaped woman with a love of bad wigs and colorful pantsuits. My uncle, who was wearing a Bama baseball cap and a shapeless bright yellow shirt, had a look of concern on his face as he took off the cap, rubbed his bald head and then put the cap back on.

"Mabel, he's not going to be eating food for a while," my mother said.

"I hope they put something in that tube of his, like some liquid protein or maybe some chitterling juice. You don't want him wasting away. People back home will see him and won't believe that he got shot. They'll think he got that disease that causes folks to lose weight," Aunt Mabel said.

I noticed my pops shake his head and roll his eyes.

"Why are you looking at me like that? Ray Jr. is still funny that way, ain't he?"

"Look, woman, you need to go and take your food talk to the cafeteria or the waiting room. We need to let some of Raymond's other friends come in here and say hello," Pops said.

"But we're family," Aunt Mabel protested.

"Mabel, you heard Raymond. Come on, now," Uncle James said.

When Aunt Mabel and Uncle James left the room, Pops looked over at my mother and said, "And you wanted to spend Christmas with them?"

My mother pulled a chair close to my bed and placed her hand on the side of my face and started an endless stream of soft, comforting words: "Don't worry, baby, everything is going to be fine. You're in God's hands and he loves you and he knows how to heal you. Your father and I will be here for as long as we need to. Kirby is on the way, and Trent is waiting in the cafeteria. We knew you'd wake up eventually. We love you so much."

I looked at my mother and father and the sadness on their faces, and I was scared and wondered why I couldn't talk. I thought about my life, my dreams, and tears started pouring out of the sides of my eyes, and I didn't have the will or muscles to stop crying.

My mother wiped the tears from the left side of my face with a towel, while Pops wiped the right side with his hands.

"Don't worry, son. You're going to be fine," my pops said.

The door opened and a nurse came in with a lovely bouquet. She was followed by an attractive black man who was wearing a white coat and carrying a clipboard. When he came close to my bedside, I read *Dr. Smith* on his coat.

"So you finally woke up. I understand you're a lawyer, so you probably needed the rest," he said with a peaceful smile.

"Why can't he talk, Doctor?" Pops asked.

"Raymond has what is referred to as transient ischemia of the cord. The bullet nicked his spinal cord. The condition should be temporary, and hopefully in a couple of days he'll be able to talk again. Right now all he needs to do is rest," Dr. Smith said.

"Is he in pain?"

"He's probably sore from the surgery. But I can give him something to make him as comfortable as possible. Can you two come outside with me? I have a couple of things to talk with you about, and while your son can't talk, his hearing is still intact."

I looked at my parents and then at the soft, muted light from the ceiling, and I closed my eyes. I felt my mother kiss my forehead, and then another kiss that I assumed was Pops from the brush of hair I felt on my skin.

❖   ❖   ❖

I guess I must have fallen asleep again, but when I opened my eyes I couldn't remember any of my dreams. I smelled a familiar scent, so I moved my eyes to the left and saw Trent sitting in a chair. He was asleep.

Trent looked the same way on so many mornings when I would wake up before him and just gaze at him, looking at his face, handsome and peaceful. A nurse walked into the room with more flowers, and Trent jumped up. Our eyes met briefly as Trent stood and walked over to the edge of my bed.

"Mr. Tyler is the most popular patient on the ICU floor," the nurse said.

Trent gave her a polite smile. When she left, he gently rubbed my arms, which were cold and covered with goose bumps.

"I let you out of my sight and you come to New York and become the big hero. You've been on television all across the country. People are talking about how you dived in front of Yancey B. and saved her life and most likely several other people's. I know your parents are proud of you, and of course I am too," Trent said. When he spoke, his voice was low and unsteady.

"I've always been proud of you. I know this might not be the time to tell you, but I'm sorry. I think I treated your love lightly because I was insecure. I always thought one day you'd leave me. I realize my actions hurt you deeply, because you haven't told your parents we broke up and I know how close to them you are. I was surprised when your father called me with the news of the shooting and offered to pay my way to New York because he knew you'd need me. Don't worry, I didn't let him buy my ticket or tell them we've broken up and that I'm married. You tell them when you feel it's right."

I began to stare at the ceiling and wished I could talk so I could tell Trent that although I appreciated his being there I didn't need him to feel sorry for me. I knew that it wasn't my fault that he couldn't be the lover he pretended to be. I wanted to tell him I wished him and his new family well and that I would survive. I was a Tyler man.

"Are you comfortable? Oh shit, how stupid can I be, the doctor told me you can't talk. It seems like you've made a lot of friends since you've been in New York. I met Zola, and she's really worried about you. I met some of her friends and Davis McClinton. I saved some of the newspaper clippings with pictures of you. It seems Yancey B. is grateful as well.

I saw her on *E!* and *Access Hollywood*. They even talked about you on *The View* and *BET Tonight*."

Trent's monologue was making me tired, so I closed my eyes and counted to one hundred, but he continued talking. When I heard him say he had met Basil and how Basil had been at the hospital a couple of times, I had to concentrate on not opening my eyes and suppressing my smile at the mention of Basil.

❖   ❖   ❖

For the next four days my family and friends must have felt as if I were a member of the clergy since I couldn't talk and all I could do was listen. Didn't they know that if and when my voice returned there was nothing to keep me from repeating some of the things they shared?

Zola dropped by and told me the shooting had brought her back together with her best friend, Justine, who had shown up at the hospital when she heard of the shooting on the radio involving Yancey B. and *Bling Bling* personnel. Zola also told me that Yancey B. had dropped the lawsuit and how I needed to get well because her friend Kai was having an Oscar party as a kickoff for Zola's new magazine, *Urban Soul*. Zola added that she wasn't worried about her agreement with Davis because it was probably going to take three years to raise the funds she needed.

Davis surprised me by telling me he didn't know how or when he would correct some of the mistakes he'd made. He didn't mention Zola or Sebastian, but he seemed sincere.

Some of Trent's confessions made me uncomfortable. He told me how much he loved being around his children but he thought his new wife had the wrong impression about his financial situation. She had the notion that she wouldn't have to work another day in her life, despite the fact that he explained the reason he and I were able to live in the neighborhood we did was that we were a two-income household. Trent said she didn't want to hear about his life before her and became a nervous wreck anytime he spent more than an hour at the gym and didn't want him to come to New York. He told me he wanted to stay and make sure I was going to be fine, but he had to get back home.

Chris, Debi and their son Luc came, and Chris offered me not only a job but a place to stay. When Chris and Debi found out that my parents, Aunt Mabel and Uncle James were staying in a hotel, they insisted my family stay in their rambling apartment on Central Park West.

Kirby and Sebastian showed up on New Year's Day and watched football games and shot the breeze like nothing had happened. It was the first time I realized I'd missed Christmas. When they got ready to leave, Kirby popped back into my room and said, "You know you can't scare me like this anymore. I'm a man now, and we don't like to cry, even for our big brothers who mean more than anything in the world. I love you, Ray-Ray." Kirby was wrong about men crying, and he came over and hugged me tight. Tears rolled down my face, and I felt wetness on my neck where Kirby had buried his face.

The friends and flowers continued into the New Year, but still no word from Basil. I assumed he had returned to Atlanta. Jared and Nicole came to New York for a quick "hello" but could only stay overnight. Nicole was on her way to London to direct *Dreamgirls*, and Jared wanted to get back to their kids. They suggested that I consider moving back to Atlanta, or at the very least coming and staying with them while healing and sorting out my life.

A week later, Dr. Smith came into my room and told me that I was doing well, my voice would return soon and I would be transferred out of ICU.

I was happy about my prognosis and I was hopeful that I was going to be released in a couple of days, even though I didn't know what I was going to do when I got out.

My left side was a little sore, and Dr. Smith had told me to use a cane for a couple of weeks. I was searching around the room for the cane when I heard the door open and smelled the strong scent of masculinity.

I turned around and standing there with a huge smile on his face was Basil.

"You don't look so bad to me. You look damn good. Are you ready to go home?"

I smiled at him and said, "Yes, I'm ready."

Epilogue

I Won't Last a Day Without You

THE CARPENTERS

It was Oscar night and you'd think that I'd been invited to the main event at the Kodak Theatre instead of a dinner party that Kai was throwing in my honor. I was looking delectable in a stunning black sleeveless cocktail dress with oversized sequins lining the bottom and I had on a new pair of Jimmy Choo's. My hair was whipped into an elegant bun and I was wearing a pair of diamond studs and a beautiful diamond necklace that was in one of the many boxes Davis had sent but I had refused to open.

Finally, I decided I deserved the gifts after all I'd been through in the last three months. Not that things had been all bad. I had Justine back

as my best friend and I was actually getting excited about being a brides-
maid in her upcoming June wedding. We'd always planned to be in
each other's weddings.

Justine was still spending a great deal of time at church but I think my
letter touched her and she realized that God wanted her surrounded by
people who loved her. I had even ventured back for Sunday services and a
Monday night Bible study. I felt comforted when I walked into the church
and could understand what Justine said when she told me that giving her
life to God was the first time she felt she had a love that would never leave
her. I told her I wanted the same thing but with the exception of my family and friends, love for me was like waiting for stars that never come.

I spent the first half of the party chatting with some of the people Kai
wanted me to meet who she thought might be interested in investing in
my new magazine, *Urban Soul*, which was closer to becoming a reality
since Davis unexpectedly released me from my non-compete clause. In
a personal letter sent by messenger, Davis had even offered me my job
back or start-up money for my new venture. I politely declined both in
a short note. I had learned an invaluable life lesson and knew only I
could make my dreams come true, with my brains and not my body.

I stepped into the library of Kai's beautiful home, where several people were watching the Oscars as waiters circled with champagne on silver trays and distributed mock Oscar ballots that doubled as coasters.
The well-dressed guests were selected from Kai's powerful social address
book.

I looked around the room hoping to see Hayden or Justine, who had
promised to drop by with Deacon after church services. I had come to
like Deacon because I could tell he really loved Justine.

I didn't see Justine, but I spotted Hayden in the hallway talking with
a tall, black man with an Afro who had obviously been bitten by the
Hayden bug. I could tell by the way he was smiling. I noticed him take
Hayden's glass and disappear and I darted over to Hayden and pinched

his back and whispered, "Looks like he's all up in your Kool-Aid."

Hayden turned around and gave me a big hug and kiss and said, "I hope you're right, honey, because my pitcher is ready."

"Nice party, huh?"

"I know you didn't expect anything less," Hayden said. He was wearing leather pants with a "Free Winona" T-shirt and a black silk jacket.

"Not at all. This is Kai we're talking about," I said.

"Step back, let me see. You look amazing. That dress is the truth!" Hayden said.

"This ole thing? If I told you how long it took me to get ready you wouldn't believe it. I bet I took longer than Halle Berry. Did you see Halle and Eric walk the red carpet? If they aren't the best-looking couple in Hollywood then I don't know who is."

"You think she's going to win?" Hayden asked.

"I don't know. I hope so, but this is her first time and everybody's talking about Sissy Spacek."

"What about Denzel?"

"I just hope one of them wins," I said.

Hayden's new friend returned and I decided to get a drink. I picked up a glass of champagne off one of the trays and walked out to the terrace where a few couples were drinking and smoking. I started to walk back inside because I didn't want to smell like smoke, but the night air felt wonderful and I decided to enjoy a few sips of champagne.

I glanced up at the dark blue canopy of sky filled with stars and it looked like magic. Suddenly I heard someone call my name. I turned, and standing a few inches from me was Jabar. I blinked to make sure my eyes weren't playing tricks on me, because while the face and easy smile were Jabar's, somehow he looked different.

He was dressed in a tux with blue enamel cuff links and matching studs and there was a gentlemanly look of elegance about him.

"Jabar, what are you doing here?" I asked.

"I knew you'd look beautiful in the necklace," Jabar said as I noticed him gazing at my necklace.

I touched it nervously and looked away.

"You didn't answer my question," I said.

"I'm an invited guest," he said.

"I didn't know you knew Kai," I said.

"I don't," Jabar said.

Just as I was getting ready to ask another question Kai came to the terrace door and announced that the buffet was ready and that they were getting ready to announce the Best Supporting Actress Oscar.

The other couples picked up their glasses and rushed through the door. But I couldn't move as I noticed Jabar's eyes dance flirtatiously over me.

"You look beautiful, yo," Jabar said.

"Thank you. You don't look so bad yourself," I said.

"Didn't know I could clean up so well, did you?" Jabar asked.

"You still didn't tell me how you know Kai," I said.

Jabar explained to me that his mother's company had catered several parties for one of Kai's socialite friends and the two of them had become friendly. Kai's friend had secured the invitation for his mother and Jabar was filling in for his dad.

"So your mother's here?" I asked.

"Yep, she's somewhere glued to the television. She's always loved award shows, but tonight she's beside herself with excitement."

"What have you been doing?"

"Since you kicked me to the curb?" Jabar asked, laughing.

I was trying to think of an appropriate reply when I heard Justine call my name. I was so happy she and Deacon had decided to come. I gave them both hugs as Jabar looked on.

"How are you doing?" Justine asked as she looked at me with a sly smile and then at Jabar.

"Good. How was church?"

"Wonderful but empty. I think this is one of those nights when a lot of people, especially black people, are sitting in front of the television," Justine said. "I was glad when the minister announced he was going to make his sermon short just in case the good Lord wanted to make some history tonight."

"Wouldn't that be wonderful," I said as I eyed Jabar who had a gentle smile on his face.

"Hello, I'm Justine Rice and this is my fiancée Deacon Fisher," Justine said as she extended her hand toward Jabar. I realized I had been rude by not introducing them.

"I'm William Jabar Lewis," he said.

I looked at him and rolled my eyes not in annoyance but surprise. I never knew Jabar's first name was William.

"Nice meeting you, William," Deacon said.

"Call me Jabar. That's what my peeps call me," he said, sounding for the first time tonight like the Jabar I knew.

"Let's go get some food and watch the awards," I said.

"Sounds like a plan," Jabar said as he gently touched the small of my back to guide me inside. He was acting like a real gentleman allowing Justine and me to walk through the door first. He even waited for Deacon before following us into the large dining room, where guests were loading their plates with chicken, ham and several different pastas, vegetables and lots of caviar.

We found seats at a brass-rimmed table in front of a giant-screen television and watched the Oscars and chatted about the dresses and speeches.

Several hours later, I was sleepy but stunned as I was once again reminded how life can be filled with such wonderful moments. When Halle won best actress I cried like I had won. I was trying to compose myself when Julia Roberts announced with unbridled joy that Denzel Washington was the best actor. Then the tears began again.

Jabar got up from his chair to retrieve some tissue for me and I excused myself for a few minutes to touch up my makeup. When I returned, the crowd had thinned and I noticed Jabar talking to an attractive middle-aged woman who I assumed was his mother. I said goodbye to Justine and Deacon and then checked with Kai to see if I could help her clean up.

Kai told me the staff would take care of everything but asked me to join her for a toast to Sidney Poitier, who had received an honorary Oscar, Halle and Denzel. We moved to the terrace and talked about what an amazing night it had been. Kai asked me if I had noticed how all the African Americans at the party had gone wild when Halle and Denzel won, and how some of her guests, even those wanting the pair to win, didn't quite understand the excitement.

"I thought I was the only one who noticed," I said.

"Sometimes the world takes a step forward and then back. I hope I live to the day when we really are one," Kai said.

I was getting ready to tell Kai how much I agreed with her when I heard Jabar call my name. I turned and there he was, looking so handsome.

"Come here, I have someone I want you to meet," he said.

Jabar introduced me to his mother and then disappeared, saying he was going to get the car.

We spent about ten minutes talking about the Oscars, and how this was an evening that wouldn't be forgotten for a long time. I was surprised that Christine, Jabar's mother, knew that I had run a magazine and that Jabar talked about me all the time. I guess I was wrong assuming Jabar viewed me only as a weekly booty call.

"He does?"

"Does that surprise you?"

"Yes," I said. I couldn't believe that I had responded so honestly, but Christine's warm smile made me feel comfortable.

"He was really disappointed when you broke things off with him.

Even I was surprised when you didn't respond to the gifts and flowers. I told Jabar classy ladies like nice things."

"What gifts?"

"You didn't get all the little gifts from Tiffany's and the flowers?"

"Yes, but I didn't open them until recently, and even then I didn't read the cards. I thought they were . . . ," and then stopped myself. "I had no idea they were from Jabar. How could he afford such nice things?" I said as I touched the diamond necklace.

"The boy lives at home and he trains people about nine hours a day. You know how popular he is and what he charges per hour. That might change now that he's at the academy," Christine said.

"The academy?"

"I guess he didn't tell you. He's training to be a fireman," Christine said proudly.

"No, he mentioned he was thinking about it," I said.

"Zola, I know you're a smart girl, but sometimes being so focused on your career and protecting your heart you miss some of the wonderful gifts God has planned for you. My son is a gift," she said.

I started to tell Christine that I was beginning to know that when Jabar came up and asked what we were talking about.

"You, my sweet son," Christine said as she touched his cheek and then kissed him. I felt tears forming again.

"Mama, the car's out front. I want to say good night to Zola," he said.

"Zola, it was so nice meeting you. I hope the next time I see you will be in my kitchen. I would love to cook you a meal and continue our conversation," Christine said.

"I would love that," I said as I took both of Chistine's hands.

She gave me a kiss on the cheeks and then looked at Jabar and said, "Son, I can drive myself home. Why don't you catch the train?"

"Are you sure? I don't want Dad upset with me. I promised to look after you," Jabar said.

"And you did. I'll be fine. You make sure this beautiful young lady gets home safely."

Jabar walked his mother to the car. I went to retrieve my wrap and say good night and thanks to Kai.

"That Jabar is a real cutie. Now I see why you were keeping him on lock-down," Kai teased.

"He seems different tonight. I can't figure it out, but I like it," I said.

Jabar returned and we rode the elevator, acting nervous like we were on a first date. Jabar did mention he was surprised when he didn't even get a thank-you note for all the flowers and gifts he had sent. When I explained I thought they were from someone else he scolded me for underestimating him. I told him I was willing to accept my punishment if he would accept my apology.

As we stood at the front door of Kai's building waiting for the door-man to hail a taxi, Jabar reached for me and pulled me close to him and whispered, "I've missed you, Zola. I've missed you bad."

Then Jabar kissed me like never before, flushing my body with love and not lust. I was happy that I remembered the difference. When the doorman interrupted our kiss I couldn't help but notice that the sky was filled with stars. I also realized that it was Monday morning.

Sidney, Halle and Denzel were probably somewhere in Hollywood celebrating their historic victories with family and friends and the golden man called Oscar. Being with Jabar, I felt like I was the biggest winner of the evening, and I got to take my prize home too. Life, thank God, was still surprising and wonderful. And love, like stars, always returned.

"How are you feeling, Raymond?" Dr. Few asked.

I thought about it for a minute, then looked at her and smiled. "I feel great. Life is good."

"I guess your family and friends were worried for a little while," Dr. Few said.

"Yep, it's not the way I would recommend spending Christmas and the New Year. But I came through with God's grace and I'm ready to move on. I'm looking forward to the rest of my life," I said.

"Have you decided what you're going to do?"

"About what?"

"Your career. Life?"

"No, I haven't. I'm still taking things one day at a time. I realize now how important each day is," I said.

This was my first visit to Dr. Few since the shooting. I had talked to her a few times by phone after I had completed my rehabilitation and speech therapy. I hadn't decided if I was going to continue seeing her, but I had so much going on in my head that I thought it would be good to talk it out with someone objective.

I was eager to tell Dr. Few how wonderful Basil had been, taking care of me and allowing me to stay at his apartment. He was still going back and forth between New York and Atlanta, but when he was in New York he gave me the majority of his attention.

I reported how Rosa had turned down Basil's marriage proposal but had forged a positive relationship so they could raise Talley in a loving environment.

When I asked Basil if he was disappointed, he said he was relieved. Basil told me that his proposal led to an honest conversation where he and Rosa admitted that the love they felt for each other wasn't romantic. I think it was noble of Basil to want to do the right thing by his daughter.

"How do you feel about Basil?"

"I love him," I said calmly.

"Does he know that?"

"Oh yeah, he knows, and I must say this time he's handling it pretty well. I'm proud of him," I said, smiling.

"Did you tell Basil you loved him?"

"Yes. I also admitted to him that I might have loved him for a long time but was too afraid of the heartbreak. Now I'm willing to take more chances. Good thing I did, because Basil said he loved me and suffered the same fears."

"What about Trent? You told me he came to New York after you were shot."

"If anything, I feel sorry for Trent. He's called a couple of times to check on me," I said.

"Why do you feel sorry for him?"

I thought for a moment before answering. "Because even though he's almost forty he still feels the need to please the world. I know he loves his children and they will bring him a lot of joy as he gets older, but I don't hold out much hope for his marriage."

"Why do you say that?"

"Once when Trent called, he told me how much he loved me and how he had made a big mistake."

"What did you say to him?"

"I told him I appreciated his honesty and for not making me feel like I had done something to deserve his treatment. But I let him know that I was moving on with my life. Did I tell you that Basil met Trent at the hospital? Basil told him he could head back to Seattle because he was going to take care of me," I said, smiling.

"How did that make you feel?"

"Loved."

"So are you going to pursue a relationship with Basil?"

"I love it the way it is now. Sex sometimes complicates matters," I said.

When Dr. Few asked me to explain, I told her how Basil for the last several months had made sure I never wanted for anything. He'd cooked for me, gave me massages and held me tightly every night he was in the city. I told her we hadn't made love yet and Dr. Few gave me a what-are-you-waiting-for look. Maybe she wanted to hear about some hot male-on- male sex.

"I want it to be perfect. I want Basil to understand what I expect from a relationship. He's making progress and I think we're pretty close," I said.

"What happened to the woman who shot you?"

"Ava is one of the reasons I'm still in New York. Her trial is coming up next week and I have to testify against her. It'll be interesting being on the other side in the courtroom," I said.

"How do you feel about her?"

I didn't have any real feelings for Ava Middlebrooks. I told Dr. Few I thought it was so sad that a mother and daughter held such contempt for each other. I wondered if black families were now becoming as dysfunctional as the white families I saw on television.

Davis had also called recently and wanted to talk to me.

"Are you going to see him?"

"I might. I want to know what on earth can make a person turn his back on his family. I hope it's not because he was embarrassed that they were sharecroppers," I said.

"How is the young lady you worked with? The magazine editor."

"Zola is doing fine. She invited me to an Oscar party and I felt well enough to go, but Basil suggested we stay in bed and watch them together. So we did. He ordered some food and I had my first taste of champagne in months. I fell asleep right after Sidney Portier's wonderful speech, but Basil woke me up with a kiss right before they announced best actress. I'm sure glad God let me stick around to witness that," I said. I didn't share Basil's confession that night. He had realized how he might lose me for good, and on the morning after the Oscars, he told me he never noticed how the sunrise flooded his bedroom until that moment.

"What are you smiling about, Raymond?" Dr. Few asked.

I realized I was smiling too much so I told her that Zola was starting her new magazine and had asked me if I wanted to come and work for her. I turned her down because I wanted to make sure my next job would be something I could do for a while. Magazine start-ups were too risky.

"So are you going to stay in New York?"

"For now. I'm thinking seriously about moving to Atlanta, but that will depend on what happens with Basil and me."

"What are you waiting for?"

"A sign. I'll know when it's time to take the next step."

While Dr. Few was jotting down a few notes on her pad, I looked at her mantel and noticed a beautiful picture of the ocean with two lovers, a man and a woman racing toward the water. I remembered the dream

I had while I was in the hospital about Trent, Kelvin and Basil. When I told Basil about the dream, he shared a recent dream about the time we had made love in the pool when we first met. Basil told me how that night was one of the best nights in his life, both physically and emotionally. I asked him why he'd felt that way and he surprised me because he said, "I felt like I was forever swimming in your love." I couldn't even respond. I just placed my head in his arms.

Reflecting on how much Basil had changed in the last three months caused an easy flow of tears. Dr. Few asked me why I was crying.

I let the tears continue to fall and then looked at her and said, "Sometimes love just fills you up. I'll never complain about not having love in my life. I have a great family, wonderful friends and Basil. I have my life and I realize how precious it is."

"So what are you going to do, Raymond?"

"Live like it's my last day and love like I'm going to live forever."

Bling Bling Confidential is back in business—July 30, 2002

Retired diva Ava Parker Middlebrooks was found guilty of attempted murder and sentenced to fifteen years in prison. Former *Bling Bling* editor Zola Norwood announced December 1, 2002, as the release date for the first issue of *Urban Soul* and her engagement to William Jabar Lewis. John Basil Henderson was named *Bling Bling Sexiest Brotherman Alive* and picked up his prize with his daughter, Talley, and partner, former Bling Bling CEO, Raymond Winston Tyler Jr. Davis Vincent McClinton will hold a press conference on August 5, 2002, to comment on an *Ebony* cover story concerning his background.

About the Author

E. Lynn Harris is a former computer sales executive with IBM and a graduate of the University of Arkansas at Fayetteville. He is the author of seven novels: *Any Way the Wind Blows, Not a Day Goes By, Abide with Me, If This World Were Mine, And This Too Shall Pass, Just As I Am* and *Invisible Life.* In 1996 and 2002, *Just As I Am* and *Any Way the Wind Blows* were named Novel of the Year by the Blackboard African-American Bestsellers, Inc. *If This World Were Mine* won the James Baldwin Award for Literary Excellence. In 2000 and 2001, Harris was named one of the fifty-five "Most Intriguing African Americans" by *Ebony* and inducted into the Arkansas Black Hall of Fame. In 2002, Harris was included in *Savoy* magazine's "100 Leaders and Heroes in Black America." In 2001, Mr. Harris fulfilled a lifelong dream and made his Broadway debut in a production of *Dreamgirls.* Harris divides his time between New York and Atlanta, Georgia.